ENDORSEMENTS FOR PAT SIMMONS

Simmons shines in this godly romance. This avid reader was overwhelmed by the compassionate writing and Scriptures that spoke to my soul. There were points that I identified with each character that led me to further investigate other Scriptures. She uses family history, murder, prison, and postpartum depression along with Scriptures to show God's ultimate sacrifice and constant forgiveness of sins. The character development and storyline pace will have you mesmerized as two families face their demons. Crowning Glory *is a masterpiece of Christian romance which is definitely a MUST read.*

—MONIQUE "DELTAREVIEWER" BRUNER

Talk to Me *is a great book! I am an avid reader and* Talk to Me *is one of the best I've ever read. I found myself laughing out loud—sign of a good book, grinning from ear to ear, and then saying "no she did not"! Once I started reading, I couldn't put the book down. The storyline was intriguing and the characters were well developed. I finished it in two days! You definitely will not be disappointed. Pat Simmons is definitely gifted to write a good story! Thanks, Pat, for sharing your talent with the world!*

—LESLIE HUDSON, BALTIMORE, MD

Guilty of Love *by Pat Simmons was my first experience with Christian fiction and I must admit that I truly enjoyed reading this novel. I thought that Ms. Simmons did an excellent job of inserting the character's spirituality into the dialog in such a natural manner that didn't come across as being preachy and she was also able to interlace a multitude of rich African American history in the process. I felt each and every emotion of the heroine and it touched me deeply within. This story centered on a very difficult, heartbreaking issue, and how Cheney dealt with it came across so incredibly real to me. It was astonishing to find such strong characters in a novel, even with the weaknesses evolved from their past experiences. I advise the* reader to keep a big box of tissues handy because you will need them on numerous occasions. Thanks go to Ms. Simmons for a truly inspirational story.

—NIKITA, REVIEWED FOR JOYFULLY REVIEWED

The author provides great lessons for someone going through any aspect of their life in terms of health, relationships, bearing children, and family values. She truly deserves an encore for Not Guilty of Love as she distinctively uses faith as her theme for the book. I look forward to the continuation she has in store!

—EKG LITERARY MAGAZINE

Still Guilty was a really good and powerful story. Pat Simmons brought it to the line. As I read this book, it was just what I needed. I was going through my own personal struggles and all of the Scriptures that Cheney and Parke recited I jotted down for my own personal use. I have told SO many readers about this series and I'm looking forward to reading more books by Pat Simmons!

—CARMEN FOR OOSA ONLINE BOOK CLUB

I felt as if I was part of this story. I found myself wanting to help the characters. I loved Still Guilty. I want to read other books by this author. She is a talented author. LOVED IT!

—READERS' FAVORITE "BOOK REVIEWS AND AWARD CONTEST"

guilty
by THE JAMIESON LEGACY
association

PAT SIMMONS

MOODY PUBLISHERS

CHICAGO

© 2012 by
PAT SIMMONS

Scriptures taken from the *Holy Bible, New International Version®*, NIV®. Copyright © 1973, 1978, 1984, 2011 by Biblica, Inc.™ Used by permission of Zondervan. All rights reserved worldwide. www.zondervan.com.

Edited by Kathryn Hall
Interior design: Ragont Design
Cover design: Faceout Studio
Cover image: iStock, Sshutterstock, Masterfile, Veer
Author photo: Naum Furman

Library of Congress Cataloging-in-Publication Data

Simmons, Pat.
 Guilty by association / Pat Simmons.
    p. cm. -- (The Jamieson legacy)
 ISBN 978-0-8024-0368-1 (pbk.)
 1. African Americans--Fiction. 2. Domestic fiction. I. Title.
 PS3619.I56125G85 2012
 813'.6--dc23

                         2011038313

            1 3 5 7 9 10 8 6 4 2

Printed in the United States of America.

Praise God for the youth of today—
for Jesus shall deliver them from all temptation.

The term "angry black man" is widely used throughout the African American community. However, it's not limited to one ethnic group to describe the disobedient and rebellious spirits directed toward family and society. Yet, be encouraged. God has a plan:

In the last days, God says, I will pour out my Spirit on all people. Your sons and daughters will prophesy, your young men will see visions, your old men will dream dreams. Even on my servants, both men and women, I will pour out my Spirit in those days, and they will prophesy.
(Acts 2:17–18)

Boston, Massachusetts

"*H*e called again," Sandra Nicholson told her son, Kevin "Kidd" Jamieson, as soon as his commanding figure cleared the doorway of their Hyde Park condo.

Grunting, he shut the door. Kidd's nostrils flared as he swaggered across the hardwood floor. The persistent caller claimed to be Cameron Jamieson, a distant cousin who had tracked down Kidd and his younger brother, Aaron "Ace" Jamieson, through some genealogy nonsense.

In one of his frequent attempts to reach Kidd, Cameron mentioned to Sandra that he was completing his second engineering degree at Massachusetts Institute of Technology. Ever since this so-called relative's first attempt to call, Kidd wondered if the whole thing was a prank. After all, in the Black community, everybody claimed to be a cousin.

"I told the man we weren't interested in whatever he was selling," Kidd spewed, before brushing a tender kiss on his mother's cheek. Fighting hunger pains, he headed to the kitchen.

"Kevin Jamieson," she snapped, following him. Whenever she felt the need to "scold" her grown-up son, she called him by his given name. Then, planting her hands on her hips, she noted, "He isn't pedaling goods. He represents your father's side of the family—maybe the good part. At least feel him out."

Family, huh? More like . . . Kidd didn't finish the thought. "Okay, I'll put an end to this, once and for all. You have his number?"

Kidd didn't need this added frustration. He was the older of two sons born to a never-been-married mother. He found no fault with her, just his absentee father. Kidd's priority was, no matter what, to take care of his mother. That charge had become a little harder after he was laid off from the Gillette Corporation—a job he labored at for eleven years. The unfortunate turn of events also forced him to give up his apartment.

His mother tore off a sheet of paper and handed it to Kidd. Studying the number, he punched in the digits and leaned against the granite countertop.

"Hello?" Music blasted in the background.

Assuming it was Cameron who answered, he didn't waste his words on preliminaries. "Let's meet."

And Cameron didn't play dumb. That earned him a point of respect. Kidd heard him muffle the phone. "Hey, it's my cuz. Turn it down," then repeating his order, he added, "lower!"

Kidd grunted. *Cuz?* The man didn't know him, yet claimed him anyway. That seemed odd, considering his worthless father had turned his back on him and his younger brother.

"I'm ready whenever you are."

"Now," Kidd demanded. Let the man come on his turf.

Cameron didn't stutter or skip a beat. "You name the place, and I'm there."

Kidd did and disconnected.

"You could have invited him here, honey. He's very polite when he calls, not rude like you just treated him. Don't make me ashamed, Kidd."

8

Shaking his head, Kidd washed his hands in the sink and dried them on a paper towel. Grabbing a plate out of the cabinet, he explained to his mother. "He may have our number, but he doesn't need to know where we live."

Seemingly without a care in the world, he began lifting lids and peering into pots. "Mmm, sweet potatoes and collard greens. Thanks, Ma."

Sandra sat at the table, folded her hands, and then cleared her throat. "How long do you plan to make him wait, Kidd?" She didn't mask her irritation with him.

"He's interrupting my dinner plans, and I'm hungry. Job hunting isn't what it was when I finished junior college."

Kidd took a seat at the table, after piling enough food on his plate to feed him and his mother. He bit off a chunk of cornbread without saying grace and then made the mistake of glancing at his mother. She raised a censoring brow that prompted him to bow his head and sanctify his food.

As he chewed, he reflected on the pending meeting. What was the purpose? It never was one of Kidd's goals in life to build a relationship with *any* Jamieson. As a matter of fact, he had considered changing his last name a couple of times. To his mother's displeasure, he would have preferred to use her surname. At the end of the day, Kidd viewed Samuel Jamieson as a reproductive donor bank that held the power to replenish the earth—nothing more.

It wasn't until he was a teenager when his family learned—thanks to debt collectors trying to track down Samuel—that he had already been married twice and spawned eleven children. Unfortunately, neither of those marriages was to Kidd's mother. The memory of his "hide-and-seek" dad began to fade as he grew into manhood. Now at thirty-one, it had been more than twenty years since he'd last seen Samuel.

When Kidd finished eating, he went upstairs to change clothes and pack his pistol. He wanted to be ready for whatever would go down.

Driving the short distance and parking, he wondered, *What does this man expect? For us to shake hands and shoot some pool?* Kidd got out of his car and nodded to a few men loitering near the parking lot. For some, their presence might seem suspicious, but not for him. He could easily blend in with those men. In fact, he knew two or three of them from tinkering on their cars. If this Cameron was a true Jamieson, surroundings like these wouldn't intimidate him.

"Whatz up, dawg?" Black Eye, a convicted felon, greeted him at the door of the club and slapped his back. He looked around and glanced over his shoulder. "Kidd, some light-skinned brotha walked up in here a few minutes ago like he was a regular—and he ain't. The guy claimed he was your cousin and you're expectin' him—a big guy. Got two other fellows with him. One could fit in and the other . . . ain't no way. A tie? Up in here?" Black Eye roared. "You know, I've got ya back if you need me." Black Eye thumped his chest.

So Cameron had sense enough not to come alone. Kidd smirked. "Don't know him. I came to check him out."

Black Eye patted the waist of his pants. "I got this."

Kidd reached out and stopped him. "No, I got this."

Nodding, Black Eye stepped back and let Kidd enter. As he wound his way through the lounge, he fist-bumped some, winked at a few ladies, and nodded at the bartender. Then he paused and took a deep breath. Yeah, this was his turf. If the relative imposter tried to put anything over on him, Kidd would personally break all two hundred and six bones in his body.

With the back room in sight, he observed the three occupants. The light-skinned guy was buffed, maybe six-one or -two. Kidd had been a wrestler in high school and a boxer in the streets. Either way, he could take him.

As he edged closer, his heart suddenly slammed against his chest. What if . . . what if this man really was his relative and knows something about his father? Kidd had no idea how to process that information. He took a deep breath. The only Jamiesons he knew in the world was him and his brother. He had never met any at school, at work, or anywhere else for that matter.

As if sensing Kidd's presence, Cameron glanced over his shoulder. He stood. Standing face-to-face, they eyed each other. Kidd squinted, looking for any familiar features—nothing—until Cameron worked up a cocky smile.

The moment of recognition was swift. The cousins weren't a mirror image, but enough similarities were noted. Some of the same expressions that flashed across Cameron's face when he grinned matched Kidd's brother, Ace. Where Cameron was fair-skinned, Kidd had the richest deep-brown tan a person couldn't buy in a bottle or get in a tanning booth. Both had thick, wavy hair.

"Thanks for coming."

Shrugging off his jacket, Kidd grabbed a chair, whipped it around, and sat without taking his eyes off Cameron. "Show me what you got."

No argument. Cameron retook his seat and opened a thick folder. His two friends sat back, looking as if they didn't want to be there. Cameron appeared to be confident and not intimidated in the least. He whipped out a long sheet of paper with a maze of lines and names. The document piqued Kidd's interest for a minute when the name "Samuel" stuck out amid the sea of Jamieson descendants.

"I brought copies for you—"

"I didn't come to read. You said we're cousins. Break it down, beginning with Samuel Jamieson."

Cameron grinned. It was smug like his, and Kidd didn't like it. "I don't have to read it because it's all up here," he announced, while pointing to his head.

"My tenth great-grandfather, Paki Kokumuo Jaja, was the firstborn son of King Seif and Adaeze, which means princess. A member of the Diomande tribe, he was born in December 1770 in Côte d'Ivoire, on the Gold Coast of Africa. His name means 'a witness that this one will not die.'

11

"In the fall of 1790, he and his warriors were attacked and savagely beaten by slave traders, chained, and kidnapped. Paki was among hundreds of thousands who were hauled to the Gates of No Return castle. As they waited, many captives prayed they would die, including my tenth great-grandfather. They were unmercifully stacked together in the bowels of a ship—not the ironic *Good Ship of Jesus* under the command of Sir John Hawkins—but *Snow Elijah*. The biblical reference is uncanny, isn't it?"

Kidd's head was spinning with the information. "Listen, my black skin could rival a panther's, so there's no doubt I'm from Africa. Why don't you cross the water and stick to relatives who lived in the twentieth century?"

Cameron lifted a brow. "It's rude to interrupt. You didn't want to read the notes, so I'm giving you information verbally. I'll bring you up to speed in less than five minutes."

Backbone. Kidd admired that, but it didn't mean he had to accept the man as a blood relative.

"*Snow Elijah* landed first in the Caribbean and dropped a payload of human cargo. Then it headed off to the coast of Maryland, a state known for harsh slave laws. Automatically, my tenth great-grandfather was separated from his bodyguards. Because of his stature and strength, Paki was sold at the highest bid of $275 to a wealthy slave owner, Jethro Turner, in front of Sinner's Hotel. That purchase gave Turner exactly one hundred and thirteen enslaved people."

"I'm warning you, Cameron, get to the point. Or, do I need to draw blood to get a DNA sample?"

"And I told you I don't like to be interrupted when I'm on a roll," Cameron snarled. "Paki married Turner's daughter, Elaine. Besides my great—you know—grandfather, they had four other sons: Aasim, Fabunni, Abelo, and Orma. Orma was your eleventh great-grandfather. His name means 'free'. Although he was born free, he sold himself back into slavery for a woman, Sashe, who was a runaway, but recaptured."

12

Cameron concluded and leaned back.

Figures, a fool from the beginning. Kidd had had enough. "That tells me nothing about my old man and how you and I are related."

"Sure it does. It tells you that my tenth great-grandfather and your eleventh great-grandfather were brothers. Your father and his children are direct descendants of Orma. If you want to know more, I have stipulations."

"You sought me out. Not the other way around." Laughing, Kidd stood and grabbed his jacket. "Whatever you want to drink, it's on the house."

Cameron also stood. "I can buy my own drink. And for the record, I'd make a better bouncer than that gatekeeper at the door. The Jamieson men are a force to be reckoned with."

"I wouldn't say that too loud. Black Eye has a short temper, and he's not empty-handed."

"I never leave home without mine."

Kidd looked Cameron up and down. "I'll be in touch." He walked out without looking back. Kidd would never admit it to anybody, but he liked Cameron, whether he was a Jamieson or not.

month later, Kidd still hadn't reached out and touched Cameron—as the nostalgic AT&T commercial jingles suggested. Regardless of whether he was too stubborn or proud, his mother called him ornery. It was the principle of the thing.

As far as Kidd was concerned, it was too late to connect with that side of the family. Of course, his stubbornness didn't stop him and Ace from bonding.

There were more pressing matters. If things didn't get any better soon, he would have to relocate to find work. He took money out of his 401(k) for the down payment on his mother's condo, even though she could have easily afforded it without him.

It was Kidd's bribe to get her out of a rough neighborhood. She was his mother, and he took care of his own. That's what a real Jamieson man did. Even if he lived on the West Coast or in Australia, he would still send money home.

Stretching out on the sofa after another exhausting day of attending job fairs and filling out applications, Kidd had to find another way to supplement his severance pay.

Most of the time, he earned his money honestly. His childhood dream had always been to collect antique cars. He got the fever once he and his friends started tinkering with anything on four wheels. It wasn't long before he was known as the neighborhood mechanic, so making money was never an issue. When the bug hit him, he would cross the border into Connecticut and gamble at MGM Grand Casino.

Even though money had never been a problem, things were changing. He sighed. Although his eyes were closed, Kidd could hear a pin drop. Having a keen awareness of his surroundings was a skill he had picked up from living in the ghetto until he was in his late teens.

Kidd heard the car before the garage door was activated. His mother was home from work. A few minutes later, her high heels clicked on the hardwood floor. Sandra Nicholson's actions were so predictable. She dumped her purse, keys, and whatever else she was toting on the counter near the back door.

"Good evening, son," she said, seconds after walking into the living room.

"Good evening, Ma."

Leaning over the back of the couch, Sandra kissed his forehead and hugged him. When she came around and sat next to him, she asked, "Any leads?"

Kidd shook his head, knowing she was referring to a job.

"Kevin Lawrence Jamieson, there's one thing I can't stand, and that's a moody man. Now open your eyes and look at me," she demanded, then softened her voice.

The authoritarian in her worked since he was a boy. As a thirty-one-year-old fearless man, who once lived on his own, he still obeyed as a sign of respect. His deference was also fueled by the knowledge that Sandra Nicholson would fight him like a man if she had to.

At fifty-one, she was still beautiful. She could be a cougar or an heiress to an old tycoon. Either way, the man would have to pass Kidd's security check.

"Maybe it's time for Plan R—relocate."

Before they could get into a deeper discussion, Ace turned the lock in the front door. He strolled in with Cameron, and two other guys brought up the rear. Before any introductions, Kidd ID'd them. He thought he and Ace favored each other but the three stooges were obviously Cameron and his brothers. Their resemblance was uncanny.

Kidd sat up, crossed his ankle over his knee, and stretched his arms across the back of the couch.

"Hey, bro," Ace greeted. "Hi, Mom. These are Cameron's brothers, Parke and Malcolm, from St. Louis." He grinned, as if he had just found stray animals and brought them home to keep.

Sandra stood and smiled. "Hello."

"How are you, Miss Nicholson? I'm Parke Jamieson VI," he said, taking long strides and introducing himself with a handshake.

What family, outside the British monarchy, keeps track of numbers behind their names like that? Kidd wondered.

"I'm Malcolm. We're this knucklehead's older brothers."

Sandra laughed. "Oh, you have one of them too."

Reluctantly, Kidd stood and welcomed his guests. "Whatz up? I'm Kidd."

After the men made themselves comfortable in the living room, Sandra headed into the kitchen to warm up leftovers for their company.

Parke was the first to speak. "Kidd, Cameron has been telling us a lot about you and Ace."

"Well, it's secondhand information." Kidd shrugged.

"Ace and I agree that you've been extra moody lately. I know the job market in Boston has taken a hard hit, so I came up with the perfect solution—my brothers," Cameron said, proudly.

"Kidd, if you want to come to St. Louis, you will have a job—professional or technical—with a top salary. Plus, free room and board for as long as you want . . . or four months, whichever comes first," Parke offered, while Malcolm just watched him.

Kidd grunted. "You two traveled all the way from St. Louis to offer me a job?"

Sandra stopped banging pans. "Praise God! Thank You, Lord Jesus! Thank You!" she exclaimed, hurrying from the kitchen.

"Actually, you can choose from three jobs. All you have to do is say the word and we'll set things in motion . . . and it will be yours."

"I'm saying the word." Sandra jumped in. "My eldest analyzes things too long."

"I don't need handouts." Kidd's nonchalant attitude didn't seem to faze Parke or Malcolm.

"We're staying for the weekend, so I'm hoping we can get to know each other better. Swap stories, you know—"

Parke's iPhone interrupted him. "Excuse me. Yeah, baby." He listened for a minute and then frowned. "What is she doing in the emergency room?" Parke stood and walked to the door for more privacy, keeping his back to the group.

All discussion ceased while everyone tried to follow the one-sided conversation. "She shoe-whipped somebody?" Nodding a couple of times, Parke mumbled something and disconnected.

"Is everything all right?" Malcolm asked.

"Yeah. Some guy tried to rob Grandma BB. She beat him up real bad and then waited for the ambulance to come. To make matters worse, she rode inside with him to make sure he didn't regain consciousness."

Malcolm nodded and chuckled. "Of course she didn't tell the police that those were her footprints all over him."

"Of course not. She's still on probation for another six months."

Kidd didn't see anything funny.

"Is she okay?" Sandra inquired. Her genuine concern was evident by the expression on her face. "Do you need to get back home?"

"That old woman is tough," Malcolm answered, shaking his head.

"Yes, she is. Grandma BB called my wife for a ride back to the

17

shopping center to pick up her car. That woman has more drama than a television show."

No old person would get into that much trouble. Kidd was convinced Grandma BB was a nickname for some tough, young *sistah*. After all, who would believe a person named Kidd would be a thirty-something year-old man and more than six-feet tall?

Parke clapped his hands as if to resume the prior exchange. "So, Kidd. What do you say? Use the weekend to get to know each other?"

"No" was on the tip of his tongue. Kidd had planned to hang out with Black Eye on Saturday night. He had no intentions of changing his plans for the Jamiesons, until his mother and brother shot down every one of his excuses. Outnumbered, he finally conceded. "I'll think about it."

After that, he was no longer the center of the conversation, so his mind wandered. Boston was home. Did he really want to start over and leave his mother without his protection? Ace would be here, but his carefree lifestyle most times overruled his common sense.

The group eventually gravitated toward the kitchen where their chatter continued over black-eyed peas, beets, cornbread, and smothered pork chops. Kidd found himself smiling when Ace recalled some of their mischievous childhood deeds. It was late when Sandra called it a night. Not long after that, Cameron left with his brothers.

When Kidd awoke late Saturday morning, his mother was whipping up omelets, waffles, and sausages for brunch. As if cued, Cameron rang the bell at the same time Sandra was setting the table. Like the previous night, he and his brothers said grace before everyone dug in.

Kidd noticed how his mother seemed pleased as the Jamieson brothers spoke highly of their wives and lovingly about their children. When they pulled out their cell phones, Parke and Malcolm whizzed through a collage of photos that made Kidd think he was visiting a photographer's website.

After stuffing themselves, no one seemed to be in a hurry to leave.

As the day progressed into evening, Kidd found himself having a good time. Parke and Malcolm declined an offer to go clubbing with Ace and Cameron, so nobody went anywhere. It was another late night of talking. This time the discussion was around sports: the St. Louis Cardinals and the Boston Red Sox.

On Sunday afternoon, Kidd tagged along as Ace and Cameron drove his brothers to the airport for their flight back to St. Louis. When he returned home and walked through the door, his mother's downcast face and misty eyes instantly put him on guard.

"What's wrong, Ma?" He had to repeat himself before she answered.

"It's Black Eye." She swallowed hard. "He's dead. He got shot multiple times last night."

Kidd felt the blood drain from his face. Yeah, he knew people who had gotten gunned down in gang fights and such. That's why he tried to keep a handle on Ace, but Black Eye?

"Not Black Eye." He choked. They attended grade school together. He cleared his throat. For as long as Kidd could remember, he and Black Eye always had each other's back in the neighborhood.

"It was an ambush, the news said. Black Eye didn't have a chance," his mother reported. Then, turning her attention to him, she begged, "Kidd, please take a chance. Pack your bags and give St. Louis, or anywhere, a try."

Dazed, Kidd couldn't speak. He and Black Eye were supposed to be together last night. If it wasn't for the Jamiesons' visit . . . He shivered, not wanting to think about it. "What about Ace? He's the one you should be worrying about, Ma."

"I'll get rid of him next. I don't want the same fate that happened to Black Eye to fall on you. What if . . ." She paused and took a deep breath. "Those jobs in St. Louis . . . look at the relocation as a blessing in disguise. Prove that you can be a better man than your father."

But Kidd didn't believe in disguises. If a blessing was to be had, then it should be out in the open. As far as competing with his phantom father, Samuel Jamieson? It didn't take much to outdo him. But if he decided to accept Parke's offer, what drama would be waiting for him in St. Louis—with people like Grandma BB around?

"I'll check it out."

Chapter Two

St. Louis, Missouri

*B*arely a month later, already there was trouble in Kidd's promised paradise. He shifted on the sofa of Parke's magnanimous turn-of-the-century home in the historic neighborhood of Ferguson.

At the moment, he was being chewed out royally by Parke's wife, Cheney; Malcolm's wife, Hallison; and another woman whose identity escaped his memory. They were livid because he refused to accept or retain any of the jobs they labeled as great opportunities.

Other than having the fear of God somewhere deep, deep down inside of him, he wasn't afraid of man or beast. But a double dose of beautiful, tongue-lashing, long-legged females—with their hands hoisted on their hips, shooting darts his way—somehow made Kidd rethink his fearlessness. Their mug shots resembled his mother when she was about to take down him and Ace, once they began to tower over her as teenagers.

Even a pint-sized, adorable little girl named Kami stood staring at him with her arms folded. With two thick braids and wearing a karate outfit, she was the spitting image of her father. Without saying a word, the group's expression conveyed their sentiment: *"Looks are deceiving. We've got just enough 'tude to back up our demands."*

"My father-in-law was cordial when he learned you walked away from that factory position. He had been tirelessly pursuing it for you since the day you got off that plane. Although Papa P. held his tongue," Cheney smarted off. "Parke will be steaming that you did it again—turned down a job that hundreds of people want."

"Same here," Hallison added. "Malcolm even tried to set up an office position for you, and you declined it."

"I don't have a hubby yet, but if I did, he would have their back," the third woman chimed in. "I see a beat down coming your way."

Kidd grunted. "If you're a fortune teller, then I'm sure you'll see I'm not the man down," he said smugly. It irritated him that he couldn't recall her name. "And, you are again?"

"Part of this family." The woman was a looker: cute, shapely . . . and White. There's no way she could be a blood relative, could she? She triple-popped a wad of bubblegum to indicate the question-and-answer period had just ended.

"Really?" Kidd baited her.

"Never mind that, Imani," Cheney said. "Our husbands are a piece of cake compared to a woman's wrath." She added, snickering, "Put it this way, you might want to start shaking in your boots right about now, because we happen to love our men. And we're not going to let anybody take advantage of them—including another Jamieson."

"Just in case you don't want to listen to them, I've got my rig outside, and I'd be happy to repossess that nice ride of yours. Give me any reason. As a matter of fact, I don't need one." Then Imani added proudly, "I haven't earned the company title of 'repo woman of the month' for nothing."

He contained a smirk at their bogus terrorization. What a joke, and they professed to be peaceful, loving Christians. Kidd sneered. He didn't doubt many people tangled with these Jamiesons, but he was just as much a reckoning force single-handedly.

Acknowledging their month of hospitality was probably about to expire, Kidd decided to speak his mind. "Your family sought me out—not the other way around. I was happy in my Hyde Park neighborhood in Boston."

"Mommy's talking. Don't interrupt," Parke and Cheney's daughter, Kami, warned. "Please." Then she shifted into a martial arts stance and looked for confirmation. "Right, Mommy?"

"Thanks, sweetie."

Kami beamed when Cheney nodded and gave her a heartwarming smile.

Is there a law against spanking someone else's child? he wondered. In fact, he was about ready to strangle everybody in the room. If they had owned a bird and a dog, Kidd wouldn't spare them either.

"You ladies must think I'm a kid—"

"That's what your name implies. What kind of nickname is that anyway?" Imani tempted him for a response.

"Don't let the nickname fool you. Last time I checked, I'm old enough to drink and drive."

Kidd flexed his muscles. His father—whenever he made an appearance—addressed Kevin as "kid," as if he couldn't remember his name. When Kidd's younger brother came along five years later, Samuel tagged Aaron as "Ace." That nickname claimed the younger Jamieson to be his father's "Ace in the hole" when Samuel gambled. What Kidd couldn't understand was why his deadbeat dad was adamant about them having the Jamieson last name. What a joke.

Soon, Ace began calling his big brother "Kidd" as an endearment, and it stuck. Even the neighborhood children labeled him "Kidd." Considering how much he disliked his father, Kidd didn't know why he didn't nip that name in the bud before he reached puberty.

Although at times, the name did have its advantages. How many people would feel threatened by someone named Kidd? That was until they saw him. His six-foot-three inches and two-hundred-plus pounds of bulk could back up whatever he said.

Kidd eyed Imani. "Regardless of my first name, it's the last name you all seem to appreciate. So don't test me."

Not surprisingly, their husbands chose that moment to open the front door and enter with more force than necessary. They stalked into the living room as though they were the new sheriffs in town. Malcolm strolled over to his wife and planted a kiss on Hallison's cheek, while Parke fixed his attention on Kidd. Standing face-to-face, the two cousins matched in height and build.

Kidd lived by two rules. The first: never bring children into the world without a commitment of marriage. That one was thanks to his father. The second: never fight with family, was courtesy of his mother. "Family always has your back," she would say. However, judging from the way Parke's nostrils were flaring, something in this family was about to change.

Parke growled like an attack dog. "What is your problem? Your Jamieson family food stamps are about used up. I have to work," he said, thumping his chest, "and Cheney likes her job. Even my children clean up behind themselves for an allowance. And here you are passing up job opportunities. From now on, please feel free to contribute to the household income. The Bible says if you don't work, neither shall you eat, so I guess that's one less plate at the table."

"I'm not a heathen, Parke. I may not go to church, but I do own a Bible, so don't start quoting Scriptures to me." As far as Kidd was concerned, the Bible was for reading in specific situations. At certain times, usually after some tragedy hit—like Black Eye's funeral—or if he was in desperation mode, he would refer to it. In his mind, this wasn't one of those times, so Kidd didn't bother to pack it.

Parke's good graces were exhausted. Twisting his mouth, he looked like he was furious with his cousin. "Good. Glad you're familiar with 2 Thessalonians 3:10. Let me add a footnote. In my house, if you don't work, not only will you not eat, but you won't sleep here either."

Kidd's mother would be ashamed, but he was seconds away from throwing the first hook. "Let's cut our losses. You wanted to get to know me. Done. I thought it was a good idea at the time. It didn't work out, and now I'm out of here. Done."

His next move was to head upstairs and pack his bags. He was streetwise when it came to a matter of survival. Or he could be a charmer when the situation called for a subtle approach. Either way, he was getting out of there.

Kidd wasn't accustomed to taking orders. That was a task for fast-food workers. When the mood hit him, he lined his pockets without working the traditional nine-to-five gig. Whether he made petty bets with strangers at the bars or played poker and slot machines at the casinos, he won more often than he lost.

"It's not time to fold up, Kidd. We're family. We have your back. If one of us does well, we all look good," Malcolm's wife pleaded softly, taking on the role as a peacemaker. With her next breath, her voice strengthened. "But it can also go the other way too. If one member is a bad apple . . ."

Kidd grunted. "I guess I'm spoiling the whole bunch. Excuse me, ladies." He tried to walk past them.

"No." Kami signaled with her hand for him to stop. "You have to listen to Auntee Hali. She's good with kids—I mean children, because kids are goats."

Kidd inwardly groaned as Hallison winked at her niece. Could these women cut him down any more? Cheney cleared her throat as Parke shot daggers. With his arms folded, Malcolm held an unreadable expression.

"Kidd . . . Kevin," Cheney corrected, "we're a family who believes in sharing the wealth and knowledge. Being a manager for the phone company, I handpicked a position for you as a U-verse technician. Good pay and benefits. You had it wrapped up with your engaging personality and Jamieson good looks. But you turned down the offer because you didn't want the excessive overtime the position required. The extra work was unacceptable to you because it would interfere with your weekend plans."

Cheney glanced at her sister-in-law and continued talking. "Have you lost your mind? Do you know how much money you could've made in a year? Then, Hali, a human resources director"—Cheney glanced at her sister-in-law—"secured you a position in her bank's call center. What do you do? Refuse to take the mandatory number of calls a day. In four weeks time, you've destroyed some good job opportunities."

Imani *tsk*ed.

Kidd shot Imani a final warning. Like a feline cat moving around the room, glancing at him every few seconds, she was beginning to grate on his nerves. "One customer had a list of complaints," he offered. "I put her on hold—"

Suddenly Paden, Cheney's toddler, yelled for her from upstairs. Kami took off for the steps. Cheney was right behind her, dismissing Kidd and giving Kami instructions. "After I check on your brother, I want you to stay upstairs and play with Paden until the adults finish."

Out of three children, Paden was Parke and Cheney's youngest. Pace was the oldest, and Kami—their only daughter—was in the middle. *At least the girl's name doesn't start with a "P,"* thought Kidd. It was already confusing enough.

Kami nodded. "Don't let our cousin bully you because he's big, Mommy."

Even a child thinks I'm terrible. Kidd groaned inside.

He regretted thinking that this change of scenery could give him a fresh start in life. He should have stayed in Boston and stuck it out. Eventually, he could've made things work. Although it was ultimately his own choice, Kidd blamed Cameron for his present predicament. It would have been better for him if his cousin hadn't called in the cavalry of Jamiesons from St. Louis.

The phone rang and nobody seemed to make a move to answer it, as the standoff continued. Finally, it stopped ringing. Cheney must have answered it upstairs or it went to voice mail.

Almost immediately, the likelihood of a fist fight was put on hold when Cheney raced down the steps, crying and ranting hysterically. "Grandma BB . . . Silent Killer . . ."

Uh-oh, here we go, again. Who did the woman whip this time? Kidd had yet to meet her.

Imani didn't seem alarmed, as she folded her arms. Rolling her eyes, she shook her head. "Not again. I told her to put up that dog before he attacks someone else," she fussed. "Silent Killer's just as dangerous now as when he was a trained police mutt. Even though he was shot in the vocal cords, bark or no bark, that dog still has fangs."

"No, it's not the dog this time! It's Grandma BB! She's had a stroke—the silent killer!" Cheney clarified.

Pandemonium exploded at the severity of the situation. Kidd's employment status was shelved. He was trying to figure out how a dog and a disease were related when he was shoved into a makeshift circle. Malcolm gripped one hand and Parke squeezed his other. The next thing he knew, everybody was praying—except him. As the prayers lingered, calmness washed over Kidd seconds before his cousins loosened their holds.

As the "Amens" faded and sniffles ceased, the women gathered their purses and jackets to leave. Parke nudged Kidd aside. "This isn't over, cuz."

Wrong. Kidd was returning to Boston. He'd made up his mind. There was nothing for him here—nothing. He could pack in record time.

"We've got to get to the hospital. Do you mind staying with the children?" Parke asked.

What? Shock must have registered on Kidd's face. Reconciliation? Where was the fight in Parke now, if he was going to back down like that—crisis or not? Plus, Kidd was definitely not a babysitter.

"No matter what, we're family," Parke added. "I can beat you down later. Right now, I need to make sure my little Jamiesons are okay while we go to the hospital."

There is a time to love, and a time to hate; a time of war, and a time of peace. God spoke Ecclesiastes 3:8 to Kidd.

Huh? Kidd sucked in his breath, a little shaken. There was no mistake; he'd heard the same words from his mother's lips when she broke up fights between her sons. Now it was God who took the time to intervene? There was no memory of that ever happening to him before. Blinking, he refocused and eyed his cousin. Kidd was speechless, as his opinion of Parke moved up a notch.

"Thanks." Parke took his silence as a given. Holding up his fist, he telepathically forced a fist-bump. After Kidd succumbed, Parke ushered everyone out the door before his abandoned protest resurfaced.

Chapter Three

*T*he door had barely closed when Kami snuck up behind Kidd. He didn't even remember her coming down the stairs.

"My Grandma BB is going to be all right because I prayed for her." Kami's lips trembled, as tears hung in her eyes. This frightened little girl didn't resemble the fierce warrior of minutes earlier.

"Right," said Kidd, appeasing the child.

Whether she believed him or not, she headed back upstairs with her shoulders slumped amidst sounds of sniffles.

Evidently Kidd didn't do a good job of convincing her. His maternal grandmother had died from a stroke many years ago. He knew that wasn't something to be taken lightly.

"I've lost my mind. What did I just volunteer for?" His head was spinning when he collapsed on the sofa. He was still reflecting on what he had indirectly agreed to do—be the "on-call nanny." Not only that, he was very much perplexed over what he had heard—a Scripture Kidd knew he couldn't quote. Vaguely he recalled a saying about the sheep hearing or knowing God's voice, but Kidd didn't consider himself a sheep.

Closing his eyes, he was drained and hungry. First, his day began at a factory where he'd walked off the job after the first morning break. Assembling devices for dry-ice blasting didn't seem like the path to an exciting and challenging career. Second, a pack of angry women—okay, three—plus, a threatening little one, chewed him out. Third, he squared off with his cousin in his cousin's home. Now he was stuck babysitting while a lady's life was in question. "A busy day for an idle, unemployed man," he mumbled.

Rubbing his hand over his face, he was reminded of the stubble he'd missed while shaving that morning. The pendulum of the grandfather clock sitting in a corner of the room caught his attention and began to hypnotize him. Kidd's lids were drifting closed when Kami reappeared.

Her older brother, Pace, scrambled down the steps, but the toddler beat him to the landing by sliding on his belly. Kami was ready to grab Paden, but he had a mind of his own. At full speed, he raced away from her, giggling.

Reluctantly, Kidd got up, and the children led the procession to the kitchen. The room had a wow effect. It was a showcase for the latest in cooking artillery and a library of the newest cookbooks for every occasion known to man. Pace sat first, then anchored his elbows on the table and stared at what probably seemed like to the child, his giant of a cousin.

Independent, the toddler climbed into a high chair and Kami secured the tray and strap around him. Turning to Kidd, she placed their orders. "We want hot dogs, and pork and beans, please. You have to chop up Paden's hot dogs because he'll choke. You do know the Heimlich maneuver and CPR, right? And we keep ipecac syrup in the cabinet in case of poisoning, but you should still call the poison control hotline. Can we have juice instead of milk, please?"

The young girl had his head spinning. One moment, she was reciting a version of Wikipedia's medical diagnosis and treatment plan. The next, she was asking for juice. And for the record, he was certified in CPR and first aid. His mother made sure of it.

She must be trying to get one over on me. Kidd didn't answer right away, as he stared from her angelic face to the two young boys. Their handsome, manly features would break through at the appropriate time after the stroke of a razor. Both of them were a tinge browner than their parents' fair skin. Only the girl was a carbon copy of her father.

He had to give Cheney and Parke their kudos. At least the Jamieson rug rats were well behaved—so far—except for Kami. Something told him he had to keep an eye on her. At least Parke was married before he replenished the earth, unlike Kidd's father. Ace wasn't a single father yet, but there were too many close calls for Kidd's comfort. In actuality, Ace was the one who needed to be away from Boston, if anyone.

Without asking, Kami took charge of placing the plates on the table. Pace got up and retrieved the hot dogs and buns from the refrigerator, as the toddler waited patiently. How could he deny such dutiful children their requests? Caving in, Kidd served them juice.

Before the hot dogs were nearly burned and rescued from the skillet, Kidd put a serving of pork and beans on each child's plate. Then he listened, as they recited a children's prayer to bless their food. They were so innocent.

With everyone eating contently, Kidd shut them out to evaluate his plight. Pride kept him from wholeheartedly accepting the Jamiesons' help. From the first day, he and his cousin had bumped heads on whether he would stay in a hotel or not. Kidd wasn't penniless, and he was only considering a permanent move. It wasn't written in stone yet.

Parke had tried to argue his case. "I'm not a sensitive man, but don't hurt my feelings and insult me at the same time. My house is opened to you for as long as you need it. Like I said before—four months tops— or whichever comes first. You better believe the next time I go to Boston, I'm bunking in your bed, and you can have the couch." Parke wasn't smiling when he said it.

The jobs that the Jamiesons had paraded in front of him were good paying, even if they held little interest to him. More than that, Kidd wanted to dislike his cousins simply because they were Jamiesons. And up until last year, *Jamieson* was a bad word in his book. He had found himself resisting them and their help. It was as if they were trying to make good the Jamieson name that his father had tarnished so badly.

Kidd gnawed on his lip, contemplating. Maybe he should stay and work out their differences. He loved Boston, but he did need to make a change in his lifestyle and some of the people with whom he associated. Crime was up in certain Boston-area neighborhoods; nearby Mattapan was fast becoming known as "Murderpan." Then there was the death of Black Eye. Plus, the opportunities for a Black male were stagnant.

He chided himself. Maybe he needed to realign his attitude. If another position came his way, Kidd would accept it gracefully and give St. Louis an honest try. It's not as if they were insulting him with minimum-wage pay.

Glancing at the children's plates, he forced his mind to stop drifting. "How old are you?" he asked Kami, knowing he would forget as soon as she told him.

"Almost seven." She smiled and sat up straight at the sound of it.

"I'm eight." Pace didn't wait to be asked, as mustard lingered on his top lip. He tilted his head. "Paden's two."

If he ever got married—if—and if he ever fathered children—a bigger if—maybe God would bless him. Then again, God hadn't really blessed him when he had to grow up without a father. As far as he was concerned, God let too many questions go unanswered. Like, why had his father deserted them?

After their makeshift nutritious meal, the siblings began to argue over which cartoons to watch or games to play. Rather quickly, their perfect manners were thrown to the wind. Finally, Kidd assumed control and designated their duties until the kitchen was restored.

When the work was done, the children led him into what Cheney described as "Parke's cave"—the sun porch—where virtually every new electronic gadget on the market was housed. An enormous flat-screen TV was the main attraction.

"We can't come in here unless we're with an adult," Kami advised. Jumping on an overstuffed chair, crossing her ankles, and then her arms, she appeared triumphant. Paden protested, wanting the seat for himself. When his sister didn't relent, he was possessed with a tantrum and hurried over to his big brother. Pace picked him up and patted his back until the toddler quieted.

Good. He couldn't stand tears on a boy, or a man. Lounging in Parke's cave, Kidd wished for a beer.

Kami asked, "Can we call you uncle? You're too big to be our cousin."

"All our cousins are small like us," Pace explained.

Picking up the remote, Kidd chuckled at their curiosity. He aimed it at the screen and replied, "I don't care."

A basketball game between the Dallas Mavericks and the Chicago Bulls was in the second quarter. Kidd was immediately drawn in and the boys settled near him. Seconds later, out of the corner of his eye, he snuck glances at Pace. The boy had begun to scoot closer to him until his bony elbow dug into Kidd's muscular thigh.

Ouch. To relieve the discomfort, Kidd was about to stretch his legs and rest them on a coffee table, but the two older children stopped him in unison.

"You'd better not."

"Bossy Jamiesons make me sick," he muttered.

Pace stared. "Don't you like being a Jamieson? Are you adopted too?"

Adopted? What is he talking about? Adoption would have been too good of a fate in Kidd's life. There was no way these children weren't Parke's flesh and blood. Stunned, he felt as if he had just learned the truth about Santa Claus. That didn't make sense. They were a carbon copy of their parents.

He frowned, noting the child's curious expression. "I wish." Kidd returned his attention to the game to dismiss the tale they were spinning. Before long, his curiosity got the best of him. "Are you adopted?"

"Yeah." Pace's neutral tone indicated it didn't matter. "I'm a Jamieson, because he's my real daddy." Pace stated that with pride.

"I was adopted before you!" Kami protested.

"Umm-hmm," he responded in confusion. They were trying to run a game on him. A father didn't have to adopt his own son, did he? Kidd stared at Pace. And he would like to analyze Kami's DNA too.

"I've got a nickname like you. I'm really Parke K. Jamieson VIII, eleventh generation descendant of Prince Paki Jaja of Côte d'Ivoire, Africa. That's what my dad taught me."

What was it with this family's fascination with Africa? Who cares? Kidd was darker than all of them. *I don't even know some of my immediate family members. I'm definitely not concerned with African dynasties.*

"I'm older and smarter than her." Pace pointed at Kami.

"Uh-uh. You got a C on your homework. I got a A . . . I mean an A!" she boasted. The two seemed poised for battle. If Pace studied martial arts like Kami, the pair could tear up the house.

"Okay. Okay," Kidd said sternly. He scrutinized them again, looking for any sign that what Pace said wasn't true. *Nah.* The resemblance was too uncanny. Then he realized the boy was off a number. "You mean, you're the seventh," Kidd corrected.

Pace shook his head. "Nope. He died."

What? Their tales were getting more colorful. *Died? Right.* Before Kidd could catch them in a lie, the security alarm beeped, alerting them someone was coming through the front door. Kami jumped up and raced off yelling, "Mommy, Daddy!" Her brothers scrambled behind her.

A few minutes later, Parke strolled into the room. He looked beat.

Kidd got on his feet, not sure where things stood between them. "How is she?"

"Grandma BB had a partial stroke." He swallowed hard and explained. "Her German Shepherd, despite the inability to bark, knocked a phone off the table and kept scratching the numbers until 9-1-1 was hit. Thank God, the police came to check out the situation with Imani, her next door neighbor, who had a key. One of the officers who responded to the call recognized the dog as a former canine from his unit. He commanded Silent Killer to sit and the dog followed his order. The officers called for an ambulance and paramedics rushed Grandma BB to the hospital."

It was the oddest story Kidd had ever heard.

"They're going to keep her for a few days and run some tests, but she definitely can't return home and live alone. And she refuses to come to our house—stubborn."

Anticipating Kidd's thoughts, Parke held up his hand. "Before you use that as an excuse to leave, we have plenty of room. Since Cheney and I are considered her next of kin, we'll look into a place where she can get rehab care. That won't be until in the morning, though." He paused. "Kidd, you haven't met her yet because she's been busy traveling with the Red Hat Society ladies. Then she came back and started setting up her Rent-a-Grandma local franchise."

This woman sounded like an action figure on steroids or something. "I'm sorry to hear that she's ill. Is there anything I can do?"

"Hold that offer. Right now, I've got to get some rest. I'll think clearer tomorrow. Thanks, man, for being here for me." Parke held out his hand. Kidd accepted the shake and the slap on the back. "Good night. We'll get back in the ring later."

"Yeah." Kidd smirked. "When the bell rings, my gloves will be on." Chuckling, they retreated to their respective corners of the house.

Chapter Four

A few days later, Kidd was about to stretch out in Parke's favorite chair when Parke strolled in. Rubbing the back of his neck and then squeezing it, Kidd recognized Parke's sign of frustration because he had the same habit. In fact, he'd done it minutes earlier.

It had been a grueling week. Kidd was exhausted after hours of morning group interviews, networking luncheons, and evening seminars. His job prospects didn't seem any better than in Boston. One thing he had to admit, this family really did have connections. Too bad he had burned so many bridges.

"Hey, man. Whatz up?" Parke didn't wait for his response, as he took residence in another recliner. "I've come to collect on your offer."

Kidd froze and frowned. "What did I offer?"

"About Grandma BB."

His heart sank. Strokes weren't anything to play with. "Look, man, I'm really sorry she passed away." Kidd felt like a jerk for giving Parke a hard time on the same day his close friend had suffered a stroke. Now she was dead.

"Are you kiddin' me? Grandma BB is very much alive. We made

arrangements for her to stay temporarily at Garden Chateau. It's a skilled nursing and assisted living facility. The director is a friend of mine, and I'm also her financial planner. Hopefully, Grandma BB will be out in no time.

"But the way that woman was swearing at Cheney and me when we had her transferred today, I would say she'll need an extended stay in order for her to repent. I was so close—" he used his finger and thumb to demonstrate—"to scooping her up and dumping her in the prayer room until praise and worship filled her mouth." He exhaled. "She clowned so bad at the nursing facility, we literally had to leave the building before we got put out. Cheney and I were down the hall and could still hear her carrying on. Slurred speech and all. Needless to say, I don't think our presence was going to aid in her recovery at that moment. Everyone agreed.

"The director of nursing will give us a call when she feels Grandma BB has accepted her diagnosis. The sassy-mouthed senior has to be willing to become an active participant in her recovery. The nurse cautioned me that it could be weeks, or maybe a month, depending on Grandma BB's frame of mind. At this point, she seems agitated because she likes to be in control."

"Sounds like a character to me." Kidd wanted to laugh at his cousin's embellished description of some old woman.

"To say the least, Mrs. Beatrice Tilley Beacon, aka Grandma BB, is a spirited personality. She needs almost twenty-four-hour surveillance."

"I wish there was something I could do," Kidd stated offhandedly, as he stood and was about to head toward the kitchen. Mrs. Beacon sounded feisty. Too bad he'd never met her.

"There is. I have a business proposition. You may not think you need us, but we desperately need you right now."

Suddenly, Kidd had a bad, sinking feeling that he wasn't going to like it. Business propositions were usually meant to take advantage of something or somebody. And he was nobody's fool.

"Okay, here's the deal. Grandma BB is somewhat of a displaced matriarch in our family—albeit a crazy one. But God's working on her. Yesterday, I called in a favor. The nursing facility has a few openings. The director says whichever position you want while you're undercover, is yours. You can keep an eye on Grandma BB and keep us posted on her progress." Parke looked hopeful.

"What?" Kidd roared. "Me? In a nursing home? You've lost your mind! I am not nursing-home material or old-folks friendly. That's a definite no." He laughed and shook his head.

"I'm serious. She seems to have aged from the episode. I don't think she wants us to see her like that, but she doesn't know you. You could be our eyes."

"The woman had a stroke. How much trouble could she get into?" Kidd stated what seemed to be the obvious.

Parke lifted a brow. "Where there's a will, there's a way. Believe me, Grandma BB is headstrong and will find a way. All you have to do is keep us updated on how she's doing—"

"Can't your friend do that? You know, the one who did you that favor?" Kidd was having an onset of shortness of breath, and his palms were getting clammy. *I'm getting ready to have a heart attack. Lord, anything but that,* he silently petitioned. Could he fake passing out? Wait a minute. He wasn't a sissy. A bold, flat-out "no" was on the tip of his tongue.

"One thing the Jamiesons share is pride. Not a good quality all the time, but it's in our blood." Parke stood and exhaled slowly. "I'm begging you. Hopefully, she'll be out of there in a few weeks, maybe a month—tops. Then you can do one of your specialties—quit."

Kidd ignored the last comment; he was feeling like a deer caught in someone's headlights. Soon he calmed down and all his earlier symptoms seemed to vanish. He had never been in a work environment around seniors who needed help to the restroom, to eat, or to dress themselves.

"I don't think I'm the one for that. A nursing home? Listen, Parke, if this is about a payback, I'll swallow my pride, eat crow, and take any of the previous offers. And, believe it or not, I've even been job hunting on my own. It's just that I'm allergic to smelly, teeth-missing, bladder-incontinent people."

"Keep living. You'll get there. Besides, Garden Chateau is the Cadillac of nursing facilities," Cheney said, as she entered the room from nowhere. Had she been eavesdropping on their conversation? Kidd immediately added nosey to the list of the Jamieson family's faults.

Sure it is—Cadillac, huh? Like the Jamieson brothers lying about St. Louis being a Mecca of job opportunities. If he hadn't fallen for the "land of milk and honey" story, the Promised Land, or the "green pastures" fantasy, Kidd would be at No Name Restaurant on the Boston Pier, getting ready to devour a delectable swordfish dinner.

"The answer is still no." Kidd was a man who meant what he said and said what he meant. For him, this was a no-brainer.

Then strangely enough, on Sunday evening, he didn't know what had hit him or what was in the food they fed him, but he had a sudden change of heart. He concluded the family must have lifted him up in prayer while they were in church that morning. How else could his mouth betray him by saying, "I'll do it for a few weeks."

Ten minutes before 8:00 a.m. on Monday morning, he was about to report for duty. Talk about guilt? The Jamiesons went for the overkill.

The moment he stepped through the door to the facility, his foul attitude dissipated. A lady was posted outside the administrative office, watching the entrance. Somehow he forgot why he didn't want to work there.

As though drawn by a magnet, he approached her direction. Mesmerized by her beauty, he couldn't take his eyes off of her. The woman's hair seemed to have every hue of brown in it. In some way, her maroon nurse's uniform complemented the red undertones in her lovely skin. Her luscious lips appeared to be made for resuscitation. She was beautiful. Kidd sucked in his breath. Should he thank Parke now or later?

Chapter Five

*D*on't drool, Eva warned her mouth when Garden Chateau's automatic doors opened. Her eyes were fixed on the six-foot-plus inches of male perfection and temptation that suddenly graced the entrance. Removing his sunglasses, he glanced around. Once they made eye contact, he swaggered toward her. A suit never looked so good on a man.

Semidark chocolate drenched the skin of this fine Black man. The crisp white shirt against his neck complemented his dark suit. She wondered if he was the new hire the nursing home staff was expecting. Or, was he visiting a loved one? When he greeted her with his infectious smile and baritone voice, he reminded her of a broadcaster, a world-renowned politician, or an Ivy League professor. For a fleeting moment, Eva felt if they were in a room with a thousand people, he would stand out. Almost instantly, she knew her friend and coworker, Dawn Wright, would make a mad rush to stake her claim.

"Good morning, I'm Kevin Jamieson. I'm the new community resident liaison." He nodded as he towered over her by at least a foot. "Family and friends call me Kidd and I answer," he joked. "Are you one of the nurses?" His speech indicated he wasn't a native Missourian.

"I'm studying to become one. I'm Eva Savoy." Yep, Dawn's man radar would pick up Kidd any minute now. Her coworker prided herself with scoring three or more dates a month. Then too, Dawn didn't believe any place was off-limits to find romance, even the workplace. That's where Eva drew the line. She didn't want to work with a man by day and then date him by night. The idea seemed to violate a woman's code of freedom.

"Hope you succeed. I'm sure your patients will feel better once you give them that smile. You lifted my spirits the moment I saw you."

Breathe. Nothing touched Eva more than a genuine compliment. And she felt that his was sincere. The phony ones really bothered her. If she had a bad hair day, she didn't want to hear someone say how cute she looked.

How did Garden Chateau snag him? Not that a good-looking man couldn't work in a nursing home, but his piercing dark eyes, ebony smooth skin, and fine, wavy hair were assets that could back up the line at the express checkout lanes. Although he had a hole pierced in one earlobe, the stud was absent—smart professional choice.

Finally, her employer had taken Eva's suggestion seriously about adding someone whose sole focus was to address the residents' concerns. The board had left her in limbo for months about a decision. Then, seemingly out of nowhere, she blinked and there was a liaison. They had created the position, posted an opening, and hired a candidate—all in one week and behind her back. Amazing.

"I'm afraid you're stuck with me to show you around and introduce you to the staff." His presence was poised to spark an instant holiday; the women would break out in spontaneous celebration.

Kidd's eyes twinkled. "I'm fearless. However, if you weren't the first face I saw this morning, I probably would have turned back around and left immediately."

She nodded and smiled at his teasing. Good looking and a sense of humor. Nice qualities. Less than five minutes later, as Eva had predicted, Kidd Jamieson turned heads and interrupted conversations—staff and residents—while she led him on a tour of the facility. Up close and personal, Eva enjoyed the smell of his cologne and admired his proud walk. It was as if he built the place instead of being a new hire.

"Besides our sophisticated emergency response and security alert system, we have a state-of-the-art gym/game room/exercise room under the guise of physical therapy. Our residents can enjoy two heated swimming pools and flat-screen televisions in every common room, formal dining rooms . . ."

Her voice trailed off, as she caught a glimpse at one of her favorite charges. Mrs. Ollie Valentine was sitting in her room, nodding as she babbled on. Her steady stream of conversation could either be directed toward a phantom visitor or a recently admitted roommate.

Eva wondered how the stroke victim was faring with Mrs. Valentine's constant monologue. At times, the woman was known to talk, even in her sleep. It was harmless chatter, but when brought to her attention, Mrs. Valentine became so tickled by her own behavior. Unfortunately, her last two roommates weren't entertained and requested different rooms.

"You are the perfect ambassador for this place. I feel so much passion in your voice. I hope one day I can catch your enthusiasm about something," he said, thinking out loud. He cleared his throat. "Seriously, I'm impressed. I hadn't expected all of this."

Tilting her head, Eva frowned. "Really? A tour is usually a standard part once the interview process is complete."

"I was interviewed at the last minute, and there wasn't time."

Hmmm. She nodded. Yes, Kidd was a total package with the charisma of a youth minister, the build of a quarterback, and mannerisms of a diplomat. But there was a thing called qualifications. What were his? Garden Chateau prided itself on doing a thorough background investigation, which included drug testing on every new hire, and the rule was strictly enforced. How was all that possible in such a short period? She mentally stored that little tidbit and opened the door to the common grounds.

"No expense was spared. The landscaping is as meticulous as the indoor décor." Colorful, sturdy outdoor furniture, which was scattered under trees and across the manicured grounds, was eye-catching.

She pointed to a carefree walkway to her right. A white picket fence blocked out a large area. "Over there is our miniature petting zoo. It's a win-win situation for the animals and our residents. A few buildings over is a day care center for the children of our employees."

Next, they veered in the opposite direction down a path that parted a wall of trimmed hedges. Stopping, Eva sighed. A slight breeze ruffled her hair and she finger-combed it back. "This luscious ten-acre campus is breathtaking with its centerpiece water fountain. My only complaint is the annoying geese." She wrinkled her nose.

Kidd laughed. "Yes, Canadian geese, who seemed to have forgotten their way home."

Eva didn't want to pry information from Kidd that he wasn't willing to disclose, but she was curious. "I detect a dialect." She hoped he would keep her from guessing. After all, it was part of the "getting-to-know-the-new-kid-on-the-block stage". No pun intended. "No hints?"

He wiggled his brows. "I guess I haven't been in St. Louis long enough to lose it."

She shook her head, not wanting to take the liberty to nudge him in his side or playfully swat his arm. It wasn't as if they were old friends. He seemed to have a personality that exuded calm, and Eva enjoyed being in his company. However, it was only Kidd's first day. So she refrained from becoming too relaxed too soon around him.

"It's part of you. You can never lose your roots. Anyway, I was about to say, this is a front-row seat for God's handiwork to captivate any observer. Of course, every one of our residents has to have an escort when they're outside. If they don't, their security bracelet will activate a special alarm system."

Kidd stuffed his hands in his pockets and stared at the water fountain. He had become so intense; Eva thought he had forgotten about her. Obviously, there were hidden complexities in this man. She spoke softly. "Whenever your life is in turmoil or a workday is stressful, this is one of the many benches planted throughout the property. It's a good place to meditate."

"I'll keep that in mind."

"We'd better head back," she said, as they retraced their steps. "I know you can't wait to meet and greet our residents. Besides, I need to complete my ADL charts."

"ADL?"

That was basic terminology. What exactly were his qualifications? "Activities of daily living—you know, combing hair, brushing teeth, toileting—all the stuff healthcare workers are required to do. That is, to assist our residents in starting their morning."

She quickened her steps toward the front offices. "Well, Kidd—I mean Kevin—that's your abbreviated tour. I hope you'll like it here."

"You're giving me every reason to. Trust me."

Flirty. Eva hoped she hadn't blushed. She never expected in her drab maroon scrubs to garner so many accolades in one day. "Now, if you'll excuse me, I have to assist some stroke victims with their ADLs."

She had almost made her escape when he called after her. "Perhaps, we can enjoy lunch together."

"Can't promise that," she said over her shoulder. "I plan to spend most of the day with a new patient, Mrs. Beacon, so don't wait for me. The food is good, and I'm sure the lovable old residents will clamor for your attention."

"I prefer the attention of my tour guide."

Friendly or flirty, Eva didn't have the time to dwell on it. New hires were always nice. They wanted to be liked. Kidd had already accomplished that mission with her and several others.

As she hurried to the nurses' station, she hoped Kidd would make

44

a spiritual connection with the hearts of each soul. It wasn't fair to judge them when they're wrapped in an outer shell of failing health and disabled bodies. Eva absentmindedly shrugged. Kidd applied for this job. He knew what he was getting into, so she wouldn't have to worry about that silly notion.

Eva was certain he would be the talk of the facility for a while. She anticipated some impractical accessories would emerge: some woman would risk wearing dress heels with her scrubs, sport dangling earrings, or drape pearls around her neck in order to get his attention. She would definitely expect to witness a few new hairdos she had never seen before.

"Oh, well." Eva was just glad to have a committed voice for all residents. Grabbing her chart, she headed down the corridor.

"Good morning, ladies," Eva greeted, walking into a Victorian-decorated suite. Although the walls were white, the curtains, accents, and furniture were explosive shades of green. It was tasteful décor. Many of the double-occupancy rooms were spacious enough for a small sofa, chairs, and personal items from home. This particular room had plush rose carpeting, yet a thick, emerald green rug covered the center of the floor.

"Hi, Eve. Where's your Adam?" Mrs. Valentine smiled after her standard greeting.

"God hasn't made him yet," Eva always replied. Except this time, she wondered if the woman had seen her earlier with Kidd and was making reference to him. *What an odd thought,* she silently observed.

Although her name was Eva, people called her Eve more times than not. Of course, that name automatically seemed to be connected with the name Adam, like peanut butter and jelly or milk and cookies. It was simply expected that she would have an Adam. Unfortunately, Eva hadn't had an Adam, Charles, or Jared in her life in a while. She tried to keep her mind off that void and focus on the task at hand: school, church, and her yearly volunteer projects with Habitat for Humanity.

Mrs. Valentine needed little assistance getting out of bed in the morning. On a good day, she could wash and dress herself independently, but at a slower pace. When she suffered severe bouts of arthritis, any movement was intolerable. Plus, she had weakened after suffering a mild heart attack. But today, she appeared to be in good spirits. Radiant in a pink lounging set, Mrs. Valentine's only limitation was her struggle to remove a few foam curlers from the back of her hair.

Eva completed the task before moving on to Mrs. Beacon's bed. A certified nurse's aide had her already cleaned and freshened up, but the woman was still wrapped in her robe.

"Good morning."

"Mornin'." Her response had a tinge of a slur, barely noticeable.

Eva went to the woman's side of the closet. Her clothing mainly consisted of colorful jogging suits. She pulled out one outfit after another until Mrs. Beacon's selection was indicated through the sparkle in her eyes, before she ever voiced it.

"Lilac, it is." Mrs. Beacon's clothes were made of quality fabrics. She definitely wasn't destitute or a Medicaid recipient. In compliance with federal law, every facility had to set aside a certain number of beds for patients with little or no means to pay.

"Did you sleep well last night?"

"She talks too much." Mrs. Beacon appeared frustrated, as she sat with her left fist resting in her lap. As discreetly as possible, she used her right hand to pry the fingers open on her left hand. Eva noticed the woman's frustration, but didn't say a word.

A few days earlier, when Eva assessed the new resident, Mrs. Beacon was irritable from a plague of short-term memory lapse and failing hand-and-eye coordination.

"Can't hear anybody talkin' in my dreams," she mumbled.

Eva wanted to smile at Mrs. Beacon's complaint, but maintained her poker face. It appeared yet another one of Mrs. Valentine's roommates was ready to change residency. Unfortunately, at the time of Mrs.

Beacon's transfer from the hospital, this was the only space available.

"I'm sorry, Mrs. Beacon. I'll see if we can find you another room."

"I'm Grandma . . . Grandma BB," she scolded, then swallowed. "Let me be. Her constant yip-yakking reminds me to doze with one eye open. All I need is my gun and my dog, and I'll be fine."

Right. This woman was going to be a handful. "You're safe here. The staff is available twenty-four hours a day if you need us."

Mrs. Beacon's expression hinted she was doubtful.

At that moment, God reminded Eva of a familiar tune. As she sung the words to "He Lives," the woman's eyes danced along with the melody. Maybe Eva should come prepared with a song in her heart every morning to win the new resident over. Even Mrs. Valentine stopped talking and listened.

Eva's singing ceased by the time she had helped Mrs. Beacon get dressed.

"My hearing is sharp, and you're off-key. My little god-grand-daughter can hold a note and knows the words of any song she sings. I miss that little angel, but I don't want her to see her granny like this."

The more Mrs. Beacon talked, her words became less slurred. Still, Eva listened carefully.

"Miss Lena Horne, I'm not." She attempted to recall a name from Mrs. Beacon's era; someone she would quickly recognize. Eva chuckled as she brushed the older woman's glossy silver tresses.

"You got that right—a Beyoncé or a Rihanna, you ain't either."

Eva laughed. "See . . . and I thought I had a slight chance." Maybe she and the woman with the colorful personality would get along after all.

"Nope. Your cute, little shape will get a man's attention. But limit your singing career to humming only," she said with a twinkle in her eyes. Almost instantly, the humor was gone. "I'm serious."

"Good advice, Eve," Mrs. Valentine chided.

"Okay, I see what's going to happen here, two against one." She hoped Mrs. Beacon's loose tongue wouldn't corrupt her charming, kind roommate.

The women's banter continued until Eva had to move on to the next room. "I'll see you two lovely ladies later. Grandma BB, your speech therapist will be in shortly. From our conversation, you won't need Hattie's services long. But you'll need to see your occupational therapist this afternoon. You're sure to get a good workout today."

"Humph." Mrs. Beacon frowned. "Don't think they're not gonna get one too."

Eva didn't doubt it a bit. During the next few hours, she caught glimpses of Kidd, entering one room after another. He might as well have been speed walking, hardly spending enough time with any resident to memorize a first and last name.

Midmorning, she eyed Kidd slipping outside where the cooks and custodians took their smoke breaks. Immediately, Eva was disappointed to think he indulged in the unhealthy habit. For her, it wasn't just the health issue; it was a turnoff. Yet it wasn't even her business.

There I go again. Eva chastened herself rather than putting the Lord through the trouble of doing it. She was a work in progress, trying to stop judging people for their vices. "Prayer covers a multitude of sins," was her mantra. Walking past the thin storm door that led to the patio, Eva slowed to eavesdrop, careful to stay out of view.

"Whatz up, Kidd? I'm Matt. I like your threads, man. They got a brotha up in here in a suit and tie. Cool. Don't forget us, man." Matt offered Kidd his pack of cigarettes.

"We're in this together. Don't smoke, but I ain't turning down a drink when I want one. And I do believe in having a good time. Plus, my momma drilled into my head not to forget where I came from."

Bumping fists, the group nodded. "You're all right. You play cards or go clubbing?"

"You know it. It's second nature. Can't have a good time without those pastimes. I wouldn't be a Black man, if I didn't."

"All right, dawg," somebody said. A few laughed; one or two used profanity in a joking manner.

Why was she relieved when he confessed he didn't smoke, but had no comment about his other vices? If he hadn't been dressed in a shirt and tie earlier when she met him, from his demeanor alone, she would be convinced he was a gangbanger. His speech had easily slipped into their casual lingo.

Two of the men he spoke with were recent high school dropouts. Brad Lewis bragged that he had skipped the first day of high school, and it was downhill from there. At least the other young man had just passed his GED. Eva was proud of him for not settling and for striving to get an education. Hopefully, Brad would keep trying as well.

Bored with snooping, Eva walked away and almost collided with Dawn as they rounded the corner.

Eva did a double take. Her coworker was decked out in blue eye shadow, long lashes, and bright red lipstick. Dawn's hair was swept up in a do that she probably couldn't duplicate the next day. There were no pearls or heels, but the overbearing scent of body spray was gagging. For a fact, Eva knew that Dawn wasn't dolled up when she came to work this morning.

"Girl, when did you do all this?" Eva swept her hand in front of her friend.

Dawn shifted her hips. "I took an early lunch and kinda upgraded my appearance." She leaned closer. "Is it a bit much?"

Eva swallowed. She wasn't about to tell her friend that her appearance was over-the-top. Despite their difference of opinions in almost everything, she and Dawn Wright, an RN, became fast friends on Eva's first day on the job a little more than a year ago. "Well, considering old Mr. Whitman has a crush of you, you might have to fight him off."

When Dawn laughed, she had the prettiest smile. "Girl, he had to go to the hospital last night, so I'm okay. I'm talking about Kidd. He is one gorgeous man." She exhaled.

"You changed like this for him?" Eva wasn't about to let on that she had already predicted Dawn's actions.

"Girl, you know me. I don't miss great opportunities."

Eva wanted a special someone in her life like any other woman since biblical times, but she made a silent pact that even her older sister wasn't aware of. She refused to compromise her looks, personality, or lifestyle to lure a man. Now a distant memory, she recalled the time when she was in the seventh grade. As a young girl with a crush, Eva begged her mother for heels. Along with her struggle to conquer them, she wore her hair in curls to impress a boy named Harold Cunningham. But none of that counted.

Whatever a man saw in Eva was what he would get, 24/7. Although practicing what she preached netted Eva fewer dates lately, she tried to keep her mind occupied with good thoughts. Philippians 4:8 was her motivator: *"Finally, brothers and sisters, whatever is true, whatever is noble, whatever is right, whatever is pure, whatever is lovely, whatever is admirable—if anything is excellent or praiseworthy—think about such things."*

Although she had to admit it, sometimes it was hard to think on anything else besides her loneliness.

"Check the smoking area." What Eva wanted to do was shake Dawn and remind her of the past heartaches she suffered after chasing men who didn't chase her back. How many times had she told Dawn to be herself? Yet, in the end, Eva didn't believe in telling her friend, "I told you so."

They said their "see you laters" and Eva needed to check on another resident. During the day shift when so many residents were up walking, undergoing therapy, or enjoying recreational activities, her most tiring job was keeping track of the walkers and the wheelchair rollers. She sometimes had to break into a jog to even keep up with them. It was such a blessing when family members and friends would visit. They provided an extra watchful eye on the residents.

By late afternoon, Eva was starving. Lunch had come and gone, and she hadn't taken time to eat. Her stomach had lost its patience. Detouring to the facility's largest dining room, she stopped one of the workers who happened to be picking up discarded trays. "Marian, whatever's left in the kitchen that's hot to room temperature, can I get some?" she asked, approaching the shy, young woman.

Smiling sweetly, Marian went to check. Minutes later, she reappeared with a wrapped plate on a tray. Thanking her for the goods, Eva hurried outside to hide on her favorite bench before anyone could stop her.

Her stomach was rejoicing in anticipation of the feast. As Eva walked closer to her spot, she noticed someone had beaten her to it. This time of day, residents were usually napping, while most of the staffers were sneaking glimpses at their favorite soaps.

The broad shoulders came into view first, then the thick, wavy head of hair—Kidd. She was surprised he had taken her suggestion so soon. Eva decided against choosing another spot. She enjoyed the view of the pond from that angle.

"Mind if we share?"

As he turned to face her, Eva saw the beginning of his smile. He had loosened his tie and the weariness was evident on his face. Kidd performed a quick sweep of her; his eyes seemed to dance as they came alive. Surprisingly, his appraisal wasn't the offensive gesture of a man's bold, lustful assessment of her body parts. She appreciated Kidd's respect and adoration, but detected a hint of mischief as well. Eva would definitely keep her guard up.

He glanced at her tray and gave her a cocky grin. "It depends. Are we talking about you sharing your food or me sharing the bench and watching you eat?"

Eva laughed, bouncing the curls in her hair. "Not the mac-n-cheese—that's nonnegotiable—so it has to be the bench."

"Selfish," he teased and shrugged. "I had two helpings at lunch. I don't blame you."

"I know. It's only this good when Miss Gertie's in the kitchen, which is a couple of times a week. Wait until you taste her fried chicken. Her sandwiches are great too—club, veggie, or chicken salad. In fact, I've never had anything of hers that wasn't good yet." Preparing to take a bite, she added, "I'm surprised there was some left."

Suddenly, Eva felt bad for imposing. "Oh, I'm sorry if I'm interrupting your solitude."

Kidd stood and took one step, towering in front of her. "I would love to share my solitude with you." He eased the tray out of her hands, never losing eye contact.

Swiping a paper napkin from under the plate, he used it to clear a spot for her. It was as if she was wearing a ball gown instead of a pair of scrubs that had probably picked up more germs than she wanted to know. Kidd held the tray as she took her seat. Before he gave it back to her, she placed another napkin on her lap.

Bowing her head, Eva said grace. She sighed and enjoyed the stillness of the moment. A minute or two later, she wasted no more time before sampling bits of meatloaf and stuffing her mouth with the cheesy pasta.

Leaning forward with his arms resting on his thighs, Kidd quietly studied the water fountain. "I don't think I'm cut out to work here," he admitted out of nowhere.

"So soon? What do you mean?"

He huffed. "I've never worked in a nursing home before, and it's more than the sweet old ladies who want me to dote on them. It's everybody. Even when I walked past the petting zoo, the puppies were barking for attention. I'm overwhelmed."

Eva withheld her chuckle about the animals. "One hundred and seven beds are demanding." Maybe when she saw him earlier he was dodging her coworker's advances. Running from Dawn would wear out any man. *Oops. Two chastenings in one day.*

While spending time around him, she hoped she wouldn't break any records for prejudging his commitment. Eva knew it took a special kind of person to minister to more than the physical needs of the mostly elderly residents.

"Kevin, you applied for this job, and God gave it to you. You have a mission here."

"Don't be so sure about that," Kidd replied in a cryptic manner that made Eva rack her brain to read between the lines.

ive days. Kidd had survived almost a week with his sanity intact—barely. No thanks to Parke Jamieson the fifth, sixth, or whatever number followed his last name. Every day, his cousin had been like a dog waiting for a bone. No matter how small, Parke was ready to devour any update on Mrs. Beacon's condition when Kidd arrived home. If this was what he had to look forward to until the woman was released, then he would either move or resign. After all, it was only Eva's alluring presence that kept him from quitting before he completed his W-2 forms.

"Seen any signs of Grandma BB improving, or is she still a loose cannon?" Parke crunched on his cereal, as they ate breakfast at the kitchen table.

Mrs. Beacon was the furthest thing from Kidd's mind. His primary goal was to limit interaction with the old folks as much as possible. He had said maybe two words to the woman in passing. She looked her age, whatever that was, and harmless. Not the viper Parke had described.

"Cheney's called a few times and was basically told Grandma BB is coming along. What does that mean? You're our only eyes."

"Parke, if you want her to have around-the-clock security detail, then you should have hired a bodyguard. You know I won't think twice about quitting."

Parke scooted back from the table, folded his arms, and stared. "You're right. I'm not going to dare you because I'll lose. I'm not going to lay another guilt trip on you either, because I've done that, and you took the job . . ."

What else did the man want from him? Suck out all of his Jamieson blood? "Don't pat yourself on the back if you think your guilt was so burdensome that I caved in," Kidd said. Then he added, "I'm doing this as a favor—nothing more."

Parke's eye twitched. "I challenge you to think of somebody else for a change. Knock that mountain off your shoulder and be a—"

His nostrils flared; Kidd was fuming. *I know he is not going to say what I think it sounds like, because I will not be disrespected.* He didn't care in whose house he temporarily resided.

Lifting a brow, he baited Parke to finish. "I guarantee you that I didn't take a nursing home job for selfish reasons. Now, what were you about to say?" Kidd cupped his ear. "What, cuz, be a man? Just because I didn't have a father in my life doesn't mean I didn't grow up to be a man."

Pounding his fist, Parke leaned across the table. "That's obvious. I held back because I didn't know how you would take what I was about to—"

Kidd folded his arms, grunted, and then twisted his mouth. "Try me, and I promise I won't take the first swing."

"Be a Jamieson. That's what I was going to say."

"That name means nothing to me."

"Yeah, I got that the first time we met. But it still means everything to me, my family, and our tenth great-grandfather who was captured in Africa." He pounded a fist again.

"Save it, Parke." Kidd held up one hand and pulled his keys out of his pocket with the other. "History was never my strong subject. I'd better head to work." He emphasized the last word, as if it left a bitter taste in his mouth. "I wouldn't want to be late and get fired." He walked out, spewing a mocking laugh.

Clearly, the large house wasn't big enough for two Jamieson men. Clearly. They were too much alike, but on opposing teams: pro-Jamieson versus anti-Jamieson. He should have left town the night of their first big blow-up. That way, he wouldn't have known about Mrs. Beacon. He would have been back in Massachusetts and not in this predicament.

In the driveway, Kidd turned his focus to something else. He climbed behind the wheel of his classic silver Maxima—his car was a thing of beauty. It had been parked in a driveway in his cousin's neighborhood when he noticed it.

The deal he got for it alone was worth the trip to St. Louis. The "as-is" sign planted in the windshield was his clue that the owner was fed up with it. Calculating the vehicle's worth, Kidd made an inquiry, then tinkered with it for less than an hour. Once he diagnosed the problem, he haggled over a fair price, an amount that was a bargain for the buyer.

Parke had been amazed at Kidd's mechanical know-how when he completed the repairs and parts replacement in no time. A good wash and wax made it appear new. The new Jamieson in town not only had technical skills, but intellect—whether Parke respected and accepted that or not.

Kidd shifted to refocus on the present. After strapping himself in, he leaned against the head rest and closed his eyes to regain mental control. "You don't know me, Parke," he whispered. Taking a quick assessment of his current situation, he considered the fact that he was still in St. Louis, wasn't he? He took a crummy job to appease his cousin, didn't he? And he was living in another man's house. "I would say that makes me a saint!" Kidd concluded.

After this latest stint, it was doubtful they would even like each other. He and Parke didn't make a love connection in Boston, but they remained civil. Ever since Parke had picked him up from Lambert Airport in St. Louis, they had been bumping heads. Their newfound relationship was going downhill fast. Parke was going to learn he couldn't run this Jamieson.

Kidd might not get on his knees and pray every morning like Parke's household, but he knew how to thank Jesus for one day at a time. As a matter of fact, he was a card-carrying member of the Lukewarm Club. He wasn't hot for Jesus, nor was he opposed to Him. Again, his mother didn't rear any heathens.

On any other morning, his Maxima offered pure driving pleasure, as he drove the short fifteen-minute distance to Garden Chateau. After the morning's argument with Parke, he really couldn't stomach the place. He'd already stayed two days longer than he would have.

This was not going to be a good day. He turned into the complex and parked in a random space. Kidd punched his steering wheel after he turned off the ignition. He didn't even get the chance to finish his bowl of cereal. Parke ruined his breakfast. He loved Corn Chex. Taking a deep breath, he got out and stalked up the walkway to the building's entrance, grunting his greetings to anybody he passed on the way to his office.

Behind his closed office door, Kidd flopped in his chair and gazed at the ceiling. "God, my prayer for today is, why am I being punished? Living with Parke is torment and working here is insanity. What did I do to deserve this?"

Kidd didn't expect an answer, and he didn't get one. Instead, he regrouped for the second time that morning. Instinctively, he scanned the list of residents' requests for appointments with him. The myriad of names blurred before his eyes; it was all too overwhelming. Although the facility was very nice and odors were kept at a minimum, he was still surrounded by older people who freaked him out.

That ice-blasting assembly position he worked at the factory for one day was starting to look like a dream job compared to this. Huffing, Kidd stood and grabbed his clipboard and pen. He might as well make himself look busy. Maybe, he could walk off his steam. He pasted on a dazzling smile and strolled down the corridor, entering the first room and checking off the name.

"Good morning, Mr. Johnson." The thought of shaking hands with the man was out of the question, so Kidd didn't go through that motion for the fear of contracting something.

"It's Johnston," the man snapped. "Can't you read?" Thin white hands with blue veins snaking through them gripped the wheels of his wheelchair. "'Bout time you got here, boy. I need to go to the bathroom."

Kidd stiffened. *Oh no, he didn't.* "What did you say to me, Mr. Johnson?" he asked, this time purposely mispronouncing the man's name. Pressing down hard on his clipboard, he broke the pen in two. All the while, he was hoping wax had clogged his hearing. Otherwise, the man was asking for trouble.

"I'm not gonna tell you anymore, boy. My name is Johnston, and I need to use the bathroom!"

"Humph. That's what I thought you said. Have a good soaking on me. Nobody's stopping you. I haven't been a boy since I was ten." Kidd twirled to exit and nearly slammed into Eva, who stood speechless with a horrified look on her face.

"He started it," Kidd stated with a tilt of his head, as he moved past her and exited the room.

He hated that Eva probably heard the ugly side of him. But coming from any man, "boy" would always be a derogatory word to a Black man. To keep from getting arrested and tainting the Jamieson name anymore than he had, Kidd made a notation on the chart next to the man's name. He scratched out the "t" in Johnston as a reminder to steer clear of his room or be ready to face jail time. At thirty-one, he had never been in jail—although he had come close a few times with rowdy friends. Nothing was worth him going now.

Although Garden Chateau was paying him a good salary for a job he didn't like or want, no amount of money could compensate him for humiliation.

I give grace to the humble. God spoke from 1 Peter 5:5.

The words sped by him like lightning. What? Kidd frowned and glanced around. Nobody else seemed to be looking for the owner of the voice. Was that God? If so, it was the second time he felt some type of spiritual intervention since he came to St. Louis. Kidd shook himself and moved on.

Every other resident he met after that incident—Black or White— wasn't nearly as belligerent as Mr. Johnston. A couple of residents were comedians, including Miss Nora who was reciting her third joke when he waved good-bye and made a hasty exit. A Black man wearing faded brown jogging pants and a long-sleeved white T-shirt steadied himself using a bamboo cane and the wall. He couldn't have been older than fifty, if that. Kidd felt pity toward him. Why was he here with these old folks? Kidd wondered.

The man seemed relieved to see him. "Do you mind helping me to the bathroom?"

What is it with these people? Kidd thought. Did the staff give them too much to drink? He panicked. He peeped around the corner, searching the halls to see if someone was coming to the man's rescue—anybody, but him. While Kidd contemplated what to do, the resident shuffled away.

The man was within feet of his destination when he had an accident. Kidd groaned. "Come on, dude." Turning up his nose, he frowned. "Clean up in aisle . . ." looking around for a locator wall plate, "Hall C," he shouted to anyone who would listen.

"Kidd, this is not Kmart," Eva hissed, rushing out of a room at the same time a nurse's aide hurried to assist the man. "This is a group effort. We all pitch in to help." She went into a utility closet and grabbed a sponge mop.

"What are you getting ready to do with that?"

"Didn't you just yell aisle cleanup?" Eva scowled.

"Yeah, for the custodian."

She gritted her teeth. "Well, for the moment, I'm the acting custodian until Larry can get around here. In a few minutes, we'll start to bring residents this way toward the dining room for lunch. If this isn't cleaned up immediately, you may see more than your share of hip fractures. We can't have our residents slipping and falling."

"You really take this job too seriously." He shrugged and walked away.

As he predicted, the day got worse. There was a pending food fight during lunch when three sets of elderly women saved Kidd a seat at their tables. They all waved frantically to get his attention. One lady grabbed his arm with a death grip as he strolled by. That prompted someone else to pitch a corn muffin at the offender.

Kidd escaped, but without eating. For the remainder of the afternoon, he sought out hiding places from the residents. It was definitely going to be his last day. An hour before it was time for him to clock out, his stomach growled. Spying the halls to make sure the coast was clear, he headed to the kitchen, as if he was running for a field goal. The aroma of dinner was permeating the air. He opened the door to the kitchen and stuck his head inside.

"Hello," his voice echoed. A gray-haired woman with an apron loosely tied around her waist poked her head from behind a corner. Kidd cranked up the charm. "I missed lunch. Do you think I can get a sandwich?"

"You're Kidd, right? The new kid on the block. Get it?" she mused.

"Yes, madam. Actually, I get that pun all the time." He quickly stepped inside and took one last peep before closing the door.

She chuckled. "I reckon so. What do you have a taste for, baby?"

"I'll take any kind of meat and cheese between two slices of bread. Bless you." Kidd knew when to turn on his spirituality too.

"Coming right up, handsome." She opened the door to a wide, stainless steel, walk-in refrigerator. Pulling out a couple of containers and condiment jars, she made a sub sandwich before his eyes and wrapped it with a napkin. Lastly, she plucked a miniature juice carton off the shelf. "There, baby. Now get out of my kitchen. I've got folks to feed."

"Are you Miss Gertie?"

Her hands landed on her hips, as her nostrils flared. "Do I look like Gertrude?" She cranked her neck. "Don't mention that woman's name to me. Every time she's here, she rearranges my things. I'm Miss Mary, younger and better looking."

Nodding, Kidd winked. "Well, thank you, Miss Mary." Cracking the door, he looked both ways. He didn't want any witnesses to follow him outside to the pond, or whatever they called it.

He hustled his way to the familiar bench and collapsed. "There's got to be a better purpose in my life." Kidd shook his head in disappointment, mumbled a few words over his food, and tore off a hefty bite. Immediately, he spit it into his napkin. "Blah." It was horrible. How could a person mess up a sandwich? His little seven-year-old cousin could probably do better than this. "Yep. It definitely couldn't compare to Miss Gertie's hoagies." He reached for the carton of juice to wash away the nasty residue.

"If I were a man, I would beat you down."

Kidd flinched and glared over his shoulder at the threat—Eva. He was about to smile, but one arched brow accenting her game face indicated it wouldn't help.

"Considering my lovely opponent, I'm a lover, baby, not a fighter." What possessed him to say something so cocky? Blame it on the counterfeit sandwich.

Eva laughed. "You would first have to love yourself, which you don't seem to do! Then you could love others. I'm still trying to convince myself that those mean-spirited words actually came out of your mouth to Mr. Johnston—"

"Wait one minute, Eva. I don't need to defend myself. But did you not hear what the old man said to me? Those are fighting words. I'm not apologizing for that one."

"You're an imposter. This is our job, Kevin. We are here for the residents because we want to be. What a loser. When you first walked through those doors, I thought you were a blessing in disguise. Well, it didn't take long for you to come out of your costume. This whole 'fighting words' thing is thuggish."

Kidd sucked in his breath, as if she had delivered an uppercut.

"I was in your corner, Kevin. I was pulling for you. I expected you to succeed, but now another Black man bites the dust." She turned and stomped away. Then, swirling around, she snapped, "God doesn't like ugly, and today you looked horrible."

Chapter Seven

*L*ater that evening, sequestered behind the closed doors of her
two-bedroom condo, Eva was slumped in her favorite overstuffed chair. Glancing around her living room flustered about
her earlier behavior, she could have earned the first runner-up spot if
there was a contest for the poster child of those famous airline commercials "Wanna Get Away?"

At first, she was too embarrassed by her actions to call Dawn or
her sister, but her only sibling knew her better than anyone. So far, they
had been on the phone for more than a half hour.

I've lost my mind, Eva thought while her sister was talking. When
it was her turn to speak, she confided, "I just can't believe I turned 'pre-
nursezilla' on the man. What was I thinking?" She rubbed the same
patch of hair until her scalp became sore.

"That's exactly what I want to know. That man could've hurt you.
I don't care if he thinks he's a kid, or whatever." Her twin, Angela, didn't
back down. The tongue-lashing had been going on for—she blinked
to read the time on her wall clock—forty-five minutes.

Standing at five-foot-six, Angela and Eva were identical twins. At times, their mother could barely tell them apart. They had brownish-streaked hair, light-brown eyes with the clarity of a new marble, and skin that was fair, but just dark enough to camouflage freckles.

They both could turn heads.

But their personalities were distinguishable. Eva had no problem dining solo to savor exceptional food in solitude. On the other hand, Angela was a chatterbox from the time she placed her order, during the meal, and after paying the check. It was no surprise when Angela's food was often room temperature by the time she started to eat it.

"I was definitely having an 'out-of-body-and-out-of-mind' experience. I just couldn't believe my ears. I was shocked to hear such an exchange—and with a resident no less. It caught me off guard."

"Put yourself in his shoes," Angela scolded. She tried to be the voice of reason when Eva made an error, but Angela chased wisdom away when it was time for her to exercise good judgment.

"From what you told me, it sounds like that resident provoked your coworker. How did you expect him to react when an old geezer called him 'boy'? That's slavery terminology—a word we think is obsolete until it resurfaces without warning." She paused. "And you know, I'm not chummy with senior citizens either, unless they're related to us. My only exception is the yearly pre–Mother's Day project I do with you. Besides that, I'm not visiting."

"Come on, Angela. I'm not talking about being chummy. I'm talking about simple cordiality, regardless of sex, creed, race—or age."

Angela sighed. "God gave you a specific gift for geriatrics. Some gifts aren't meant to be shared—although we know God freely gives—check your Bible on that one. What I mean is, everyone doesn't share your passion. Besides, this man isn't your responsibility. If he doesn't do his job, let the powers that be deal with him."

Eva nodded, admitting her sister was right. Still, she wanted to have the final say. "All that sounds good, Angela, but forget about my passion. A person doesn't retaliate against ignorance. I've heard derogatory comments from residents—and some have come from people who aren't as old as Mr. Johnston. That doesn't give me ammunition or an excuse for rudeness. I just ignore them and keep doing my job. That's called being professional."

Eva didn't believe in living in the past. Her blessings were in the future. Yes, sometimes their words were hurtful, but who was going to stand up and be a Christian?

Her sister wasn't letting up either. "No, that's called you being desensitized." Eva imagined Angela was wagging her finger at the phone. "Everybody doesn't 'get over' everything easily, especially a Black man—I don't care how intelligent he is. Plus, if he isn't a practicing Christian, then his reaction was strictly textbook. And speaking of being a Christian, it appears you missed the mark today, sister. You got mad at your coworker for putting some old man in his place, and what do you do—"

Eva groaned. "Turn around and act the same way." Forget having the last word. Angela snagged that spot. Still, Eva was looking for some justification, even if it was a dot of being right. "Angel, you should have heard him. He sounded deadly."

"Did you interrupt a murder in progress?"

Now her twin was grating on her nerves. This is where their shared compatibility ended. Angela always wanted to be right, and Eva refused to be wrong. "Are you kidding? Not if Mr. Johnston had anything to say about it. He may be weak in his body, but he has spit, kicked, and yelled when the mood hit him."

"Hmm, violent nature. Does he have a touch of Alzheimer's?"

"Nope. His mind is sharp."

"Then he meant what he said. Case closed." Angela's line clicked as if on cue. "Hold on."

Eva thought about disconnecting and letting Angela return to dead air. Her sister was trying to back her into a corner. It was definitely time to go and put something together for dinner.

Pushing up from her cozy position in her chair, Eva stood and stretched. The sun was setting, but faint rays of light sneaked through her miniblinds. It was just enough illumination to provide a path to the light switch on the wall.

With the skylights beaming in her kitchen, Eva still contemplated hanging up on her sister. She was simply looking for support to justify her bout of out-of-control behavior toward Kidd. She wanted Angela to be outraged by his actions; instead, Eva got a spanking.

"Sorry. I'm back," Angela said, breathless as if she had run a marathon around the house. "The bottom line with this Kidd guy is to pray for him . . . and for you to apologize."

Eva dreaded the thought. She didn't mind apologizing, but to him? "I guess so; since I started it, it's up to me to end it." She opened her refrigerator and grabbed a bowl of leftover chicken salad.

"Yep. Listen, Lance will be here any minute and I want to be ready. Are you sure you don't want to tag along with us to his cousin's fiftieth birthday party? It'll be fun."

Eva had had enough of Angela tonight. She'd rather sulk in silence, but couldn't. "Sorry. I've got a date with Watson and his *Theory of Nursing* textbook for an upcoming test."

This was her second semester in St. Louis University's nursing program. The fall semester had been difficult, but she survived. Now the spring session was making her question her choice to return to school at twenty-seven. After all, her first degree in business landed her two dead-end jobs. Although she really wanted to obtain a second degree, the course work was a struggle.

Once they disconnected, Eva replayed every word she had uttered to Kidd and his every reaction. She was reminded of Isaiah 55:11 where once God's Word left His mouth, it never returned, but accomplished the task that God ordered. "If only I could have recalled my words so they would never have hit my intended target." Then she would have bypassed Angela's scolding and her need for repenting.

Eva garnished her salad with shredded cheese and olives, then glided across the hardwood floor to her oak wood bar table. Out of habit, two place settings were always staged for an unexpected visit. She carefully laid her teal bowl on a gray place mat; both colors inspired the décor throughout her condo. Without children or pets to clean up after, Eva couldn't resist the white shaggy rugs scattered throughout a few rooms.

Before getting situated at the table, she strolled into her bedroom closet, where a stash of bridal magazines was hidden from view. In case she had company, Eva didn't want anyone to get any wrong ideas and ask questions. They were purely for entertainment purposes only.

She reached for a thick edition of *Brides* magazine. While she ate dinner, she needed a diversion to keep her mind from returning to the scene of her crime. Just as she was about to flip through the pages, her hand froze. A wedding dress embellished with layers and layers of ruffles swallowed up a blushing bride on the glossy cover. The caption read "Let the Fairy Tale Begin." The photo took her breath away.

In another world, Eva's career choice would have been anything connected with weddings—hers or that of a family member, a stranger, or a mail-order bride. It didn't matter in what capacity: cake decorator, planner, dress designer, or florist. It was just a fantasy.

She wondered if Angela and Lance were meant to walk down the aisle. If so, Angela would be Eva's first test case, unless Dawn snagged someone beforehand. Physically, Angela and Lance complemented each other. He was a looker, and they were inseparable. They could almost be each other's twin. In Eva's eyes, his vice was placating Angela's domineering personality. The couple never had an argument during their one year of dating. How was that possible? Lance was a wimp. Some women would love to have one just like him, including Dawn.

However, in his defense, Eva had also been on the receiving end of Lance's generous nature by default of being Angela's sister. Lance never hesitated about including her on outings, and he never made her feel like a third wheel. As it turned out, when Angela got a boyfriend, Eva got a big brother. Yet, despite Lance's handsome looks and winning personality, men like him never intrigued her.

Eva was drawn to a strong Black man, and she wasn't talking about his strength alone—although firm abs, biceps, quadriceps, and every other muscle in the human body were added bonuses. She wanted a man who possessed convictions and acted upon them. She preferred a man who was confident in spite of adversity and satisfied in an exclusive relationship—and the biggest attraction was his love for God.

That combination was her weakness, or it would be if that kind of man existed. She had yet to meet someone who had the complete package. But she could hold out. Either God would send the right man for her, or He would send His Son in the rapture for her.

Either way, Eva pondered, she would remain a closet romantic and occupy her time with other interests. When she assisted with an occasional volunteer project for Habitat for Humanity, it was definitely rewarding. Eva always shed a few tears after witnessing the joy on a single mother's face when she finally had a place of her own to call home. Plus, she concluded, her so-called soul mate or knight in shining armor probably didn't know how to ride a horse.

After dinner, she cleaned up her mess. Once again, she revisited the incident at work, trying to make sense of what caused her to lash out like that. As a Black man in a key position, Eva was Kidd's cheerleader from the moment he swaggered through Garden Chateau's doors. She had prayed he would succeed and dispel the myth that all Black men were sitting behind bars, mixed up in gangs, or using drugs. However, Kidd's mannerisms suggested at times that he'd have no problem sitting behind bars or participating in gang activity. He just had a fearless spirit.

Eva returned the magazine to its proper hiding place before going back into her living room. This time she went directly to the nook that served as a condensed home office. Unzipping her book bag, which was dangling from a sturdy wall hook, she pulled out her nursing book. Then stretching out in her oversized chair, she rested her bare feet on a makeshift ottoman. Without any distractions, she began to read and highlight sections to review.

A few hours later, Eva was glad when her phone interrupted her thoughts. "Up for a late movie? The next one is at ten-fifteen," Dawn asked when Eva said hello. The woman's energy always amazed Eva.

"You should have asked me before my lesson put me to sleep. I was trying to get a jump start on studying for my test next week." She yawned.

"Oh, I just felt like getting out—dinner, dancing, movies, skating. I would even borrow someone's dog if the mutt would let me take him for a walk. I just didn't want to go by myself." Dawn sounded disappointed.

"Why did you wait so late to plan a night out on the town?" Eva rolled her eyes.

They definitely were opposites. Eva was content as a homebody, while Dawn considered home a place for sleeping only. Dawn had been an RN for six years, since she was twenty-seven; Eva was twenty-seven and trying to become an RN. Dawn was divorced; Eva had never been married or engaged and remained abstinent to honor God. Close friends knew Dawn battled low self-esteem, but she always bounced back. At times, Eva's confidence could be overbearing, and Dawn always put her in check. When all was said and done, their differences complemented their friendship and they respected each other's point of view.

"You know, at this stage in my life, I thought I would be happily married with at least one child." Dawn sighed. "Look at me, no husband and no brats."

Eva hated these conversations with Dawn because she never knew the right thing to say. Personally, if Eva had survived a bad marriage like Dawn's, she would be glad there were no ties. She felt bad for even thinking that and dared not voice it.

"I'm venting," Dawn continued. "Recently, I overheard a woman say every woman should be limited to one shot at love. If it doesn't work, too bad. I guess I never really thought of it that way. I've lost my chance."

"That's the craziest thing I've ever heard. Some women have several chances . . ." Eva stopped herself from saying others had none.

"Maybe. I guess I could've stuck it out with Gary and his drinking. But, girl, after the first punch, I made sure that was his last. I didn't stick around for an encore."

"Dawn, stop second-guessing your decision to get a divorce. Gary was a decoy, not God's blessing." Eva did her best to pump up Dawn's spirits. So their conversation bounced from one topic to another, until finally Dawn settled on a taboo subject for Eva.

"So what do you think about our Chateau hottie? Kidd's not only fine, but he's got the killer charm too. He has a smile for everyone. And I see him winking all the time at the little ladies. They get such a kick out of it. The board members really outdid themselves when they tapped that guy . . ."

Eva cringed as she listened to her friend sing the praises of a man who she had chewed out less than twenty-four hours ago. Despite what her sister said, Eva felt it was for a good cause.

"So what vibes do you get from him?" Dawn pressed her.

Eva would never tell.

Chapter Eight

"Kevin?" The intruder sounded hesitant, approaching his bench on the facility's campus.

Eva. Stirred by the light breeze, her perfume had preceded her. He liked the pleasant fragrance and immediately recognized her by it. Then it all came back to him: what she said; the fury behind how she said it; and the beauty of her stormy eyes when she said it.

The fear that shivered through his body didn't come from her threat to beat him down. Kidd doubted he would even feel her most powerful blow. What he feared was that she may have been right. He struggled with that possibility all weekend, and he still didn't like it. In fact, he returned to work simply for the challenge of bumping heads with Eva, definitely not for the love of and the commitment to his job.

"Kevin?"

Stubbornness wouldn't allow him to immediately acknowledge her. Instead, he scrutinized several male geese bold enough to leave the rim of the facility's water fountain and mosey his way.

"I come in peace," Eva said softly.

"Wasn't that a line from the old *Mars Attacks* movie, and the beautiful creature is really the evil enemy?"

"I'm not your enemy, Kidd . . . Kevin."

As Eva inched baby steps toward the bench, one goose seemed poised to protect its territory. Kidd was in a position to defend his with one movement if the beast second-guessed itself about bothering Eva.

"I had no right to judge you, and I'm sorry."

"Accepting apologies isn't part of my makeup. I believe in saying what I mean and meaning what I say. Don't you mean what you say?" Shrugging, Kidd angled his body to glance over his shoulder. Once he made eye contact, he didn't blink.

The last time he said those very words, they backfired on him and he was sentenced to this nursing home. So much for his conviction set in stone, but Eva didn't have to know that. He didn't take mess off any man. He sure wasn't going to let a woman—a pretty one at that—run over him.

"Accepting apologies is the centerpiece of humanity and Christianity." She flopped down next to him.

"Spoken like a textbook."

She practically growled. "You're a frustrating man when you're crossed, Kevin Jamieson. I was wrong to think you had a chip on your shoulder. Your weight is the size of the Rocky Mountains—no, Mt. Rushmore—and we know how hard it must be to chip through that granite."

If it was anyone else invading his space besides Eva, Kidd would have demanded, *"Who invited you to sit with me?"* Instead, he snickered and focused ahead.

"Kevin, I deserve your cold shoulder." Through his peripheral vision, he watched, amused as Eva toyed with her fingers. "I mean, you haven't known me for more than a couple of weeks, and I go berserk on you. When I thought about my actions later on, I realized that if I had said what I did to the wrong person, I could have gotten hurt."

Kidd snapped his neck around and gave her his full attention. It only took a second for his eyes to focus like the lens of a camera. Eva's freckles, moles, and the subtle lines around one side of her mouth became sharp in his view. Her hair was twisted in a loose ball anchored on the top of her head, accentuating the youthfulness of her features. What he didn't like was the drab green uniform she should have left in her closet. One day, he might tell her his opinion.

"I don't strike women. I live by standards and that's one of them. I would never touch a woman, except to kiss her or make love to her."

Even with all Eva's attributes, Kidd was not a chump. He didn't take kindly to a woman—however beautiful—cutting him down with words.

She straightened her posture, and Kidd braced for an impending challenge. He flared his nostrils in a stare dual. Suddenly, Eva nodded, as if she had made up her mind about something.

"Okay, so I'm safe with you, and so is the rest of the female population." She paused and lifted a finger. "What about an old, defenseless, senile man in a wheelchair?"

He leaned closer. Whatever snack she had indulged in before coming outside, the fruity scent lingered. "You're pushing it." He winked.

"You're an arrogant one." Eva put some more distance between them.

"Keep that up, and you might be apologizing for the next words coming out of your pretty mouth."

"To set the record straight, I am genuinely sorry and ashamed. I like to think of myself as a peaceful, loving creature." She emphasized the last word.

"Don't forget the attractive part," Kidd teased. He enjoyed their banter. He liked the vulnerable side of her fighting for dominance over her self-assured persona.

"So you noticed." She didn't miss a beat, as she lifted her chin nonchalantly. Still, a blush was apparent.

"Nothing gets by me, Eva—nothing."

"Hmm, I'll keep that in mind." She stood. "So, are we friends . . . again?"

When she extended her hand, Kidd snickered. Did she really expect him to accept an antiquated handshake? Kidd held his tongue. In these surroundings, they were nothing more than colleagues, but that could change in the future—if he wanted it to. He wasn't even friends with his cousins, Parke and Malcolm.

Not wanting to hurt her feelings, Kidd reached for her hand and held on to it. It was soft. He didn't realize he was daydreaming, until Eva's voice shattered his reverie.

"Thank you," she whispered. "And, I'm truly sorry."

He watched her retreat into the building until she was out of sight. There was something magnetic about Eva, besides her passion and exquisiteness, and Kidd just needed to figure it out. Clearing his head, he squeezed his knees.

"Might as well get this over with, Mrs. Beacon," he mumbled. She had been the source of yet another argument between him and Parke over the weekend, until Kidd had had enough. Parke accused him of not keeping his end of the bargain when, technically, there had been no negotiation.

"What do you want me to do, Parke? Stay by her side with a clipboard and constantly take notes?" That comment had seemed to chop down his tree.

"You're right," Parke replied, conceding. "Just you being there for her and us means a lot. I do appreciate your sacrifice."

Up until that argument, Kidd hadn't planned to spend any significant time talking to Mrs. Beacon until he was ready. When he did make his move, he had every intention of identifying himself to her upfront and revealing the real reason for his presence at Garden Chateau. Rethinking his strategy, he determined that would have been juvenile and petty. Plus, it wasn't his style.

For the time being, he decided to make an effort to track her progress. And when she was discharged, Kidd planned to discharge himself of his involuntary obligation. Aside from his ego trip, Parke wasn't such a bad guy, so Kidd could play this charade for a while.

An image of Eva flashed through his mind. She wasn't part of the bargain, but there was something about her that kept him questioning his attitude toward things and people.

Standing, Kidd flexed his biceps and began his trek back inside. He was ready to perform his so-called covert mission of checking on Parke's family friend—the crazy woman—in Kidd's opinion.

He caught a glimpse of Eva not far away down the hall. Her back was to him before she slowly turned around. Kidd froze and took a mental snapshot as they made eye contact. He winked to convey everything was cool between them—almost. She responded with the most engaging smile he had seen in a long time. That is, aside from the smile and hugs his little cousin, Kami, lavished on him before her bedtime. Then the toddler, Paden, would copy his big sister's actions. Even the oldest, Pace, clung to him whenever he was home.

Reflecting on Kami and her brothers made him think of Parke, which reminded Kidd that he was supposed to be somewhere. He turned away and headed down another corridor, searching for Mrs. Beacon's room number. His intention was to give her a little more than the quick hi and bye he usually said in passing.

During those brief encounters, the woman didn't appear to be in any distress. Otherwise, Kidd would have stepped in. Plus, this passive little woman didn't fit Parke's explosive description of being a shoe-whipping somebody. Then again, he had to admit he hadn't spent enough time with her to really know. Five minutes tops, then Kidd would be on his way.

Gathering a smile, he knocked on the door frame of suite eighty-seven, without looking inside. "Hello," he called out.

"Come in," a sweet voice echoed from within.

Entering the room, the décor reminded Kidd of a parlor in an old Western movie. Two pairs of women's eyes lit up; immediately, they worshiped his company.

"Good morning, ladies. My name is Kidd, with a double *d*." He grinned. It was right on the tip of his tongue to say his last name just to spite Parke.

"Kidd? Weren't no fellas on my block who looked like you as a boy, or I would've married sooner. You're fifty years too late, young man. I'm Mrs. Ollie Valentine." She blushed and batted her eyes. "It means love, you know."

"Then it looks like I already have my valentine for next year," he said, charming her. He could tell she had been a striking woman in her heyday. The remnants were evident. Mrs. Valentine's hair was white as a cloud. It was combed in some type of style he couldn't describe, but it was flattering on her. The way she moved her mouth suggested her teeth were indeed hers.

Kidd stared at Parke's friend.

"Friends call me Grandma BB. Foes are restricted to Mrs. Beatrice Tilley Beacon." She squinted. "Give me time to check you out." After making a bold appraisal of Kidd, she glanced around the room, as if she was seeing it for the first time. Looking back at him, she nodded. "Humph. You pass. I'll grant you permission to address me as Grandma BB."

Kidd laughed. What else could he do? The two definitely didn't fit Kidd's old folks' profile. He shook his head and smirked, enjoying the woman's spunk. Maybe she did say all those things Parke accused her of uttering. Perhaps this visit wouldn't be an in-and-out assessment after all.

Mrs. Beacon was also an attractive senior with silver hair and the clearest skin tone. She was all dolled up. Jewelry hung around her neck and dazzling earrings drooped from her ears. Her gold velour jogging suit gave the impression she was young, spirited, and nobody better not tell her otherwise.

She had all the outwardly feminine appeal, except when his eyes traveled downward. On her feet, she wore black Stacy Adams shoes. That appeared to be a problem. Perhaps they were from another resident's room. He would have to ask Parke if Mrs. Beacon was a kleptomaniac. When he spied the wheelchair near her bed, he wondered, *Why did she need shoes at all?*

"Are you my 'boy-toy,' ready to whisk me off to therapy?" she asked.

The woman actually made him blush. His reply was stuck in neutral.

"Oh dear, where are our manners?" Mrs. Valentine seemed embarrassed, as she clamored for attention again.

"Humph," Mrs. Beacon slurred, then recovered, "I left mine at home on Benton Street."

Mrs. Valentine shook her head, ignoring her roommate's snide remark. "Please make yourself comfortable on the sofa, dear."

Kidd eyed the dainty piece of furniture. He frowned. How old was that thing anyway?

"Go on. It's sturdy enough to hold a Kidd." Mrs. Valentine giggled.

He followed her directions, as they watched him intensely. Not only was the sofa sturdy, but surprisingly comfortable. "I've been the new resident liaison for a few weeks, and I'm still making my rounds and introducing myself. Sorry it's taken me so long to formally meet you."

"Is Kidd your birth name?" Mrs. Valentine asked with a smile.

Tilting her head, Mrs. Beacon seemed interested in his answer too.

He grunted. "Might as well have been on my birth certificate because that's all he called me."

"Who?" Mrs. Valentine questioned.

"The old man."

"What about your last name?" Mrs. Valentine followed up.

Kidd glanced at Mrs. Beacon, who seemed satisfied to let her roommate conduct the probing. He shook his head. "Don't like that

77

one either." *Good save*. He gave himself an imaginary pat on the back.

"No?" Mrs. Valentine lifted her brow.

"It means nothing to me. Neither does the man who freely donated samples of his DNA, wherever he is. He had the nerve to demand his rightful claim to us in name only, but not in love."

"Touché," Mrs. Beacon said, egging him on. "Need a gun?"

Mrs. Valentine frowned at her and leaned forward. "You can't change your parents like you do cars and husbands—I've done that twice, but I still come back to my maiden name of Valentine."

After two attempts, she stood and wobbled toward the sofa where he sat. Kidd stood and helped make her comfortable. "Thank you, young man. I like your manners and cologne." She took a deep breath and crossed one bony leg over her bony knee. "Now, many of our ancestors died without their parents having a right to name their children. Plus, many were lumped together with the same last name."

Kidd hated lectures, and he was about to bring this one to an end. "I know. Enslaved people were forced to take the name of the person who caged them."

He thought he just checkmated her, when she seemed to take on a faraway expression. Then Mrs. Beacon started to doze. *Great*. He needed to talk to her in private and see if she had any concerns, but her roommate's mouth was a well-oiled machine.

"How about having 'Negro' as your last name on your birth certificate?"

Negro? That was just like the old man calling him boy. Kidd hadn't expected to hear terms that should have been buried in the twentieth century.

"Humph," he grunted. "Don't like that name either."

"Can you imagine thousands of people having that name?"

Hmm mmm, truth or fiction? "And how would you know that, Mrs. Valentine?"

"Don't you know there are books that list all the dead folks," she said, sounding indignant. "Their county, state, age, date, and what they died from. And it wasn't always from lynchings."

"Wait a min—"

"Hush, chile." Mrs. Valentine gave Kidd a disapproving look. "I'm trying to explain. On some of the entries, the deceased were identified as black or white. On others, no classification was needed. Without having a massa's name, upon their death, Black folks were listed with the last name of Negro. Annabelle Negro, Esther Negro, Fanny Negro, even Female Negro was a name—first and last."

Mrs. Valentine was on a roll. "Now what kind of identity is that?" she asked. "I heard one woman was ninety years old with that name. And there are pages, hundreds of them, with the last name Negro— Henry Negro, Pleasant Negro, all the way down the alphabet." She *tsk*ed and shook her head.

Suddenly, Mrs. Beacon came alert. "Ah, Valentine, I don't believe a word of that stuff. Call me Negro. That's what I am. I'd rather have that name than some outrageous, thoughtless, idiotic names we had to bear," she snapped.

"Look, Beacon, you would've been among the defiant, enslaved folks who renamed themselves. Papa told me when I was a youngun, it wasn't unusual for a runaway to call himself something more dignified. I've got a great-great cousin somewhere in Arkansas named Major Wilson, but that was his birth name. You couldn't say his name without giving him some respect. See, us colored folks had pride, even back then."

Colored? Maybe Eva was right. Maybe he had been too hard on Mr. Johnston. Evidently, these people couldn't detach themselves from another era. Kidd smirked at the mention of pride—that he didn't lack. He blinked. His focus was to determine Mrs. Beacon's mental stability and report back to Parke. Instead, he was entertaining the ramblings of an old woman who had the ammunition to start a brawl with her roommate. Kidd stood to leave.

"Sit back down," Mrs. Beacon ordered.

Caught off guard, Kidd did as he was told.

"Since you started this whole war on names, let me tell you something. Another way for slaveholders to exercise control was to forbid mamas to name their babies. They called our kinfolks Moses, Hagar, and Ishmael from the Bible. They gave us the names of Greek gods and goddesses, Roman history figures like Caesar, Pompey, Nero . . . Napoleon—" Her words slurred, as she tried to talk faster.

When Mrs. Beacon took a deep breath, Kidd took that as an intermission for him to leave. He leaned forward to stand, but Mrs. Beacon began twisting her mouth. Kidd didn't know if she was exercising her muscles or about to make him her spit can, so he eased back in his seat. She grinned. It was a little lopsided, but the teeth seemed to be all hers too.

"When I was little, I knew girls named York, Africa, and Jamaica. Your black skin would have prompted the name Dark or Sable. I believe a lady just died a few years ago named Mississippi. She was one hundred and thirteen years old. I don't know if I want to get that old, but I've been seventy for a couple of years now."

Kidd looked from one woman to the other. Were they finished? If he was a doctor, he would diagnose both of them as borderline senile.

"Back to your daddy," Mrs. Valentine said, picking up the original topic. "If he insisted on you having his last name, it means you're somebody to him."

"Do you expect me to believe that?" Kidd grunted, and this time he got to his feet defiantly. He eyed Mrs. Beacon to make sure she wasn't moving her mouth again.

Mrs. Valentine jutted her chin. "With your intelligence, I expect you to look it up in the *Mississippi Morbidity* book." She tapped her chin, displaying long, bony fingers with pink nail polish. "It was 1860, or maybe it was 1850. It could be 1840."

Annoyed, Mrs. Beacon scolded her. "Make up your mind, girl. If you can supposedly remember all that stuff like an encyclopedia, why can't you remember dates?"

"Never been good with numbers. Plus, my brain power is only charged for so long. Humph." She shrugged. "Anyway, it's there in them books. If I'm lying, I'm dying, and I feel rather good today." She got up unassisted and dragged her feet back to her rocker. She slumped down and closed her eyes, apparently exhausted from her storytelling.

I guess too much talking exerts energy. Kidd was about to turn around and leave when one of Mrs. Valentine's eyes popped open. "I'm parched. My pay is one can of brisk iced tea."

"She'll need a wheelchair taxi to go get it because she ain't getting mine," Mrs. Beacon said. Then she added, "You know, you sure look familiar. Your expressions remind me of somebody. I hope I like them, whoever they are."

Chapter Nine

Why do tests always come when a person isn't prepared? Eva asked herself. "Lord, please help me." Her voice cracked, as tears choked in her throat. She decided to skip lunch, not because she was fasting, although she wished she had started off the day with that commitment. The truth was, Eva needed every minute to concentrate on her upcoming nursing test.

Keeping her eyes on the time, she desperately hoped her anatomy terms would finally begin to stick in her memory. "Lord, open my mind to remember every note and page I've read." The more she prayed, the more overwhelmed she became. Nearing the end of her break, the time came when she realized she had done all she could. Now it was time for her to trust God for the rest. Eva concluded with "Amen."

Sniffling, Eva took a deep breath at the same time the bench shifted beside her. She froze, too embarrassed to open her eyes and verify that someone had witnessed her frenzied state. That was Eva's fault. She had taken advantage of the tranquil spring day and traded her usual spot in front of the fountain to another bench. Her hope was that she would go unnoticed and not be disturbed.

"Eva." Kidd's voice was low and concerned, almost soothing.

Couldn't he see this was bad timing? She wanted to be alone.

"I'm not God, but tell me how I can help you," he continued to coax her.

How could she talk to this man, fearing she looked shipwrecked? Plus, she wasn't one to publicly exhibit weakness. It was strength she wanted to portray. Her eyes were puffy, and a Kleenex would be her first necessity. How compromising indeed.

"Go away, Kidd. You can't help me. What do you know about physiology, anatomy, or biology?" Eva mumbled with her head still down. She refused to open her eyes and face him.

"Why? Because I don't walk around with a stethoscope?" He shoved a napkin in her hand.

Was he an idiot? Couldn't Kidd see his timing was off for teasing or provoking her? She had hoped their spat was long forgotten. Apparently not. Covering her face with the rough paper and hoping it was unused, Eva inhaled.

Reluctantly, she prepared for the last humiliating act. She blew her nose hard, sniffed, and then blew it again. Taking a deep breath, she gathered her thoughts to deal with the distraction next to her. Unable to prolong the inevitable any longer, she opened her eyes and turned to him.

"I'm only capable of one drama at a time. Your being here right now is not one of those times. When you said you forgave me, I took you at your word." Why did he have to test their cease-fire and bring bits and pieces of their conversation back to the surface?

Kidd shrugged. "I can deal with your fire. I can't deal with your tears."

He paused, so Eva searched his eyes. There was a hint of compassion and vulnerability. His complexity made her heart melt. Kidd was the definition of a man's man: strong, fierce, and no-nonsense. But she also saw a heart that guarded hurt, pains, and failures. With a blink of his eyes, he shut down his defenselessness and looked away.

"What made you say I didn't know anything about anatomy? Hmm . . . if I had a dirty mind . . ." He chuckled. "I don't, even though around you that is a possibility. But did you think so little of my intelligence? Is it because, in your eyes, I'm nothing more than—what? A gangster all dressed up?" Before she could speak, he lifted his finger to silence her. "The truth, Eva."

She panicked. What could she say? Again she had uttered something without thinking. Because of him, she would constantly be on her knees, praying.

"Honestly . . . can I answer this at another time? I really need to study. That's why I called myself hiding over here."

"The truth, Eva," Kidd pressed, ignoring her plea.

She took a deep breath. "When I said you didn't know anything about anatomy, it was an assumption based on your lack of interest in the residents and in the medical field. You also made a curious comment about not fitting in."

Eva withheld saying anything further. One thing she had learned from being friends with Dawn was that whenever someone asked for the truth, they were seldom ready for it or wanted it. Eva was ashamed because that's exactly what she thought. The subject was already challenging for her. She didn't expect him to know any better.

"Really?" His smirk was a tease. "Just so you'll know, I've got a little hood in me, among other strengths and weaknesses. But let someone try to mess with you, and we'll see how much you'd appreciate the hoodlum in me."

His expression was deadpan, which frightened her, causing mixed emotions. Should she be afraid for herself or someone who would be on the receiving end of his eerie threat?

Her sister's boyfriend, Lance, made it clear on numerous occasions that he took his role seriously as a protective big brother. However, she doubted Lance's backup was any match against Kidd's. Eva would cast a ballot for Kidd any day.

"I believe in you, but you know what folks say. If you mimic the lifestyle of others, you become guilty by association."

"Sometimes people see one thing in a person, and that person is forever condemned by their perceptions." He shrugged. "I have nothing to prove to anyone. Besides, I left those days behind me in Boston. But I assure you, I can pull my former ways out of my back pocket if necessary." His piercing dark eyes backed up the fact that he wasn't bluffing.

"Boston? You're a long way from New England." She had to get away from this man. Grabbing her things to stand, he gently restrained her.

"Don't take this the wrong way, but you have bits of napkin lint on your lashes." He took the liberty of disposing of them with a few gentle flicks of his finger.

She shivered under his touch, while momentarily thriving from his personal devotion to her. Her coworkers would be jealous. Dawn would be floored. While everyone was vying for Kidd's attention, he happened upon her at a spot where she didn't want to be found. Why was his presence comforting? *Lord, I cried out to You for help. Why did he show up?*

Kidd angled his body. "Since we're friends and everything . . ." He lifted a brow. "I felt I should be honest with you, now that we've established this level of trust."

She held her breath and braced for the unknown.

"You look—what do you ladies call it? A hot mess—when you cry." Kidd delivered the insult and then had the nerve to snicker. A gray strand on his mustache glistened.

Eva glared, growling like a Rottweiler ready to attack. He right-out laughed, further taunting her.

"Hey, you don't have a good sense of humor, do you? The truth is, I couldn't stand to see you cry. I guess in my uncouth way, I picked a fight." His childish grin was priceless. "Since I didn't feel like hanging out with the guys, talking about cars, sports, and—"

"And probably women," she finished.

He shrugged. "Maybe that too. I decided to wander out here and, for some reason, I veered in your direction. Maybe God sent me."

Yeah, the devil sent a decoy. Locking her poker face in place, she waited to respond. His last remark wasn't funny. She didn't play that. When a person prayed for help, God sent the best person, not just anybody.

"I can't handle tears, Eva—especially my mother's. Or when I was younger, my baby brother's. Even my little cousins can get my attention when they're crying."

Eva was touched that he would put her on a plateau with his loved ones. Squinting, she tilted her head. He was hard to figure out. There was more to him than she had first thought, or maybe it was her second opinion of him. Kidd Jamieson was something besides his clean-shaven face, trimmed mustache, and bulging biceps. Yes, she noticed and made note. Oh, she forgot his baritone voice and one faint dimple when he smiled.

"Now." He wiggled a brow mischievously. "If you're finished with your appraisal of me, which I don't mind at all . . . don't worry about your appearance. You always look cute, even when you wear those ugly yellow and blue uniforms. Of course, you're flattered by shades of red, or burgundy, like you wore on my first day here." He lowered his voice. "Now, tell me what's wrong, Eva?"

Kidd had skillfully flipped the subject again. Shaking her head, she felt hopeless. "I don't have time to explain."

He reached for her textbook, which was as thick as a phone book, and gently pried it out of her hands. "Let's see. *Anatomy and Physiology: The Unity of Form and Function*. Hmm."

"I have class tonight. I was just stressing over the quiz and—" .

"Where are your test questions?"

"Why?" Eva sighed. "Parts three and four. What difference does it matter to you?"

Quickly, Kidd scanned the sections. "What makes up the nervous system?"

A no-brainer. That question wasn't her challenge. The other twenty-nine were. "The central nervous system and the peripheral system." She looked at him expressionlessly.

"Hmm. Not quite." Kidd tugged on his mustache.

"What? Kevin, do you wear glasses? Did a contact fall out or something?"

"Actually, I have 20/20 vision. What does the central nervous system do?"

Rolling her eyes and knowing his efforts were useless, she humored him. "Control the brain and spinal cord."

"And the periph—" Kidd demanded.

"Is the nervous system outside the central nervous system, such as glands and muscles?"

Kidd winked and began drilling the questions out of order. "Very good, Miss Savoy. Name the four stages of pressure ulcers."

Frustrated, she pinched him—or attempted to. But he didn't budge if he wasn't satisfied with her answer. The strong man with the soft heart was like no other man she had ever met. At this moment, what was there about him not to like? Clearing her throat, she refocused. The stages were her stumbling block because she couldn't visualize the examples. "Stage one is intact skin . . ." She rambled off the definitions.

He patiently waited until she was finished. "You had stages three and four backward. Although both have full thickness tissue loss, don't confuse visible subcutaneous fat with the exposure of tissue, bone, and tendons."

Eva's mouth dropped; she was stunned. He wasn't reading from the textbook. His explanation signified that Kidd Jamieson knew what he was talking about.

"How do you know so much? I mean . . ."

"This isn't about me. My friend is studying for an important test.

We have a few more questions." He glanced at his watch. "Come on, you're wasting time."

Sitting straighter, Eva's heart continued a slow melt. "Thank you, Kevin."

He winked and immediately his demeanor changed. Kidd proved to be an unmerciful taskmaster not to be crossed. He closed her textbook when he was satisfied she was as prepared as she could be in the short time.

"I guess you're more than a handsome face," she complimented, teasing.

"Yes, I am." It wasn't a boast or tease. She had learned within this setting that when Kidd was serious, he locked eyes with her and held her stare until she looked away.

"Come on." He stood and swiped up her notebook and textbook so she could get to her feet. As they strolled back to the building with Kidd carrying her books, Eva felt like a schoolgirl.

"You mentioned you're considering elderly care. Why? Isn't seeing blood disgusting enough? Then mix in urine and vomit . . . Yuck."

Eva didn't have to think. She knew at this point in life what she wanted. "I think older people are time travelers. They've weathered the storms of the past and braced themselves for the future. They already have the wisdom that we go to school to grasp. Spending time with them can help a young person to avoid a lot of mistakes. In the Bible, chapter two of Titus advises older women to teach younger women. I know it references marriage and loving our husbands too, but—"

Kidd stopped midstride and frowned. "Have you ever had a husband?"

Tilting her head, she squinted at the odd question. In the three or so weeks since he'd been there, he had never seen a ring on her finger. "No."

"Okay, finish," he said, shifting the book behind his back as if he was impersonating a school principal.

Once they entered the building, Kidd didn't leave her side when she headed to the employee locker area to get her purse. They met a few curious glances from coworkers, which Kidd ignored and to which she offered a faint smile. Eva was almost at her locker when she realized her purse was dangling from her shoulder. Kidd was definitely a distraction.

"You'll do fine tonight. I have faith in you, and you have faith in God. Just stay focused." He handed her the textbook and notebook and squeezed her hand. Kidd walked away like a man in control, definitely leaving her feeling out of control where he was concerned.

For the remainder of her shift, Eva never saw him again—not even a glimpse. She briefly wondered if he was rescuing another damsel in distress. Did it matter to her? For a reason unknown, it did.

At five, she clocked out and hurried to her car. Her mind was on her quiz and getting to St. Louis University's campus early enough to go over the material one last time.

"Ready?" Kidd stood in the center of the parking lot.

Spooked, Eva jumped, then relaxed. Kidd was her hero of the day. If for no other reason, he cared about what mattered to her. Taking a deep breath, she nodded.

He escorted her to her car. Once she deactivated the alarm and was about to climb behind the wheel, Kidd stopped her.

"Let me." Welcoming his act of chivalry, Eva handed over her keys. Kidd then opened the door, but not for her. Instead he got into her Ford Focus and adjusted the driver's seat. "Your leg room is terrible."

"What are you doing?" She jabbed her fist on her hip. She didn't have time for this.

Turning the ignition, he *shh*ed her. As he listened—for what? She was clueless. With the motor still running, he stepped out and towered over her while holding the door for her. "Make me proud, Savoy."

What was that all about? She wondered, but didn't have time to ask. She had to get going. Smiling at his military order, Eva gave a mock salute. When she tried to close the door behind her, Kidd wouldn't let it go.

"Although I may answer to the name Kidd, I'm a serious man who knows how a lady expects to be treated. And I can deliver." Kidd closed the door and stepped back.

Eva sucked in her breath and gritted her teeth. Why did he say that? How was she supposed to take a test when the only thing in her head was his words, instead of her medical terms?

Chapter Ten

"*N*ever judge a book by its cover, and never let a woman think she's got a Black man all figured out," Kidd mumbled, as he slid his hands into his pants pockets.

I calculate a man's worth, God whispered into the breeze.

Kidd held his breath. Another cryptic message. Why? Why was God singling him out and why now? He had nothing to offer God during this phase in his life. He considered himself an occasional Bible reader, casual prayer—not a prayer warrior—but certainly a merciless sinner.

He sighed and twisted his mouth. Parke had invited him to church a couple of times, but Kidd had declined. Why was God getting into the picture? Maybe he would be a one-time visitor to Parke and his family's church on Sunday in hopes of figuring out why God was singling him out. Maybe.

Refocusing on the present, he closed his eyes as Eva's taillights faded into traffic. He genuinely hoped she would ace her test. *Ace.* Kidd smiled. He hadn't spoken with his younger brother, Aaron, in a while. Initially, they talked almost every day when Kidd first arrived in St. Louis. Then their routine slipped into every other day. Now it appeared they had downgraded to a biweekly schedule, if that. Kidd would definitely have to call him.

Again his mind switched back to Eva and her dumbfounded expression. This time he grinned in a boastful way. It was the first time he hadn't had to spend money to impress a woman. Who would have thought that his fascination with anatomy and physiology books when he was a boy would have paid off? His mother's former boss, Dr. Robert Franklin, had loaned him the books. The doctor would be proud.

Thoughts of his mother made him long for home. Kidd just wasn't sure if the Midwest was a good match for him, especially in terms of seafood. So far, he was adjusting and Eva was unknowingly making his decision difficult. Still, he missed his family. He longed to hear a familiar voice, see recognizable surroundings and landmarks, and not feel like a fish out of water. Lifting his cell phone out of its case, Kidd punched in his mother's number. While he waited for her to answer, he spun around and headed to his car.

Distracted, he bumped into a figure that blocked his path. Ready to defend himself, Kidd disconnected the call. Instantly, his body tensed as he observed his soon-to-be injured assailant. Recognizing the familiar face, he groaned.

"Parke? What are you doing here?"

Parke gave him a weak hug and pat on the back, acting as though he hadn't seen Kidd in weeks instead of the day before. "It's been almost three weeks since Grandma BB suffered her stroke. My children are clamoring to see her. Cheney and I noticed she's back on Facebook. Instead of her long posts, her messages are short. Thank God for social media. But you would tell us if something was wrong, right? Cheney and I came by in hopes that Grandma BB's temper has calmed since that first day."

"Grandma BB doesn't come across to me as a person who changes her mind. She seems very willful, in my opinion. But hey, you know her better. Visit at your risk."

"What do you mean?" Parke rested his hands at his waist, as Cheney got out of their SUV and strolled up behind him.

"I'm not an expert, but I think the stroke affected her hormones. That woman had on some man's shoes."

Cheney started laughing and Parke joined her. Kidd frowned. "That isn't normal. I don't care what you say."

"For her, it is," Parke and Cheney said in unison, nodding and grinning.

"First, a dog called Silent Night—"

"Silent Killer," Parke corrected him.

"Whatever, man. Then there is this undercover assignment. Now she's a cross-dresser."

Shaking her head, Cheney stopped him. "Believe me, she's all woman, just a little eccentric. Her Stacy Adams shoes are a keepsake from the years she spent with her husband. She doesn't wear any other men's apparel."

"It's a long story," Parke added, "but let me just say it's her unique fashion branding."

The smile Cheney gave Kidd was warm and inviting, nothing like the stinging darts she fired at him the day they got the news about Mrs. Beacon. Aside from that incident, Cheney had been quite welcoming and treated him warmly as a close family member, not a prodigal Jamieson.

Giggling, Cheney explained, "If they're Stacy Adams shoes, those are hers. She has at least three pairs: black, brown, and gray. At least, I think I packed her gray ones."

"You know, she's strange. In fact, you all are. She had on the black ones—polished, not a scuff in sight."

"At least Grandma BB's in good spirits," Cheney replied.

"When I last saw her, I would say she was in a feisty spirit, with her sharp tongue. I've heard a slight slur at times, but her comeback is amazing. Oh, I do have a question. Is she known to spit on people? Because that's where I draw the line. Overall, she seems a little irritated from not being in control of her body. When she goes to therapy, they say she puts up a fight."

"Yep. That sounds like her." Cheney reflected. "Same old stubborn self. Every time I call for an update on her condition, the nurses tell me the same thing: she's going to need four to six more weeks of therapy to steady herself on a walker."

Four to six weeks longer? Kidd had no clue about her prognosis, but Mrs. Beacon's willpower could get her through anything. "So I guess there's no need for you two vigilantes to storm the place."

"Oh, we've come at night when she's sleeping, so she won't see us. But since we're here, I thought we could chance a face-to-face visit today."

Kidd shrugged. "Go for it. Now if you two will excuse me, I'm hungry. I think I'm going to run by the Whistle Stop and grab a sandwich. Maybe I'll go to the movies afterward."

Usually, he didn't plan out his evening. He was becoming restless. He had to make a decision. Maybe it was time for him to consider getting an apartment, but that sounded too much like permanent relocation. Was that what he really wanted? Keep the job for the next four to six weeks, which didn't seem appealing, except for being soothed by Eva's passion? Or quit? Maybe it would take that much longer to make up his mind. He also had to consider this business of Mrs. Beacon's antics. And he still didn't know what to make of her roommate, Mrs. Valentine, and her tall black tales.

A few days after his arrival in St. Louis, Kidd came to the conclusion that, as much as he appreciated Parke and Cheney's hospitality, he wasn't comfortable in the idyllic setting the two had created. They had a neat little package going on and he didn't seem to fit. It's no wonder their children appeared to be happy and well disciplined, which had to do with their overpowering affection.

There was the three-story turn-of-the-century historic house, fully restored and updated. In addition, their SUV and Altima weren't top of the line, but the features in both screamed luxury for the price. The bottom line was that their overall lifestyle was foreign to him, except for the love, which he would never admit out loud that he craved.

In the mornings, he tried to delay his jogging until after they left for work. Every once in a while, it didn't turn out that way. In particular, he wasn't able to avoid his cousin the day after he and Parke had the blowup about Mrs. Beacon. A few times, Parke joined him on the trail.

"There's no need to eat out. I made smothered pork chops, mashed potatoes, snapped peas—" Cheney started.

Kidd's stomach growled at the sound of her menu. "I'll race you home." He pulled out his keys from his pants pocket and took off sprinting across the parking lot.

"You'll win," Cheney yelled, "especially if she'll be glad to see us."

Kidd looked back with a smirk. "Enter at your own risk."

"You too. By the way, Imani is babysitting. Be nice."

He slowed down and turned back toward them. Cheney knew that Imani wasn't his favorite person. Kidd made that determination the third time he saw her, which was on the day of the trio's verbal assault. "How is that woman related again? Is she someone you dug up from the past too?"

"Nope. She's adopted," Parke answered.

The children. They had said they were adopted, and Kidd meant to ask Parke about that. "Is everybody around here adopted?" he muttered offhandedly.

"In the body of Christ," Kidd heard Parke say.

Having said that, they parted ways. Kidd jumped inside his car and took off.

Maybe this would be a good time for me to file for divorce from the Jamieson family and their crazy entourage, Kidd thought, as he headed home. Then he mumbled to himself, "Don't tempt me."

Chapter Eleven

*A*nticipating the taste of home cooking caused Kidd to weave in and out of five o'clock traffic. As he drove past the majestic homes on the east side of Old Ferguson, it reminded him of Beacon Hill, Chinatown, Back Bay, West Roxbury, Roslindale, Dorchester, Jamaica Plains—the list was endless.

When he first arrived, Parke had given him a brief narrative about his historic neighborhood in North County. In 1905, the creator of the famous Maull's Barbecue Sauce, Louis Maull, purchased a home in the area. Kidd crossed over South Florissant.

Suddenly, he thought about Eva and wondered how she was faring on her test. The brief interruption of his thoughts made him miss his turn and enter into a dead-end street—Adams Street. His detour had brought him to an unusual structure, and Kidd recalled what Parke had told him about it. The owner had the house built with an extra-wide front door so caskets could be brought in for families to conduct wakes. Interesting.

By the time he arrived at Darst Street, Eva continued to invade his thoughts. A few minutes later, Kidd parked his Maxima. With the thought of being this close to a delicious meal, he hurried down the short, winding pathway to the porch. Before he could turn his key in the lock, the front door opened.

"What are you doing here?" Imani questioned, as if she didn't already know that he had a room there.

The woman had a high ponytail anchored on her head and a fist rested on one hip. Long ago, he withdrew his initial thought that she was pretty. She was too irksome for that. What was it that made him her enemy? He wondered for a brief moment and decided he didn't care.

Kidd had already been warned, so he didn't plan to answer her question. He knew his response could potentially make him ten seconds from spinning around and sleeping elsewhere for the night—or permanently.

"Imani," Parke said. His steely voice startled them both, as he and Cheney came around the side of the house. "Stop fooling around. Let my cousin inside our house."

Perplexed, Kidd tried to figure how he and Cheney arrived so quickly. Perhaps they had to cut their visit with Grandma BB short because the lady wasn't in a hospitable mood. He had tried to warn them. Then again, he had to take a longer route home; his constant thoughts of Eva had delayed his arrival.

As if she was a puppet on a string, she twisted her mouth, then plastered on a smile and stepped back. "By all means, Kidd, please come in."

Grunting, Kidd stepped into the house where he was greeted by three miniature Jamiesons.

"Cousin Kidd!" Pace shouted, while he remained rooted to his spot on the living room ottoman.

"He's going to be our uncle," Kami argued. The toddler, Paden, raced straight to Kidd and gripped his legs, giggling.

Kidd laughed and lifted him up. He had handsome Jamieson features, but Cheney's genes were dominant. When he planted the baby back on his feet, Paden raced for his parents while Pace waited for Kidd's attention. Parke welcomed his small son with open arms, and Cheney hugged Kami tight.

The tender moment reminded him of when he was small. The few times his father did visit them, Kidd soaked up Samuel's presence and clung to him until he once again disappeared. Ace did too.

The only difference was these three Jamiesons—adopted or not— had a stable home environment. He guessed the children wondered about his whereabouts when, at times, he purposely came home late. When he wasn't in the mood to deal with the overpowering aspects of love that filled the atmosphere, he deliberately waited until most everyone in the home was asleep.

On those occasions, Kidd utilized his time after work to explore St. Louis's bars, casinos, shops, or whatever caught his attention. That was also the reason he had considered catching a movie tonight. In a sense, he felt like the hide-and-seek great, great whatever number removed cousin in the Jamieson dynasty.

"I cooked, Uncle Cousin. I helped Momma before she left." Kami grinned proudly, her arms still wrapped around her mother's waist.

Kidd gave her a wide grin in return, before Cheney responded, "That's my big girl. Okay, everybody, go on and wash your hands while I set the table."

"I already did when you phoned and said he was eating here. Besides, I set an extra one for me," Imani spoke up, putting extra emphasis on "he." "Got to keep an eye on who you let come in your house." She lifted a suspicious brow.

Cheney nudged Imani toward the kitchen, giving Kidd an apologetic expression. "I'm glad we made it back in time for all of us to eat together," she said, as some kind of concession to Kidd.

Once behind the door, Cheney lit into her friend. "What is wrong with you? You are starting to antagonize every man you meet lately. You're too young to be going through the change . . . but, girl, I wonder.

First, it was Parke's friend Duke. Now, you're ready to put your claws into his cousin. What gives? You've been living next door to Grandma BB too long."

Kidd focused his attention on his little cousin, as he angled his body toward the kitchen. Why was he curious about what the women were discussing?

"Listen, Imani," Cheney continued. "I know that your divorce was hard on you, and you know my past devastated me. But God did something wonderful when he brought Parke into my life. You can't go around hating everything male, so—"

"Eavesdropping can be a lovely thing. Ain't it?" Parke came up behind Kidd and slapped him on the back. "Pay Imani no attention. Unless, of course, she's behind the wheel of the repo truck. Then you'd better keep an eye on your ride. Unfortunately for the debtors, Imani does have close to a 100 percent recovery rate. Otherwise, she's really harmless."

"Right," Kidd said sarcastically. Good thing he didn't believe in running up a tab. He didn't like to be indebted to anyone, which was what he was starting to feel. Switching gears, he strained again to hear the women's conversation.

"I guess it doesn't hurt to know what a woman is thinking. It's better than trying to figure her out."

"Imani is just bitter over the way her marriage ended. Since then, she's had a string of bad dates, but we've been praying for her," Parke defended.

"Well, it goes to show, we all have bitterness rooted somewhere in us."

Minutes later, they sat around the table. The children ogled Kidd as if he was their idol.

"Let's bow our heads, so we can bless the food," Parke instructed, then prayed. "Lord Jesus, we thank You for the food. We thank You for providing it, the hands that prepared it, and the company to share it with around this table. Bless my children and my lovely wife, and our family far and near. Lord, pour Your abundant blessings over all of us. In the name of Jesus. Amen."

When Kidd opened his eyes, he nodded at Parke, and then there were no further words spoken. Like the others, he wasted no time digging in. He was famished, and before it was all over, he found himself fighting Imani over the remainder of the snapped peas.

After dinner, the two men rinsed dishes and then loaded the dishwasher. It was the children's chore to wipe off the table. Following a brief struggle with his sister over who would sweep the floor, Pace won.

Kidd waited until he and Parke were in the sanctuary of the entertainment cave to inquire about his visit with Mrs. Beacon.

"So what happened?"

"We couldn't stay too long. That woman cursed me out—without profanity—like I was some stranger on the street. Slur and all."

Kidd frowned. "How does one curse without using choice words?"

"Oh, she can piece together curse words like a serger sewing machine. Among other words, she used 'your momma', some body parts, and Ebonics." Parke gave Kidd a pointed look. "Before you ask, some things aren't worth repeating. Enough said." He paused, shook his head, and lifted the remote to aim it at the flat-screen.

Then Parke's comments turned more serious. "I witnessed with my own eyes her baptism to wash away her sins in Jesus' name. I saw firsthand how she rejoiced. I guess she's the kind of vessel Matthew 12:43–45 refers to."

"A what?" Kidd had no idea what Parke was talking about.

"Sorry." Parke chuckled. "I always assume people know what I mean. Matthew 12:43–45 says, *'When an impure spirit comes out of a person, it goes through arid places seeking rest and does not find it. Then it says, "I will return to the house I left." When it arrives, it finds the house unoccupied, swept clean and put in order. Then it goes and takes with it seven other spirits more wicked than itself, and they go in and live there.*

And the final condition of that person is worse than the first. That is how it will be with this wicked generation.' Well, this evening, her spirits were having a shindig."

Kidd had nothing to add to that topic, so he nodded. Why should he go to church when Parke brought it home with every opportunity he got?

During a brief period of silence, while Parke surfed channels, one of Kidd's favorite sports talk shows grabbed his attention. He hoped it would grab Parke's too and bring an end to the impromptu witnessing tirade.

The hosts of *Pardon the Interruption*, Tony Kornheiser and Michael Wilbon, were involved in a heated discussion about a doomed athlete. Uninterested, Parke flipped channels again, and the Yankees and the Dodgers were in a pitching duel. Kidd would have rather finished watching Tony and Michael.

During the first commercial break, Parke lowered the volume and faced Kidd. "Cuz, I want you to know, I appreciate the sacrifice you're making to work in the nursing home. I realize it hasn't been easy for you. Out of all the jobs we tried to match you with, this one is probably the most incompatible and uncomfortable for you. It may not seem like a big deal to check up on Grandma BB, but it's important for us to keep an eye on her. She thrives on her independence, and this has to be cramping her style. She's always into something; we never know what the woman is capable of doing."

Kidd listened while Parke continued to open up. *Who knows?* he thought. Maybe he'd learn something that could help him deal with this difficult person.

"From the glimpse of what I saw today, it looked like she had aged a bit since the incident. I think deep down she's afraid of becoming incapacitated and dependent on others for the rest of her life. Even with her spunk, it doesn't seem like this setback is coming to an end any time soon. That's why she never discloses her real age of eighty-one—we found out by the slip of her tongue. Usually, she tells folks she's in her seventies. I don't know. Maybe she feels like she's counting down the days before her death and wants to clown up until her last breath. But we love her and prayer changes things. That's why we'll keep on praying for her."

Kidd was choked with emotions at his cousin's heartfelt sentiments. The moment was one of a handful where he didn't feel they were drawing enemy lines as the eldest of two Jamieson families. So who was indebted to whom?

"I hope you've come to accept us as your family, whether it's for the better or worse. Blood is blood. You can dilute it or transfuse it, but the DNA will always be there. Christ's blood will always be there for you too, Kidd, if you decide to embrace Him in your life."

He went there again. How Parke could mix Jesus in during the seventh inning stretch was pure skill. Kidd had to admit, but only to himself, that he would give his cousin's words some thought. He could no longer deny that Parke's influence was changing his whole perception of what a Jamieson family could be like.

Still, there was nothing anyone could do about the fact that it was too late for Kidd to embrace what he longed for as a child, but never obtained—his father's love.

Chapter Twelve

*K*idd. Eva was giddy as she drove home from her night class. She felt good about her answers on the quiz. With both hands gripped around the steering wheel, her mind was elsewhere when she stopped at the red light. "Lord, I asked for help and You sent Kidd. Unbelievable."

Shaking her head, Eva still couldn't believe the grilling process that he put her through had actually worked. She was overflowing with joy, until there were too many songs in her head to choose just one. So she pieced together words and notes and created her own song of praise to God.

Eva was still a ball of energy when she walked through the door of her condo and dumped her keys, books, and purse on the table. Reaching for the nearby cordless phone, she called her sister's cell. As she strolled into the bedroom, Eva was disappointed, but not surprised when she got Angela's personalized voice mail greeting. Her sister changed it every day. Angela treated it like a Twitter account, briefing callers on her constant whereabouts with Lance. Talk about making it easy for criminals to track her.

What about her mother? Nah. Rita Savoy would read too much into her daughter's jubilation over a test that a good-looking male coworker helped her to pass. For her mom, that would be akin to announcing, "I just got engaged!"

In her bedroom of white walls, curtains, and comforter, all the furniture was bleached wood. Eva kicked off her tennis shoes and peeled off her socks. Wiggling her toes, she took a moment to admire the red polish. Kidd said the color complemented her, referring to her uniform. She briefly wondered if he would like her pedicure.

Removing her scrubs, she dumped them in the multicolored hamper and threw on a T-shirt and shorts. Eva retrieved the cordless phone from her bed and headed to the kitchen. On the way, she was distracted by the vertical blinds that adorned her terrace doors. They beckoned to her, and she responded by stepping out onto the balcony.

While taking a few moments to absorb the view, Eva glanced around her little space and smiled. She was pleased with a recent purchase of a bamboo wicker patio set. Relaxing in the chair, she rested her feet on the miniature table.

Eva bit her bottom lip, wondering if any chemistry existed between her and Kidd. Why did that ridiculous question even pop into her head? Kidd was different and too complex for his own good. Most times, Eva was abhorred by his rough and insensitive reaction to situations. Especially people.

The more she pondered over this man, one thing for sure, she admired Kidd's confidence. Then too, in her book, very few men could compete with his intoxicating looks. Not only was he attractive, his physical strength dictated that one punch from him could leave bruises and broken bones. But the thing that most offended her was his unpolished manner. It seemed like he wasn't comfortable in his position at the facility and would rather interact with the low-paid maintenance crew.

Their chance meetings in front of the fountain would be romantic if she was reading about them in a novel or watching the scene play out in a movie. However, at this point, it didn't matter if he was attracted to her or not. The breaking news was that she had standards and Kidd didn't meet them—period.

Purposely, she steered clear of the members of "the angry Black men" club. Unfortunately, there was an entire generation of them. Kidd's "I don't care" attitude ran people away, including her. She couldn't change a grown man who had apparently slipped through the cracks as a child.

Closing her eyes, she prayed for God to help him and all those men who were like him. Those who deep down inside were good men, but reached for their anger as a survival tool every morning. "Lord Jesus, there is no guarantee the Prodigal Son will find his way back home, but You are the Great Shepherd and You know where Your lost sheep are. Lord, please gather them, nourish them, and restore their hearts and minds. I pray that You will toss into the sea of forgetfulness whatever it was that drove them from Your presence. Jesus, I know You promised me salvation and that You will be faithful until the end. I thank You for the assurance that You are preparing a wedding feast for Your church. Although I'm Your bride first, Lord Jesus, I would like to meet a flesh-and-blood groom before You return. In the name of Jesus. Amen."

I keep My promises, Jesus spoke.

His whisper gave her the intended comfort. The only sure thing in life was His promises, which were too numerous to count.

Opening her eyes, she squinted as a star struggled to make an appearance before dusk. Eva's thoughts returned to class where she had prayed until the moment her instructor said that time was up. Although Kidd's assistance boosted her confidence, Eva still had to trust God that her answers were correct.

A tempting thought entered her head. If she had his number, would she be crossing some kind of employee line to call and thank him again? What signal would that send? Kidd was definitely fine. Eva made a resolve: as a woman, she would always be attracted to good-looking men—but that didn't mean she would entertain any ridiculous notions that the two of them could ever be romantically involved. That is, without the sex part, of course.

Mentally, she flipped through the pages of her bridal magazines, picturing her reflection in many of the designer dresses, rehearsal dinners at the cozy restaurants, and the faceless groom at the altar. With his dark hand reaching out for hers, Eva took a deep breath and smiled. Her lids drifted closed again; this time, she refused to open them until she could see the face of the man whom God had set aside just for her.

It wasn't long before Eva was awakened. Dazed by the surrounding darkness, she was startled when the phone rang. "Hello."

"Hey," Angela greeted. "Are you asleep already? Why do you call me and not leave a message?"

"Hold on." Eva stood and stretched. She quickly stepped back inside her living room before the mosquitoes feasted any further. After closing the sliding door, she locked it and turned on a few lights. Remembering she was hungry, Eva headed straight to the refrigerator to grab something quick to eat. "Well, since you let your social network of followers know you and Lance went to a movie, I didn't want to interrupt."

Angela laughed. "Right. My cell number isn't posted on the Internet. Anyway, at the moment, Lance and I are in line to get some Ted Drewes Frozen Custard—yummy."

Eva's mouth watered at the mention of a St. Louis favorite summertime novelty—ice cream as thick as concrete.

"What's going on?"

"Remember that test I was stressing about last week?" Eva's giggles exploded before Angela could respond. "I asked God to send help, and minutes later, Kidd came along. Can you believe he quizzed me? He broke down some questions, and I used his study tricks. I was amazed that it worked . . . and just think—"

"Wait a minute. Not your nemesis?"

Eva sighed and gritted her teeth. She was chiding herself for sharing that negative description with her twin. "I misjudged him. He's very intelligent, and I'm ashamed to say how I got his attention." Shaking her head in embarrassment, she didn't even want to think about that scenario.

Angela covered up the phone. "It's Eva. She had a run-in with that guy again." Lance yelled in the background, "Does she want me to go up to her job? Because I will . . ."

Eva rolled her eyes and bit into the ready-made sandwich she found behind the bottle of milk on the top shelf. No wonder she had to constantly repeat herself to her sister. Angela never got information right the first time.

"Listen to me, Angel. First of all, tell Lance to back off. I wasn't threatened." Eva began to pace the stone-tiled floor as she nibbled. "I was at my weakest moment, sobbing uncontrollably, freaking out about the test. I guess it was the tears that got to him. He could have ignored me, but the man has more compassion than I gave him credit for. His kindness was so tender, I would've cried all over again if I wasn't already bawling. I would never have thought in a zillion years he had that much knowledge in him."

"Now I think you've gone too far. You said yourself he doesn't seem to fit in a nursing facility environment. All of a sudden, he quizzes you and breaks down complex medical terminology. I don't know anything about this Kidd, but I do know you sometimes don't give yourself enough credit. You were prepared for that test, and he probably convinced you of that. I'm proud of you, sis. You've been holding back from me all these years," Angela teased, then muffled the phone and conversed with Lance.

Shaking her head, Eva said good-bye, but doubted her sister heard her. Placing the phone on the counter, she finished her sandwich. Minutes later, she padded into the bathroom to run some bath water. As she soaked, she recalled a day in eighth grade when she and Angela switched places to take a test. The outcome wasn't worth it. Eva—the imposter—scored high on the test, but she and Angela barely escaped their mother's punishment for their dishonesty. That was the last time she and Angela traded places for anything.

Angela's true calling was in secondary education, and she excelled in it. Eva, the indecisive twin, needed more time to ponder her purpose. Careerwise, it took Eva until after her first degree to reach all the way back into her childhood to find her passion. As a little girl, first she wanted to be an opera singer. Eva had purposely shattered one of her mother's favorite glasses, feigning she had hit a high note. Her mother had ended that career goal, and she was sore the next morning.

Then there was the time she had aspirations to become a chef. After two close calls, the fire department advised her mother to keep her away from the stove without adult supervision. At the time, Eva was an adult of twenty-three. Finally, she stumbled into her calling when a neighbor thought he was bleeding to death. In a panic mode, she grabbed some soap, alcohol, bandages, and aspirin for pain. For coming to the rescue, her reward was a twenty-five-dollar gift card. Long after that event, she kept a makeshift emergency medical kit under her bed—just in case.

Still, her purpose in life didn't come without challenges. She would never admit to anybody, especially to Kidd, that the facility residents' ill-mannered comments tossed at her did sometimes hurt her feelings, but she pitied them and prayed.

Eva climbed in bed after a soothing bath and started to review material for her May final, which was weeks away. Tomorrow wasn't coming soon enough; she couldn't wait to see Kidd.

Chapter Thirteen

*O*n Monday morning, Kidd took long strides to Mrs. Beacon and Mrs. Valentine's room. He knocked and waited for permission to enter.

"Hi, Adam. Where's Eve?" It didn't take long for Mrs. Valentine to adapt her signature greeting for him.

"Let's just say, God's molding her to my perfection." Kidd winked.

"I've been waiting for you, Jamieson." Mrs. Beacon spoke without hesitation. "So I guess since Parke couldn't babysit me himself, he sent you."

If the woman was about to go multi-crazy spirits on him, then she was sure to get some of his own spirits, lurking to come out at her. Kidd had another rule he lived by—people did not curse or hit him without his retaliation—so he might as well walk away now.

"What's the matter? Cat got your tongue?" Mrs. Beacon ironically slurred the last word.

"Actually, it's sheer willpower." He didn't blink, as his nostrils flared and he folded his arms.

"Ah, sit down. Don't get testy with me. Nose expanding, biceps pumping, and height never meant nothing to me." She met his stare. "Listen, if I get a crook in my neck looking up at you . . . watch the damage I can do from a wheelchair."

Oooh. Kidd wanted to test her. Instead, he huffed and took a seat on their dainty sofa. "Happy now?" He crossed one ankle over his knee.

"I've already sent Parke a tweet. It took me less than 140 characters to let him know, the next time he decides to spy on me, not to send another Jamieson."

"Really? I was wondering how long it would take you to figure it out." Kidd snickered, taunting her.

"Don't test me, Jamieson. Last Friday, he and Cheney called themselves sneaking in here. I may have a little trouble staying steady on my feet, but my mind is sharp as a tack . . . I think. Your bloodline is strong; I see the resemblance. Plus, Eva mentioned your last name earlier that same day, long before they showed up. So for now, everyone will have to continue tracking my progress on Twitter or my Facebook page until I'm ready for visitors—and not a day before. I'll bust out of this joint first," she said with a slight slur.

Kidd shook his head. This woman was a force to be reckoned with. They might be able to get along after all.

Mrs. Valentine cleared her throat, indicating she was about to take advantage of the cease-fire. "Just before you walked in, I was tellin' B about the sundowners last night. They were on the prowl."

Now they were down to one syllable names—B? "What's a sundowner?" Kidd frowned.

"Every now and then, when the sun begins to set, Vince Williams gets confused and thinks he's the butler for a man named Randolph Franklin. He sneaks out of his unit and walks the halls, asking us if we need anything else, bowing as he backs out of the room. He's harmless." Mrs. Valentine waved her hand in the air.

"But the worse of them all is that Jack Miller. He's a nasty old fool. It's a good thing he can't get out of his room half the time. I heard he was something else back in the day. Some nights, you can hear the staff fighting him off."

"So the freaks come out at night, huh?" Kidd racked his mind to place the name with a face. When he did, Mr. Miller didn't seem strong enough to lift his head. He chalked it up to another one of Mrs. Valentine's tales coupled with Mrs. Beacon's collaboration.

"Give me a few minutes with the sucker. I'd leave my carbon footprints all up and down his body," Mrs. Beacon stated, without a hint of jesting.

Kidd kept a straight face. If it wasn't for her stiff leg, Mrs. Beacon just might deliver a blow. "There's no need to make threats."

Jutting her chin, she boasted, "Humph. You think I can't back mine up? I shot a man. My bullets are marked, and I always hit my target. Ask Cheney. It was her father."

This woman *is* crazy. Something told him that friendship ties would have been severed if Grandma BB carried out such a plot. Garden Chateau sure knew how to pair up the residents. Kidd smirked and decided to have some fun. "Hmm. Well, I beat down two guys at the same time for messin' with my brother. I don't need a gun. I used my God-given talent."

"I'm sure God didn't give you strength for that, Samson," Mrs. Valentine chimed in.

"No need for you to bring God into this, V," Mrs. Beacon warned her, shooting daggers her way.

Actually, the two were quite amusing. He would have to visit them more often.

Mrs. Valentine won the duel. Leaning forward, she batted her eyes and looked at Kidd. "I've been thinking about your dislike of your last name. You can change it like many of our ancestors. You know any Freedmans? I bet ya they're descendants of former slaves who took on that name with pride after slavery ended. That's why they called themselves—Freed-man. Now me, I'm taking Valentine to the grave."

111

Kidd remembered the old woman telling him that before.

She continued talking like a runaway train from the station. "I'm from descendants of Robert Valentine. He bought and sold Blacks as if he was on that Wall Street. Our ancestors were valuable currency—silver and gold. Can you imagine the price of Jesus' blood for our sins? Ooooo weeee." Mrs. Valentine's expression took on a faraway look.

"After the war, folks would call for a Reunion Day throughout the South, hoping to find kin who had the same former slaveholder's last name. If some had changed their names, the connection could be severed forever. Back then, Reunion Day stood for more than a good time. It was a way to track down family. You see, there was this man with a funny name who had enslaved some of the Harris family from Wilmington, North Carolina. Let's see." She paused. "There were the twins, Ross and Burr . . . and their sisters, Ceila and Mahaley. They were separated during the war. Ross ran an ad in the *Christian Recorder* newspaper. I think the year was 1893. Anyway, those were our distant kinfolks."

Mrs. Valentine eyed him. "Now back to your disdain for the Jamieson name. It can't always be about what the enslaver called you. To hate your name is akin to hating yourself. You've got to love yourself. Christ loved you way before your great-great kinfolks were even born."

First Eva, now Mrs. Valentine. They really didn't know him. Otherwise, they would know that he was all about self-preservation. And that translated down to loving himself. What did Eva and Mrs. Valentine do? Compare notes?

"If your daddy made a bad name for himself, change the value of it. It happens all the time, especially with those celebrities. Don't matter if their papa ain't no good. The sons and daughters grow up to be successful. Don't you know the good always shows up the bad? Let your light shine, boy. Let it shine."

Boy. Somehow that word coming from Mrs. Valentine made him want to make her proud.

Chapter Fourteen

*E*va went on the hunt for Kidd Jamieson. His car was parked in his regular spot, and his office door was open. But he was nowhere to be found. Not to worry. She had all of eight hours to track him down, so she went about starting her shift.

In between residents' care, she checked outside on the bench. Eva even searched some of his known hiding places that he didn't know she knew about. It's funny. When she wasn't looking for him, she saw him all the time—ducking and dodging residents.

Throwing her hands up in defeat, Eva gave up. As she strolled down the hall, she heard Mrs. Valentine's harmonious voice in a one-sided conversation. She was about to knock on the door frame when she halted.

The object of her search had his bulky body squeezed into a dainty white chair. Relaxed with his ankle resting on his knee, Kidd was entangled in the tale Mrs. Valentine was weaving. She had full command of the floor; even Mrs. Beacon was captivated.

Mrs. Valentine looked up and paused. "Hi, Eve." She smiled as if she had won bingo, her favorite game. The woman looked forward to playing it in the recreational room on Wednesdays. "I've got me an Adam."

Lifting her brow, Eva nodded at Kidd. She wanted to drag him out of the room and share her good news. Of all days, he was doing something he was paid to do. That forced her to tuck away her news for another time.

"Good morning, Adam—or should I say Professor Adam?" she teased, hoping it would prompt him to ask her to explain.

Dense or unconcerned, he chuckled. That was all the intermission Mrs. Valentine granted Eva. She continued her story, regaining Kidd's attention.

"Mistress Sarah Cowan had one slave named Miss Hannah. In 1860, she was 120 years old. Let's see . . ." She tapped her chin and gnawed on her red lipstick. "I guess that makes her born in 1730 or '40"

"How can you remember details from a hundred years ago and can't do simple math?" Mrs. Beacon snapped. Beginning to use her arm again, she reached for her cane, but came up short.

Kidd was swift to assist Mrs. Beacon and then sat again. Without missing a beat, he spat out his objections about the old enslaved woman to Mrs. Valentine. "And Miss Hannah lived her life as a caged pet, with mental and invisible chains. Humph. And people can't understand our anger—our hate. Miss Hannah was somebody's daughter."

The twinkle in Mrs. Valentine's eyes faded. "Why, shame on you. Anger is a cancer that will eat you up. Miss Hannah adapted and *lived*. She was a survivor from disease, deceit, and dishonor—but she survived. Will you survive all the darkness around you, or will you give up right now? Miss Hannah had twenty-three children. My grandma didn't say if they were all living, but . . ."

The angry Black man syndrome was the unofficial, but obviously verified diagnosis for Kidd. Jesus was the only remedy to replace that anger with peace. Eva's excitement about her test performance dimmed as her heart ached for him.

Slowly backing out of the room, she said a prayer. The bitter words frightened her. *Lord, how can I reach him? Even though I'm far from perfect, give me the wisdom to help.*

Mrs. Valentine's mindless stories were fueling Kidd's fire. This was one resident of whom he definitely needed to stay clear. If only Kidd would believe that Christ nailed his burden to the cross with Him. She prayed for whatever was tormenting Kidd. It had to be deeper than Mrs. Valentine's tales.

He stayed on Eva's heart for the remainder of the day. The bright spot came when she logged into a computer at the nurse's station and accessed her class grade. Her heart pumped as she waited for the screen to reveal her test results. Running her finger down the column to the previous day, Eva gasped. "Ninety-one!"

Not believing her eyes, she blinked profusely, but the score didn't change. She had never earned a ninety-anything on her other nursing tests. Eighty-seven had been her highest grade, and that was only one time. Usually, she scored in the low eighties. "Thank You, Jesus!" She pumped her fist in the air.

Ready for an impromptu celebration, Eva began a marathon to the snack machines. This called for a high-sugar-content grape soda and a bag of caramel popcorn dripping in highly saturated fat. The nursing student within her scowled, but at the thought of junk food, her taste buds were already salivating. She almost stumbled when she saw Kidd guarding a vending machine as if he was a defensive tackle.

Amused, Eva quietly observed him assaulting it. When she giggled, he paused and did a quick glance over his shoulder. His expression definitely wasn't like he had gotten his hand caught in the cookie jar. She sashayed toward him. "Whatcha doin'?"

Whirling around to face her, he leaned against the machine, blocking Eva's view of the goodies. Kidd crossed his arms and stared into her eyes first. "Nothing illegal—yet."

"Hmm. Need a loan to get something out of the machine?" she teased.

"No," he responded, as he twisted his lips in a seductive tease. "I need for this thing to give me my bottle of iced tea. Do you have any suggestions on how to make that happen, considering I've already pumped in six dollars so far?"

She swatted at his arm and Kidd flexed his muscle. "You're a sucker for Mrs. Valentine."

"My secret is out. My affections are known." His voice was almost husky. "Well, she is my valentine. I've got to keep her happy. How did you know?"

"She's always parched and in need of an iced tea after her stories." They chuckled. Then Eva sobered. "I'm glad you like her. One never knows what her monologue will be from one day to the next. Pay Mrs. Valentine no mind when she talks about slave times as if she were there. She fabricates those stories. When I walked into their room today, you seemed disturbed by what she was saying."

The cockiness evaporated. Kidd broke eye contact and glanced over Eva's head. "I'm tough. I can handle anything."

"What about your heart, Kidd? Can it handle anything?"

No response. Eva mentally stepped back in her place. What made her believe that, just because he quizzed her, they would suddenly become more than coworkers? Why did she think she could speak her mind without him taking offense?

Swallowing, Eva changed the subject as she eyed his arsenal of bottled drinks—Pepsi, water, and two cans of root beer—on the nearby table. "Thirsty?" she joked.

"Nah." Kidd shrugged and jingled the loose change in his pants pocket. Pulling out some dollar bills, he turned around and fed the machine more money. Within seconds, he grinned victoriously when it finally released the correct item.

"Somebody needs to talk to your vendor," he complained, scooping up his change from the slot. "Any word on your test?"

Eva's heart fluttered that he remembered something important to her. "I only missed three." Her excitement erupted again. "Yay!"

He stopped what he was doing and turned her way, wearing a smirk. "Congratulations, Miss Savoy." He gave her a high-five. "You made me proud, girl." His eyes danced with merriment.

The man had so many personalities. The intensity of them all scared her. She loved it when he smiled, though. They always seemed genuine. On the downside, his anger was raw. What had sparked it earlier?

"I haven't been this happy since Jesus washed my sins away." Eva didn't let his blank expression stop her. "I needed to score high on this last quiz before the final. Then if I do mediocre on the final, I'll still average a low B, but it's still a B."

"So we'll have to make sure that happens. Can't have you missing your calling. Mommies and nurses know how to kiss it and make it feel better."

Their eyes locked, and Eva didn't know if the man was flirting with her or not. If so, why did it thrill her so when Kidd wasn't her type?

Taking a deep breath, she turned and eyed the vending machine. Instead of sugar, she needed a bottle of water to cool her hormones. She could feel his presence behind her back. Eva willed him to disappear.

"I've offered to help again."

"You have," she confirmed.

"Would you accept?"

Was it her imagination, or was it the manner in which Kidd asked that made Eva wonder if they were still talking about her class.

"Your tutoring services? I couldn't refuse."

"How about anything else from me?"

Okay, she wasn't going to toy with any innuendos. Eva cleared her throat. "Hey, I meant to ask you how you knew those definitions so fluently that you could explain minuscule terms."

"I don't play games, Eva. If you want to evade my question, fine.

I'll ask again, but when I get tired of asking, I'm done."

That sounded like a threat, but she kept her poker face in place. He wasn't in a position to issue any ultimatums.

"To answer your question, when I was younger, my mother worked for a doctor. He would let her borrow his medical books as a way to encourage her to pursue a degree in medicine."

"Did she?"

"Yes and no. She couldn't get past the blood, so she did the next best thing. She paid medical claims after all the bloody procedures were done.

"So before you turn me down again, think about my qualifications," he whispered in her ear and swaggered down the hall.

Are we talking about the same subject? Eva wondered.

Kidd stopped in his tracks and glanced over his shoulder. As if he was staring into a camera, it was her eyes he commanded. "By the way, I like your hair."

Dawn appeared from nowhere and grinned. "He's a keeper, Eva. Don't worry, if you kiss him, I won't tell." She winked and glided away.

Chapter Fifteen

*E*va excited Kidd. He craved her smile in the mornings. There was something about her passion that he wanted to capture and emulate. His desire to touch her lips hadn't diminished, even when those very sweet lips were hurling bitter comments about his character. She was beautiful when she was angry.

He had catalogued her features. She was pretty, not drop-dead gorgeous. But then again, who could surmise that dressed in those nondescript scrubs. He wanted to take her out and see how long they would last before they disagreed about something. Kidd needed to set that wheel in motion.

The work environment was not an ideal setting to spark a romance. But he didn't believe in one-sided attractions. If she didn't feel something for him, then Kidd could walk away and look elsewhere. He even ceased his friendly flirting with the old ladies. Actually, Kidd had become fond of them, but even in their old age, they acted very territorial.

He was an admirer of natural beauty, and Eva had it—period. She didn't need the one-inch lashes he had noted on some women or the rainbow hair extensions that made him wish he was color-blind. Until now, he didn't know that a loose-fitting uniform top and pants could be so form-fitting with a little imagination.

Kidd ended another workweek in a great mood. The pay was exceptional for a man with an associate's degree. Even after he routinely sent money home to help his mother, he had a chunk left to save. He offered Parke money for allowing him to stay in his home. But Parke refused. His anger at Kidd had dissipated and he'd changed his mind again, stating that his cousin's watchful eye over Grandma BB served as extremely adequate compensation. So Kidd regularly stuffed money into his three cousins' penny banks.

Earlier in the day, he asked his coworkers about fun-natured trouble to get into over the weekend. Some of them suggested The Loft in the city, near downtown. They said it was the night's hot spot, so Kidd considered that as an option. Their recommendations had been right on point since he arrived. Matt, a custodian, raved about Envy, a club not far from Garden Chateau. Kidd had stopped by and had no complaints.

Before he made any definite plans, he needed to touch base back at home. When he stopped at a red light, he fumbled with his iPhone, tapped his mother's cell number, and then touched his Bluetooth. The moment she answered, Kidd felt something was amiss.

"What's wrong, Ma?"

Hesitantly, Sandra released a heavy sigh. "I didn't want to worry you. Your brother . . . he's in Randolph police station."

"What!" Kidd gritted his teeth to rein in a string of curses that was begging to get out. Now what?

"I'm on the next flight home." *There goes any weekend plans here,* he thought. Kidd disconnected the call, realizing too late that he had hung up on his mother. Pulling over to the curb, he accessed the Internet via his phone and searched the Southwest Airlines flight schedule. Within minutes, he booked a nonstop flight to Boston. If Ace was in Randolph, he had probably been at Vincent's Nightclub. What had his brother done this time?

Operating on autopilot, Kidd didn't remember arriving at Parke's home. All he knew was that he was standing on the porch about to turn the key. Giving his car a glance, he chided himself for leaving the driver's door open. He stomped back and shut it while his mind was still on his twenty-six-year-old baby brother, who should be acting like a man. It appeared Ace had set a goal to visit every jail around Boston. This was his fifth trip, in how many months? Kidd was sure it was only because of their mother's prayers that no serious charges had been filed.

He stepped inside the house and groaned. Malcolm, Parke, and their sons were sitting around the dining room table. Too bad they weren't hanging out in Parke's entertainment cave. Apparently, the men were babysitting. Kidd took a deep breath; he wasn't in the mood for any brotherhood camaraderie. Nor did he have the time. He coaxed himself to breathe and headed upstairs to pack lightly, so as not to generate questions. His goal was to get out of there as fast as possible.

Before Kidd could make his move, Parke interrupted. "Hey, cuz. It's just us men tonight. The women are at a baby shower, and the men rule." Parke grinned and held up a finger. "My wife made a big pan of tetrazzini and garlic bread. Help yourself."

"And my baby threw down on some serious red velvet cake." Malcolm patted his stomach. "I left you a few slices. Afterward, maybe you'll want to hang with us. We're taking the boys to the NASCAR Speed Park at the Mills."

Pace's puppy eyes were hopeful. "Come on, Cousin Uncle. You can ride in the same bumper car with me."

Parke rubbed his son's head. "Hey, what about your old man?"

"You can ride with me after him." Pace grinned, favoring his father and displaying a missing tooth.

They all laughed. Even Kidd had to chuckle at the boy's possessiveness, then he sobered. "Sorry, I'm going to have to pass."

Malcolm frowned. "On the food or going to St. Louis Mills?" He sat up straighter.

"Both. I've got a plane to catch."

"What's going on, Kidd?" Parke squinted, as he went on alert.

"I'm flying home for the weekend or longer. As a matter of fact, my plane leaves—" Kidd checked his watch and grimaced—"in less than two hours." He headed for the steps. "I'll talk to you later."

Parke stood. "Is everything all right?"

"It will be."

Once upstairs, he dragged shirts and pants off the hangers. He went into the bathroom and grabbed whatever toiletries were in sight. Throwing everything in his bag, Kidd headed back downstairs. Parke and Malcolm were waiting for him.

"We're going with you."

Kidd didn't have time for this. "Parke, stay here with your family, and I'll go see about mine." His attempt to walk around Parke failed. His cousin was blocking him as if he was Chicago Bulls' Derrick Rose.

"Listen to him, Parke." Cheney stood in the open doorway unexpectedly. "He's a Jamieson—stubborn. Good looking, but stubborn. Good-hearted, but stubborn."

The woman could never give him a compliment without tacking on the other stuff.

"Hey, babe, what are you doing back so soon?" Parke went to her and brushed a kiss on her cheek.

"I left the gift card here, so I came back to get it." She scanned everyone's faces. "I didn't hear everything, but I think he knows by now, we have his back." Smiling, she walked up to Kidd and hugged him. "I hope you know that if you need anything—money, prayers, moral support—we're there before you finish uttering your request. Don't let your Jamieson pride get in the way. Like I told you earlier, don't let pretty faces and peaceful, loving families fool you. We're armed with spiritual armor, and we use it."

Kidd's mind was too jumbled to register that conversation. "Right. I've got to go. I'll leave my car at the airport—"

"Wrong. We're driving you," Parke said with finality. "Your bag looks light. I hope you packed underwear and mouthwash."

"Shut up, man." Kidd shoved him, as if he was going around him for an imaginary layup to a basket. "If you're my limo driver, let's go."

Chapter Sixteen

Kidd's plane couldn't land soon enough at Logan International Airport. When he disembarked and rounded the corner outside the security checkpoint line, his mother was waiting for him. She had a strained smile on her face as she hurried toward him.

Preferring soft colors and stylish casual clothes, she never failed to catch men's eyes—young and old. But Ace was on the road to aging their mother before her next birthday if he kept up with his foolishness.

Reaching out, Kidd engulfed her in a hug. She didn't seem to mind his smothering. He inhaled the scent of her hair and perfume, imagining she was about the same height as Eva. That is, if ever he was in a position to hold her. Kidd froze and blinked. How did Eva travel through his mind and end up in Boston with him at a time like this?

"What's going on, Ma?" He stepped back and squinted, his arm remaining around her shoulders. When she stalled, he added, "I guess that explains why I haven't spoken with the knucklehead in a while, and he's been on my mind." Exhaling, Kidd rubbed his head in frustration. "I knew I shouldn't have left him, or you, to stay with those do-gooder cousins in Missouri," he chided himself.

Sandra squeezed his arm and broke free of his embrace, then steered him toward the parking area. "You can't keep running to Ace's rescue every time he makes a bad decision. The separation was about clipping wings, your protection over him, and his dependency on you."

"What about you?"

"God's got me. There's only one thing I want out of life for my sons," she said, sighing, "to know I reared two strong Black men, ready to take on the world with their intelligence and confidence—not fists, guns, and knives. Besides, I was prepared to let him stew there until his trial date. But no, after a few days, Cameron intervened. He argued that was no place for his cousin or any other Jamieson man."

Charity from Cameron. Kidd would weigh the pros and cons about his involvement later. "I don't like it."

"Me either. I think Cameron maxed out his credit cards to put up bail money. The paperwork should be completed on Monday, and then Ace can be released." His mother was no pushover. As long as Kidd could remember, she didn't expect handouts for her children. She would do without—and she had—before her boys would miss a meal or a school field trip for lack of funds.

"How did Ace get locked up?" Once in the parking garage, Kidd spotted his mother's black Kia Forte. "I'll drive. I need the practice anyway. I miss outwitting the cabbies on the obstacle course. St. Louis is no fun."

Sandra smiled again, and this time it reached her eyes. Kidd kissed her cheek as he opened her car door. "What did he do, Ma?"

She waited for him to get in and click his seat belt. "Hanging out with people as stupid as he was acting. Of course, it involves disorderly conduct outside a nightclub. Drinking and flirting with the wrong woman is a bad combination."

Kidd swore under his breath out of respect for his mother and the fear of getting smacked upside his head.

"I think I pressured the wrong son to move out of town. Ace

should have gone." Sandra sniffled, but quickly composed herself. Kidd reached over and squeezed her shoulder, and she looked at him.

"God is telling me to trust Him, and I've been imploring Him to show me how. I hate to say this, but Ace is your father magnified a hundredfold. Thank God I'm not a grandmother."

Kidd already knew that. Why couldn't Ace see that he was fulfilling a generational curse, thanks to their loser father? Nothing had changed in the months Kidd had been gone. As a matter of fact, things seemed to have gotten worse. He gripped the wheel as he got on I-93 South. Kidd tried relaxing as he prepared for the thirty- to forty-minute drive to Hyde Park, but he was too tense.

"I'm not going back to St. Louis, Ma. Ace needs direction."

"No, Ace needs to find his own way, even if he has to earn scars to get there. Whatever it takes, he can no longer depend on his big brother, or me, to bail him out. I had money in my account, but I would rather have spent it on a lifetime spa membership or a cruise than bail him out."

"Even knowing he was sleeping in a cold cell?" Kidd quizzed her.

"I've had my share of sleepless nights and enough of them to go around. Unfortunately, it comes with the territory for any parent, especially for those who have African American sons. We worry about the crowd you run with. And when you drive, we pray you're driving under the speed limit so you won't be targeted by cops because you're a Black male behind the wheel or 'driving while black' as we say."

"Either way, it's a dangerous world for our Black sons. They have to excel like President Obama. They have to." She spoke with conviction, as she stared out the window. The weariness in her voice was evident. "I also pray to live to witness Ace's transformation—and yours too."

Kidd squirmed in his seat, and then honked his horn when a driver jumped in his lane. "How did I get lumped into this? I'm not stirring any pot." His mother was putting too much faith in God to change the behavior of a person who was content with his lifestyle. "Well, it appears Ace has found another crutch—Cameron."

"Yeah, and I plan to put a stop to that too." Sandra faced him again. "I'm thankful the opportunity came along so you two could split up. With you in St. Louis, Ace no longer had a unified front—that is, until Cameron filled in the gap. I believe the hard attitude that has taken root in you will soften. There's so much good in you, Kidd. I believe Jesus brought Cameron into our lives to show you the good in the Jamiesons. I believe God is going to save your soul and heart."

"I don't have an attitude." He squeezed his lips in offense, ignoring her comment about God saving him—from what?

Sandra reached out and patted his hand. "My dear firstborn, you do have an attitude, even while you deny that you have an attitude. How are things coming between you and Parke?"

He genuinely didn't have an answer. Their relationship—as long as Parke didn't try to run his life and agreed to jog on opposite side-walks—would work. Honestly, it was getting harder to find fault with Parke. Kidd wasn't ready to admit that.

"Give it time, son. I have to believe God knows what He's doing; otherwise, His Son's death on the cross was in vain."

"Ma?" Kidd asked, as he checked the rearview mirror, clicked on the blinker, and changed lanes. "Do you really think God is concerned about your two sons, who you bore out of wedlock? I mean, I know we've talked about this before, but it just seems like . . . never mind." He was not about to hurt his mother's feelings; she was already hurting enough.

She chuckled. "By that, you mean, am I sleeping in the bed I literally made? Sometimes women have stronger feelings in a relationship. I loved Samuel and thought he loved me. If I had known he was married with other children, he wouldn't have gotten a second glance. Did I sin? Yes. Am I paying for it with Ace's craziness? No, I don't believe that, because Jesus paid my debts on the cross. Nevertheless, we all reap what we sow, and I'm reaping."

She lifted her brow and smirked. "But my God owns a high-powered weed whacker. He knows how to destroy the weeds without touching the delicate vegetation of new believers."

"I hope so," Kidd stated, unconvinced Ace would find some type of purpose—instead of continuing his destructive behavior. After all, Kidd was still searching for the meaning of his own life.

Crossing River Street to Hyde Park Avenue, Kidd suddenly craved grits and sausages from Brothers' Deli and Restaurant in Mattapan Square. It was only blocks away from the place he called home for years, until he moved his mother to the condo.

Kidd pulled into his mother's parking space. Taking a deep breath and turning off the ignition, he stared at the attached homes. He could sense that his mother was watching him.

"Come on, son." Sandra motioned for him to open her car door.

"One sec." Kidd got out and strolled around to assist her, then reached for his duffle bag from the backseat. His mind was already made up. He would stay through Monday; he would call the facility and let his boss know. Family—his family, Sandra and Ace—meant everything to him, and he had to preserve his own at all costs.

Within thirty minutes, Kidd was sitting at the table, wolfing down everything in sight that his mother had prepared for his homecoming. After he brought her up to speed on what was going on with him in St. Louis, they brainstormed ideas concerning what to do about Ace.

Fatigued, Kidd retired to his old bedroom. It was smaller than the guest room Parke had reserved for him. Suddenly, a feeling of discontentment washed over him, as if he had outgrown his surroundings. It wasn't so much the physical aspects, but an emotional attachment to what he once called home. The cell phone chimed.

"Hey, man. Ever heard of letting someone know you landed safely?" The sarcastic question rolled out of Parke's mouth before Kidd could finish saying hello.

"Sorry." He wasn't. "I've got a lot on my mind."

"I can imagine." Parke asked a few questions short of prying, but Kidd didn't really know what was going on, so there was nothing much to pass on. He was only able to disconnect after his little cousins took turns speaking to him. Kami was the ringleader. Parke had allowed them to stay up past their bedtime just so they could talk to him.

If nothing else, Kidd missed the children. They insisted on calling him Uncle, sometimes Cousin Uncle or Uncle Cousin. He never wanted to be an uncle, especially if it was a result of Ace's irresponsible behavior, but the St. Louis Jamiesons had him rethinking his opinion. That was the last thing on his mind when he drifted off to sleep—that and Eva's smiles, lips, lashes, hair, figure . . .

The next thing he knew, it was morning. Kidd had hoped to sleep late on Saturday, but the aroma from his mother's homemade waffles foiled his plan. He got up, showered, dressed, and made his way downstairs. Soon after stuffing his face, he pulled out his cell and punched in Cameron's number. He controlled his breathing, so he wouldn't explode.

"Hey, cuz. Welcome back," Cameron greeted.

"What were you thinking?" Kidd barked.

"That Ace is my cousin."

Hmm, so Cameron knew why he called. He appreciated that he didn't have to play games with the man. "Ace is my brother. I can take care of my own. And by the way, since I'm in close proximity of you, I should jump you now for your description of great opportunities in your hometown. I'm working in a nursing home."

"I heard you have a plush office, and you don't have to do any cleanups."

Cleanups. Eva's image came to Kidd. He wondered what she was doing today, and if she ever thought good things about him. He grunted.

"Before you elevate your blood pressure, I feel responsible for Ace's predicament since it was my suggestion we go to that club. I know he's a flirt, but I didn't realize how many drinks he'd had and that he was ready to rumble. I bailed him out because he's blood, whether he's my brother or cousin. He's a Jamieson—period."

What could Kidd argue? Cameron's logic sounded like his

brother's, despite Cameron's two engineering degrees. "Yeah, okay, but there'd better not be a next time. If you really want to help my brother, and your cousin, keep him away from riffraff. I'll see you Monday." Kidd disconnected.

On Sunday, Kidd declined his mother's urging to worship at Faithful Church of Christ on Woodrow Avenue. He was almost eight when Sandra sat beside him in the pew and repented during the sermon. Kidd recalled the alarm he felt, as tears streamed down her face when the minister finished preaching. She had stood and joined others who were walking down an aisle to the front. Concerned, he followed her and dragged Ace with him.

Elder Lane instructed him and Ace to have a seat near what he thought, at the time, was a large tub of water. Later he learned it was a baptismal pool. They sat patiently waiting until their mother walked out dressed in all white—from a swimming cap to thick white socks. She descended into that water, still crying. Kidd remembered the minister's booming voice.

"My dear sister, upon the confession of your faith in the blessed Word of God, I indeed baptize you in the name of our Lord Jesus Christ, whereby your sins will be forgiven and God will manifest Himself with power and bestow gifts to you to live right. Amen."

At first, Sandra's oldest son was about to intervene when he thought the man was trying to drown his mother. Kidd's protective nature was on high alert. But a few seconds later when she resurfaced, laughing, clapping, and singing, Kidd sat back, relieved. In his young mind, he tried hard to understand what had just happened.

For the remainder of the service, while his mother rejoiced in church, he and Ace dozed. To this day, Kidd couldn't recall one sermon, but he remembered the baptism. If Kidd included his forced attendance as a child, he was a lifelong member. Now, many years later, he would do his thinking in front of the TV. Although the only thing he could think of at the moment was his baby brother sitting in jail.

Just the other day, he heard on the news about a twenty-one-year-old man who had been in critical condition after a food fight in a St. Louis jail. The victim was rendered unconscious as soon as his head hit the ground. He later died. Kidd bowed his head. "Lord, I do have one prayer request. Protect my brother. Amen."

No, he wasn't leaving until he saw Ace and knocked some tender-loving sense into him. Later that evening, he visited friends in the old neighborhood.

Kidd couldn't wait for the alarm clock to announce Monday morning. Once he and his mother had dressed and eaten, he drove them to Randolph jail and waited. For his mother's sake, he kept his temper under control. Otherwise, he might as well hand her his ATM card, because she would have to bail him out next for assault and battery on his brother.

At last, from behind a locked door, Ace walked with a boastful strut into the lobby. Escorted by a guard, one might think he was some high-profile influential figure checking out of the Embassy Suites.

"Kidd?" His brown eyes lit up. "Whatz up, bro?" Ace grabbed his big brother into a bear hug. Kidd took that opportunity to crush Ace to his chest and whisper in his ear, "When I get through with you, you're going to wish you were still locked up."

Ace wrestled out of his older brother's grip. "Why wait? We can save the police a pickup . . ."

Sandra forced a separation between her sons with an elbow to Kidd's side and a punch to Ace's arm. At the same time the not-so-pleasant family reunion was taking place, Cameron strolled through the door.

"Let's go," she ordered Kidd and Ace. Cameron followed too.

Forty minutes later, back at the condo, Sandra, Cameron, and Ace took positions on various pieces of furniture. Kidd paced a path on the carpet, encircling his brother.

"Ace, what is it about Samuel Jamieson that makes you want to be a chip off the old block?"

Ace thumped his chest. "I'm my own man. I'm grown—"

"But not gone from our mother's house. Care about our mother, even if you don't care about yourself. Granted, the Jamieson name doesn't open any doors for us, but we're the ones who have to turn it around."

Kidd frowned. Did he just say that? Parke and Mrs. Valentine must be getting to him. "Do you know your mentality is just what's expected of you by a certain sector of society? You're feeding into the statistic that says boys from single-parent households have a greater percentage of incarceration."

"Humph. They're right about that," Ace joked, which infuriated Kidd.

"I like to prove to people they're wrong, just for the challenge. I believe we've got to have a secret weapon—"

"And that's Jesus," his mother interjected, cutting off Kidd.

Both sons shook their heads. Kidd didn't want to hear that talk at the moment. After all, he understood Ace. The two of them had to fend for themselves for so long. At times, it seemed as if they were lost in the forest and couldn't find the trail out.

Ace was destroying himself, and there was nothing Kidd could say or do to alter his path. Sighing, he flopped onto the sofa, only to meet his mother's disapproving look for mistreating her furniture.

Up until this point, Cameron hadn't stirred from his post in the corner. He cleared his throat, but didn't try to interrupt. His serious expression reminded Kidd of Parke—poker face. One thing the Jamieson men were good at was keeping people guessing at what they were thinking.

Kidd leaned back with his eyes closed. "Okay, St. Louis Jamieson, what's your two cents?"

"Actually, my opinion is worth much more than that."

"Let's hear it," Kidd ordered.

"Pray."

"Amen," his mother whispered.

132

"That's what my brothers and parents always say when I call home. Personally, I don't know how that works as far as making a person change. I do know I'm here for my cousin for the long haul. Nothing can change that."

Kidd opened one eye. It sounded good, but only time would tell. His mother was the last to take center stage. The fireworks were just beginning, and time was running out for him to extinguish the sparks before his flight back to St. Louis.

Everyone had a point of view concerning Ace's behavior—except Ace. He seemed to be stuck on stupid and at the lowest level of maturity. Maybe he inherited a defective gene from Samuel. That was one more reason for Kidd to hate the man.

They all seemed exhausted from lecturing Ace—to no avail. Finally, they ate an early dinner and Kidd threw his items back into his bag. Cameron volunteered to drive him to the airport. With Ace tagging along in the passenger seat, Sandra and Kidd occupied the rear. The radio wasn't blasting, but it was loud enough to mask Sandra and Kidd's hushed conversation.

"Listen, son, although I miss you, consider making St. Louis your new home. At least you're surrounded by family. Go to school, buy a house, get married, and have babies . . . eventually, become a grandpa. Your blessings aren't limited to a life here," she advised. Then, lowering her voice even more as Kidd strained to hear her, she said, "As soon as this matter is cleared up with Ace, he's getting up out of here. I have friends in Philly and Des Moines."

"Des Moines?" Kidd chuckled.

"My choice." Sandra lifted a brow. "Don't think I won't . . . one more thing, I'll visit you next time." She was issuing a silent threat, but Kidd wasn't in the mood to read between the lines.

"What are you saying, Ma?"

"I'll visit you next time," she repeated. "There's no reason for you to come back to put out fires whenever Ace decides to start one."

Chapter Seventeen

Kidd was actually happy when his plane touched down at Lambert Airport an hour and forty-five minutes later. The drama in St. Louis didn't compare with what was brewing in Beantown.

He was still mulling over—with an attitude—his mother's edict not to return home any time soon. After thirty-one years, he knew when Sandra was bluffing. She hadn't cracked a smile.

Walking off the plane with his shoulders slumped, Kidd would never admit to anyone that he felt like a failure. As far as he was concerned, he'd let down his mother, his brother, and himself. He blamed one person: his phantom father. Despondent, Kidd strolled to the escalators and rode down to the baggage claim area. Although he hadn't checked any baggage, Parke said he would meet him there.

When he made his way into the carousel area, a cavalry of Jamiesons greeted him: Parke and Cheney, their three children, Malcolm and Hallison, their son, and Parke and Malcolm's parents. Even Imani had shown up, playing hide-and-seek behind big helium balloons. Kidd wondered how they got her to do that. She was the only one who wasn't smiling. That snapshot was worth a thousand words.

Kidd laughed. Pace held a homemade sign that read "Welcome home, Cousin Uncle Kevin."

Slowing his steps to enjoy his brief celebrity status, suddenly, he felt appreciated. When the children spotted him, they cheered and clapped wildly, causing strangers to take notice. Their actions were as embarrassing as they were humbling, then comforting.

His mother was right—his future was in his hands. It was hard to dislike these Jamiesons. The scene was maddening as the women showered him with kisses and hugs, the men tested his strength with handshakes, and the children made a game out of chanting his name.

The drive from the airport to Parke's house was short. When they arrived at the house, the smell of barbecue teased Kidd as he walked through the front door. The children raced to the kitchen, including Malcolm's young son, MJ, who was at least a year older than Parke's toddler.

"There's school in the morning," Cheney reminded them. "After you eat, then it's bath time."

The little Jamiesons moaned as Hallison instructed them to wash their hands. Imani headed home. Since the day Cheney put her in check, Imani seemed bored to be around Kidd.

"You want something to eat, man—ribs, chicken? We grilled hot dogs for the children, but it's your choice," Parke offered.

"It's barely the end of April, why the cookout on a Monday?" Kidd asked him.

"Sort of a 'welcome back to your new home' celebration. We have plenty, including side dishes. You left stressed. It was our wives' idea."

Harmonious was the only way to describe the moment, until Kidd walked into the crossfire in the kitchen. Kami, Pace, Paden, and MJ were clamoring for their favorite color of Jell-O treats. Despite eating at his mother's, he helped himself to potato salad, spaghetti, and a few pieces of chicken. After all, it was an hour earlier in St. Louis, thanks to Central Standard Time.

If Malcolm and Parke ate beforehand, there was no evidence of it.

They grabbed plates and served themselves as if they had missed two meals or more. Instead of eating at the table, the trio headed to Parke's cave.

"I am not a maid—volunteered or paid—remember to load those dishes up when you all are finished," Cheney yelled after them.

Half-listening, Parke nodded and rested his plate on an ottoman. Kidd went along with the program and bowed his head while Parke recited a blessing. They said a string of "Amens," then Parke scooped up the remote and angled it toward the screen. Surfing the channels, he found a St. Louis Cardinals' game. Within minutes, the men jeered when the outfielder dropped the ball. Not long after that, the Red Birds lost. Parke clicked off the television and faced Kidd. "Welcome home, man."

Kidd nodded and smirked. "Thanks."

"So what's going on with our family in Boston?" Malcolm asked.

"You mean, my family," Kidd corrected.

"Kidd—"

"No, Parke and Malcolm, let me say this. There is no way I'd believe 'meddling' Cameron didn't call and give his big brothers the scoop. You had a transcript before my plane taxied off the runway to Boston."

The brothers exchanged glances. Their silence confirmed Kidd's suspicions. "See what I mean. I'm entitled to my privacy. You don't need to know everything about me, including the color of my under-wear."

"You didn't have to go there. The only male behind I want to see is when I help with Paden's potty training. Bottom line, Kidd—if Ace is in trouble—we all are."

Kidd growled and threw up his arms. "Excuse me, if I don't join in this 'all-for-one-and-one-for-all' Jamieson solidarity. My brother is self-destructing, and my mother is barring me from coming home to knock some sense into his head. She's putting her money on God to handle this."

"I second that. If you let Him, God will come through," Malcolm said, trying to encourage him.

"See, cuz, that's where I have a problem, letting other people handle my business."

"Kidd, if your mother says she's trusting God for Ace, then we've got her back. We'll keep praying while we're trusting. Ace needs spiritual strength," Malcolm advised.

"Ace needed a father to show him how to be a man. You two can't imagine how it feels to suffer from the loss of a parent. Even though Samuel Jamieson wasn't dead when we were growing up, he was missing in action."

Looking away, Parke seemed to choke. "No, I've been a blessed man to have both Mom and Dad, but you talk about pain. Wanna swap pain? How about almost losing three children?" His nostrils flared. The emotion in his eyes was raw. "I think that qualifies me to know something about hurt."

Whoa. Kidd backed off. "Yeah, Pace did mention something about his brother dying. I really didn't believe him. I thought he was pulling my leg." So the boy did know what he was talking about. Kidd could have asked Parke, but that would have shown he cared.

"When Cheney and I first got married," Parke explained, "the doctors said she would never be able to have children. Heartbroken, we accepted that, but God had other plans. When Cheney conceived, the doctors didn't believe it until their tests confirmed it. They warned us that Cheney was still high risk, but we believed God."

Parke took a deep breath and seemed to stare through Kidd. "We lost that baby, Kidd. We lost our baby." When Parke bowed his head, Malcolm slapped him on the back a few times and lovingly squeezed his neck.

"It's okay, bro," Malcolm comforted him. "God is good anyway."

Kidd chided himself for forcing Parke's hurt to resurface. No, he had never lost a child. He'd only lost his father when he was a child, but that still wasn't the same. The three were quiet while Parke gathered his thoughts and composed himself.

"Before we got married, Cheney and I had been foster parents. Kami was our first—"

"Get out of here." Kidd shook his head, still doubtful. "She's a carbon copy of you and a replica of your wife's attitude. How can that be? She is going to be something else when she grows up."

"Yeah, you're right. That was all God's doing. She's something else now, and most of her attitude comes from Grandma BB."

"Why doesn't that surprise me?" Kidd chimed in.

"I know." Parke chuckled. "We miss her. Anyway, do you know Grandma BB threatened to marry me, if Cheney didn't?"

Kidd and Malcolm filled the room with hoots. Parke shuddered.

"It ain't funny. You don't know her like we do. I wouldn't put it past her to drug me, then bribe someone to drag me to the altar—the ultimate cougar. She owns a gun and knows how to use it. She shot Cheney's father, Dr. Reynolds."

"Are you serious?" Kidd's eyes bucked. "When she bragged about that, I thought she was delusional, so I played along. What happened?"

Shaking his head, Malcolm interjected, "She called it a retaliation hit."

"That's a whole other story in a different book." Parke waved his hand. "But the end result is, Dr. Reynolds is alive and sitting in prison for a felony hit-and-run that killed Grandma BB's husband. Grandma BB got ninety days shock time for firing a weapon."

Kidd bowled over, laughing. Tears squeezed out of his eyes. "That woman—with or without a stroke—is something else. You'll have to fill me in on the details later."

Parke laughed along with them and then sobered. "Sorry, I got sidetracked." He bowed his head and took a deep breath before looking up again. "Kidd, I really want you to get my message. This family knows pain. We don't understand why God told us to trust Him, only to later suffer the loss of our baby. But He will have all the answers when we get to Glory.

"God gave us Kami, and she's a handful." Pride shone in his eyes. "It wasn't long until Cheney was pregnant again with our second child—a son. We lost him in her last semester—I mean trimester." He paused. "Cheney delivered Parke K. Jamieson VII, a stillborn, on October third at 2:45 in the afternoon. He was perfect to us. We had a chance to hold him in the hospital before we allowed doctors to take him and run tests to find the cause of his death. Seven days later, we buried him."

Stealing a gulp of air, Kidd slowly exhaled. He wasn't a crier, but his cousin was pushing his threshold.

Parke continued his monologue. "While Kami was in foster care, our social worker recalled seeing a name similar to mine for a little boy in the system. Thank God for Kami because without her, there wouldn't have been a social worker who recognized my name and put us on the hunt for Pace. Thank God for every incident in our lives that advances us to the next part."

Malcolm sat straighter. "You may not have noticed, but Kami will fight anybody over her daddy. Both she and Pace have excelled in martial arts. When MJ gets old enough, he'll join them." Malcolm chuckled and shook his head. He and Parke were both grinning proudly.

"Oh, one more thing." Malcolm added, "That girl can sense evil. She did with me."

"What do you mean?" Kidd asked, eyeing Malcolm.

"Hali had my faithfulness, commitment, and surrender, even before I proposed. God had other plans. When Hali gave her life over to Christ, me—a stubborn Jamieson—wouldn't budge. So the Lord told her to choose, and I lost."

That was the craziest story Kidd had ever heard, but he didn't interrupt.

"Us Jamieson men don't take no for an answer. You may know

something about that. So I gave Hali my ultimatum. If we were really meant to be together, I told her we would find our way back to each other. If not, we both had greater loves waiting for us. Man, I can talk a good game, but I was miserable without her—"

"Make that pit-i-ful," Parke taunted his brother.

"You don't even want me to start in on you . . . Cheney—"

"Okay, okay, finish your story." Parke backed down.

Kidd smirked. They behaved like he and Ace probably would, once his brother grew up. Both were muscular, in shape, and stood about six-two or six-three. Even without martial arts, they looked like a force to be reckoned with. Parke was fair-skinned, with a mustache. Malcolm had more sun, with piercing eyes and a cocky, sinister look. His thick beard just added to his mysterious persona.

"Anyway, as I was saying before Parke interrupted, I hooked up with this hot, sizzlin' chick named Lisa. The woman could make any man lose his mind, literally. But Kami didn't like her at all. At first, I thought it was because she wanted me to be with Hali, which probably did have a little to do with it.

"But more than that, I believe God allowed Kami to discern Lisa's spirit. That woman was dabbling in witchcraft. Whoa." Malcolm held up his hands. "Even before God saved me, I had my standards. No drugs, no gambling, and no Wicca. In hindsight, I believe God was letting me know He had the cream of the crop waiting for me. If I wanted Hali, first I had to repent and be baptized in Jesus' name.

"Once I stopped denying the whole 'I have to repent, be baptized, and accept God's gifts' mantra, Jesus filled me with His promises and power. You know, when it comes to the Lord's promises to His apostles, we often tease each other and say, 'Don't leave home without it.'"

Malcolm smiled a confident smile, as he reminisced about his crowning achievement. "Yeah, I've been good-to-go ever since. So I had a choice: the cream of the crop or the bottom of the pot." Grinning, he folded his arms behind his head, and reclined on the sofa.

"That's deep." Kidd shook his head. The man was in love with his wife. Kidd didn't see cheating anywhere in Malcolm's future. Out of nowhere, Eva's smile flashed across Kidd's mind's eye. It was just for a second, but the intense pounding of his heart lingered. He had never denied her beauty and freely gave compliments. Still, he had to get inside her head to see how she felt about him.

Parke switched back to his story. "Man, I was like a dog chasing after a bone—a fifty-pound turkey bone. I hired my private investigator friend, the Duke, to see if I had an illegitimate son who, by birthright, was Parke K. Jamieson VII."

Kidd's respect for Parke moved up another notch. No telling how many illegitimate children Samuel had sired and had never "fessed up" about them or bothered to seek a relationship with them. That's why Kidd's sexual escapades were well-orchestrated steps of protection. He would not repeat his father's mistakes.

"The Duke found my son. Pace had already been adopted and his name changed to Gilbert Junior. That really made me mad." Parke scowled. "What kind of name is that for a Black man? It wasn't any better than the name my 'few-nights stand and ex-lover,' Rachel, gave him—Parkie. I believe that woman jacked up my son's name on purpose."

"Stick to the story, man," Malcolm taunted him, mumbling something else inaudible.

Parke shot Malcolm a death-threat stare. Kidd grunted. He had exchanged that expression many times with Ace. After that brief intermission, Kidd resumed the conversation. "Why was Pace in foster care in the first place?"

"His mother died in a car accident. Rachel had no close family and my name was missing from his birth certificate. The state took over, traumatizing my son and terminating my rights. But my God can overturn any of man's laws. I changed his name to—"

"Cheney threatened to put Parke out if he tampered with their deceased son's name. She didn't care if Parkie-Gilbert was Parke's firstborn or not. He wasn't *their* firstborn," Malcolm butted in.

Parke cut his eyes at Malcolm as if he didn't want that tidbit disclosed.

"In a nutshell, Cheney and I compromised. Out of respect for our deceased child, we legally changed Pace's name to Parke K. Jamieson VIII. Anyway, to make a long story short, Gilbert didn't want to give up Pace without a fight. But again, the Lord intervened, and it worked in our favor when Gilbert's wife became pregnant. The rest is history. Suffice it to say, it was a stressful time."

Parke shrugged and fanned the air with his hand. "Anyway, Cheney became pregnant again. I guess you can say the third time was a charm. Sometimes, God's way isn't ours. The result is that little terror, Paden. Regardless of the biological beginnings, we love our children. They are all Jamiesons."

Whew! Kidd hadn't expected this revelation. All he saw was their happy ending. In a million years, he would never have guessed how their stories began.

Unfortunately for him, Kidd didn't see a happy ending in his future. Parke must have sensed what he was thinking.

"We can't change the past, Kidd. I don't know anything about your father, and I'm sorry he wasn't in your life. But I believe you need to confront him and let him know . . ."

Kidd held up his hand. "I know there's somewhere in the Bible that says it's disrespectful to curse out your parent. Right now, knowing the path my brother is taking—and no one can convince me that it's not a direct result of our father not being around—I would hurt him, Parke."

"That may not be a bad thing. A little beat down is good for the conscience," Malcolm stated.

"You're not helping, man," Parke snarled and slapped him in the chest with the back of his hand, with no malicious intent. "To put it in a more tactful and Christian way, we have your back. Whenever you're ready to track him down, we can do it."

"That may take a long time." Kidd meant it. The fact remained that Ace was going downhill and nobody—not even Kidd—could stop his brother from crashing.

Chapter Eighteen

K idd. Eva's heart fluttered as his broad shoulders cleared the entrance of Garden Chateau on Tuesday morning. She, along with the other coworkers, was curious about his absence on Monday. The only information the executive director passed on was that he was away on personal business.

That made Eva worry. She wanted to hug him, but not only was that inappropriate, she had no warrant for it. Eva sighed in relief just seeing him. She wondered what had come up—death, debt, or whatever else. But she didn't have the right to ask, or did she?

Eva was perplexed. She had never seen him in a mood so brooding; it matched the stormy weather rolling through the city that morning. His usual conceited manner, as if he owned and operated the facility, was missing. Today his steps were angry, squashing anything underfoot. How could Kidd's hard expression appear so masculine? Was this what attracted women to the bad boys?

"Kevin." Eva smiled, but grew concerned when he didn't return her cheerful greeting. "Is everything all right?" She could understand his hesitancy about confiding in her, but the cold shoulder was unexpected.

A five o'clock shadow clinging to Kidd's face suited him. If a woman preferred a man with a clean look, he wouldn't make the cut today. Eva wasn't complaining.

"I don't know how to answer that." Kidd twisted his lips, never making eye contact. The usual tasteful tie, starched shirt, and creased pants were absent, replaced with a white polo shirt and tan Dockers. His attire reminded her of a school uniform, but he was still good-looking.

"It's a multiple-choice answer—yes, no, or maybe."

"I choose none of the above." He didn't crack a smile and kept walking.

Eva wanted to toss out "don't come back until you find out," but she held her tongue. Who was this guy? How many sides to this man were there? On one side of his personality, he was too arrogant to mingle with his charges. On the other, he was compassionate enough to assist her with preparing for a test.

"I would say you woke up on the wrong side of the bed, but now I'm wondering if you're awake, Sybilian."

"Who?"

She finally seemed to get his attention. He stopped and stared at her, waiting for an explanation.

"I like your hair," Kidd said, without blinking.

How could the man drop a compliment like that without a smile, purr, or twinkle in his eyes? Eva squinted, as Kidd anchored his fists at his waist.

"Now, who is Sybilian?"

"You." Eva pointed. "Sybil's brother. You know, the woman who had sixteen personalities. A movie was made about her in the seventies and then a remake several years ago. I'm wondering . . . will your personalities outnumber hers."

"Start counting. No telling how many may come out before the day is over." Kidd grunted, before he proceeded on.

"I've seen enough already." If he was going to act like a jerk this

145

week after being so kind to her last week, so be it. She spun around to head in the other direction. "Well, I hope all of your personalities have a great day."

Bear one another's burdens, God spoke.

"I have to know his burdens before I can bear them, don't I? He can't even bear them, Lord. How can I do the impossible?" she mumbled. "I don't even know what his problem is today," Eva ranted, as she made her way down the hall.

The man was as complex as a fruitcake recipe. It seems like no one knew all the secret ingredients. He was the poster child of the type of man Eva didn't date or want. She pitied the woman who had her eyes and heart set on Kidd Jamieson. Her new resolve was—if he didn't want her friendship—then she wouldn't extend it. A good tutor or not, she would avoid him like a weed on the lookout for Roundup pesticide.

Hurt that she was snubbed, Eva refocused and completed her activities of daily living requirements with the residents. She strolled into Mrs. Valentine and Mrs. Beacon's room with a smile on her face.

"Good morning, Eve. Where's Adam?" Mrs. Valentine's eyes were bright with life.

"I sent him back to God. He had a few missing parts." Eva froze. That wasn't her standard reply. Was Kidd still on her mind when she answered that way? Mrs. Valentine beamed, but didn't comment. Eva assisted her first with her morning routine. Before long, both ladies were clean, fresh, and jazzy.

"Ladies, are you ready for breakfast?"

"Have you seen that Kidd today?" Mrs. Beacon queried.

Yes, and I don't plan to see him again, she thought. Before she could answer, two CNAs came into the suite with wheelchairs to transport the women to the dining room. She dodged answering by quickly slipping out of the room.

Eva managed to steer clear of Kidd for the rest of the morning. After lunch, she rounded a corner and angry voices coming from a nearby room caught her attention. One of them was Kidd's. *Figures. Now what?* She gritted her teeth and hurried in that direction.

"Listen, old man, you forgot who's calling the shots."

She braced to yank Kidd by his polo collar and knock some manners into his head. *What in the world is going on? Did this involve another potty break because Theodore Abraham is wheelchair-bound?*

Before Eva took a step into the man's room, he snapped, "Back off." Eva froze. Was that a call for help?

"You cheated. That's the third set of doubles. If you take away my applesauce, that's my dessert from lunch." Mr. Abraham's voice trembled.

"I don't have to cheat. I've got skills. You either hand over that bowl, or game over," Kidd threatened.

Slowly, Eva peeked inside. The two men were involved in a card game. Instead of chips, Mr. Abraham had fruit, a snack-size container of applesauce, and miniature home-baked chocolate chip cookies. Kidd's arsenal was cans of soda—no doubt from the same vending machine she witnessed him raiding the week before. At least they weren't playing for cigarettes. Mr. Abraham had emphysema, and she had seen employees slip him one or two when he was outside on the grounds.

Eva backed away before she could be noticed. Kidd was a challenging formula to decode. Inside his "mad at the world" exterior was a tender heart. There's only one problem: pulling it out was like delivering a thirteen-pound baby.

She strolled down the hall to check on the resident who would never be on Kidd's list of favorites—Mr. Johnston. She changed the bandage on his arm, covering a sore that had suddenly appeared. Doctors wanted the staff to observe it three times a day.

"Hi, Mr. Johnston, how are you feeling today?"

"I don't need you asking me how I feel. Don't you think I know, gal?" he spat.

Be the Christian. She took a deep breath. The calmer she talked, the more indignant he became. Finally, Eva finished her task and left the room.

"Thank God the good outweighs the bad," she said under her breath, as she rounded the corner. She was just in time to see Kidd leaving Mr. Abraham's room with his winnings.

Eva felt like pivoting and going the other way, but this was her turf first. She wasn't going to let him make her act like less than the professional she was. That fact made her decide to confront him. "Well, I see you're still alive. What about Mr. Abraham?"

"Theo is fine, the old goat." Kidd shifted the stash in his hands.

Eva nodded, noting the menacing tension that had a stronghold on him when he walked through the door was gone. She relaxed and silently forgave him for his earlier rudeness. "Did you leave him with anything to eat?"

Kidd shrugged. "He won't starve. Besides, Theo forced it on me. These are his snacks, not a whole meal."

"You can't gamble with food. You'll get yourself in trouble and be sitting in jail," Eva teased, but Kidd's eye twitched. Evidently, she struck a nerve.

"If I want motherly advice, I'll call 617-208-1 . . ." he shot back, rattling off a number. Out of nowhere, the brooding personality was back. She never met such a moody man.

Eva's nostrils flared. "Kidd, you are an evil, mean-spirited, grouchy loser . . ."

"Are you taking a breath, or do you need a thesaurus?" He smirked.

Be the Christian. Eva didn't answer, as she spun around and stormed away. If she hadn't, she would be one breath away from telling the man she hated him. She had never said those words to anybody, and Kidd wasn't going to provoke her to lose her salvation.

For the remainder of the shift, Eva didn't know who avoided who. Although other staff members were glad to see Kidd, he was the last person she wanted to be near. She couldn't wait for her shift to be over. A few hours later, she left work at 5:02 p.m.

Later that night, Eva flipped through the pages of the newest bridal magazine, trying to take her mind off the standoff with Kidd. Articles about fairy-tale romances didn't help. She needed to flush out her frustrations to anyone who would listen. Picking up her cordless, she dialed.

"Hey, Angel," Eva greeted when her sister answered. Then she took a deep breath before exploding, "I hate men."

"What?"

"Actually, just one. Kidd was—"

"Kidd, again? Maybe you need to go to a supervisor about him. That man sounds dangerous."

Eva twisted her lips. "And looks it too."

"What is his problem? Does he have multiple personalities?"

"My diagnosis exactly. But he doesn't act like that with everybody, just me and a few other residents he doesn't like. I'm clueless."

Her sister ran through a list of possible things Eva could have done unknowingly to aggravate him. Finally, Angela sighed. "The only thing I can say is that it's the Jesus in you he doesn't like. If that's the case, stay clear and pray from afar."

"Hey, sis." Lance must have taken the phone. "This dude could like you in a juvenile kind of way. But I agree with my baby, stay clear. I would never treat your sister like that. Do I need to make my presence known, because I will?"

Eva contained her giggles. Lance was in good shape, but there would be no contest if he took on Kidd Jamieson. It would be like a semitractor trailer Transformer meeting an electric car. "No. I just needed to vent. I don't feel threatened."

"Are you sure?" Angela and Lance said in unison on the phone.

Eva reassured them and signed off. It was a mistake to talk to her when Lance was around. He always jumped in the middle of their conversation, as if he didn't need permission. Eva liked Lance, but was it too much to ask for a little confidentiality between sisters—and twins at that? No doubt, this was what she had to look forward to if Lance became her brother-in-law.

Eva ran her fingers through her hair. It had been a while since she had her stylist give her tight curls. However, she liked the natural crimp once the curls began to fall. Kidd complimented her on her hair. At the same time, he seemed clueless about her concern for him.

When her attempt to study failed, she scoured over three wedding catalogs, folding sections or ripping out pages of exquisite dresses. Attempting to work off her stress, she multitasked this way, while consuming two bags of sour apple licorice. If she didn't feel better soon, she would make a root beer float.

An hour later, she gave in and made that float anyway. Up until that point, she hadn't succeeded in clearing her head enough to concentrate on her final exam. After downing the float, she gave in and went to bed.

Wednesday morning, the weather was breathtaking. Eva was in a good mood, despite a stomachache during the night. She vowed to return to her healthy eating habits, especially after detecting an extra five pounds.

At the facility, the afternoon was quiet. Many of her residents were either on a shopping field trip or in the activities room. Going to her locker, Eva pulled her nursing book from the shelf. She strolled outside to watch the geese and enjoy the flowers blooming around the campus.

Her first order of business was to take a few minutes to talk to Jesus. It had been a while since she carved out time for Him. "God, I praise You for allowing me to see another beautiful day. I worship You for Your salvation. And Lord, I thank You for Your abundant blessings. In Jesus' name. Amen."

Feeling spiritually renewed, Eva continued her walk, lifting her face to the sun and enjoying the kisses of the rays. She laughed at the antics of the puppies competing for her attention. Suddenly, she stopped in her tracks when she registered the figure occupying the bench through the trees—her bench. Making a swift detour, Eva wanted to put as much distance between her and Kidd as possible. She wouldn't allow her moment of praise to be in vain.

By the time she heard footsteps behind her, she was almost at a random bench. Glancing over her shoulder, somehow she wasn't surprised to see Kidd. What did he do, have sensors on when she was within arguing range or something? She ignored him. They probably needed a restraining order against each other.

"I'm sorry, Eva," he said, as his long stride overtook hers.

"I accept." She kept walking, bypassing the bench she had chosen for her quick respite. She had to get away from him. He made her moody and her lips loose where she would say things to him she dare not say to another individual.

Rounding a corner, she spotted another bench and claimed it. She pulled out her textbook and did her best imitation of concentrating for her final exam. Kidd sat, too, but had enough sense to keep his distance. The air was thick between them, but Eva refused to initiate a conversation.

"I had a lot on my mind, and—"

"And it came out of your mouth," she finished.

He nodded and bowed his head. Eva closed her eyes and silently applied the tricks Kidd had taught her to remember the medical terms. This was it and her semester would be over.

She fluttered her lids open, as she felt him scoot closer. With her back slightly turned, he was stretching his neck to peer over her shoulder. Slowly, he started calling out the terms. Eva shut her book and stood. "Look, Sybilian, I'm not used to encountering multiple personalities outside of the movies."

"I deserved that."

"And so much more. You are a good-mood killer, do you know that? And I'm so sick of you right now that I have to start praying when I see you coming."

She hurried away with a mind to pray for him on Sunday at church. Why wait? She started at that moment.

"Eva."

Irritated, she spun around, darts aimed and neck craning. "What, Kidd?"

"You mentioned you weren't married, but are you getting married?"

Frowning, she exhaled. "What?"

As he approached her, she couldn't help but admire his swagger—cool, confident, and overbearing. His arms were hidden behind his back. "I asked if you're getting married."

Squinting, she tried to remember the smart-aleck line he gave her yesterday, but couldn't. "That is not your concern."

They engaged in a quiet showdown. The tension was thick, as if two superheroes were battling for supreme power: Wonder Woman vs. Ironman.

When Kidd produced pages from her bridal magazine, she gasped and snatched them from his hands. In her stressed-out state last night, she absentmindedly stuffed them in her book. Hurrying to get away from him, they must have slipped out.

"Ah, thanks."

What a time for them to appear. How embarrassing. She turned back inside. *If I ever get married, it wouldn't be to a man like you, Kevin "Kidd" Jamieson. Or my possible future brother-in-law, Lance.* There had to be somebody in-between.

Chapter Nineteen

*E*ngaged? Kidd had never seen a ring on Eva's finger or heard her mention a boyfriend. What was her availability? He didn't believe in gathering information from other sources about an intended target. Kidd asked her a direct question and there was no misunderstanding her answer. Why did he care? Because he wanted her—whether she was attracted to him or not.

Two days later, Kidd was still mulling over his troubles. Between his desire for Eva and Ace's predicament, his mind was saturated.

Honoring his mother's wishes—more like her decree—he held out from calling home. But he needed some type of distraction. One of the guys at work had invited him to the Lumiére Place Casino for a night of gambling and entertainment. He was tempted to go, that is, until he got home, where there was a buzz of activity for a Friday night.

"Are you coming with us, Cousin Uncle Kidd?" Kami asked.

"Heading where?" Kidd pulled the untied tie through his collar.

Parke walked up behind him. "Sorry, man, we meant to tell you earlier, but it's family game night, and we're heading out to Malcolm and Hali's. It's their turn to host it."

Kidd still hadn't grown accustomed to the "family" term thrown around so loosely. He wasn't able to decline when Paden came out of nowhere and ran circles around him, screaming for attention. When Kidd bent down to scoop him up, the toddler took off, squealing.

"Parke, please grab another game besides Life as a Black Man," Cheney yelled from the kitchen through the clatter of pots and pans.

Lifting a brow, Kidd smirked. "Oh, it's no game. I can tell you all you want to know about the injustices of life as a Black man."

"Yeah. Me, too, but that's not the object of the game. It's surviving the temptations lurking on every corner to get the keys to the city."

"A game, huh?" Kidd's curiosity was sparked.

Parke nodded.

"But you're not playing it tonight," Kidd said.

Stuffing his hands in his pocket, Parke glanced over his shoulder at the kitchen door. He leaned closer to Kidd's ear. "We could, if you insisted. My wife happens to like you. Me, she tolerates."

"And loves," Kidd added, a little envious.

"You know it."

Winking, Parke bent over and blocked Paden from running by him. The toddler squealed again. Pace jumped down the stairs, dressed in a navy polo shirt with bold white letters stretching across his chest, spelling out Team Parke. "Hi, Cousin Uncle!"

Kidd nodded and then squinted. "What's with his shirt?"

"Oh, we all have one—Kami, Cheney, me, and that little monster there. Since Malcolm and I both have families, we've established teams. Come on, you'll have a good time."

Kidd didn't think so. The absence of the polo shirt bearing his name would be a reminder that he was a borrowed Jamieson.

Cheney walked out of the kitchen and reached for Paden. "Hey, Kidd. You'd better get ready if you're going."

"I'm not."

Suddenly, he became the center of attention. Even the baby stopped giggling.

Pace groaned. "Ah, man. I wanted you to be my partner." Shoulders slumped, he turned dejected.

"Please, Uncle Cousin," Kami begged.

"Well, I didn't know anything about it. It's last minute, and . . ." Kidd racked his brain for more excuses. "Plus, I don't have a uniform."

Cheney frowned. "Yes, you do." She headed upstairs. Within minutes, she returned with a navy polo with room for his muscular arms. "See, Captain Kidd." Cheney beamed. "You've been part of our family since day one."

Touched by their thoughtfulness, Kidd was tongue-tied.

"Since you two like to bump heads, I figure game night could be your arena," Cheney added.

"Daddy's the captain of our team. You might have to borrow some kids—I mean children—so you can have your own team," Kami advised. Out-voted, Kidd dismissed the idea of going to the casino in favor of spending time with his family.

Family. He had never seriously contemplated having children. He first had to get a wife, and he wasn't in a rush to make that happen. At least, not until this week when he saw Eva's pictures of wedding gowns. All of a sudden, he wanted what some other man had, a fiancée—Eva. But Kidd planned to beat him to it.

Cheney is going to kill or strangle her husband for grabbing that Life as a Black Man board game, Kidd thought, laughing to himself. He was imagining the fireworks, as he trailed Parke's SUV over the Blanchette Bridge, crossing the Missouri River into St. Charles County.

In the passenger seat, Pace bobbed his head, listening to music from his headset. Kidd was dumbfounded over how he had become the young boy's idol. It made him want to not only deserve it, but also live up to the boy's expectations.

"I'm glad you're coming with us."

Kidd smiled. "You are?"

"Uh huh. And I'm glad you're wearing your shirt too. We're going to beat 'em aren't we, Uncle Cousin?"

Kidd slowed down to exit on First Capitol Drive, a road that retained its name after Missouri's capitol was moved from St. Charles to Jefferson City. But St. Charles still boasted some impressive stats, such as the 225-mile Katy Trail and a historic downtown overlooking the river. Kidd was impressed by those tidbits, shared courtesy of Parke's eldest son. Only for his little cousin would he be willing to cheat to win—maybe.

"Watch out for Team Kidd!" Pace said with his excitement running high.

"Yeah." Kidd held his hand up for a high-five. Pace slapped it.

He passed Lindenwood University campus as Parke turned onto Elm Street, which was supposed to take them to New Town. The area was a newer development that focused on a "walkable" community situated around natural habitats.

Ten minutes later, the caravan of Jamiesons pulled up and parked in front of a newer home construction. Parke unloaded his precious cargo. Pace was already out of his seat belt when Kidd got out, but waited impatiently for his cousin to open the door so he could join his siblings.

Malcolm and Hallison were standing in the doorway. She was holding MJ's hand. The little toddler was excited at the sight of his cousins. Eventually, Hallison released him only for Cheney to pick him up and smother him with kisses.

Parke's parents, Parke V. and Charlotte, brought up the rear. Everyone seemed to have synchronized their arrival time. Parke and his father carefully balanced dishes in their arms. Kidd and Pace's task was to bring the paper products.

"Oh, no, not another Jamieson team," Hallison teased, as Kidd stepped into their spacious home and greeted Malcolm with a fist-bump.

"You know it." Kidd grinned and flexed his biceps.

As the women situated the food on the dining room table, the children dutifully set out the napkins, paper plates, and cups. Pace didn't participate and remained at Kidd's side.

Parke shoved Kidd into a huddle with Malcolm and his father, who was fondly known as "Papa P." Pace squeezed in among them. "Okay, this is the deal. I brought Life as a Black Man. You know they're going to have a fit, so I need you all to back me up."

"Got it," the men agreed in unison and separated, as if they were on a football field or a basketball court.

Kidd scanned the home. Everything looked new—from the window treatments to the furniture—to the shiny hardwood floor. The house resembled a model home until he glimpsed a room down the hallway with toys littering a brown carpet. He chuckled to discover that Hallison and Malcolm were able to contain the evidence of a toddler to one room.

"Okay, everyone, time to eat. Papa P., do you want to bless the food?" Hallison asked her father-in-law.

He waved her off and turned to Malcolm. "This is your castle, son."

They gathered around the table and linked hands. Kidd bowed his head.

"Father God, in the name of Jesus, we thank You for another family fellowship. We thank You for Kidd being among us today. I hope we have been a blessing in his life, as he has been in ours. Sanctify the food we are about to eat, and let our behavior be pleasing in Your sight. In Jesus' name. Amen."

After the chorus of "Amens," Cheney chuckled. "As long as we're not playing Life as a Black Man, we'll be fine."

Kidd cut his eyes at Parke.

"Baby, what game did you chose?" Cheney asked, as she prepared plates for her children.

Parke feigned ignorance. "Hmm. Let me see." He strolled over to the bag, opened it, and gasped. It couldn't have sounded any less genuine. "Oops. Look what I grabbed, Life as a Black Man."

The uproar was simultaneous. Kidd ducked as the first pillow from the sofa flew passed him. It was the most comedic scene he had ever witnessed. Even the children turned on their father. They retrieved the pillows for their mother to reload the ammunition until Papa P. whistled and ordered a cease-fire so they could eat.

"Considering I know my husband, it's a good thing I grabbed the Oware game. Since its origin is from Cameroon, Africa, I thought you might want to impress Kidd." She lifted a brow.

"Good choice, daughter-in-law." Parke's father nodded. "Although I don't know the whereabouts of my game that I had as a child, I still might have some of my original forty-eight seeds that are needed to play." He rubbed his chin in thought. "We should all know how to play this game," he said, as he connected with every face around the table. "It's called Awalé in our homeland of Côte d'Ivoire."

The elder Parke unwrapped the box and pulled out a wooden board that had several pits carved out. "This is a game of strategy for serious adults. One will overtake the other, but the journey is slow and calculated."

"Aren't we all playing?" Kidd questioned.

"When one plays, we all play. Even though it calls for two players, it's a very social game and a good source for African children to learn their math."

"It's all about sowing seeds in this game. In this life, you'd better believe God has more than forty-eight seeds," Parke added.

There he goes again, always interjecting God into a conversation. "What happened to plain old Monopoly, Scramble, or Bingo? Isn't

PlayStation still the game of choice these days?" Kidd asked.

"I like PlayStation, too, Cousin Uncle Kidd. But Daddy says Oware will make our brains big." Kami stretched. "But Life as a Black Man will make Black people strong. Right, Mommy and Daddy?" She looked to her parents for confirmation.

Cheney winked. Parke grinned proudly and boasted, "Yes, and I'm the reigning king to survive Glamourwood Districts, The Ghetto, Corporate America, and Prison before advancing to Freedom and winning life as a Black man!"

Groans echoed among them.

"Team Kidd, it's your call. You're our guest," Malcolm announced.

Kidd ignored Parke and a few others' hand signals. "Let me check with my partner." He squatted, eye level with Pace. "What do you think, cuz?"

Pace's eyes widened, surprised that he had been consulted. He grinned.

"Remember that video game you want, Son." Parke jumped in, attempting to bribe his firstborn. Cheney elbowed him.

Cupping Kidd's ear, Pace whispered, "Jambo! Traders who sell the most to customers in Central Africa during colony time wins." He turned to his aunt and smiled, proudly.

I guess Milton Bradley isn't a household name anymore. Kidd frowned with a chuckle. When he was a child, his pastime was bike riding, basketball, or hanging out with his buddies.

As if cued, Hallison left the dining room and went into the hall closet, rumbling through items. She pulled out a colorful square box.

"Yay!" Pace pumped both fists in the air. "Auntee Hali bought it for me when we went shopping."

"Sounds like a setup to me," Parke complained. "Traitor. There goes a perfectly good game night."

As Parke complained, the whole family laughed at his expense. Kidd noted how everyone was paired off. He was the captain with no team unless he borrowed Pace. Truthfully, there was only one person he wanted to be on his team—Eva—and that desire wasn't limited to a game at all.

Chapter Twenty

*I*n a million years, Kidd never would have guessed that he might enjoy a night of playing games. To him, it was a foreign concept. Although family night with the Jamiesons had been fun on Friday, Saturday night belonged to him. He drove to some hole-in-the-wall sports bar—another recommendation by coworkers—and actually had a decent time. It was almost one o'clock in the morning when Kidd headed back to Parke's.

As soon as he entered through the front door, Kidd heard a faint sound coming from the back of the house. Curious, he quietly walked in the direction of Parke's cave. There was no way he was still up. A late night for Parke was ten-thirty, and not a second later.

Images from the television screen caught his attention, but the noise was actually jazz music, streaming from four miniature surround sound speakers. Parke was sprawled on the sofa with Cheney cuddled up next to him. She appeared comfortable; Parke didn't. Kidd smirked, debating if he should leave them be, or save Parke from a crook in his back or neck.

Parke stirred, which caused Cheney to yawn. His eyes popped open—alert—as if he hadn't been knocked out in the first place.

"Hey, man. Sorry. I didn't mean to wake you. I heard something and came to investigate," Kidd whispered.

Stretching, Parke shifted Cheney's body as she fought against waking. "It's all right. I was waiting up for you, until she came and bothered me." Parke grinned, nodding at his wife.

Cheney smiled when her ears registered her husband's comments. She swatted at Parke's arm. "Don't blame me. I came to keep you company," she accused Parke, while he helped steady her on her feet.

"Well, you both failed. I could've been a burglar."

"Burglar? Ha. I doubt it. I heard the alarm on the front door when you opened it."

Liar. "Right. Sure you did, cuz."

"And we have a pretty thorough neighborhood watch team. They practically provide a twenty-four-hour surveillance of the streets in Old Ferguson. But nobody could outdo Grandma BB." Cheney became quiet and reflective. Slowly, she seemed to muster a weak smile. "She was the ringleader on the block where I used to live. Grandma BB was the inventor of watch mistress."

Cheney sighed. "I sure do miss her sass. It doesn't come through as strong on Facebook. She posted on her Stacy Adams fan page this morning that the pickled beets in the joint aren't worth the wheelchair she needs to get them." She laughed.

"Her spirits seem high," Parke added, "so I guess her therapy's going well. It's a shame she won't let us step another foot in the place without causing a scene."

"Grandma BB is one of a handful of determined residents. She's a'wight. I check on her at least every other day. She'll make it, Cheney." Kidd tried to placate them.

"I know you're right. We've been praying for her. Maybe God is trying to get her attention. Playtime is over. God is married to the backslider, but Jesus has to be losing patience with that woman. Again, I can't thank you enough."

"Yeah, your visit blew my cover. She wasn't too happy about that."

"But you're still here with us and there too, watching over her." Cheney brushed a kiss against Kidd's cheek. "Well, I guess I'd better head to bed. Parke, don't stay up too long. You know my feet get cold."

After lifting a brow at Parke, Kidd pivoted on his heel and watched Cheney disappear through the kitchen to take the back stairs. "I would say the lady doesn't want you to keep her waiting."

"Right, and don't get used to that. There'll be no more kisses coming from her. Get your own woman." Parke didn't crack a smile.

"You have no worries from me. I'm faithful to my convictions. Anyway, I'm about to call it a night. Good night." He turned to leave.

"You're good people. If I thought you were a threat, you wouldn't be here. Got a sec?" Parke motioned to a chair.

"Actually, I don't. I'd rather have a pillow and blanket. Whatz up?" Kidd sat and slipped off his shoes.

"We really enjoyed you at family night. We weren't so bad, were we? I'm hoping you'll consider going to church with us on Sunday. I've tried not to nag you about it, but we would really like for you to accept our invitation. It's the third one, you know."

"You're counting?" *So much for no pressure,* he thought. Kidd didn't make a commitment.

"Listen, Kidd, I know we didn't get off to a good start. And I know it's been up in the air whether you want to hang around—"

"I'm thinking about staying . . . in St. Louis, but not at your place much longer."

Parke's grin stretched across his face. Then he sobered. "Oh, man. Sorry, you're leaving so soon."

They shared a laugh.

"Well, I guess it's good night, and hope to see you at service tomorrow. You've got the address to Faith Miracle Church?"

Kidd strained his brain. When did he actually say he was going? "Considering you have church programs strategically placed in the kitchen, on the coffee table, in bathrooms, and I even found one in the laundry basket." Kidd gave him a suspicious frown.

"Hmmm, imagine that. Children hide the strangest things." Parke's smile was anything but angelic.

"I don't think I'll have a problem finding it."

"Good." Parke stood and walked out of the room.

It wasn't long after that Kidd clicked off the TV and retired to his room. Sure enough, Parke had slid another church program under his bedroom door. "So much for subtle hints."

Kidd disrobed and got under the covers, but he was far from sleepy. He thought about his mother and brother. He wondered if God held the same disappointment in him as Kidd held for Ace.

"God," Kidd whispered, "thank You for letting me be here . . ." There was so much he wanted to get off his chest, but refrained. "Just thank You, Lord. Good night."

The next morning, the sun's rays pounded against Kidd's window, nudging him awake. With one eye, he glanced at the clock—8 a.m. He moaned and rolled over. "Parke didn't say anything about Sunday school."

An hour later, Kidd woke up and propped himself on his elbows. "Might as well get this over with."

Planting his feet on the thick, multicolored rug, he padded to the bathroom. Parke didn't beg him to go to church—verbally. Otherwise, Kidd would have disowned him as a Jamieson. Jamiesons do not beg. But when it came to Parke's friend, who ironically had shot his father-in-law, he overlooked that big time. To Kidd, it didn't sound like an accident. He didn't get it; Parke was a different breed.

In record time, he showered, dressed, and grabbed breakfast to go. Bottled orange juice and a bagel would hold him. The church wasn't far from where Parke lived.

Fifteen minutes later, he arrived late. Kidd cruised down the aisles of the church's packed parking lot a couple of times before securing a space. The next task was spying out his cousins. With the aid of an usher, he found them. Malcolm and Parke created an opening between them as if it was a trap to hold him in position for the Lord to pounce on him.

After settling into his seat, Kidd stretched his legs and scanned the sanctuary. All eyes were riveted on their leader, who was standing at the podium with his Bible open. Kidd was later than he thought. He missed the good stuff—the music.

"He's our pastor." Parke identified him, in a low voice. "Pastor Scott."

"God promised Abraham he would be a father of many nations in Genesis 17, but Abraham is not my focus today. It's what happened after God issued the edict that I want to talk about. When God promises us anything, let's take it to the bank. It won't bounce, because God's Word cannot return to Him void. The Bible says His Word will complete the mission. Oh, and while I'm at it, God doesn't need us to tinker with His promises. He's got this!

"Here's an example: Isaac was Abraham's chosen son, but what about Hagar's son? After all, Ishmael was the offspring of a slaveholder and a slave woman, who happened to be his wife's handmaiden. Inferior to some, but despite Ishmael's background, he was still important to God and didn't get left out of the blessing."

Pastor Scott shouted, "Hallelujah!" And the congregation responded the same. Then the man of God continued. "Now let's fast-forward to the New Testament. God—wrapped in a body called Jesus—hung on a tree. I guess in modern terms we might say He was lynched. He was humiliated, despised, and bruised for our sins. Yet—"

The pastor lifted his finger and wagged it at the congregation. "Jesus redeemed us, paid our debt in full, not with currency or human bondage, but with His blood. We are no longer slaves to any man, thing, or sin. We are, as 1 Peter 2:9 reminds us, 'a chosen generation.' Read it for yourselves. The entire chapter addresses our struggles and sufferings in life."

Kidd frowned, failing to see the correlation. He began to daydream until Parke nudged him to stand for altar call.

"What is your hold out?" Pastor Scott labored.

Others, who apparently felt the conviction, walked down the aisle to the front. Ministers were waiting to pray for them or prepare them for baptism. Parke felt the need to explain what was happening to Kidd, as if he didn't already know. He had witnessed his mother's moment of repentance and what happened after she was baptized. He knew what was up. Yet Kidd didn't feel any stirring, so he quietly observed.

Finally able to relax after the service had concluded, he felt a sense of immediate satisfaction. It was never his intention to succumb to any pressure for a conversion he wasn't seeking. After the benediction, Parke and Cheney were more than happy to introduce Kidd to several people, who raved about the sermon. He was mostly silent as they all shared in the excitement of how their pastor broke it down.

When his cousins started to parade one church sister after another to greet him, he knew it was time to go. Only one woman, Eva, enticed him without trying. And she was a tough act to follow.

Kidd said his good-byes and walked out of the house of God. When his shoes touched the parking lot pavement, God's voice seemed to zap him like lightning.

The day you hear My voice, harden not your heart.

Swallowing, Kidd slowed his steps and looked over his shoulder. There wasn't a soul nearby, which meant only one thing. God was indeed talking to him again.

Chapter Twenty-One

*E*va gritted her teeth. She was helping her mother carry home large plastic bags of clothing they bought from the Goodwill. Dragging the heavy bags into her parents' house, she was beyond frustration.

"Mom, something must be wrong with me. I can't be attracted to the wrong man. It's a trick of the devil."

Rita Savoy chuckled. "Honey, there are worse things. You could be married to the wrong man."

"Mom, aren't you listening? Out of nowhere, my heart is starting to fight against my common sense. Instead of sending out warning signals, it's telling me to 'stop, feel him out, and give him a chance.' A chance for what? To become an angry Black woman with an attitude like his? I must have lost my mind!" She mocked. "How can I be drawn to Kidd—he's a . . ."

"A man with a good job," Rita filled in the gap. "That's a big plus right there."

"Yeah, well, he acts like he doesn't want to be there."

If Kidd could only shed his negative vibes, what wouldn't there be to like about him? But he was like a scalding hot pot with legs. And when he boiled over, how could anyone, far or near, not get burned—including her?

"Sometimes, we all feel that way at work. But he's there."

"Please don't take the underdog's side, Mom. He doesn't bring out the best in me. You know, like the Marvin Sapp song says. So it boggles my mind how I can long for a man who is probably not the best fit for me."

"Have you ever thought you could bring out the best in him?"

"Nope. It's hard getting blood out of a turnip. If I can't shut down these feelings, I'm afraid I'll find myself falling in love with him. Worse yet, I won't know how or when it happened. God, why me?"

"Love?" Her mother stopped untying bags. "Hmm. Really? Are your feelings that strong? If so, then are you going to resolve within your heart how much patience you'll give him? Remember, *Love is patient, love is kind. It does not envy, it does not boast, it is not proud. It does not dishonor others, it is not self-seeking, it is not easily angered, it keeps no record of wrongs. Love does not delight in evil but rejoices with the truth. [7] It always protects, always trusts, always hopes, always perseveres.'*"

Eva sighed. "I know 1 Corinthians 13 says love never fails, but love has made fools out of many women," she argued, fighting what was becoming obvious in her heart. At the same time, she realized the impact of her off-handed remark.

"Mom, I didn't mean that . . . I'm not referring to you personally . . ." Eva backtracked quickly. "The point I'm trying to make is that my salvation is at risk around that man." Eva couldn't stop harping. She walked to the kitchen sink and scrubbed the germs off her hands, after sifting through the piles of used clothes.

Glancing out the window, she blinked. Her mind was playing tricks on her. Kidd's handsome reflection winked at her as she dried her hands. She growled back.

How the thought of a man's moodiness flustered her. Eva couldn't imagine the intensity of so-called sexual frustration. It was enough for her to deal with a mind game with Kidd. The challenge of it all was whipping her like a switch on a naked behind.

"Mom, remember your old saying, 'If it has three, let it be'?" It was a rule of thumb her mother used for how to identify poison ivy leaves. "Well, this man—Kidd—acts like an overgrown brush with more than three personalities. Whoever came up with the cliché, 'be careful what you pray for,' should win an award."

Eva shook her head in exasperation. "My intentions were good when I suggested the creation of a position to better serve the residents. If only I had known the type of person they would handpick to spearhead it, I would've kept my mouth shut."

Rita was a good listener and a wise counselor. But at the moment, Eva wanted her mom to condone her desire to stomp on Kidd's foot, spike his soda with vinegar, or do something else out of her character. However, Rita knew that Eva was facing a serious matter of the heart and just needed to vent. So her mother remained quiet.

Eva could have had this one-sided conversation from the balcony of her own home. She couldn't care less about making a field trip out of shopping. But her mother had convinced her it would be a good day for them to bond. As it turned out, their bonding was nothing more than a smoke screen. In reality, she was called upon to act as chauffeur to fulfill Rita's thrift-store-hopping addiction.

Now that her daughterly duties were satisfied, her mother would sort through the three large plastic bags of clothes and other household items. Then every garment would be washed and made ready for Rita to donate to their women's ministry program at church the next morning.

How convenient that Angela had somehow dodged the bullet for their day of affinity. She wasn't a thrift-store junkie either. If Angela couldn't buy a name-brand item in a store at the mall, then she didn't want it. Eva didn't believe it was a coincidence that Lance whisked her clever sister away for a surprise early morning breakfast.

Taking a seat at the kitchen table, Rita patted a chair next to her. Squinting, her mother took pleasure in scrutinizing Eva, which made her squirm under the examination.

Rita Savoy was stunning in her younger years. Now, in her middle age, she was beautiful. Eva and Angela took after their father, Kenneth. The twins had his lashes, eyes, and lips—and that image hadn't faded into adulthood. He often boasted, "Once daddy's little girls, always his big girls." They were still considered pretty, but what Eva wouldn't give to have her mother's thick hair and dark-brown skin tone.

Rita was ready to offer her opinion. "From your description, his moods do appear to be antagonistic. I'm wondering," she paused, "could he like you and be too shy—"

"Shy?" Eva laughed. She thought about the times the man couldn't hold his tongue around residents. Bold was definitely his forte. "This isn't a grade-school crush. I'm twenty-seven years old. Shoot me now and put me out of my misery."

Her mother smiled as she reached for an apple in a bowl on the counter. "Could you like him and be misreading his signals toward you." She definitely wasn't posing a question.

"How absurd." Gritting her teeth, Eva stiffened. "Then shoot me twice. He's not the kind of man I would want to bring home to meet my mom and dad."

"I don't know. I wouldn't mind meeting him."

"Mom, you aren't helping. Granted, Kidd's looks are worth a second glance, and I don't mind looking. But not touching," she admitted.

Rita gave her daughter "the look," as if she knew something Eva didn't. A smirk followed.

Eva held up her hands. "But the charm stops there." She didn't want her mother fantasizing about marriage and grandchildren. "Kidd's got this raging 'mad-at-anybody-who-breathes-on-him' mentality. He barely hides his attitude, even while he's dressed professionally in a shirt and tie. His hard edge and rough persona is deep-rooted. All he needs is gold teeth, some bling draped around his neck, and tattoos scattered all over his arms." She turned up her nose in disgust.

Her criterion for any man was that he had to hold her attention and attraction. But Kidd didn't pass the test. With his see-saw personalities, Kidd's qualities weren't even worth entertaining. When he smiled and was in a pleasant mood, Eva enjoyed his company and conversation. When his demons seeped out, she wanted to bathe him in holy oil, call 9-1-1, and rush him to the nearest church for baptism. He desperately needed his soul cleansed.

"Have you forgotten verse 21 in Romans 12 about not being overcome with evil, but overpower it with good? Since you really don't know the man, he may be going through something. We're too close to Jesus coming back, so don't let his negative vibes be your downfall. When you're around him, notch up your compassion. You realize we might not be having this conversation if you had invited him to church. Have you?"

Eva swallowed. "No." She sighed heavily. God must be disappointed in her for not reaching out to Kidd. Her mother was placing the torch in Eva's hand to bring him to the finish line.

The phone rang and Rita stood to answer it. Eva used the reprieve to reflect on her mother's counsel. It was easy to be a practicing Christian when Kidd was in a good mood, but look out when some unseen cause kindled his wrath. She had allowed the flesh to override her oath to God to draw people to Him with loving-kindness. Not to mention the judging-people habit she was trying to overcome. From time to time, it reared its ugly head.

Silently, she asked God to forgive her behavior and give her the strength to be a victor over a small obstacle such as this man. Rita ended the call and returned to the table, appearing to be ready to pick up where she left off.

With the front door slightly opened, Eva and her mother watched as Angela and Lance approached the porch. Something must have distracted them when they pivoted and crossed the lawn.

"Probably Miss Penny, wanting to show off her garden." Rita smiled. "If she can snag you, she's got company for at least ten minutes." Tilting her head, as if she was thinking, Rita commented, "Lance is a sweetheart. He's good-looking and adores your sister."

Even with all those accolades, the vibes between the pair came off as platonic. Eva twisted her lips. "Yeah, he's the son you never had and the big brother I never wanted. If Angela ever says yes to the question he seems hesitant to ask, he'll be a wimp for life."

"At least she's closer to the altar than you." Rita tweaked Eva's nose and switched subjects. "I haven't seen Dawn in a while, and you two haven't gone shopping lately. What's going on with her?"

"Ha!" Rolling her eyes, Eva exhaled. "Mother, I shop for clothes, shoes, furniture—"

"Yeah, and Dawn shops for men. What does she think of this Kidd guy? That girl is scandalous. If there's a man within ten feet, she knows about it," Rita said with a chuckle, not condemnation.

"Dawn's exact words were, 'He's a man's man. They always have an attitude.' In Dawn's book, Kidd can do no wrong." Eva shook her head and chuckled. "She's a piece of work all right. Remember a while back when she tried to convince me to go to Harrah's Casino with her to see the Chippendales?"

Rita laughed. "What was that she told you?"

"You don't have to touch, just drool," they said practically in unison.

"That's when I told her the only man I plan to drool over is the one who has a gold band on his finger that matches mine. I mean that, Mom."

"Dawn doesn't profess to be saved or practice an ounce of Christian living, yet you see the good in her. God paired you two up in a friendship. Surely, if we can see a redeeming quality in her, you can find something good in Kidd," Rita said. She had always been fond of Dawn

172

because the woman had bounced back after enduring an abusive marriage—with a makeover and a new attitude.

"I never said Kidd wasn't kind and didn't have some good qualities. It's the dormant anger that's unexplainable. It's sad, really. What a waste of energy." If she could tap into whatever was the cause, perhaps she could drain the poison. But for a man as complex as Kidd, she would need a fire hose to flush it out.

Eva did admire his limited interaction with the residents; he always had a smile for Mrs. Valentine and Mrs. Beacon. Kidd even had patience to play boring games with Mr. Abraham. Plus, she had heard the rumors about him fixing minor car problems for a couple of the custodians who didn't have the money for repairs. Why couldn't he overcome the bad things in his life with his goodness? She wondered.

Because he has no power. God reminded her of a portion of Acts, chapter 1. *Once the Holy Ghost comes, he shall receive power to live right.*

Christianity was the root of so much of Black people's endurance. So why did people neglect to nurture their spiritual birthright? At times, Eva knew she was guilty of it too. How often had God bailed her out of trouble, only for her to forget about what God had done, moments after her drama was over? Yep, Eva was guilty of it too.

"Take Dawn for instance," Rita said, interrupting Eva's musing. "That girl could have become bitter after being loyal to a husband who didn't return her loyalty. Praise God, she moved on. I've learned there's a Scripture for every situation. There are two classifications of people. First Timothy, chapter 1 says, *'We also know that the law is made not for the righteous but for lawbreakers and rebels, the ungodly and sinful, the unholy and irreligious; for those who kill their fathers or mothers,'* and the list goes on. But in the end, you know the verse that says, *vengeance is the Lord's and He will repay.*"

Romans 12:19. Yes, she knew it. Eva shivered at the thought of God paying out wages on the day of judgment for the lawless and disobedient. *Jesus, help me to be forever faithful.* Quietness descended between mother and daughter. Although they started off talking about Dawn, it seemed to end with an innuendo about her father's unfaithfulness. The "other" woman had been successful in breaking up her family, and Eva's parents had eventually divorced.

While in the clutches of that home-wrecker, God caused her father to have a repentant heart. The woman was dumbfounded that the man she had stolen turned around and rejected her. During that dark time in the Savoy household, Angela stumbled across a news article about an antiquated "alienation of affection" law. It was still on the books in seven states where the wife could sue her husband's mistress. At the time, it sounded like a plan to her and Angela.

Kenneth earnestly repented, but it wasn't an easy task to win back his wife and daughters. Eva had never seen her parents so tormented and conflicted. Her mother was not only a prayer warrior, but an astute Bible reader who held fast to the six powerful, but short, verses in Psalm 1. Rita would not sway to the counsel of her girlfriends, coworkers, or churchgoers. But in the end, after consulting with God and standing on His Word, Rita made her decision to forgive her husband and remarry. Oh, if only she had an ounce of temperance like her mother.

No one would ever have guessed that Rita and Kenneth Savoy could have been separated for six months. It was difficult to believe they had been divorced for a year before finally having their marriage restored. The second time around, they had been going fifteen years strong.

Her mother knew firsthand about heartache and forgiveness. Kenneth was the prodigal husband, prodigal father, and prodigal backslider. He, too, knew about temptation and the snare of the devil. Maybe her conversation should be with him. If there was a male code of craziness where Kidd was concerned, Eva's father could decode it.

Rita cleared her throat. "I kinda like Dawn's innovative ways to find dates, keeping a pocket calendar of weekly hot spots, going where the men are—"

"I'll never forget the time I tagged along with her to a medical conference when I was thinking about going back to school. The woman's got skills, and it's a major production watching her in action . . . then there was this bodybuilding competition, but I refused to go with her."

"Her success rate is amazing."

"Yeah, but she's in a slump lately. She may be getting tired of the game. If nothing else, she's developed some solid friendships. By the way, next month, Dawn and I are doing our part to help with Habitat for Humanity's last spring project."

"Good." Rita stood and threw the apple core in the trash bag. "At least you haven't let her drag you to any sports bars to pick up men. When the time comes, a confident, strong Christian man will find you."

"When the time comes, I hope so too."

Usually her mother's next statement was about Eva's unrealistic standards for men. Eva wanted to lighten the mood. "Of course, he's got to have his body odor under control and have dental insurance," Eva joked, and her mother fell into the trap and joined her. But she really wasn't joking. The man had to smell as good as she suspected the gorgeous, muscular actor, Isaiah Mustafa, in the Old Spice commercials smelled.

"Seriously, with my nursing classes, I'm blessed to get six hours of sleep at night. I need a man who will challenge and respect me. Plus, he has to be a man's man. Only one wimp allowed in our family . . . Lance—"

"Hey, I heard my name." Lance followed Angela into the house and strolled into the kitchen, smiling.

Eva rolled her eyes. If the man only knew her requirements, Lance would be disqualified at registration.

After spending a few extra minutes to chat with Angela and her mom, Eva said her good-byes and went home. She spent the rest of the day and into the evening studying for her final. Kidd was constantly in her thoughts. *It would be nice to have him as my study coach,* she kept thinking.

On the way to Sunday morning service at Salvation Temple, Eva had Kidd on her mind once again. It was getting harder and harder to shake him these days. There had to be a reason; she vowed to pray more fervently for him.

The pastor of her church, Elder Taylor, read from Galatians 6:9. *"Let us not become weary in doing good, for at the proper time we will reap a harvest if we do not give up."*

As she prepared to listen, Eva thought, *How many times have I held my tongue with Kidd?*

Not many lately, her conscience answered.

Elder Taylor continued. "Maybe it's time for a refresher course on verse ten: *'Therefore, as we have opportunity, let us do good to all people . . .'"*

As he began preaching, the Elder asserted, "Beginning right now, today. Delays should only pertain to road construction and airline flights."

Her burden for Kidd became so overwhelming that she bowed her head. *Lord, whatever has been festering in him, deliver him from it. In Jesus' name,* Eva silently prayed, as she sat in the pew between her parents and the lovebirds, Angela and Lance. She was beginning to feel like the fifth wheel.

Her mind drifted back to Kidd during the altar call, the baptism, and the benediction. As the congregation filed out of the sanctuary, Eva waited. She sat thinking about her next move, then gathered her purse and Bible and stood to leave. Eva pulled her father aside.

"Daddy, do you have a few minutes to talk?"

His eyes sparkled. "I'll make time. When?"

She glanced around. Her mother was off looking for the person who would take her donation. That would give her a good fifteen minutes with her father.

"How about now?"

"Sure."

They found a pew that was the farthest away from the crowd. "Before you say anything," Kenneth said, holding up his hand. "Your mother told me a little bit about your conversation yesterday."

Deflated, Eva was about to protest the violation of her right of confidentiality. When she opened her mouth, her father stopped her.

"She didn't tell me everything. All she said was you were attracted to a man who didn't seem to meet your standards. Am I right?"

"Yes." She nodded. "I need your insight, Daddy. He seems to be so wrong for me, yet I'm drawn to him."

"I've never met this young man, of course, so it's hard for me to judge him."

"Since the time I met him, I haven't always been impressed. He's difficult to work with," Eva was quick to say.

"Bring him around the house. We can chat and I can observe him, then I'll tell you what I think." Kenneth smiled.

"Daddy, that sounds like a plan. But I'm not sure he even likes me like that."

"What's not to like about my beautiful daughter? Watch and pray, and the Lord will show you a sign." He hugged her and whispered his love.

Groaning, she returned his affection. So far, Kidd's signals had been like arrows, warning her to run the other way.

Chapter Twenty-Two

*E*va shivered when she caught a glimpse of Kidd on Monday after-noon. She was unsure how to interact with him after her con-versations with her parents. Her first instinct was to duck into the nearest room to collect her thoughts. The room happened to belong to Miss Jessie Atkins, who was resting.

Her heart warmed when she glanced at the older woman. Miss Atkins was another one of Eva's favorite patients, with her smooth dark skin and bluish-silver curls.

The woman was the most polite, soft-spoken resident, even when she was in excruciating pain. She was prone to sores that wouldn't com-pletely heal, despite the prescribed antibiotics and ointments. But the kind lady never complained.

While adjusting Miss Jessie's covers, Eva gave herself a pep talk. This was her turf. Then just before she reached the level to become puffed up in pride, she remembered all her mother had said. Eva closed her eyes and asked God to help her overcome the trial that tormented her, which happened to be more than six feet tall. She could only avoid Kidd for so long. Opening her eyes, Eva sighed before stepping out of the room. A quick scan of the corridor proved the coast was clear.

Mrs. Valentine's voice could be heard doors away, whether she had an audience or not. Eva was about to round the corner when she practically bounced off a solid figure. Stumbling, she blinked and tried to regulate her breathing.

"You're just the person I'm looking for." Kidd steadied her.

She lifted a brow as she glanced down at his hands fastened around her arms. His grip was strong, and within a few seconds the firm grasp of his fingers would be pinching her skin.

"Please let go of me."

He did, but not before massaging his point of contact on her skin. It was soft and smooth. "Your forest-green uniform threw me off.

Oh no, you're not getting a blush out of me. I'm not falling for it. Eva hid her grin and lowered her lids. She was definitely going uniform shopping, and maroon definitely wouldn't be on her list. Eva didn't believe in dressing to impress a man. If he didn't like the way she looked, then he could move on.

Kidd's piercing eyes seemed to weigh what he wanted to say next. "Can we talk? I owe you an apology."

"Again? That makes how many now?" She fixed him with a stare. His five o'clock shadow was now a trimmed beard, which boasted of his masculinity. Was that Old Spice she smelled?

Seven times seventy, Christians are to forgive, God spoke forcefully, putting her in check.

She really wanted to give him a sample of his variety-pack personality and rude behavior toward her. Eva debated between smarting off or listening to the Lord and holding her tongue.

"I've tried to be a friend to you, Kidd, but I can't. You won't let me."

"You know, when things go wrong in a relationship, it's always the man's fault. I have to agree with you on this and accept the blame for my mixed signals."

"What relationship? Is that what you call bumping into each other on the bench in front of the fountain? You are the most irritating, arrogant, and double-minded man I've ever met. Be consistent."

Instantly, she trembled at God's warning, recalling Sunday's message from Galatians 6:9. How could she not be weary in doing good? How long would the season be with Kidd before she could reap—if there was anything for her? She hoped she wouldn't regret her loose lips later.

"Okay." He cupped her head and brought her lips to his, startling her. The hairs of his mustache tickled, but his lips were soft. The kiss was slow, as if asking for permission, but it was too late. Eva was in no position to make decisions this close to Kidd. Light-headed, she couldn't remember her response, but she did hear her name called faintly. Was it God?

"Eve . . . Adam, is that you?" Mrs. Valentine's voice sliced through the moment.

Breaking away slowly, but not before delivering another gentle kiss, Kidd waited for her to respond. A slap would have been forthcoming, but she was a willing participant. What were they thinking—no—what was *she* thinking? One moment she was telling him off and the next, she was succumbing to his charm.

So this was how he responded to her loose lips. A storm was brewing in his eyes, and Eva could no longer doubt that he was attracted to her. She'd better get him to her dad quick and then to the altar for prayer and redemption, but not in that order.

"Eve?" Mrs. Valentine repeated. "Can you hear me?"

Taking a deep breath, Eva stepped back as Kidd twisted his lips in a smirk.

"I can be more consistent than that. I promise you that kiss was nowhere close to satisfactory," he declared.

Eva was about to go off—again. How dare he rate her kiss? Granted, she wasn't an experienced smoocher, but did he have to insult her? If she said anything, she would be repenting for days. She had to get to Mrs. Valentine's room, but Kidd continued to deluge her with more words.

"Eva Savoy, you've been the best thing since I've come to St. Louis. To satisfy my thirst for you, I need more time for your lips to resuscitate me."

What does he mean . . . she has been his best thing? Eva needed clarification.

"Can we talk later?" His voice was husky.

Eva nodded because her voice was slow in coming. "Not here and don't ever kiss me at work again."

Kidd's nostrils flared as if he was weighing how to respond. "Give me your number and we can talk and kiss later."

Her head was still spinning and her lips sizzling. Eva needed a clear head when she conversed with Kidd Jamieson. And kissing him? She could never prepare herself for the onslaught of his kiss again. She almost fainted.

"Let me think it over. I've got to go." Before he could protest, she hurried off and probably left a trail of smoke. For the rest of the day, Eva stayed busy with the residents—from providing emergency help to simply keeping them company. When the next shift was short-staffed, she volunteered to work a few hours overtime, stalling to give Kidd her decision.

Before he left for the day, he sought her out. Eva gathered up enough strength to decline. She didn't have the nerve to say yes. Amazingly, Kidd accepted without any further comment. The rest of the week, the two were cordial in passing and he never asked again. Although Eva missed their spirited interactions, she needed breathing room.

On Friday, he approached her as she was leaving the nurses' station. His expression was comical: a brooding frown and a sexy pout.

"I'm not a patient man, Eva, but with you, I have been. You've ordered me not to touch you. That's like asking a Bostonian not to cheer on the Red Sox. But when you thought I wasn't looking, humph. I drank in the sight of you until I quenched my thirst. When I was a child, my mother would put me and my brother on punishment for a week. After that, I was free." He stepped closer. "Am I free now? Is my punishment over yet?"

Eva swallowed, as she locked with his piercing dark eyes and inhaled his cologne. How was she supposed to answer him when he had her in a trance?

"Since I've honored all your demands," he continued, "I have one of my own."

"Okay," Eva's voice squeaked.

"Go out to dinner with me after work."

"That's in a few minutes."

"Yes, it is, but first . . ." He retrieved his iPhone from his belt. "May I have your phone number—please?"

She couldn't resist him any longer. They needed neutral territory to discuss their hot and cold emotions. "I would like that. I'll make sure to order the most expensive thing on the menu."

"I don't think White Castle burgers will break my bank."

"Try and take me to White Castle and see if you don't get stuck with a sack of gas burgers to feed the geese," Eva teased and relaxed, as they shared a laugh.

When she gave him her number, Kidd immediately dialed it and then disconnected right away. "It's a good number." He nodded with a satisfied grin.

Putting a hand on her hip, she lifted a brow. "You didn't believe me?"

"It was a test of the Emergency Broadcast System. I had to make sure the number you broadcasted was a good signal." He winked and leaned in as if to kiss her, but caught himself. "I'll meet you in the parking lot in ten minutes." Straightening his body, he grinned and walked away.

What have I gotten myself into? Eva mused. Part of her was ecstatic; the other part was scared to death. Kidd Jamieson was too much man for her. All of a sudden, she realized the need to go home and freshen up first. There was no way she was going out with a man in a suit and tie when she had on scrubs.

Eva was about to call him and give him her address to meet her at her condo, but she saw him heading outside. Since she had already clocked out, she grabbed her purse to catch up with him and tell him.

Once outside, he walked in the opposite direction—away from the parking lot. Tilting her head, Eva frowned and wondered where he was going. He crossed the street and disappeared inside a two-story brick building. She knew it held several businesses and a few doctors' offices, but she never had a reason to go inside. Instead of calling him, out of pure curiosity, she decided to follow him.

As Eva waited to cross the street, she realized she had no idea where he would be inside. Once the light changed, she dashed across the four lanes. The automatic sliding door opened and she stepped into a wide corridor. Eva looked from her left to right. In one direction, there was a travel agency and Kidd wasn't in there. She passed a few more businesses until she came to a florist shop. Through the large glass window, Eva saw Kidd.

Careful to remain out of sight, she stepped inside to hear the conversation. He was standing at the counter and she heard the woman say, "So Mr. Jamieson, let me make sure I have this right. That's two sets of a dozen roses. One to Cheney Jamieson . . ."

They must be for his mother. Eva smiled at Kidd's thoughtfulness. But now, before they were about to go to dinner? Talk about bad timing.

"The other one to Hallison. What about . . . Miss Imani Segall? Did you decide whether she gets flowers or not?"

Eva was getting a bad feeling. *Who's Hallison and who's Imani?* Eva didn't move as the clerk continued.

After a moment of silence, he finally answered, "Yeah. I don't want her to be left out. She's having a hard time after a recent divorce. Hold Imani's order. I need to double-check her address."

Did he say her recent divorce, his recent divorce, or their recent divorce? Eva's heart dropped. She really didn't know him.

"And Sandra Nicholson in Boston gets the 'expressions of love' bouquet?"

"Yes, I want her to know I still love her, even after our recent disagreement . . ." Kidd's voice faded.

Sandra? Was she a "baby mama" back in Boston? Is that why Kidd had to rush home a while back? She never did hear what the emergency was. And who is Imani? *Oh no, he had me fooled.*

"I'm sure she will. I've never met a woman who has turned down flowers."

Should I march up to that counter and raise my hand? Eva silently fumed.

"And I'll take these with me. I owe a special lady a peace offering."

"That bouquet is beautiful. She'll love hers, and so will the other ladies. Peace offerings keep us in business," the clerk said.

"I'm counting on it."

Eva snarled. She imagined Kidd was standing tall, thinking he was the man. Humph! Peace offering? Eva had heard enough. How many blow-ups with women did he have at one time? Either he had a lot of mothers, or too many "baby mamas."

Okay, Daddy, I got my sign, Eva thought, as she hurried out of the building before he discovered her.

Chapter Twenty-Three

"*F*inally," Kidd said, strolling out of the florist shop. Within a half hour, he and Eva would be lounging on the back patio of Hendel's in Old Town Florissant. There was no way he was going to take Eva out to dinner—formal or informal—without presenting her with flowers.

Hendel's Market Café and Piano Bar was another recommendation. This one came from a brother who was a facility vendor. During his last visit, they were talking about sports when Eddie mentioned he had to hurry and finish up. He was taking his wife out to dinner. Kidd perked up when Eddie said the place was voted top ten for crab cakes and outdoor dining.

"Really?"

Eddie nodded.

Hailing from Beantown, the seafood capital of the United States, Kidd doubted it. But he promised Eddie he would check it out. Glancing at his watch, he realized ordering the flowers took longer than he thought. He hadn't planned to, but once inside the store, signs were everywhere about remembering Mother's Day. So he ordered flowers for all the women in his life, including Imani, so she wouldn't feel left out.

Surely when Eva saw the flowers, she would forgive him for being late. He called her cell phone and got her voice mail but didn't leave a message.

Kidd walked to the parking lot. He knew where Eva was parked, but her car was gone. He called her again, and this time left a message.

"Sorry to keep you waiting more than ten minutes, but I don't see your car. I'm still at work, so call me back with your address, and I'll pick you up."

Kidd double-checked inside to make sure she had left. She had. He walked back to his car and Eva still hadn't called. He glanced around the parking lot, wondering what could have happened. Finally, he made one last attempt to reach her. "Eva, this is Kidd again. You have my number. Call me."

Mad, he disconnected. Eva had just stood him up. Deactivating his car alarm, Kidd threw the bouquet in the backseat and slid in behind the wheel.

All the while driving to Parke's house, his temper was building. He was not a man to be played with, and she had played him. If Eva wasn't ready to take things farther, then she should have told him.

"Grrrr." He pounded the steering wheel and accidently hit the horn. A driver honked back. When he glanced to his left, the woman behind the wheel was waving frantically at him. She looked to be about a hundred years old.

Kidd groaned and pulled off when the light turned red. He was clueless to what could have caused Eva to change her mind. Arriving at home, he parked and activated the alarm.

As he ambled up the walkway and stepped up to the porch, Kidd heard voices coming from the backyard. It was an area that opened to a small common ground, which the Jamiesons shared with a couple of neighbors. Kidd walked around to investigate and found Parke playing softball with Pace and Kami. Paden was off to the side, pulling up colorful tulips.

Kidd smirked, wondering who would get in trouble from that violation—Paden, probably not—Parke, big time. He opened the wooden gate at the same time Pace connected with the ball. Parke yelled for him to run to first base, which was a tree trunk. At the same time, Kami yelled she had the ball: "I got it! I got it, Dad!"

She didn't, and she was mad about it.

Amused and shaking his head, Kidd walked further into the yard. There he detoured to the customized double deck with a gazebo on the second level. It was huge, running from one end of the back of the house to the other. Setting the flowers on a side table, he eased down on a lounger. *What happened?* He refused to let that question plague him all weekend.

"Hey, old man," Parke called out and waved. "Come on and get some exercise."

"Nah. You need it more. I jog every morning, remember?"

Paden lost interest in the flowers and trotted Kidd's way, climbing the few wooden steps. He grinned at Kidd, holding a broken stem with one petal clutched in his small fist. Mischievous. Kidd loved it.

"Hi, Uncle Cousin!" From his spot at the tree trunk, Pace shouted with his hand cupped to his mouth.

"It's Cousin Uncle!" Kami screamed from her position in a makeshift outfield.

While Parke ordered them to stop arguing, Paden dropped his flower and set his sights on the bouquet. Kidd scooped him up in his lap and lounged back. What reduced his romantic dinner for two on a hidden patio to a backyard baseball brawl with him as a spectator, sitting on a wooden deck?

Suddenly, his iPhone chimed. Pace ran across the yard and made a beeline to the seat next to Kidd, as if it was home plate. Reaching down to pick it up, Kidd had to wrestle his iPhone from Pace's baby brother Paden. He read the text:

Kevin, let's keep us simple. I want nothing from you, including your flowers. I hope not to see you at work. Eva.

His eyes bucked as he reread the text. He frowned. "What in . . ." Catching himself, Kidd paused and eyed his audience. After clearing his throat, he finished his thought, ". . . the world is wrong with her?"

"Are you having women problems, Uncle Cousin?" Pace asked in a serious adult tone.

Kidd groaned at being busted by a third grader. "What makes you think that?"

"Your face looks sad, like the men in the movies Mom watches. She says they're romance classics."

"Never seen them." Kidd slid his iPhone back in his case, which was hooked on his belt.

Pace glanced around the yard and back at Kidd. "It's okay to be scared. I hope I can get a wife too someday."

"A wife?" Kidd stuttered, stunned by the assumption. "I'm not trying to get a wife, little cousin." *I'm perturbed that a woman had the nerve to stand me up.*

Tilting his head, Pace twisted his lips. As if he was a doctor about to make a diagnosis instead of a child in a Cardinals baseball uniform, he declared, "I think you need a wife."

Chapter Twenty-Four

Kidd Jamieson was a liar, a cheat, a hustler . . . and an array of other endless adjectives Eva silently called him, as she drifted off to sleep Friday night. On Saturday morning, it seemed as if her mind picked up right where it left off the night before.

At least she and Angela were committed to work on a weekend project. Eva hoped that would keep her mind occupied with thoughts other than about Mr. Jamieson.

Before she overheard Kidd's deceitfulness, she could have imagined a weekend with him, filled with so many possibilities—a picnic, bike ride, roller skating—anything fun. On Sunday, their time together could have culminated with them sitting side-by-side in church, enjoying an electrifying sermon.

Her very next thought was about the names that had rolled off his tongue: Imani, Sandra, Cheney, and another name she couldn't recall. Her mind began reciting another laundry list of words that collectively painted him as a monster. She was becoming a regular walking, talking thesaurus.

Eva felt like a fool. If it wasn't for her following Kidd into the flower

189

shop, she might not ever have known he was a charming womanizer. At first, she scolded herself for not confronting him. However, in hindsight, the day after the disaster, Eva decided she had done the right thing. Not only was she disappointed in his lack of sincerity—he had been stringing her along—but she was disappointed in herself for letting her guard down. Thank God, Kidd hadn't tried to call or text her after she sent that message. There really was no reason; she had busted him.

"Would you concentrate on what you're doing," Angela fussed, as they worked alongside each other in Eva's kitchen.

"I am concentrating," Eva defended, but just not on the task before her. She shifted her thoughts, as she tied ribbon bowties around stuffed animals. Angela's students had collected contributions to purchase the toys as part of their community service.

"Angel, you and your class are a big help again this year."

"Not a problem, sis. The students were thrilled they didn't have to beg for money. As soon as people heard them mention 'stuffed animals' and 'nursing home' in the same sentence, the donations poured in." Angela grinned.

It didn't take long for the twins to establish a routine. Once Eva finished her task, Angela smashed a hat on the animals' heads to give them a funny personality. After a few minutes, Eva ventured into her sister's personal life. "You and Lance have been dating for almost a year—"

"Fourteen months," Angela corrected without stopping.

"Touché." Shrugging, Eva mustered a smile. "So, he's everything you want in a man, besides looks? He is kinda cute."

"Cute? Girl, that man is fine. If I wanted a hundred things in a man, he has more than 50 percent, which makes the rest unnecessary."

"Personally, I think you two have the most platonic relationship ever. Mom and Dad seem to have more romance going on than you and Lance. He might as well have been born a Savoy. You two act like siblings."

"No, you did not go there. First of all, Momma and Daddy's marriage is strong after a bitter breakup. As a result, Daddy will probably romance Momma until death they do part. No doubt about it, God truly restored them." Angela aimed a red miniature top hat at Eva and fired it off.

"Lance doesn't have to prove his affections or intentions to anybody but me. He's respectful in public, but when we're alone, only I'm privy to his sweet words and sexy flirts." Angela blushed. "Platonic, ha! Plus, you know Elder Taylor counsels us. Regardless of our status—married or single—we are to treat one another as—"

Eva held up her hand, nodding. "I know. I know. We're all still brothers and sisters in Christ, regardless of our relationships with others."

So much for a casual conversation. Still, Eva had a nagging question. At all costs, she wanted to avoid revealing to Angela her misjudgment of Kidd's character again.

"Here's a silly question. Do you think Lance would ever cheat on you?"

Angela laughed. "That is a dumb question. Nope. My man has too much integrity. Why?" She lifted a suspicious brow.

"Oh, just wondering."

Her mind revisited Friday's event with Kidd, their first kiss earlier in the week, then his trifling arrogance to disrespect her in a web of deceit. Eva held in a sigh. Maybe men like Lance were worth a second glance.

A few hours later, when they completed their project, Angela left to get ready for a date with Lance. Eva retired to her bedroom to relax and watch a movie before a little studying.

The next day, after Sunday service ended, Eva drove her sister's SUV to Garden Chateau, filled with boxes of stuffed animals for the residents. The deliveries had become part of the pre–Mother's Day weekend for three years strong and counting.

191

Although Angela disliked "old folks," she believed it was a worthwhile community service. Plus, Angela admitted to the gratification she felt after watching the residents' eyes light up when they were handed the furry creatures.

Eva parked near the dining room's side entrance. Getting out, Angela waited while Eva scanned her security badge to unlock the door. Once inside, they retrieved empty food carts near the wall and rolled them back to the vehicle. After stacking boxes on the carts until there wasn't room for any more, Angela closed the hatch on the SUV.

Huffing, Eva rolled her cart inside, followed by her sister. "Okay, you ready?"

"Yep. What wing should I start?"

Eva thought about Mrs. Valentine and Mrs. Beacon. She would never get out of their suite, so she sent Angela in that direction and she would stop by Miss Jessie's room.

Once the first load was gone, they agreed to meet back in the dining room to get the remaining boxes. Eva finished first, so she relaxed in a chair, facing the window with her leg swinging over her knee.

How could she not be here and think about Kidd? Her mind drifted to their brief kiss. *I'm not going there.* Blinking, she noted the facility was teeming with more families today. Normally, it made Eva happy when residents were getting extra attention, but today her emotional happiness was on hold. Her eyes misted, and again, Eva felt beguiled.

"You think you're funny." Angela's voice broke into her reverie. "I know you purposely stuck me with those two Golden Girls."

Eva feigned innocence. "Who?"

"You know who, Grandma and Valentine. If I didn't have to use the bathroom, I probably still would have been their prisoner."

Eva laughed, and a tear escaped, which made Angela madder. "Okay, wait until next year. You'll be begging me for help."

"Okay, okay." Eva held her stomach, snickering. "I'm sorry . . . I'm guilty. Let's hurry up and get out of here."

Eva was completing her second round when she headed toward the front entrance and caught a glimpse of Kidd. Her heart pounded wildly. What was he doing here on a Sunday? If she was a crazy woman, Eva would run and jump on his back and wear herself out, trying to beat him down. Thankfully, God gave her a sound mind.

God, what do I say? How do I act? I'm not ready to see him. Could she trust herself to walk up to him, look beyond his dirt, and treat him like God expected of her?

The other option was to turn around and leave without letting him see her. She could wait until Monday to deal with Kidd Jamieson. To her dismay, her feet, heart, and head weren't in sync. She kept walking into a mental battlefield. Her feet were shouting for her to turn around, her heart said everything was a misunderstanding, and her head was gearing up to give him a piece of her mind.

His back was to her as someone was holding his attention. Eva inched closer.

"You stood me up—" Kidd accused. He folded his arms and spread his legs, mimicking Will Smith's and Tommy Lee Jones's stance in the movie *Men in Black.*

"Pardon me?" Angela replied, clearly unaware that the man standing in front of her was Eva's heartbreaker.

There was silence.

"So this is how Miss Eva looks all dressed up and in red." He whistled. "Wow."

Offended and hurt by Kidd's insincere compliment, Eva angled her body to get a better view of Angela's reaction. "Sic him, Angel," she whispered.

"I'm not Eva—" Angela had the nerve to blush.

What! You traitor, Eva silently fussed.

"I know. Your left brow's not arched. Eva has three freckles on her nose and a beauty mole behind her right ear."

Eva sucked in her breath at the same time Angela's mouth dropped open, speechless. Instinctively, Eva touched her brow, nose, and behind her ear. Her mole was so small; she doubted her parents looked for it as a point of identification. As far as the freckles, Eva never counted them. Plus, she never came to work without foundation to cover her imperfections, and then topped off her look with one brush stroke of blush powder. No lashes, no lipstick, no hair extensions, no jewelry. She kept everything simple, including her life, until she met the man flirting with her sister.

"Could your name be Kevin or Kidd?"

"Eva calls me Kevin. Kidd's the alter ego." He shrugged. "So, she has a sister."

"Twin, actually." Angela extended her hand. "Angela Savoy. It's nice to meet you. I'm impressed, which isn't done easily." She chuckled.

"Evidently," Eva grumbled.

"Believe me, that was not my intention."

Kidd's statement bordered on arrogance. Yet it was that confident personality she both admired and couldn't stand at the same time.

"That means she's probably somewhere around here." Kidd stuffed his hands in his pants and pivoted around, catching Eva in the headlights. She didn't even have a chance to duck.

"So there's the little woman who stood me up and ruined my weekend." His accusation was followed by a tender smile that indicated, *I'll forgive you for anything.*

Despite it being Sunday, Eva wasn't in a forgiving mood. It wasn't that easy for her to forget what she heard. She didn't budge. Kidd, wearing a cocky smile, took the opportunity to perform a bold assessment. Starting with her feet, his eyes began taking inventory. Her toes— adorned with red polish—wiggled without her permission. Because she loved open-toed heels, she was wearing strappy three-inch sandals.

His sweep continued upward, lingering at Eva's legs and stopping at her mouth, which bore the remains of a pinkish lip gloss. Kidd shot a quick glance at Angela, "Don't take this the wrong way, Angela, but

I withdraw my earlier compliments." Then returning his attention to Eva, he proclaimed, "You're absolutely stunning, girl."

It wasn't the first time he had called her "girl." The first was when he was encouraging her on her test, and it didn't bother her. Now Eva didn't know how she felt about him calling a twenty-seven-year-old woman a *girl,* like she was a stranger off the street. Yet somehow, coming from Kidd's lips, it made her shiver.

His eyes locked with hers, waiting for her response. Eva refused to give him the slightest satisfaction of the tiniest blush. She was still hurt by his apparent intent to add her to his list of conquests and "baby mama" drama.

"What are you doing here?" She snubbed him, while discreetly admiring his handsomeness in a gray-striped suit and a paisley tie. She noticed that his beard had thickened. There was no way to describe Kidd as less than a very good-looking, drool-worthy Black man. *But don't forget his womanizing ways,* her conscience reminded her.

Kidd folded his arms, as if he had read her thoughts. "We need to talk, Sybil."

"What?"

"You know, the personality that texted me back and canceled our dinner on Friday."

Angela formed an "O" with her lips. "Ah, I'll go get my SUV."

"Angel, wait," Eva called after her, trying to keep her sister from escaping. That only made Angela walk faster, almost breaking into a cutesy jog in heels.

"Traitor," Eva mumbled. Her twin had left her to deal with the six-foot-plus hunk of a problem.

"What happened, Eva?" She heard his baritone voice coming closer. "Why did you change your mind?"

Eva spun around and squinted. "Do you want the truth, the whole truth, and nothing but the truth?"

He nodded. His expression hovered between annoyed and

wounded. Which one should she believe? Let him stew. She shrugged. "First, why are you here, Kidd?"

"I'm surprised you don't know. It's the spring open house, or something. Since I'm the resident liaison, the powers that be informed me that I should be here and greet families. You know, good public relations and all. I'm supposed to take credit for all the good things that have improved resident morale. Even though I had nothing to do with implementing any of it."

Eva had forgotten about the date change for the yearly open house. Usually, it was held at the end of May. But, to avoid a dilemma such as this, she could have made her deliveries on another weekend. The idea of having to change her plans because of Kidd infuriated her. She had always delivered the gifts the Sunday prior to Mother's Day. That way, she could spend Mother's Day with her own mother. She was losing it.

Invading her space, Kidd took one step closer and towered over her. She suddenly remembered the kiss. "Now, no more stalling, Eva. What happened within the span of fifteen or twenty minutes after giving me your number? Don't play games with me, Eva. I don't lose."

"There's a first time for everything. The florist did you in."

Kidd had the nerve to grin. "I thought you would like a bouquet. I'm trying to woo you."

"Really?" She gritted her teeth and folded her arms. "How do you *woo* me when you're ordering flowers for several other women?" Holding her breath, she braced herself for the truth or a lie.

"What? How do you know about them?"

"Evading the answer, huh? I was about to call and tell you to meet me at my condo when I saw you walk out of the building and cross the street. Out of curiosity, I followed you into the florist shop. But then I wished I hadn't. You don't play games? Huh? What are you doing with those women who will receive your flowers?"

Kidd's response was a barking laugh, which further enraged her.

"Curiosity killed the cat. Those flowers were for my mother, my two cousins, and their wacko friend."

Smooth. A good lie always sounded like the truth. "Hmm. Or one could be your baby's mama. Are the other two blood relatives? I guess I'm asking if I can believe you, Kidd." She could probably count on one hand how many times she had addressed him by his nickname.

He stared at her a long time. "Any other woman who'd question my intentions would be wiped off my list, but I want only your name on it. Do you want to trust me?" He whispered, throwing the ball back into her court. "Eva, I do have secrets and a past. I will share anything with you. It's up to you if you want to know about my demons. You decide." He didn't blink.

How did the tables turn on her like that? This was more than she had bargained for, and why did he have to mention the word *demons*? Kidd turned and walked away, never looking back.

Eva's eyes misted. She saw Angela pull up the SUV to the entrance. Eva took one final glance at Kidd's retreating figure before walking outside. "Lord, I'm getting too many signals."

She took a deep breath as her heart pounded like something crazy. When she opened the passenger door, Angela was chatting on the cell phone.

"Oh, here she is now. I'll see you later, sweetie. Love you too." Angela ended the call. "Girl, you're right about Mr. Kidd. That man is a monster and you are his prey. Friendship is definitely not his intention. Way to go." Angela grinned and lifted her hand for a high-five, which Eva ignored.

She withheld her rebuttal. Kidd was asking too much of her, and she knew too little about him to believe him. Although saints sometimes stumble and fall, Eva refused to fall over him. She would not allow herself to ignore the red light flashing a warning signal. Eva believed in obeying all traffic laws.

"What's wrong?" Angela teased. "There are no buts about it, that man likes you. If you try to deny it, God is going to get you for lying on a Sunday."

Chapter Twenty-Five

K idd enjoyed challenges, but games with women were not his forte. There were too many goldfish in the pond, yet Eva was the most beautiful of all.

Anxious to get out of his monkey suit, he had started the countdown until the open house was over.

Later, back at Parke's house, Kidd changed clothes. Downstairs in the kitchen, Kidd stared at Eva's bouquet that he placed in a tall glass. The colors were still vibrant, but fading just as his chances with Eva. How could the woman jump to those wild conclusions?

Kidd strolled outside on the deck and sat on the wooden swing. He needed a solitary moment. If Eva didn't want him, then she didn't want anything from him. "God, what does it take for things to go right in my life?"

Seek Me, God answered.

The voice didn't startle him this time, but the request was confusing. Kidd took a swig from the bottle of water he had grabbed on the way out the door. What he wanted was a can of beer, but Cheney forbade any liquor in the house. Parke was a chump—or in love—to let his wife run him and the house.

How does a person seek God? He needed a simple how-to pamphlet to follow. Without a sound, Kami flopped next to him, putting the swing in motion. She scooted closer. Together, for the next few minutes, they sat quietly with Kami's elbow digging into his thigh. She waited for him to acknowledge her presence. It was almost as if Kami was trying to discern his mood.

Finally, curiosity got the best of her. "Those flowers are pretty, Uncle Cousin. Who are they for?"

That was a touchy subject. "For you, my favorite girl."

Kami's eyes widened and a smile lit up her beautiful face. Like Eva, she would grow up to be a heartbreaker. "Me? I'm your favorite girl?"

Kidd winked. "You know it." He tweaked her nose.

"Wow. I thought maybe you had a girlfriend."

"Nope."

"Wait until I tell my boyfriend I got flowers."

Kidd shifted, causing the swing to pick up speed. "What! Does your dad know about this boyfriend? Better yet, I'd like to meet him myself." There was no way he was going to let any boy close to Kami for at least twenty years, and then it would be his cousin's problem.

She giggled. "Cousin Uncle, you're silly. I can't have boyfriends yet, but when I do, he'll have to bring me candy and flowers to beat you out." She stood and raced back inside.

"Where are you going?"

"To tell Mommy you don't have a girlfriend and the flowers are for me."

Kidd smirked. He had come to love the little spitball, despite her original intentions to take him down. He didn't know how long he stayed outside, but the sun began to set. The back door opened and footsteps approached. Without an invitation, Cheney came and sat at the other end of the swing.

"I helped Kami put the flowers in her room. You've got a girlfriend for life."

Kidd chuckled.

"I'm serious. I would be careful if I were you. If you bring any lady friends around here, my baby will be like a momma bear protecting her cubs. She acted that way with Parke and Malcolm. You don't want to see that girl in action defending you."

Cheney scraped her sandal against the deck and started the swing again. Kidd went with the flow.

"What happened?" She paused, and when he didn't respond, she continued. "Listen, my husband is the only man I know who buys flowers just because. Who is she and what happened? Kidd, I'm a good listener . . ."

"I'm good, Cheney."

She didn't leave as he expected. "I like you, Kidd. You're a good man, but an unconvincing liar. I've never heard you talk about a lady friend, so how did you mess this up?"

Kidd grunted. "Me? If I hadn't bought her flowers, then there wouldn't have been a misunderstanding, or mess—as you call it."

"What's the name of this misunderstanding?"

"Eva Savoy," Kidd stated, yielding to Cheney's baiting. "She's the prettiest little woman, but she doesn't trust me."

"Imagine that," Cheney teased. "Kidd—newsflash. Most men aren't trustworthy, so that's an immediate defense mechanism for a woman."

"I'm not like most men—"

"I know. You're a Jamieson. Kidd, flowers are good, but I fell in love with your cousin because, besides me not being able to get rid of him—"

"Yeah, I have noticed your husband can be a pain . . ." Kidd didn't finish his statement out of respect for Cheney. "Okay, tell me how my ugly cousin wooed you." Anything to get his mind and the conversation off Eva.

"Watch it. There are no ugly Jamiesons. It's not in your genes." Cheney turned and made herself comfortable, pushing the swing again. "Anyway, my past tormented me. I had made a bad decision. I couldn't forgive myself, so I figured neither could Jesus. But He has endless grace toward us."

Cheney shook her head as if she was still having a hard time believing it. "I had demons haunting me, and Parke came on the scene as my personal demon-slayer. The only problem was, at the time, neither of us had any spiritual power to overcome the adversary." She shrugged.

"During that time, Parke seemed to take my troubled heart and safeguard it in his hands. It reminds me of 3 John 1:2 that says: *'I pray that you may enjoy good health and that all may go well with you, even as your soul is getting along well.'* Parke hung in there through my hard times. And as my soul and mind began to mend, he gave me my heart back, filled with so much love. I love Parke and he loves me, but from the beginning it wasn't so."

Kidd rubbed the hairs on his chin. "I doubt if Eva wants to be my demon-slayer," he said more to himself than Cheney.

She stood and patted his shoulder. "You're a Jamieson and something tells me God's going to give you the sword to slay your own demons. It's part of His promise and plans for us. Start reading your Bible and really study the book of Acts. It tells how God handed His power out to His believers." She turned to walk away.

"Hey, Cheney," he called over his shoulder.

"Yeah, cuz?"

"I'm not a believer." He sighed and rested his elbows on his knees to fold his hands.

"Yet." She laughed. "There's too much power going on up in this house for something explosive not to happen. It reminds me of the upper room." She strolled into the house, humming a melody that praised Jesus.

He didn't expect Cheney and Parke's love story to affect him. More than that, he wasn't going to let Eva walk away from him, even if he had to kiss her into submission. Kidd remained outside, plotting his showdown with Eva until the mosquitoes started biting.

Chapter Twenty-Six

*E*va woke disoriented, as she climbed out of bed to prepare for her fifth and final day on the midnight shift. "Why did I agree to this again?" she asked herself on the way to the bathroom. "Oh, that's right. I asked for this punishment so I could be away from Kidd for a week."

She didn't know which was worse: working nights or staying awake all night thinking about him. Lying in her own bed at eleven o'clock at night was the solid winner.

Dawn had been disappointed that Eva agreed to switch shifts with Janet. Dawn did not like Janet and accused her of always having an excuse for why she couldn't work her shift. She was forever begging people to switch with her.

This time, Janet didn't have to beg. Eva offered and Janet jumped on it. But Dawn didn't have to know that. She only wanted Eva to tag along to a movie premiere, produced by some local talent. Personally, Eva was glad she had an excuse to decline. She wasn't much of a movie-goer. Give her magazines any day, especially the bridal ones.

Eva didn't understand why she even bothered seeking God concerning Kidd. Her heart, mind, and spirit still weren't in sync, so she stayed prayerful as her desire for him increased on its own. Was he lying with his explanation about the flowers?

Sighing, she stared into her bathroom mirror. Peering closer, she verified Kidd's count of her freckles. For some reason, that had become part of her ritual every night since he made note of them. She smiled because he was accurate. At the same time, Eva was saddened because her heart wanted to trust him. The immature and insecure woman in her wanted to call his bluff and meet these female relatives. Depending on how they looked, she might believe him.

It was all a moot point anyway. In the end, if it wasn't God's will for her to be with Kidd, the trust issue didn't matter. Eva couldn't make a move until God gave her a sign.

After brushing her curls up into a high ponytail, Eva opted to forgo the foundation and blush and just smeared gloss on her lips. She dabbed holy oil on her head and prayed for safety before leaving her condo. It was a habit her mother instilled in her as a teenager; something she still did whenever she left the house at night.

Once again, Kidd was her unwelcomed mental companion on the drive to work. He was the type of man who could hold her attention, but what about those demons and secrets he mentioned? Eva shuddered. She just didn't know if she was ready for that, if ever.

His bitterness could destroy her heart. She wasn't reared in a way to accept any kind of man into her life. She couldn't do it. Eva knew the importance of having a mate who is a strong, Spirit-filled believer in Christ. She would accept nothing less.

Eva also knew Kidd would never be able to overcome the stronghold over his life until he repented of his sins and confessed that he needed God. Then he would have to continue on the Christian journey with the water baptism to wash away the filth of his sins that had him in a stronghold. Taking those steps would empower him to grow as a babe in Christ. God is ever ready to bestow spiritual gifts that Kidd could never imagine.

Eva pulled her car into the parking lot and turned off the ignition, but didn't get out right away. "God, I know You can save and keep anybody."

They have to want to be saved; then I can keep them, God spoke.

"God, You are faithful. Your Word says no one comes unless You draw them," she said, paraphrasing John 6:44. "Jesus, You are stronger than any devil trying to consume him. Please overpower the darkness in his life and draw him. In Jesus' name. Amen."

Eva strolled through the back entrance of Garden Chateau, expecting, praying, hoping, and believing that God would help Kidd. Coming around to the nurses' station, she nodded at Glenda, the RN on duty, and then clocked in.

Irene, the LPN who Eva was scheduled to relieve, hurried to the nurses' station. Her eyes came alive when she saw Eva.

"I'm so glad you're here on time. Janet has a problem with an eight-hour shift. She really believes it's seven hours and fifty minutes. I'll let you sign in and get situated before I brief you during the rounds."

After a few minutes, Eva was ready. She grabbed a flip chart and followed Irene into the first of twenty-five patients' rooms. Eva would be assigned to their care until seven the next morning. It would take her about two hours to do a thorough assessment of each resident before repeating the task again.

"Everyone on this wing had a good evening. They ate and enjoyed naps without incident, except Mrs. Beaver. She's in the mood to walk. Mr. Green was irritated and belligerent a few times. Of course, I wanted to tie him to the bed, but that was wishful thinking, and . . ."

"I thought you said it was uneventful." Eva gritted her teeth.

"For the most part." Irene shrugged. "The gangrene in Miss Jessie's toes doesn't seem to be responding to the ointment. No new orders from the doctor yet. Just keep a diligent eye on her."

Eva made notes on who would be her priority patients throughout the night. After they completed the final round together, Irene clocked out and waved a weak good-night. Eva could never get accustomed to doing her job when it was pitch-black outside. How Alaskans adjusted to darkness for six months at a time was beyond her.

Completing the first round of her shift took a little longer than expected, especially since she'd gone through the same tasks for almost a week now. Waking up residents to change bandages, or to turn them in their beds, or even assist them to the bathroom were major chores. She was already exhausted and hadn't completed half her shift yet.

It was after one in the morning. Eva had just taken one resident to the bathroom again and checked on his roommate. Walking out of the room, she stumbled. She had to be hallucinating; her eyes were playing tricks on her. Bigger than life, there was Kidd, leaning against the wall. Talk about ghosts, this one looked real. She walked closer toward the mirage.

"Kevin?" she barely whispered. At this hour, how could his gorgeous looks override his weariness? He appeared refreshed and inviting. Eva felt tired, grouchy, and self-conscious. Her hair was pulled into a careless ponytail and her face lacked any beauty enhancements. She felt justified because the night shift was more work, especially in the lockdown unit, to which she was assigned.

"Kevin, what are you doing here?" Eva frowned with curiosity.

Lifting a brow, his nostrils flared. "How many answers do you want?"

"As many as will explain why you're here at one in the morning. I assume you worked eight-to-five, as usual."

He pushed off the wall and came face-to-face with her. "Why are *you* working this shift?"

Eva jutted her chin. "I needed a change of scenery."

"That can be accomplished by taking a nature walk or getting on a plane. You deprived me—us—by working a different shift. It took me a few days to figure out your little scheme, but I'm here to tell you I plan to finish what I started."

"Really?" She arched a brow. "Funny, I thought we finished our discussion on Sunday when you walked away."

"I should have never walked away from you like that. I'm sorry, but I can't let you walk away from me without really knowing me. Despite what you insinuated last week, I want one woman—and that's you. I need you to trust me; I won't hurt you."

"What about my heart? I never planned to be a heart transplant candidate. I'd rather guard the one God gave me," Eva argued in a hushed voice.

Kidd leaned closer and whispered, "Women are not the only ones with hearts. God gave man a heart first."

He seemed so vulnerable, and it was becoming her weakness. "So, again, why are you here?" Eva changed the subject, as she headed to the nurses' station. Her traitorous mind shouted at her, *What difference does it make? His presence is comforting.*

"One, I missed you. Two, I've heard about those sundowners characters. And, three, I missed you."

Ignoring his other two reasons, which were actually the same, she explained, "Most sundowners are harmless. Their confused state is usually, as the word implies, when the sun is in the process of going down, a few residents might get agitated because they become disoriented and afraid of their surroundings. I'll be fine. Go home."

As she tried to walk around him to enter the next room, Kidd blocked her and whispered, "Listen, I've told you before, I don't take directions too well. So we can have a showdown before this sundown stuff kicks in, if you're up to it. But I'm not going anywhere."

"Stubborn," Eva mumbled, as her heart—the second traitorous member of her body—did cartwheels. The only part yet to be heard from was her soul. She hurried into the next suite, knowing Kidd wouldn't follow her. He would refrain to witness her changing bed pans, cleaning sores, or rotating patients who weren't ambulatory.

Eva walked into the room where Miss Jessie was resting. She had been an active resident until a few months ago. The ulcers on two toes, which started out as sores the size of corns, had expanded and become infected. Gangrene had set in. Now the ulcers were starting to eat away skin and expose ligaments and bone.

The prognosis didn't look good if the antibiotics didn't halt the spread of the infection soon. Eva's guess was the resident might have to undergo amputation. It was the doctor's call. She and her coworkers were doing their best to avoid that option, but it seemed futile. Carefully, she assisted Miss Jessie out of bed and steadied her walk to the bathroom.

At three in the morning, Eva returned to her first resident and began the standard care ritual again. All the while, Kidd—her fierce protector—dozed in a rocking chair. Every now and then, when she walked out of a room and looked his way, one of Kidd's eyes would pop open.

Her heart was drawn to him, and her mind was usually the voice of reason. But it was the confirmation in her spirit she was holding out for. About two hours later, Eva succumbed to a chorus of yawns. Her body was loudly protesting the switch of her night and day routines.

Eva repeated her third set of rounds. As warned, Mr. Green, who had been diagnosed with dementia, was restless. As she was about to enter his room, she glanced over at Kidd. Somehow he had managed to curl his bulky body in a chair that in no way accommodated his size. He was down for the count, although he didn't appear comfortable. Shaking her head at the sight, Eva smiled and continued into the room.

After checking his vitals, she was about to leave when the man grabbed her arm. "Mr. Green, Mr. Green." Eva struggled to break his hold, but his grip was tight.

"My wife's asleep. I've been waiting on you, baby." His voice was strong and determined.

"Mr. Green, stop it! Your wife is deceased. You're in Garden Chateau. Let me go—"

In the blink of an eye, Kidd's strong arms had yanked her out of harm's way. "Old man, if you want to tangle with somebody, here I am," Kidd threatened the resident, but the man would not be deterred.

"She's mine! Tell him, Lucy. You're my gal," he said, becoming adamant.

Eva was able to reach for the call string, and another LPN came to her aid with a sleeping pill and cup. It took the three of them to get the man to swallow, but within minutes, he had mellowed and dozed off.

"My radar has been on him since yesterday. We're going to have to call the doctor. He's becoming more combative. Maybe they can examine him for some underlying depression," Denise, the other LPN, explained. She walked away, swaying her hips for nobody's benefit—except Kidd's.

"Are you okay?" Kidd asked, as he guided Eva out into the hall.

Composing herself, she sighed, then straightened her clothes and hair. She was a little shaken and out of breath.

"Thank you," Eva whispered, hoping her eyes weren't revealing too much. "You, Mr. Jamieson, amaze me. I thought you were asleep."

"Don't ever underestimate me."

"I see." She wanted to say, *I would never do that.* Instead, she restrained herself and said no more. For the remainder of her shift, Eva never looked Kidd's way again. She knew his radar was activated and fully charged.

Finally, after seeming like forever, the sun beamed through the complex's ceiling-to-floor windows and the sound of birds chirping introduced a new day. For Eva, it signaled the completion of her good deed for Janet—and time away from Kidd. Although admittedly, she was glad he had been present the previous night.

Eva clocked out and nudged Kidd awake. This time he looked exhausted, but even in his sleep, his face seemed on guard and ready to react. She laughed. At that moment, she realized that being rough around the edges could sometimes be a good thing.

"Hey, sleepyhead. Do you need a designated driver?" she teased.

Kidd stood and stretched. His eyes were bloodshot, but the smile he gave Eva was a pure good-morning pleasure. "Do me a favor."

"What?"

"Don't ever work this shift again. My back is killing me."

She smiled. "Thank you, Kidd, for sacrificing a comfortable night's sleep to come to my rescue."

When he moaned, God's faint voice whispered, *He's the one.*

He's the one? Her heart raced as she responded to His voice within, *Oh, my Lord, what have I gotten myself into?*

Chapter Twenty-Seven

*A*fter the fireworks of the previous night, she and Kidd agreed to a reprieve on her trust issues. Before they left the facility, they freshened up with toothpaste he retrieved from the supply cabinet, along with toothbrushes and mouthwash. Relishing the moment, they sealed their newly made agreement with a good-morning kiss. It mattered to neither of them how long it lingered.

Eva was exhausted when she got home early Saturday morning. The only thing on her mind was getting some much-needed rest. As soon as her head hit the pillow, she fell into a deep slumber. It was the best sleep she'd had in a week's time.

Eva dreamed that she lived in medieval times. Locked in a tower, Kidd was her knight in shining armor. He had come to rescue her.

It was late afternoon and Eva hadn't stirred from her bed when the phone rang. "Hello?" she answered with a slur.

"You're still asleep? This is my first official phone call. Can't you sound better than this, woman?" Kidd teased.

His voice was refreshing; it seemed funny to her. As soon as God gave her the go-ahead, she released her emotional shackles.

"Not when I've worked the midnight shift for a week. You'd better be glad I answered rather than letting it go to my voice mail."

"Good point. I worked one night and thought I died." He paused. "I would love to take you out this evening."

"No way. I'm not leaving here until I go to church tomorrow morning." She had a better idea. "I would love for you to go with me," she said and held her breath.

"Then I'll go."

Eva blinked. Now she was wide awake. What? No hesitation or stuttering on his part? She was surprised it was that easy. "You mean, just like that? No argument? No fighting and screaming?"

"None."

Well, God, I can read this sign!

She gave him her address and told him what time to pick her up for service. Their first date would be at church. They were off to a good start. She grinned and decided to surprise her family about his pending visit.

Angela had already given her assessment of Kidd. "He seems like your type. But remember the fellowship of light and darkness. I'm referring to 2 Corinthians 6:14." Eva knew the Scripture; her hesitation from the beginning was based on it: *"Do not be yoked together with unbelievers. For what do righteousness and wickedness have in common? Or what fellowship can light have with darkness?"*

What would her parents think about him? Her father would have his opportunity to observe Kidd and assess his worthiness. Eva was sure Kidd would charm her mother.

Sunday morning at nine sharp, Kidd rang Eva's doorbell. Punctuality was attractive. She opened the door, and he stood there with a bouquet of flowers. He was the epitome of 100 percent male.

"Wow. You're breathtaking." Kidd's eyes danced. "Look, we're matching. I need to go to church with you more often," he said with such awe.

"You do," she agreed, stepping aside to let him enter. Eva experienced a moment of complete utopia as she accepted the flowers. "Thank you. You'll get no argument from me on that."

She hadn't seen this steel-gray pinstriped suit before. The crisp white shirt and gray-and-black tie with specks of red complemented his rich, dark skin tone.

"To impress you, anything."

"You did that Friday night at work. How's your back?"

"Nothing a good night's sleep couldn't repair. Ready?"

"I am. I'll get my purse and Bible. Make yourself comfortable. Do you need me to grab an extra Bible for you?" She yelled from her bedroom.

"Nope. My sister-in-law offered to loan me one of hers, but I don't like to rent or borrow. I believe in owning what's mine, so I went out and bought my own."

Inside her bedroom, Eva scanned her appearance one more time in the full-length mirror. Pleased with her selection, the sleeveless silver dress modestly fit her curves. The matching duster hid them in reserve. She fluffed the soft curls in her hair, checked her small studs, and adjusted her necklace. Finally, Eva took a deep breath and stepped out of her bedroom. She found Kidd looking out her sliding doors to the balcony.

At the sound of her presence, he pivoted. Kidd Jamieson was one good-looking man: sweet, tough, and—she had to admit—genuine with his compliments. Altogether, it was a good combination.

"I see your favorite color is white," he said, referring to her décor.

"Yep."

"And I see you were expecting someone at your dinner table." He arched one of his brows.

"Yep," she said, as they walked out. Why share her idiosyncrasies on the first date? Once they stepped outside, she was about to lock the front door. Kidd stopped her.

"I might as well get this out of the way." Taking her in his arms, he kissed her until she felt faint. He couldn't have timed the kiss more appropriately. Inside the privacy of her home could prove to be too tempting. She refused to lose her dedicated life of virginity and sanctification to a moment of lust. Yes, outside of her condo was definitely better.

Finally, Eva pulled away. Dazed, she struggled to find her voice. "I never knew a kiss could last that long. We'll be late for church."

He smirked, as if he wouldn't mind that at all. Then he took her keys and finished the task. Squeezing her hand, he led the way to his car.

"When a man is thirsty, he doesn't stop drinking until he's quenched his thirst. Cool me off, Eva. Whatever it is that controls your temperature, share it with me."

What was he talking about? Just because God said Kidd was the one didn't mean things would happen overnight. They had to keep things in perspective. It takes time to develop a relationship. Plus, she didn't know of any journey that was completed without an obstacle course. Eva needed to spiritually buckle up and start praying for guidance—big time.

Being a gentleman, Kidd opened the car door and helped Eva inside. While he strolled around to his side, Eva prayed within her, *Lord, help me to keep my eyes open, so that I don't make You ashamed of my conduct. Let him receive Your Word today and forever be changed. In Jesus' name. Amen.*

He who hungers and thirsts after My righteousness, I will fill him, God spoke from Matthew 5:6.

Without saying a word, Eva faced Kidd and watched him settle behind the wheel. As he turned the ignition, her eyes misted. She had to help keep his mind on track spiritually.

When they arrived at Salvation Temple, she located her family and led Kidd to where they were sitting. Her father looked up and did a double take after seeing her guest. She mouthed, *this is Kidd.*

Nodding, Kenneth stood to allow them to enter their row. Her mother scooted over, forcing Angela and Lance farther down the cushioned pew. As a sign of respect and acknowledgment of coming into the presence of God, Eva knelt and said a prayer of thanksgiving. What she wanted to do was stay on her knees and petition God for Kidd's salvation until he surrendered to Him. She planned to begin that process very soon.

For now, she finished her prayer and took her seat next to him on the pew. Kidd's eyes sparkled as he waited to assist her up. Then he stretched out his arm, inching her closer to him. Eva glanced at her parents. She leaned over him to whisper to her mother.

"Happy Mother's Day, Mom." Eva kissed her cheek. She had purchased her mother several lovely scarves two weeks ago. Distracted by the developments between her and Kidd, she had left the gift at home.

"Happy Mother's Day, Mrs. Savoy," Kidd added with a nod toward her.

"Thank you." Rita smiled, and then winked at Eva.

Kenneth watched the interaction with an intense expression. Eva glanced at Angela, who winked, while Lance scowled.

As the praise team filled the sanctuary with their harmonious voices, Eva stood and worshiped. Kidd didn't, but his shoe never stopped tapping. Too soon that segment of the service was over and Elder Taylor walked to the podium.

Eva wanted to shout out, "Preach, Pastor, until Kidd is convinced that it's God's way or no way." However, she withheld her remarks and kept her composure. At least he had come.

· Elder Taylor welcomed the visitors when he asked them to stand. Kidd and others throughout the auditorium complied. Everyone clapped, and Elder waited until they retook their seats.

"Happy Mother's Day to all our mothers," Elder addressed the audience. Then, with a series of questions as an introduction, he began his message, "Do you recall your mother scolding you as a child when you got in trouble? Did she ever tell you to be a leader, not a follower? When employers have openings, don't they seek someone with leadership skills? And in sports, everyone knows being in the lead is to your team's advantage. I could go on and on." He held up a finger and shouted, "But there is always an exception to every rule."

Although Kidd focused on the pulpit, he never let Eva forget his presence with a touch every now and then.

"It's all about Mom today, but it's about Christ every day. You can't be led astray when you become a follower of Christ. I'm sure your mother will agree. When you were a child, you thought as a child, acted as a child, and gave your mother childish gifts, which she cherished. But when playtime is over, every mother wants to see her children grow up into responsible adults, get good jobs, and have beautiful families. Finally, and most important of all, a mother's prayer is to have her children's names written in the Lord's Book of Life. For Christ's sake and yours, I need you to get a one-track mind today and decide to follow Him . . ."

Elder Taylor preached on, mingling Scriptures with examples for just under an hour.

Eva glanced at Kidd, and each time he met her gaze.

"Choir," the pastor said, turning around, "please sing 'Let Me Be a Follower of Christ.' As our brothers and sisters meditate on their present circumstances, this is the altar call. Let everyone stand and pray. For those who are conflicted, have storms raging in their lives, you need to walk with Jesus. If you have not given your life to Christ, please come."

Eva and her family stood to their feet. So did Kidd. Closing her eyes and squeezing his hand, she prayed for the man for whom she was developing strong feelings.

Elder Taylor broke into her thoughts. "Let there be no hesitation on your part. God wants to save you. Repent of your sins right where you are standing. Tell God all about your hurts, disappointments, anger, and desires. Then walk from where you are to the altar. We have ministers who will pray for you. If you want to take it a step farther, we can baptize you today, in the name of Jesus, for the cleansing of your sins. You do not need an appointment with God. Do it today. Give your mother and yourself the best gift today . . ."

Suddenly, Kidd released Eva's hand and left the pew. Tears sprung up and flowed down Eva's cheeks. She couldn't believe the man who seemed defiant at every turn was yielding his pride to God. Eva couldn't contain her joy. She held her breath and watched as Kidd allowed the ministers to anoint his head will holy oil and begin to pray at length with him. But instead of continuing to the back for the baptism, Kidd headed back her way. Eva exhaled a disappointed sigh.

Evidently, her father noticed her downcast look and whispered, "Give him time. Patience is probably the biggest gift God could give us next to salvation. He's coming. Maybe not today, but his actions show he's seeking God. Don't lose faith."

Eva sniffed. "Thank you, Daddy."

When Kidd returned, Eva was able to smile—thanks to her father's words of wisdom—and reached for his hand. Kidd accepted it and winked.

After the benediction, she made proper introductions. Her father shook his hand and chatted a few minutes, while her mother silently appraised Kidd and seemed to hold on to his every word.

"Hi, Kidd, or should I call you Kevin?" Angela asked, grinning.

"Let's stick to Kidd. No one can say my name like Eva."

"Hmmm," Angela responded and exchanged glances with their mother. As Lance cleared his throat, Angela introduced him, "This is my boyfriend, Lance." Without releasing his left hand that had been resting on Angela's waist, he shook Kidd's hand.

When Lance flinched—and he wasn't a small man by any means, nor was he out of shape—Eva decided she had seen their hand-wrestling stunt long enough. She nudged Kidd, and he released his grip.

"So you're the infamous Kidd. Well, if Eva hasn't used that can of mace I got for her yet, then I guess you passed."

Angela slapped his shoulder. "Lance!" She and Eva said at the same time.

Eva rolled her eyes. The man was going to have to get over the whole big brother kick. If Kenneth Savoy didn't feel his baby girl was in danger, then Lance had better fall in line.

Eva tugged on Kidd's hand as a signal for them to go, but he didn't budge. His eyes were locked on Lance. "Mace, huh?"

Facing Eva, he addressed Lance's comment. "You won't need it when I'm around. I've been known to break a bone with one snap, so I'm capable of making sure you're safe. If we weren't in church and I hadn't just asked for prayer, I would give a demonstration. All I need is a volunteer."

Eva elbowed him in the gut. "Stop teasing."

"Only with you. Otherwise, I'm serious."

Lance said nothing.

"Eva, looks like you're in good hands," her father joked and shook Kidd's hand again. "It was nice meeting you. Hopefully, we'll see each other again."

Kidd nodded. Eva said her good-byes and shoved Kidd toward the exit.

"Did you have to scare my sister's boyfriend like that? Now Lance will probably add on more weights at the gym."

"I just wanted him—and you—to know I can protect and serve without a badge."

When they left church, Kidd took her to Hendel's before brunch was over at two. He made a mental note to return with Eva to sample the seafood at a later date. Just before they finished their meal, he signaled to the waiter for the check.

"January Wabash Park is close by. Do you feel like a short stroll? I know you're wearing heels." The waiter returned with his credit card. Kidd tucked it back into his wallet, stood up, and reached for her hand.

219

"I can run in heels, if necessary."

"You don't have to worry about me giving chase. I gotcha now," he said playfully. After helping her in the car, they drove away toward New North Florissant Road. Five minutes later, they were strolling along a pathway that encircled a lake.

"This is so beautiful," Eva said, taking in the moment. Her joy and admiration was reflected in her eyes.

"Yes, you are. I don't stay too far from here with my cousins, but it's time for me to move."

Then Kidd quickly switched subjects. He definitely didn't want to talk about Parke and his clan. "I've changed my mind. I'd rather not walk. There's a bench. We can sit there and I can admire your legs."

Eva blushed.

"That's right," Kidd backed himself up. "I'm attracted to everything about you—from your three freckles, to your shapely legs, to your feisty spirit."

"Kevin, we just left church. I'm flattered by your compliments, but we need to talk about something else."

"Chicken," he taunted her, as squeals from children on the playground equipment entertained them.

"No, I'm saved." Eva switched the topic to the sermon. She then talked about her ambitions as a nurse, her family, and her salvation.

Kidd listened, but reciprocated with tales of his antics during his childhood. He deliberately steered clear of anything about his father. Not wanting to uncover the demons that still plagued him about Samuel's absenteeism, he desired to display his strengths, not weaknesses.

The couple hadn't realized they had talked for hours, until the hint of dusk was upon them. Somewhat reluctantly, they got up and walked the path back to the car. Neither seemed ready to call it a night, even though Eva yawned one too many times.

"Come on. Let me get you back home."

"I guess my body is still readjusting from the night shift."

At her front door, Kidd feasted on a good-night kiss. She pushed him away, whispering, "Kidd, if you respect me, then say good night."

"Good night," he said, before sampling two more tastes of her sweet lips. Watching her lids flutter open, Kidd took a deep breath and reluctantly walked away. The only thing he could think of was naughty nights of immoral pleasure.

He needed a five-minute cooldown as though he'd been running on a treadmill. "Whew." Kidd wanted Eva, but more than anything, he wanted her respect. And he was determined to give it to her. Driving the short distance back to Parke's house, he reflected on the morning's sermon. Suddenly, he remembered it was Mother's Day.

Immediately, Kidd dialed his mother's number. While waiting for her to answer, his mind was still on the sermon. Eva's pastor did preach words that spoke to his heart, yet something held him back. He wasn't quite persuaded, and he didn't know how Eva was going to respond when he returned to their pew. But, to his relief, her acceptance of him for who he was spoke volumes. It was because of her and the sermon that he had asked for prayer.

After several rings, Sandra answered drowsily. "Hey, my firstborn, there you are. I didn't know if you'd forgotten about me."

"What do you mean? To the second most beautiful woman in the world, how could I? I know it's late, Ma, but you are the only mother I've got. I have a special gift for you today."

"I used to be your number one girl. Now you've put me in second place." Kidd could hear the mirth in her voice, as she cleared her throat. "I got the flowers yesterday. They are beautiful."

"That's not all. I went to church today and actually asked for prayer. Happy Mother's Day, part two."

"Praise God! Hallelujah! Thank You, Jesus!"

"I figured you would say that." Kidd chuckled.

"This is the first time you've called to tell me that you went to church. God is calling you, baby. Just yield to His will, so He can choose you. Many are called, but few are chosen. Live so He will choose you." Words spoken straight from a mother's heart.

They chatted a few more minutes and Kidd asked about Ace. His mother brought him up to date.

"Now what woman replaced me as number one?"

"Eva Savoy."

"I can't wait to meet her."

Chapter Twenty-Eight

*A*ngela Savoy thought it would be a great idea for Eva and Kidd to double date. Needless to say, she was pleased that her sister's relationship had slowly begun to flourish. Angela took the opportunity to invite them to a barbecue given by one of Lance's family members. Eva wasn't so sure.

It was held in a West County suburb where the lawns were sculptured like a botanical garden. Kidd wore a red T-shirt intended to show off the Adonis within him. Eva decided to don a matching top, and both sported tan shorts.

Kidd reminded Eva of a server, as he balanced their plates piled high with "a little of this and a little of that" from the buffet table. She followed him across the yard to two lounge chairs that seemed to be waiting for them under a large, weeping willow tree.

"Thanks for coming with me," Eva said. She rested their cups of sweet tea on a small table. After sitting down, she reached for her plate. Kidd handed it to her and took his seat beside her.

"I can't get enough of you, either at work or anywhere else. Lance doesn't seem so bad now that he knows I adore you."

Eva playfully scrunched her nose at him and then bowed her head. Silently, they blessed their food before digging in. "I seem to talk all the time about my family, which you've met, but you talk very little about yours. All I know is that you have a mother, father, and brother."

"No father."

She stopped nibbling. "I'm sorry. Is your father dead?"

"You're starting to learn my secrets," Kidd said between bites. He didn't miss a beat on his ribs.

Watching him devour his food, Eva laughed. Then she noticed almost a wounded expression appear on his face. "I'm sorry." Responding to his pain, she held her stomach.

"It's complicated, babe."

The endearment engulfed her. She took a few moments to enjoy the word off his lips. "I don't think any relationship could have been as complicated as that of my parents." She touched his knee to get his full attention.

Kidd wiped his mouth with his napkin and set his plate aside. He seemed ready to open up. "If you were a gambler, you would lose."

"Wrong. My parents were married, then divorced, then remarried."

"I would have never guessed." Kidd paused briefly to reflect on that. "Mine aren't together." His tone was final and not to be cross-examined. A hard edge that she hadn't seen in a while seemed to overpower him.

Eva shivered under his scowl. She reached for her cup of sweet tea and slowly sipped, racking her brain on how to regain the once jovial moments they had shared. Clearing her throat, she ventured to say, "Kidd, you're so closed about your past. You're shutting me out before you open the door. So tell me about your relatives here in St. Louis."

"The women cousins, I like. Their children, I love. The male cousins are a pain sometimes, often manipulative—and definitely add 'pests' to their description." He paused, as if to think of more to say.

"I need something from you. Promise me I'll get it." She couldn't help the pleading in her voice. It was as if a demon had set up shop and changed the atmosphere. Eva prayed silently before she continued, calling on God for help. She was determined to pull Kidd back.

"Give me a smile."

Kidd lifted a brow as his nostrils flared. He leaned closer and smiled before devouring her lips with a kiss sweeter than her sweet tea. There were no fireworks, as cartoons depict exuberance, but the mood did lighten considerably.

"Better?" he whispered.

"Yes." Eva smiled and he grinned. Stuffed, she leaned back on the lounger and watched the buzz of activity around them. Music filled the air. Several children splashed happily in an inflatable pool, and a few adults had converted the cobblestone patio into a dance floor. Everyone seemed to be having a good time.

"I know we agreed not to talk shop outside of work, but since we met at Garden Chateau, it would be nice to know what paths brought us to the nursing facility."

"My manipulative cousins—"

"Kidd, I have a hard time imagining anyone manipulating you."

"My cousins perfected the art. Thinking they're family detectives, they succeeded in tracking my brother and me down in Boston while doing some genealogy research. I came here on a dare, a challenge, or as a sucker, whichever applies."

She frowned. "That's sounds like your bio. You dare anyone to cross you, like Mr. Johnston. You challenge Theodore in ridiculous card games, and you're a sucker for Mrs. Valentine."

Kidd explained his move to St. Louis and his rejections of his cousins' job offers, which led to an ultimatum—an undercover bodyguard service for Mrs. Beacon.

"Does she know?"

"Are you kidding? Not too much gets by her. Plus, she said you mentioned my name once when you were in her room."

"So I spilled the beans without knowing it. When did you plan to tell me?" Eva was hurt. She thought he had been up front with her about everything, except his past.

"If we didn't stop bumping heads, the answer is never. But Eva, I have you now. And in order for me to keep you, you have to allow me to open up to you at my own pace. I'm combustive regarding my past and I don't want to explode on you. I thought I would have outgrown my bitterness and hate by now, but I'm dealing with it the best I can."

"The way you were talking at first, I thought you killed somebody," she joked, laughing.

Kidd cut his eyes at her. "If I saw him, I would do it in a heartbeat."

It didn't take long for word to get around the facility that she and Kidd had something going on. Eva didn't deny the rumors, but she didn't flaunt their relationship on the job either. Her coworkers as a whole seemed genuinely happy that she snagged the hunk of the century, as some referred to Kidd. Her friend Dawn was her biggest cheerleader. There were a few pockets of jealous women, but Eva treated them with more patience and kindness than normal.

Thankfully, she had no more problems working around Kidd by day. Beyond that, they could enjoy easy conversation—if she didn't mention certain subjects—over dinner at night. Something had to give about his taboo topics. Or else, how could they grow as a couple?

Eva did some soul-searching. She had to make a choice to be patient with him or walk away and come back once God restored him. Although she didn't hound him about a spiritual makeover, Kidd's need for salvation constantly stayed on her mind. After all, her heart was on the line. Love was on her heels, and Eva was trying to outrun it to keep it from catching her.

Without any prodding from her, Kidd showed up at her doorstep unannounced to accompany Eva to church a few more Sundays. Once, she caught a glimpse of him in his office reading the Bible and shaking his head. Either he didn't agree or didn't understand. He never asked her any questions about it, and she never mentioned it.

However, the "bad boy from Boston" persona didn't totally take a backseat. Some days, Kidd's good mood would turn sour. At those times, it was as if demons were escorting him when he had to interact with difficult residents like Mr. Johnston. Despite going to church, humility was at the bottom of his list. The good news was when he played cards with Theodore and won, Kidd did return Theodore's applesauce. *Thank God for small miracles,* Eva thought.

One Friday in June, before leaving work for a date with Kidd, Dawn stopped Eva. "I guess it's safe to say, not only will you be at the Habitat for Humanity site tomorrow, but I assume your bodyguard will be there too."

"I don't know. I haven't asked him."

"You don't need to. If you want me there, I'll be there," Kidd answered, coming up from behind her. "Hey, Dawn."

"Told ya," Dawn teased, as she walked away.

Very early Saturday morning, Eva and Kidd met Dawn at the designated property in Old North St. Louis. It was minutes from downtown, and it was the Habitat's sixteenth of the seventeen homes planned for the year.

Years ago, Dawn had talked Eva into getting involved in Habitat for Humanity's five-day "Give Thanks Blitz Build." Because it was held around Thanksgiving, the biting wind proved too much for Dawn. Despite the coldness in the air, she stayed true to her image and tried to dress cute.

That being said, Dawn wouldn't let something like inclement weather stop her. She never missed an opportunity in her quest to scout out for good men. Gratified after their first act of volunteerism, she and Eva both returned the following year.

This time, they chose to be part of the spring crew. "What better place than where hammers pound and muscles ripple." Those had been Dawn's exact words. She would have no problem making a love connection in a work environment. The irony is that Eva had found Kidd at work—right under Dawn's nose. Eva couldn't help but smile when she thought about that.

As the project nurse on site, Dawn would be in her element. She was ready to administer aid whenever a crew member got a scrape, especially if a male worker suffered a nasty cut. On the other hand, Eva was content with painting and doing other manual labor.

Kidd proved he wasn't a slacker. He teamed up with other men who were lifting lumber and working on roof repairs. Hours later when the crew called it quits, the structure was complete. The only remaining tasks were some cosmetic enhancements and touchup work.

"Since we're in the area, do you want to eat at Crown Kitchen?" Eva asked Kidd. Walking back to the car, she leaned against him. She was exhausted and thankful that he was there to support her. "It's a neighborhood landmark corner store, and they're usually packed."

"Baby, if that's what you crave, then I'll get it for you."

Actually, she craved him and his salvation, but she thought it wise to keep those requests close to her heart.

Officially called Crown Candy Kitchen, the establishment was considered to be one of the oldest operating soda fountains in the country. These days, descendants of the two Greek immigrants who started the business kept it going.

The neighborhood around the place had been deteriorating for years, but with its proximity to the revitalization of downtown, rehabbers and investors swarmed into the area. In addition, thanks to Habitat for Humanity's efforts, low-income families were able to start anew in the longtime Black section of the city.

"I can't remember the last time I had one of their signature handmade malts," Eva rambled, as they got in the car and clicked their seat belts. She turned in her seat to give him directions as he drove off.

"Hey, this place has its own little customer challenge."

"Let's hear it."

"If a person can drink five twenty-four-ounce malts within thirty minutes, their name will be inscribed on a plaque displayed in the store. Even Adam Richman, the host of that crazy show *Man v. Food,* was there a few years ago."

"How did he do?" Kidd smirked.

"His best was downing four malts. Only thirty folks have done it in almost one hundred years. Want to give it a try?" she teased.

"Woman, not even to impress you, am I that crazy."

Chapter Twenty-Nine

On Sunday, Kidd bowed out of going to church. "This old man needs some rest." He telephoned Eva early that morning.

She laughed. "You said it, not me, but I understand." Her muscles were still sore too. "Thanks for letting me know."

"Disappointed?"

"Not really." And she wasn't. His commitment was to God, not her. "But I'd better get up now, so I can be there on time."

"I know something must be aching on that pretty body of yours. I can't believe you can still move."

"Believe me, I'm sore, but I learned a long time ago that, when it comes to God, if I don't stay on a 'praying, church-going, and fasting' schedule, it's easier to get offtrack than to get back on."

They chatted a few more minutes before she hurried off the phone. After church, Eva enjoyed dinner at her parents' home. It was a good thing he wasn't with her because every other word at the table was about Kidd. When Eva expressed her concern about Kidd's salvation progress, both her parents counseled her to be prayerful and patient.

The following week proved to be chaotic at the facility. Kidd was busy putting out fires involving residents' complaints. When a couple of staff members called in sick, Eva was called upon to work extra hours. Although their bench getaways were few, they did enjoy the short and sweet texts that bounced between them.

When the weekend arrived, it was the first time they hadn't made any plans. Eva was looking forward to a lazy Saturday at home when Dawn called.

"What do you and Mr. Fine have going on today?"

"After last weekend and the rough week I just had? Humph, I have nothing planned. No, I take that back. My plan is to do absolutely nothing," she answered, saluting an invisible partner and then taking a sip of her freshly mixed limeade. Minutes earlier, she'd put together a cheese ball, cut up a few veggies, and grabbed some crackers.

Eva eyed her hideaway. The balcony was the perk that sold her on the condo. All morning, it had enticed her to come out and lounge. The birds were on standby, waiting to perform a musical extravaganza. The sun was cued to bathe her in its warmth, while the tree branches were poised to stir a soft breeze.

"What? You and Kidd aren't attached at the hip today?" Dawn teased.

"As a matter of fact, we both decided to relax." Eva grabbed her plate of goodies and headed toward the sliding door.

"Well, if your man told you to rest, then enjoy your day." She chuckled. "See you on Monday." They disconnected.

Eva didn't mind embracing boredom, laziness, and bumming around on a Saturday. She welcomed the downtime after recently enduring another hard semester and fulfilling her yearly pledge with Habitat for Humanity. It was normal for her body to take some time to rebound after a home-building marathon. The previous weekend's back-breaking tasks seemed especially exhausting.

She guessed there was some advantage of working with the man she dated. Eva had just seen Kidd the previous day. And although she had no complaints concerning his attentiveness or attention, she yearned for his closer walk with God. That was the only way to expel his demons and get him on the right track.

The phone rang again just as she turned back to retrieve her glass of limeade. This time Angela's number popped up. "Hey, there are several Juneteenth celebrations going on throughout the city today and tomorrow. Downtown seems to have the biggest one at the Old Courtroom and the Scott Joplin House. I figured you and Kidd would want to go."

Priding herself on keeping abreast of cultural events in St. Louis, Eva couldn't believe she had overlooked the day that grass-root groups across the nation set aside so that no one would forget the dark past of American history.

"Just think, before long, we'll commemorate the 150th year after the last group of African Americans were freed from slavery," Angela reminded her.

Stepping outside, Eva situated her treats on the glass tabletop. With the cordless still squeezed between her ear and shoulder, she closed the screen door and settled in her wicker recliner. Eva blessed her snack with a quick prayer and nodded in silent agreement with her sister. She then shoved a cracker, topped with plenty of dip, in her mouth, without bothering to smother the crunch in her sister's ear.

"Then, if we add in the Jim Crow laws after that—up until the Civil Rights Era— Blacks have barely enjoyed true freedom for fifty years," Angela rambled on. "We've still got a long way to go."

"Hmmm, you're right about that. But we won't be going today. Maybe I can get Kidd to go with me after church tomorrow."

"Tomorrow? The good stuff happens today," Angela whined. Still, she failed to convince Eva to reconsider before they disconnected.

In the past, Angela would have never let Eva get away with turning down her invitation to go somewhere with her and Lance. She seemed to have only backed down since Kidd entered Eva's life.

Most folks assumed that single women liked to stay busy because it would keep their minds off of their singleness. Eva disagreed with that philosophy. She considered singleness as a season to enjoy like all of God's other seasons.

Finishing her snack, she headed back inside for seconds. Anything mixed with cream cheese was her weakness. Kidd found that out from her obsession with crab rangoon.

Eva huffed when the phone rang—again. It seemed like the whole world knew her whereabouts. Checking the call ID, she was quickly becoming annoyed. A day of rest was supposed to be just that, a day to rest. She should have disconnected the phone.

"Yes, Dawn?"

"Put your day of rest on hold, girlfriend," Dawn said excitedly. "The Kappas and Omegas are playing in a fraternity softball tournament to benefit the Mathews-Dickey Boys' and Girls' Clubs scholarship fund. You know, it's all about the children."

Eva twisted her mouth. "Right, children this weekend and another worthy cause the next. Aren't you still sore from last weekend's house project?"

"Nope. Since I hooked you up with Kidd, the least—"

Eva lifted her hand in the air, as if Dawn were standing in front of her. "I met Kidd at work. How are you crediting yourself with the hookup?"

"Humph! I kept the other females in check and their claws away from Kidd. I think that makes me an accessory to prevent the perfect crime of snagging someone. After he didn't seem interested in me, which is unusual I might add, I watched him. Without interfering, I knew it was just a matter of time before you realized the man was interested in you—credit taken." Dawn created her own sound effects to indicate she had scored a point. "I don't think Kidd would mind if you go."

"I'll pass, Dawn. Stop calling me—" Before she could hang up, Eva's phone beeped and she groaned. When Kidd's number showed up on the caller ID, she smiled. Her tone instantly changed. "Got to go! Bye.

"Hello?"

"Am I disturbing your rest?"

Eva grabbed her plate and walked back out to the patio. "You?—never. Dawn and my sister—most definitely. That was Dawn calling for the second time, wanting me to go to a charity event with her today."

"Another one? When does the woman sleep?"

"Probably on the job. Just teasing." But Eva did wonder. "Plus, Angela invited me to a Juneteenth celebration downtown, but—"

"That's why I was calling. My cousin was trying to talk me into the same event. He makes it sound like an exhibit not to be missed. If you want to go for a little while, we can, or if you'd rather stay in, I won't be upset. We could cook something together and sit at your table for two."

Her heart warmed at how easily their relationship seemed to be developing. Eva looked at her dip, limeade, and the birds perched in the trees outside her balcony.

"What time will you pick me up?"

Chapter Thirty

Kidd didn't offer Eva a verbal greeting when she opened her door a few hours later. He swiftly wrapped his arms around her waist and dragged her closer. Then he hugged her as if they hadn't seen each other in years instead of the previous day at work.

He kissed her until he gasped for air.

"You do that to me."

She reached up and wiped her lipstick off his lips, while he kissed the tips of her fingers in the process. Once Eva gathered up her purse and keys, she locked the door behind her. Kidd escorted her to the car. Along the way, he relished the moment to admire her figure and enjoy the breeze that stirred up her perfume and the hem of her sundress.

With their seat belts fastened, Kidd lifted her hand to his mouth and kissed it. He didn't let go as he drove off. "You'll meet my cousins down there. You know, the other women. Thank you for trusting me on that." He watched the sun rays play in her hair. She looked so dainty in a sundress and comfortable-looking sandals that showcased her beautiful feet. Red polish on her toes—he loved it!

Gritting her teeth, Eva turned away and looked out the window. "Yeah, the 'other woman' thing; it was a defining moment. I wanted to trust you with my heart, but the woman in me wanted their numbers. Put yourself in my shoes, what would you have done? Hmmm?"

"Me? I would have confronted you and then taken care of the competition," Kidd said. It was a no-brainer to him. Checking his rearview mirror, he exited on I-270 and headed west to I-70 downtown.

"Right. Sounds good on paper, but from my point of view, I was afraid you would lie to me."

Their banter was light until Kidd finally said, "Baby, I see your point, but like I told you, I'm true to myself. My philandering father is not my role model." Soon he was going to have to explain to her what he meant by that.

The drive downtown was less than a half hour away. Kidd got off on Memorial Drive and parked on a side street. Hand in hand, they mingled within the crowd and strolled toward Keiner Plaza.

The entertainment was already under way. A reenactment of Major General Gordon Granger leading the Colored Troops as they arrived in Galveston captured their attention. The actors were outfitted in authentic Civil War uniforms and appeared to take their roles seriously. Opening a rolled parchment, the man portraying the major read aloud Executive Order 3:

"The people of Texas are informed that in accordance with a Proclamation from the Executive of the United States, all slaves are free. This involves an absolute equality of rights and rights of property between former masters and slaves, and the connection heretofore existing between them becomes that between employer and free laborer."

The words enraged Kidd. "It took a law to free enslaved people." He twisted his mouth in disgust. It was a good thing that textbooks withheld a lot of the truth when he was in school. At the time, Kidd doubted whether he could restrain himself from retaliating against anyone who appeared to be White.

I fulfilled the law and you now live under My grace, God spoke swiftly.

Kidd frowned. *But what about the past?* he questioned God. Black people were captured and enslaved. Fast-forward a hundred years, and they were still oppressed. Kidd just didn't see a correlation between God and His benefits for Black people.

The enslaved actors shouted in jubilation; most ran into the audience as a route of escape. A few others stayed behind, wide-eyed and bewildered about what it meant to be free. Kidd became disgusted with their seeming stupidity.

Without knowledge, My people perish. God revisited Kidd.

Frustrated, Kidd didn't know if he could ever make sense of God's cryptic messages.

"Cousin Uncle! Cousin Uncle!" Kami yelled from a distance. Excited to see Kidd, she broke away from her family and raced toward him. Crashing into him, she hugged him tight around the waist. The look of contentment on her face was touching until she glanced at Eva. Still clinging to Kidd, Kami shot Eva a suspicious glare.

Kidd lifted Kami off her feet and smacked a noisy kiss on her cheek. It only took a minute for him to remember what Cheney had said, when he noticed Kami hadn't taken her eyes off Eva. He took his time and placed her back on the ground.

"This is Miss Savoy." Kidd was on guard, prepared to react to whatever Kami might have up her sleeve. "And this is Kami, my little cousin."

"It's nice to meet you," Eva said, as she bent to Kami's eye level.

"Are you my cousin uncle's girlfriend?"

"Yes, she is," Kidd answered for Eva.

"Oh." She twisted her lips, thinking. "Well, I'm his favorite girl because I got flowers. If you're his girlfriend, then he'll give you flowers."

"I'm glad I got flowers without being his sweetheart." Imani added her two cents when she strolled up behind the Jamiesons.

"That's enough, motormouth," Kidd ordered and playfully pulled on Kami's ponytail. After hearing Cheney mention that Imani had been through a rough marriage, Kidd toned down his retorts to her instigating remarks. He even went a step further when he included her as one of his recipients of flowers for Mother's Day. Kidd understood all too well about hardships.

"You can be his girlfriend because you're pretty," Kami told Eva.

"Well, thank you. I'm glad she meets your approval." Kidd chuckled, watching Eva blush.

"Hmmm." Kami shook her head animatedly. "Grandma BB says I should always tell it like it is, and I'm telling it like it is," Kami said in a grownup tone and attitude to go with it.

Eva's eyes sparkled. "I know your Grandma BB. She's a funny lady."

"And a strange one too," Kidd mumbled. Eva cut her eyes at him.

"I miss my grandma. I'll be glad when she comes home," Kami said, pouting.

"We will too," Parke said, speaking for the first time. He seemed impatient, waiting for an introduction.

"Eva, I want you to meet my cousins, Parke Jamieson and his wife, Cheney."

"Hello."

Cheney reached out and hugged Eva. Next, Hallison introduced herself and gave Eva a hug. Almost immediately, the women broke off into a personal discussion.

"Eva, it's nice to meet you. If you ever want to know something about a Jamieson man, my sister-in-law and I can fill you in." Cheney laughed.

"Thanks." Eva smiled politely, not sure how to respond to Cheney. Changing the subject, she added, "You look familiar. What church do you attend?"

"Faith Miracle Church on Highway 67."

"My church fellowshipped with yours . . ."

Oh no. There'll be no church talk on my time, he thought to himself. Kidd wasn't about to be pushed to the sidelines. "Okay ladies, I would like to spend time with my date."

"Oh, sure. Not a problem. We'll exchange numbers," Hallison said, as the three started digging in their purses for their cell phones.

Parke shrugged. "Get used to it, man. I did. When women want to get together, we can't stop them."

Kidd unfortunately had to wait while Eva tapped the numbers into her phone. Then he finished the rest of the introductions.

"These are their other brats: Pace, the oldest, and Paden, the baby. That's a mouthful." Kidd turned. "And this is Malcolm, Parke's brother and Hali's husband, and their little boy, MJ." He tilted his head. "And somehow Imani Segall is part of the family. She's also Mrs. Beacon's neighbor."

"Watch it. My number of repossessions is down for the month," Imani warned through a pasted smile. Imani never joked about her job.

"We're getting ready to explore the music venues, want to join us?" Parke invited them.

"We left home in separate cars for a reason," Kidd reminded his cousin, then looping Eva's arm through his, he proceeded to walk away. "Thanks, but we can do our own exploring."

"They seem nice. So those are your other women, huh? They're beautiful." She shoved him playfully. "The similarities between Parke and his brother are striking. You all have some good genes."

"But I'm the best looking."

"You'll get no argument from me. They don't seem manipulative to me." She elbowed him. "That's nice of them to invite you into their home. I'm sure you've enjoyed the family bonding."

"Not at all when I first arrived . . . and even still, sometimes. I was ready to move back home until they talked me into the Garden Chateau gig. You stole my heart the moment I laid eyes on you. You're like a sweet fruit that I want in my lunch box every day."

When her eyes misted, Kidd reached for her hand and squeezed it. "I'm glad you decided to stay. So," she took a deep breath, "how are you all related to each other? Brothers' sons?"

"Nope. It's a long story," Kidd replied. He wondered when it would be a good time to release the fire from the dragon demon within him. It surfaced whenever he thought about Samuel Jamieson.

Eva pressed him. "Think of it as feeding me nourishment, a little at a time. We can take small steps, and you can tell me the whole story over time." She gave him a smile that made him want to release a floodgate of his life's history.

Holding his head back, he closed his eyes and counted to three. Kidd didn't want Eva to witness his rage. "I already told you my parents weren't together. I left out the fact that they were never married. I usually omit that tidbit, not wanting to bring judgment on my mother, who is as sweet as pie. I hate him for that. I can't help it. I grew up with a little boy's memory of his absent father. Although I had friends without fathers in their lives, I wanted a father in my home like some of the other boys I knew. When I later learned that Samuel Jamieson had two other families and us—his illegitimate children—I hated him even more."

She gasped. Shaking her head, Eva yanked her hand from his and covered her mouth. "I'm so sorry."

"I'm a man's man. I don't expect pity, neither do I accept it." He didn't give her the slightest glance, as he stared straight ahead. Then Kidd lifted his shoulders and rolled his neck. He squeezed his fists so tight, his muscles flexed.

"He's to blame for everything wrong in my life. Now I believe my younger brother is on a path to break Samuel's record with his outlandish activities. I hate my father for my brother's behavior. I hate my father, period."

The more Kidd confessed, the more rage swelled inside him. He had to stop before he exploded.

"That explains your hard edge," Eva whispered in a cautious tone.

"And my edge is sharp too. I don't let people run over me, or my family, or you. Samuel Jamieson ruined my life from the cradle."

"But Jesus saved your life when He rose up from the grave."

Chapter Thirty-One

*E*va's heart ached for Kidd. Where was the man who picked her up at her doorstep hours earlier with a smile, a kiss, and a hug? Where was the man who had gone to church with her, asked for prayer, and whom she had even caught reading his Bible?

Eva had been privy to his moods; she had seen him angry. She also knew he was kindhearted. But this accelerated rage was frightening and she had to be bold.

"Kidd, something wants to destroy you, and that scares me. Not physical destruction by a knife, a gun, or poison. Your inner turmoil and your own hatred will take you down. God has already defeated the devil. The only thing you need to do is cross over to the other side—Jesus is waiting for you."

Eva paused to take a breath and gather more courage. "It's obvious to me, there's a spiritual battle going on in your life. I don't think you would try and defeat an entire gang by yourself if they attempted to gun you down in the streets. Why wouldn't you allow God to send His gang of angels to fight your spiritual battle? Kidd, you can't do this alone."

His steps slowed, but never stopped. He frowned.

God, what is he thinking? she wondered. Attending Juneteenth was definitely a bad idea. He couldn't handle his personal past. He surely wasn't ready for the haunting of slavery.

"You know I've been going to church, but I don't think it's kicked in yet. I just seem to snap."

"Oh, Kevin, you need Jesus in every facet of your life. You're so close to your salvation. You've passed the first base; don't let the devil call you out at second base. You've got to get to home plate."

"God knows I'm trying, but this is where we differ, babe. God wants me to turn the other cheek. I wouldn't be a man if I did that. I'll pray, read my Bible, and go to church, but there comes a time when a person shouldn't bother God with pettiness."

She began to silently pray. *Father, in the name of Jesus, I come boldly to Your throne of grace because You warned us that the devil comes to steal, kill, and destroy. Jesus, I'm asking You to command the devil to remove Kevin from his hit list. Lord, please restore all that the devil has stolen from Kevin. In Jesus' name. Amen.*

His voice softened. "I told you I had dark secrets, and you're still with me despite that. Eva, what I want from you . . . is your love." He paused. "Just so we're clear. I didn't stutter—I want your love. I know it's too early in our relationship to expect it, but I plan to earn your love."

Eva blinked. Confusion clouded her mind. Kidd went from hot to cold in one setting. She wasn't prepared for any of what she experienced thus far today. She wondered if Jesus was jealous. What Kidd wanted from her, God wanted from Kidd.

She didn't even realize that a tear had escaped, and she hoped the evidence of her emotions went unnoticed. But nothing seemed to get past Kidd. Abruptly, he stopped in the crowd, causing others to go around them. Cupping her face, he gently took his finger and brushed away another tear rolling down her cheek.

Was this the part in a novel where the heroine confessed her love and the fairy tale ended happily ever after? At the moment, she was on a nightmare of a date with Kidd, and he had the nerve to talk about something as romantic as love. She couldn't respond to him. Eva was still working through her own feelings. She wanted to love him, but not in his present spiritual state.

Her head moved toward his face unwillingly, as she stared into his eyes. He tapped one more kiss on her lips. Grabbing her hand, he tugged her along to the next booth. It exhibited a replica of a story printed in *The Colored American* newspaper. The article was entitled, "Fine Me to Free a Slave." Silently, they began to read.

Socialite, Mrs. Clara Middleton, defied authorities who wanted to search her dwelling for a girl child slave belonging to Mr. Henry Bogan. Confident that Sally would not be found, Mrs. Middleton took her seat in the parlor and sipped from her cup as the troops searched each room. Disappointed when they found nothing, officers confronted Mrs. Middleton about her being seen with a Negro girl in her presence. She boasted her opinion of the disgrace of the institution of human cargo and taunted them to fine her. The woman's family . . .

"Mrs. Middleton risked her life," Kidd whispered, as if he didn't believe it. "What would have happened if the little girl was found— like Anne Frank? They would have killed her. The article said she was sick with a bad cough."

"God always has good people to be a light in the midst of darkness. We can't assume every White person's ancestors were slaveholders. That would be to misjudge them. Some risked their lives and were outspoken advocates of freedom."

She glanced at the date of the publication, 1840. "It was more than twenty years before slavery officially ended on paper, but not in the hearts of many slaveholders. Black people were the root of their wealth. They couldn't buy anything without us."

"That's right." Parke's voice came out of nowhere. It was deep and strong, but Kidd's baritone held the authority when he spoke.

Eva jumped.

"I'm sorry. I didn't mean to startle you. We saw you as we were heading this way," Parke said, with his family in tow.

"Anything related to Black history, they seem to know. The baby's first diaper was probably tattooed with their ancestral chart, instead of cartoon characters," said Kidd.

Right. Eva didn't believe him.

"Pay my cousin no mind. Paden will know his family tree before he starts preschool, that's for sure. He didn't learn it from the cradle, as Kidd implies."

"See what I mean?" Kidd smirked. "So what's your commentary on this, because I know you have one?" He folded his arms and waited.

Parke shrugged. "Slavery was big business, and the capture of runaways yielded a hefty reward. Officers of the law could receive a bonus if our ancestors were apprehended. Even for wealthy people like Mrs. Middleton, a thousand-dollar fine for breaking the law back then wasn't pocket change. A person had to really love Jesus to stand up for what was right. I can't remember where I read it, but by the middle of the nineteenth century, more than fifty thousand enslaved people had escaped from the South."

"I do." His cute little daughter chimed. "That was in our game Runaway. Remember, Daddy?" She smiled.

Parke winked and the girl glowed with the silent praise.

"You're slippin', old man, when your daughter has to help you," Kidd taunted Parke, who grinned.

Eva was fascinated. These Jamiesons seemed to know their dreadful historical facts, yet their reaction was nothing like Kidd's. She didn't care how Kidd had characterized them; his cousins were good for him.

Parke continued, "Remember, enslaved people were the blue chips on Wall Street. The more plantation owners harshly treated laborers and forced them to run away, the greater their losses. There was already a Fugitive Slave Act from the late 1700s, but Northerners defied honoring it and were on the side of the fugitive slaves. But somehow in 1850, slaveholders managed to persuade Congress to pass another sinister Fugitive Slave Act.

"This time around, it was different. The law basically held everybody accountable for the recapture of slaves. If federal marshals didn't arrest an alleged runaway slave, they could be fined a thousand dollars. If citizens assisted alleged escapees with shelter, food, or anything, they could spend six months in prison and also be fined a thousand dollars."

Eva was impressed with Parke's knowledge, but it was his calm demeanor that earned him her respect. Briefly, she wished Kidd could be like his cousin, then immediately chided herself. There was a reason God gave everyone unique DNA.

"Dad, I have to use the bathroom," the oldest son said, interrupting his father.

"Me too," the toddler mimicked, as his hands flew to the front of his pants.

"C'mon, Parke. We'd better find a Johnny on the Spot. I warned you about giving Paden that second cup of water. You forgot he has only been potty trained for a month," Cheney scolded her husband to Eva's amusement. She waved bye again to Cheney, Hallison, and their friend. Eva couldn't wait to get together with them for lunch or something.

Instantly, Eva experienced an epiphany moment. She realized how much she wanted a family—children, good-looking husband, and all. As the group scurried away from them, she chanced a look at Kidd. He already had his eyes on her.

Wrinkling her nose, she playfully slapped her hand on his chest.

"Don't hurt yourself," he teased and then gave her a grin that implied everything was all right in his world. Eva was pulling for Parke to be instrumental in converting Kidd's stony heart. Admittedly, it was

246

going to take a village to help Kidd on his road to Salvation Lane.

All of a sudden, loud voices in the background drew their attention. Eva and Kidd looked in the direction of the Old Courthouse. A small group had formed near Broadway and Market where another skit was under way.

"My fight for freedom started here on these steps in 1847 . . ." the actor, dressed in period clothing, proclaimed to the crowd. "I tried to buy me and my wife's freedom from the widow of my master, but she turned me down."

"Dred Scott," Eva mumbled. That much she knew, since his account took place on the very steps where the enactment was taking place. Plus, some of his descendants remained in St. Louis. Whenever she thought about the Dred Scott case, Eva always marveled at the enslaved man's fearlessness to challenge the law where a Black man, enslaved or free, was invisible.

"He was my kind of man—a pit bull when it came to being free," Kidd said.

Eva leaned into him. "On a physical level, Dred Scott had the audacity to be a pioneer. The odds were stacked against him. My sister is a history teacher. She said that in a slave state, Dred wasn't considered a citizen or even a full person—only three-fourths of a man—but God touched the hearts of some White men to pay his legal fees." Eva smiled a knowing smile. "See, Dred Scott was no fool. He didn't let pride keep him from taking a handout to get what he had the right to have."

"It seems Garden Chateau was my handout."

"And we both were blessed because you took it. Kevin, there's one thing I've learned about you. You have a kind heart and a thick head. You may think you were coming to the facility to help Parke, but God had other plans. And what did I get out of the deal? I'm blessed with a good, strong Black man."

Kidd lifted her chin and brushed a kiss on her lips. "You have no regrets? Even after you've learned some of my secrets . . . ?"

"Oh yeah, and I've seen some little demons come out tonight, but I also saw angels coming to your rescue. I'm serving the devil notice. He's going down."

Kidd's eyes sparkled and he grinned. "You're lethal when you get mad. The devil better be scared."

Chapter Thirty-Two

*"Y*ou haven't gone to church with me since before Juneteenth," Eva stated. Kidd sat next to her on their favorite bench in front of the fountain at work. It was one Friday afternoon and the day had been hectic.

"That exhibit a week ago really disturbed me." He couldn't even read his Bible, but he wasn't going to tell Eva that. "I didn't want to walk in church, full of fight. I know that's not right."

"It is what it is. We can't change history, but the Bible says the truth will make us free. And God's Word isn't talking about physical slavery. It's spiritual bondage. Besides, my dad has been asking about you."

Kidd was thoughtful for a few minutes. "Consider it done. How about I take my girl out to dinner tomorrow night and pick you up for church Sunday morning?"

"I would like that. Kevin, you told me a while back that you were trying. Don't stop now." Eva stood and attempted to tug Kidd to his feet. "We'd better get back inside."

Kidd huffed. Eva made him feel carefree. "Do we have to?"

"If we want a paycheck, yes."

On Sunday morning, Kidd went through the motions of getting dressed, eating breakfast, and greeting his family before they headed off to church. On his drive to Eva's condo, he admitted it to himself. He couldn't shake the past—what his father had done to his family or what Blacks had suffered under the hands of a cruel White society.

He just couldn't see Jesus, the Commander in Chief, allowing His troops to suffer unfairly. By the time Kidd arrived at Eva's doorstep, he was emotionally drained from his internal battle.

Her smile and bright eyes greeted him. She seemed to read his moods and know when he needed her hug. When she wrapped her arms around him, Kidd held on tight.

The drive to church was surreal. He was almost mesmerized, as Eva rested her head on his shoulder and hummed a song he had never heard before. Once they were seated in the pew next to her family, Kidd began to shut out the singing. That wasn't like him; he didn't know what was coming over him.

The day you hear My Voice, harden not your heart, God spoke Hebrews 3:15.

Kidd shuddered. Eva touched his thigh. "Are you okay?" Concern and love shone in her eyes.

He could only smile. For the first time in his life, he didn't know the answer.

After the choir finished a song that Kidd couldn't even remember them singing, the pastor walked up to the pulpit.

"Church, it's time for a celebration," Elder Taylor began. "I'm not just talking about the Fourth of July, which is days away. I'm talking about your spiritual freedom."

Eva and several other people in the audience shouted, "Amen!"

"Please turn your Bibles to Galatians, fourth chapter. Verse 28 states we are the children of promise. Now let us read verses 30 and 31: *'Get rid of the slave woman and her son, for the slave woman's son will never share in the inheritance with the free woman's son. Therefore, brothers and sisters, we are not children of the slave woman, but of the free woman.'*

"Finally, verse 1 in chapter 5 reads, *'It is for freedom that Christ has set us free. Stand firm, then, and do not let yourselves be burdened again by a yoke of slavery.'* If you believe this, your life will change instantly because you will live these sacred words. But God knows you cannot confess and live it without a struggle in your flesh. That is why He sent the Holy Ghost. It's like the smoking gun, ready to aim and fire at the enemy on your behalf. As our nation celebrates its physical freedom, let us celebrate and rejoice in a liberty that is everlasting . . ."

Surprisingly, Kidd's heart began to soften, and he wondered what had overpowered him weeks earlier. Maybe he could walk this walk, he reasoned with himself. When the altar call began, Kidd debated if he should go down for prayer. *Take more time to consider this. Don't get caught up in the moment,* an opposing voice reasoned with him. Kidd didn't budge.

After the service, Eva's father pulled him aside. "Haven't seen you in a while. I'm glad you came today."

"Me too."

"That's good to know because Eva's been concerned about you. Kidd, I'm saying this as a man in love. I don't care how strong her feelings are for you, if you don't reconcile your hang-ups and stop holding out on Christ, she'll grow weary and walk away. . . . A word to the wise, son," Kenneth said, patting his back a few times. Then after he looked around and found his wife, they walked out of the sanctuary.

Chapter Thirty-Three

Sunday's sermon stayed with Kidd all week, but Kenneth's words haunted him every night. He wanted to tell God to leave Eva out of this, because it was between him and the Lord—but something held him back.

At long last, Kidd made up his mind. He was ready to trade in his old ways of hate and hostility for temperance. No longer did he want to be the bad guy and handle problems his way. Something inside of him made him realize he was getting too old for this bitterness.

"Yeah." He bit his lip, nodding his head up and down. "I'm ready for a change," he mumbled, as he climbed into bed one night. When God got through with him, he may not even recognize himself.

The next day at work, Kidd sat in his office, listening intently on the phone when Parke called him. Concerned about a suspicious "situation" at Mrs. Beacon's house, Parke shared his thoughts with his cousin.

"And the guy says he's Grandma BB's nephew, Bay-Bay, huh?" repeated Kidd.

"You know, Imani's been watching Grandma BB's house while

she's at the facility. She says he looks like he's up to no good, but then again, she says that about every man. I'm leaving work in a few minutes to head home and check into it."

"I'll talk to Grandma BB and meet you there."

Kidd quickly reconsidered that move. He didn't have to talk to Mrs. Beacon to know something wasn't right. "On second thought, no need to worry her. I have no problem handling this so-called nephew. I've got a Missouri license to conceal and carry. It's about to be 'show time.' Not at the Apollo, but in Ferguson, Missouri," he told Parke.

"No, cuz. Let the police handle it. I had to talk that nonsense out of Imani. She wanted to get in her repo truck and mow him down, or shoot and ask questions later." Parke sighed. "I'm so glad my wife doesn't have a gun. Grandma BB and Imani are trigger happy enough for the whole family."

Kidd tapped his desk with a pen, mumbling, "And she's a professional."

"Let's see if he shows up again," Parke advised.

"Let's not. Why wait for him to show up again—because he *will* show up again. I say, let's be proactive and go looking for this dude."

"He could be legit," Parke argued, but sounded doubtful.

"There are too many chances connected with *could*." Kidd didn't have time for this. "What's Imani's number?"

"Cuz—"

"Just give me her number, Parke." Kidd didn't play games. And he wouldn't allow anyone to mess with anyone he remotely cared about, especially a stroke-stricken old lady. However, her recovery was much improved, thanks to her therapies.

Eva appeared in his doorway as he punched in the last digit to reach Imani. "One minute," he mouthed.

"I'll be back," she whispered and blew him an air kiss.

Kidd was watching Eva's retreat. He didn't realize Imani had answered, until she screamed hello in his ear.

"Ah, Imani. Kidd. What's going on?"

"Well, this guy—"

"The condensed version," he said. Softening his tone, he added, "please."

She huffed. "Okay," she said with a heavy groan. "This man had trouble written all over him—from the sole of his shoes all the way up to his forehead. And wearing Stacy Adams don't qualify him as Grandma's kin. Plus, that old school Cadillac isn't helping his image either . . ."

As he listened to Imani finish her description of the man, Kidd wondered, *What's the story behind those men's shoes, anyway?* "Parke could be right. First things first. I'd better talk to Grandma BB and get back to you. Call me if the guy comes around again today." Kidd recited his number.

He had barely placated Imani when he disconnected and headed down the hall to Mrs. Beacon's suite. Kidd needed to find out her reaction to this shady person.

"Hi, Adam," Mrs. Valentine greeted him, before he could knock.

"Hello, Mrs. Valentine. Where is Mrs. Beacon—Grandma BB?"

"In therapy." She waved him in. "Got time for a story?"

No. "Ah, I'll be back." Kidd spun around and walked swiftly to the recreational center. Mrs. Beacon could be seen through the large glass walls as the therapist worked tirelessly to challenge her.

Kidd waited impatiently for twenty minutes, folding his arms and unfolding them. As he began to pace, he wondered if the physical therapist was stretching her treatment because he suspected Kidd wanted him to hurry up.

Soon enough, Mrs. Beacon was helped into her wheelchair. Although in a hurry, Kidd entered the room as casual as possible. "I'll take her back, William."

"Sure." The man shrugged, then gave his attention to another resident who was waiting for his turn.

Kidd hadn't even cleared the door when Mrs. Beacon squinted at him. "What's going on with you, Kiddo?"

"What makes you think something's wrong?" he asked, scouting out a private corner for them to talk.

"Probably because I wasn't born a minute before you came to escort me from therapy for the very first time." She paused, and then continued slowly with a hint of a slur. "And since my room is in the opposite direction, that's a clue too. Didn't know I was that smart, did you?"

Stopping in front of a window with a view of the miniature petting zoo, Kidd locked her wheels. He sat on a cushioned bench to face her, clasped his hands, and cracked his knuckles.

"Okay. This is what's going down. There's a guy trying to get in your house. He's calling himself your nephew, Bay-Bay." *Stupid name.* What grown man went by the name Bay-Bay? "And he's wearing Stacy Adams shoes like you." Kidd had to ask, "What's with those shoes?" Before allowing her to answer, he finished his report with the news, "Imani is ready to shoot him."

"Let her." Mrs. Beacon seemed calm, almost unconcerned. "Tell her to give him her best shot—literally. I wouldn't miss. Shoot, I target practiced on Cheney's dad."

"Yeah, I heard that. Why would you try and kill your friend's—adopted granddaughter's—father? Now that is pure wrong."

"Stop your whining," she said with a faint slur. "Dr. Reynolds is sitting in jail, where he should be."

"We're getting off track. Do you know this Bay-Bay person or not?"

Mrs. Beacon slightly moved her hand that was affected by the stroke, as if she wanted to tap her fingers. "I remember accepting a friend request from a Bay-Bay on Facebook."

"Facebook!" Kidd shook his head. "And parents worry about their children getting in trouble on the Internet. How many friends do you have on that thing?"

"At last count, two thousand. The requirement to be in my circle of friends is having the latest pair of my favorite shoes. If a person has more than one pair, he's a gold member of my Stacy Adams fan club." She frowned. "Why does he want to get into my house?"

Kidd huffed and rubbed the back of his neck. "Glad you're now concerned. What have I been trying to tell you for the past fifteen or so minutes?" Evidently, she had a bout of memory loss.

"I need to get up out of here. I know that." She gripped the chair's arm rests and fought with herself to stand. Gritting her teeth, she struggled to balance herself.

"No need. I've got this." He guided her back into the chair.

"Let that fool break into my house, if he's stupid enough. Silent Killer will be waiting for him. Imani better be feeding my dog and letting him run loose in the neighborhood for exercise. I know she tries to look cute in them stilettos, but have you ever seen a dog walk a person?" She *tee-hee*d.

Kidd stood, unlocked the chair's brakes, and made a quick U-turn. "I'll take care of this myself."

"Yeah, but you might need some backup. Man, I hate I'm going to miss this. Take pictures for my Facebook and Twitter home pages."

Hurrying Mrs. Beacon back to her suite, Kidd weaved around workers and residents who were enjoying leisurely walks with the aid of a wall or riding in their wheelchairs. While his adrenaline was pumping, he wanted to get the job done. He was serious about making a commitment to God, but he would have to put that on hold for now.

Kidd was almost outside the building's entrance when Eva called him. "Kidd, where are you going? I thought we were doing lunch."

Slowing down to respond, he took a moment to drink in the beauty of this woman. He had never forgotten about any plans he'd made with her. Kidd waited at the door, as she walked to him with a slight sway of her hips. He enjoyed watching her, whether she knew it or not.

"I have to take care of some business. It shouldn't take long."

Tilting her head, Eva gave him the oddest look. "As long as it doesn't involve four women and flowers, I guess I don't have to follow you."

Kidd loved her sass. "How about I bring you some Popeye's chicken back?"

"Hmmm. My favorite." Her eyes danced.

"I know."

"And don't forget the biscuits." Blowing him another kiss, she turned and hurried down a hall.

Now, on to extinguish this fire so he could get back to his woman. He knew Popeye's was running a special—two legs—mild, with a biscuit. Eva's favorite.

Mentally, Kidd was composing a profile of his intended target. Imani had given him the description—Stacy Adams shoes, bling drooping from his ears and swinging from his neck. Oh, he forgot about the printed boxer shorts. If the guy was bold enough to show up, evidently he was bold enough to terrorize anyone who got in his way.

Kidd's nostrils flared and he laughed. It had been a long while since he'd sparred with someone. And practice makes perfect.

No time to waste; he had other priorities. Eva wanted chicken, and he planned to get it for her. Reluctantly, he punched in Parke's cell number. Kidd liked being in charge and working solo. He was confident he could take on the imposter without any problems. When Parke picked up, Kidd didn't waste any time.

"I can check this out right now. Where exactly does Grandma BB live?"

"Just come over here first, and we'll go together."

For once, Kidd didn't argue. He would save his energy for Bay-Bay. Soon enough he turned onto Parke's street. When he unlocked the front door and stepped inside, the living room was a beehive of activity. Parke and Malcolm were hovering over some man's shoulders, as he sat tapping on a computer keyboard.

"What's going on?" Kidd asked, locking the door.

"My friend Duke is running the license plate number of the guy. Imani called in. He's back, sitting in front of the house. She's keeping an eye on him from her window. Imani still wants to confront him. She talked about getting her repo truck and dragging the car away with him inside it. I suspect Grandma BB didn't know this Bay-Bay." Parke straightened and waited for Kidd to confirm it.

"Nope."

"Instead of planning a covert operation, why not call the Ferguson police. They get paid for carrying a gun and investigating suspicious activities," Cheney suggested, with her arms folded. She appeared to be the only rational one in the house. Sitting calmly in an armchair in the corner with one leg crossing over her knee, Cheney was annoyed. "Humph. Men and their muscles."

The guy called Duke shook his head. "You don't have to be a private investigator like me to know that, if no crime has been committed, he'll be released and maybe come back. That's not good enough. We want him gone. Period. Who knows, the guy could prey on other elderly residents."

A private investigator? Kidd said to himself. Parke, Malcolm, and their friend were wasting time. It didn't take all that.

The phone rang and Parke answered. He listened and then hung up without a greeting or good-bye. "That was Imani. She thinks there are two of them now."

God, please look the other way. Kidd cleared his throat. "Listen, I've got this. I'm going to grab my gun from upstairs and somebody show me where Grandma BB lives."

"Gun!" Cheney shrieked and leaped out of her chair, as if she was propelled like a cannonball.

Suddenly, Kidd was the center of attention.

"You have a gun in my house? Around my children? Are you crazy?" Parke held Cheney back, as she scowled at Kidd. "That's it. I'll pack your bags myself and put you out. Do you know how many children die in gun-related deaths?"

"Almost a thousand, just last year," the private investigator answered in a matter-of-fact way.

Kidd ignored the PI and observed Cheney, who was almost hysterical by now. Pandemonium exploded around him. Finally, Duke managed a whistle that silenced the group.

"Man, don't let your eyes fool you. It may look like I'm holding Cheney back, but actually her grip on me is tighter. I can take you on and then go over to Grandma BB's house," Parke said through clenched teeth.

Hallison peeped out from the kitchen and matched Duke's whistle. "This is getting out of hand. Let's pray before there is any bloodshed."

"There is no need to pray," Kidd snapped, convinced there was no place for religion in every situation.

"That's where you're wrong. We're going to calm down and pray!" Hallison shouted.

Malcolm stared at his wife, and then took on a menacing look. "Consider it done, babe. Go pack your piece, man, and then we'll pray before we all leave here." Malcolm's voice dared anyone to argue. "Thank God the children aren't here."

Kidd huffed and took deep breaths. He didn't take orders. He was a one-man show and only called for backup when he thought he absolutely had to. Taking his time going upstairs to his room, he assessed his belongings. He didn't realize he had accumulated so many ties, suits, and shoes since his arrival months ago. It didn't matter.

With one sweep, he yanked an armful of clothes off the hangers in his closet and threw them into a garment bag. His underwear and shirts went into his duffel bag. Whatever didn't fit, hung out, caught in the zipper. The ruckus was still in full swing when he returned downstairs fifteen minutes later.

"That's what took you so long? You were packing your clothes?" Malcolm asked incredulously. "We said the gun, not your bags."

"I got everything. Make no mistake about this. Wherever my gun goes, I go."

"Yeah, right," Parke assured him, as he bumped everyone into a circle. Bowing his head, Parke took a deep breath. "God, we're ashamed that we stand before You in dishonor. You say a house divided can't stand. Lord, help us to resolve this unsettling situation without bloodshed and forgive us for our sins. In the name of Jesus. Amen."

Following the chorus of "Amens," Kidd left without looking back. When he got to his car, he realized he still didn't have the address.

"Follow me," Parke said, as he walked up behind Kidd. Malcolm and Duke climbed into Parke's SUV.

Parke pulled up in front of Mrs. Beacon's brick story-and-a half bungalow. Kidd parked behind him and jumped out first. He didn't have time for amateur backup escapades. A black Escalade with dark tinted glasses and an old-school Pontiac were posted there. The Delaware license plates stuck out.

Duke got out of Parke's vehicle and glanced inside the Escalade, then the car. No one was inside. Kidd and his cousins shook their heads at Duke's theatrics as he danced across the front yard, pulling out his gun as if he was auditioning for an episode on a crime series. Parke and Malcolm headed around the back.

Kidd grunted. If these men were bold enough to park in plain sight, they probably were bold enough to enter through the front door. Although they had no right to do so, audacious criminals believed their might alone gave them the right. Being streetwise himself, Kidd decided to take the direct approach, walking the short path to the front porch.

The sound of tapping on a window got his attention. Suspiciously, he glanced around. Following the sound, he looked up. Imani was next door in her upstairs window, grinning and pointing to the gun in her hand. "Put that thing away," he mouthed to her and then proceeded on his mission.

Opening the screen door, the front entrance door was ajar. "Fools," he mumbled. The thieves he knew back home preferred climbing through windows. Evidently, these crooks were out of shape. Kidd strained his ears and pulled out his S&W 638 Airweight. The house was quiet, but there was a trail of blood on the floor. *Humph,* he thought. Someone had beaten him to the punch.

Quietly, Kidd followed the trail, mindful of Grandma BB's dog, Silent Killer. The blood stopped in a puddle in front of the kitchen. At that point, it split into two paths. A set of bloody shoe prints suggested a pair of Stacy Adams might be ruined on the sole.

The gory trail stopped at the open window. Commanding voices came from outside—someone had called the police. It appeared the escapees—definitely amateurs—had landed themselves into the hands of the cops. Evidently, Delaware criminals didn't graduate with proper training.

Kidd peeped out the window. The police had the pair in handcuffs. The drama would have appeared to be over, but something seemed amiss. Why were there three trails of blood? Imani must have batted an eyelash and one slipped under her radar, or the other crook thought he could get away, reconsidered, and followed his accomplice. To be sure, Kidd followed the blood into a sitting room. Stretched out on a dark sofa was the dog—Silent Killer—posed as if he was waiting for the press or a photographer. Lifting his head, he licked his jaws.

Great. Kidd groaned. "Please don't let me have to shoot Grandma BB's mutt." Kidd frowned and tilted his head down toward the floor. There was a pair of Stacy Adams jutting out from the other side of the sofa. He squinted and leaned closer. There had to be feet inside those shoes.

Kidd took the safety off his gun. "I see the shoes, so I know you're behind that couch. Put both hands up and scoot from behind there—now!"

"Don't shoot. Don't shoot! Get rid of the dog, man. That monster bit me on the leg and on my—"

"Shut up, man. Silent Killer," Kidd called and the dog's ears perked up, "come sit by me, boy."

The dog started wagging his tail. Then he jumped down and methodically approached Kidd, who wore a guarded expression on his face. Both he and the dog seemed distrustful of the other. Hesitantly, Silent Killer sniffed Kidd's shoes and pant leg. Kidd determined he wouldn't shoot the dog, but crack him on the head if the mutt even thought about sinking his teeth into Kidd's new, Banana Republic, pin-striped dress pants. Amazingly, the dog finished his assessment and sat down.

"Okay. I don't care if you have to wiggle your tail out, but I got a date with my lady, and I don't like to be late. So it's me or the dog. You've got five minutes. Scratch that. You have thirty seconds. I'm impatient."

"I'm coming, man. Don't shoot, and keep that dog away from me!" His voice trembled. As Kidd watched ankles emerge, it reminded him of the scene from the *Wizard of Oz* when the house landed on the wicked witch.

Slowly, the crook's legs and backside appeared. There were several rips on his pants. With his behind in the air, the intruder wormed his way out until finally, a head came into view. The man moaned as he struggled to get up and keep his hands in the air. Pitiful. If the dude was going to break and enter, at least he should have been equipped with more meat on his bones.

"Get on your knees," Kidd ordered, as Silent Killer locked eyes on his potential prey's every move. "Hold it." With the gun pointed at the man, Kidd pulled his iPhone off his waist belt with one hand, while he kept the gun aimed at his target.

"Don't shoot!"

"It's a phone, you idiot! Now, be still!" Kidd clicked and snapped a picture. "It's for Facebook. Now get up slowly, or you're bound to make the dog nervous. And walk toward that door."

Silent Killer growled.

Timidly, the man followed orders. Kidd and Silent Killer followed him out the house where the police were interrogating the other suspects.

"What do we have here?" An officer ran up to them with one hand on his holster. Removing his weapon, he ordered, "Turn around and put both hands behind your back. I'm sure there'll be some pants to fit you where you're going." When the officer pushed the injured man to the ground, Kidd put the safety back on his gun and stuffed it in his sock.

A few neighbors were standing around and started cheering. Parke nodded with a smirk. "Good job, Jamieson."

Duke's eyes widened in disbelief, and Malcolm grinned, as he, Parke, and Duke began a round of applause. Within minutes, some in the crowd started chanting his last name, as if it was his first.

Before the suspects were manhandled into a police car, the officer in charge approached Kidd.

"Thanks for your help. We need you to stick around. After we conduct a full sweep of the house, one of our men is going to get a detailed report from you. I'm sure you have a license to carry that weapon."

"Sure officer, I'll be happy to speak with you. But if you don't mind, in the meantime I'll take some pictures. I'm sure Mrs. Beacon will want to post them on Twitter and Facebook."

Kidd took out his iPhone and aimed the camera at the crooks. "Can I get a smile, please," he taunted.

When they didn't, Kidd bent to Silent Killer. "Okay, boy, get ready."

"Okay, okay," one snapped.

"Fine!" A tall, dark brotha wearing Stacy Adams on his long feet shouted. Something about his attitude made Kidd surmise that he had to be Bay-Bay.

"Say, cheese."

Their toothy grins were wide, displaying plenty of gold.

Kidd snapped away.

Chapter Thirty-Four

*I*t was almost six o'clock when Eva opened the door. She had a serious attitude and didn't hesitate to show it. Frowning at Kidd standing in her doorway, she asked, "Where did you go for my chicken? To Perdue farm to ensure it was fresh? Kidd, you left work and never came back. When I tried to call you, I got your voice mail. What's going on?"

Kidd lifted the bag. "I got your Popeye's chicken and biscuits!" He grinned and stepped around her to walk inside.

Eva squinted, locked the door, and twirled around. There was a whole block of missing information. She stared, waiting for more. He had the nerve to break eye contact, which was something he usually didn't do.

With a self-assured smile, he held up the bag again. "Paper, plastic, or china plates?"

She grabbed the bag. "I should feed you on paper. It's a good thing I'm hungry, almost eight hours later. Miss Gertie wasn't cooking at the facility today, so you can imagine what was being served." Still curious, she lifted a brow. "Why the disappearing act?"

"Baby, if we can just eat first, then I'll tell you everything."

Why did the man have to look so innocent, handsome, and devilish all at the same time? She narrowed her eyes. "Why do I have the feeling I'm not going to like whatever you have to say?" Reluctantly, Eva gave in. "Okay, wash up." She pointed to the bathroom right off the kitchen.

Kidd scrubbed his hands and lifted his voice over the running water. "I didn't curse, maim, or kill anybody, so no repenting is necessary," he gave as a peace offering.

Minutes later, they had blessed the food. Eva was famished but listened intently as Kidd began to weave a tale that was hardly believable. However, she was clearly beginning to build trust in him. Actually, she found some of it funny. The story about the Stacy Adams shoes and the part about the pictures of the thieves seemed almost laughable, but that was all. It seemed like the entire stunt was pushing him farther away from a fine line and his walk with God.

"A gun, Kevin? I don't blame Cheney's reaction."

"She called?"

"Yep. Cheney said you were a hero, but wouldn't go into details because she thought you would want to tell me yourself. We chatted about other things, and she invited me to go shopping with her, Hali, and Imani this weekend."

Eva resumed her reprimand. "How could you keep a gun around children?"

"They were never in any danger. Plus, I didn't need it anyway. Her dog got to the jokers before I did. I don't know why Silent Killer didn't attack me."

"Besides Jesus watching over you, the only reason I can think of is maybe you had Grandma BB's scent on your hands or clothes."

Kidd snapped his fingers as if he'd just experienced a eureka moment. "That's it! I guess it was a good thing I didn't wash my hands before I left work, like I usually do."

He was acting as if they were having a casual conversation, but Eva wasn't buying it. "Back to your craziness. You should've let the police handle it. You've got to decide which walk you're going to take. God only knows, it's beyond me. I don't have enough spiritual intellect to discern whose side you're on: God's or the demons that seem to override your common sense."

Chapter Thirty-Five

*T*hat night, Kidd couldn't sleep because he was thinking about Eva's indirect ultimatum. Having booked himself into a room at a four-star hotel didn't make matters any better. The pristine environment was too cold and impersonal for him to get any rest.

If it was any other woman besides Eva, Kidd wouldn't have had to ask if he could stay overnight until he found an apartment or made some other arrangement. The invitation would have been gladly extended indefinitely. However, he wouldn't disrespect Eva by asking, and he knew she wouldn't offer.

When Kidd finally drifted off, he was in a semiconscious state until Eva called late Saturday morning.

"I'm checking up on you. Are you okay?"

"I'm okay, babe." He sighed. "I thought about my actions yesterday and our talk . . . I don't want you to feel like I'm out of control."

"It's your spiritual world that's out of control, Kevin, not you. We've prayed. So my confidence is in God. I take comfort in the fact that He won't stop until His work in you is completed. Meanwhile, you're a hard man to love."

His heart pounded at the mention of that four-letter word coming from her lips. "Does that mean you can't love me, or you can't help but fall in love with me?"

Eva didn't answer right away. Kidd prompted her again, this time directly.

"Do you love me, Eva?"

"Yes, I do. But, Kevin Jamieson, it's not Beyoncé's *Crazy Love.* Don't force me to walk away. I need a commitment," she said forcefully.

Kidd knew what she was talking about, but he baited her anyway. "I love you, and if I thought you would say yes, I would put a ring on your finger. Beyoncé would have it no other way."

"God needs a commitment from you first—either to repent of your sins or die because of them. It's a no-brainer, Kevin."

Kidd sighed. There was no hiding her frustration. It seemed like he had the same level of frustration all his life. He softened his voice and spoke from his heart, "If you really believe that God started a work in me, please pray that He will finish it. I can sense the tug-of-war in my soul. And I did call for spiritual backup before this whole fiasco went down. I am serious, Eva. You know I don't play games. You love me and that's all I've wanted from you, so I have the home-field advantage."

"Well then, imagine that's the same kind of relationship God has with us, Kevin. We love Him because He first loved us."

As the mood lightened, they talked a few more minutes. Finally, they agreed to go to the theater in the afternoon and watch an old movie.

"Can't wait to see *Jumpin' the Broom* again."

He couldn't believe how many times she said she'd seen it when it first came out. The first time with her sister, next with her mother, and then with Dawn. Now it was his turn.

On Sunday, Kidd attended church with Eva. At least he didn't have to repent for the Bay-Bay episode. The sermon was powerful, and again he went to the altar for prayer. When he returned to the family pew, Eva reached for his hand.

"Do you still love me?" he whispered.

"I never thought I would fall for a bad boy from Boston. Yes, my heart won't let me stop, but—"

"Shhh." He hushed her. He remembered what her father had said about losing her. Eva herself had voiced a concern about his commitment. Yet she continued reaching out to him.

"I love you and you are worth fighting whatever demon for."

"Prayer changes things," she whispered in his ear before Elder Taylor said the benediction. Kidd's heart swelled with emotion.

Monday morning after a decent night's sleep, Kidd was in a fairly good mood. He hit the hotel gym. Energized by his workout, he showered, trimmed his beard, and dressed. After eating a complimentary breakfast downstairs, he headed to work. His hotel was farther away from the facility, but he made it on time.

Wearing a grin, he opened the doors to Garden Chateau, and there she was. Posted outside his office, waiting for his arrival, was none other than Mrs. Beacon.

"You got pictures for me . . . and how's my dog?" she fired at him, not wasting any time.

Kidd withheld his chuckle. Did she not have any concern for her house or outcome of the thieves who tried to break into it? "I'd say Silent Killer is well-fed."

She nodded and started to roll away before he stopped her. He imagined Grandma BB couldn't wait to check out the pictures he posted for her.

"Hey, don't you want to know about the bad guys?"

"Nope. I figured between you and the other Jamiesons, plus Imani, those ba—oops, those gentlemen are no longer visiting."

"No, they're not. They were arrested on the spot. The police mentioned something about violating parole, so they won't be back. Now the bad news . . ."

Mrs. Beacon flinched and her body stiffened. "What?"

269

"I think they messed up a good pair of Stacy Adams."

Grimacing, this time she did curse, before Kidd charged a nearby aide with returning Mrs. Beacon to her room.

Kidd was still laughing as Eva rounded the corner. "Good morning, babe. You want to be my real estate agent and help a homeless man find shelter?"

She smiled and slapped his chest, but he grabbed her hand and squeezed it. Lifting his brow, he felt like kissing her breathless this morning. He settled for caressing her hand with kisses.

"Kevin, I can tell by the look in your eyes that you're up to no good." She scrunched her nose. "While you're hiding from residents in your office this afternoon, look up some properties. We can take a look after work."

"Sounds like a plan."

Chapter Thirty-Six

*I*t wasn't until the following Saturday that Kidd and Eva had enough time to do some serious house hunting. Eva had spent the previous Saturday with Cheney and the girls. She confessed they—or more like she—had badmouthed him. Amazingly, despite the big hoopla about his gun, the women couldn't sing enough of his praises. Including Imani.

Kidd didn't know what to make of the Jamiesons' love; it was quite humbling. His heart warmed when Eva relayed how upset Kami had become when anyone tried to utter a bad word about her cousin uncle.

During the first week of house hunting, Kidd was amused to watch his woman nitpick over the smallest details about properties. The second week, he learned his lesson the hard way; and by the third week, he simply remained quiet. Once, to no avail, he folded his arms and refused to budge from the front door of a property. A short distance from his job, it was tucked away into a neighborhood of mature trees and quiet streets. She was prepared to leave him there.

As he and Eva continued to compare houses, Kidd realized he could get more for his money within Old Town Florissant. New homes filled gaps between older maintained two- and three-bedroom bungalows.

Eva glanced over her shoulder and frowned. "Honey, I thought you liked this house."

"From the outside, it's nice."

"Don't you want to see the renovations and floor plan?"

"If you like this one . . ." he said, a little too nonchalant for Eva's taste. Then, holding up his hands when it appeared she was about to protest, he completed his thought. "If the price is right, I'll take it."

Eva's mouth dropped. "Just like that?" She snapped her fingers. "Don't you want to check out the furnace, plumbing, roof . . . you know, that important stuff?"

Kidd walked over to her and tilted her chin. His kiss swallowed up the rest of her words. "Baby, you should know by now; no one is going to take advantage of me. I'll check out all those things. Okay?" he whispered sweetly, as she nodded in submission.

The Realtor cleared her throat to remind them of her presence. When Eva and Kidd turned around, the woman grinned and Eva blushed.

"So when is the big day?" the realtor asked.

"Big day?" Kidd repeated.

"Your wedding."

"Oh, we're not getting married or even engaged," Eva corrected.

The older woman looked embarrassed. "Oh, I'm so sorry. I forget couples move in together without marriage. I'm really sorry."

"We're not one of those couples. If you don't see a ring on this third finger, you won't see my pantyhose hanging out to dry. When Jesus comes back, I don't want Him to find me in a compromising situation."

The Realtor nodded, but was clearly uncomfortable as she glanced at Kidd. He gave her a shrug. He would buy a ring before he bought a house, if he thought she would say yes. Women and their stipulations. He was a good man. It was just taking him a little longer to walk with Jesus.

"Okay," the woman said, clapping her hands together. "Shall we continue the tour?"

When Eva nodded, the woman relaxed. The two of them disappeared into the dining room.

God, I know Eva is my blessing. A woman I probably don't deserve, but man to Man, if You can give me a little more time, I'll come on Your terms. I'm not playing with You, Jesus. I just need to be 100 percent ready to stay. I want to be faithful to You, unlike my father was to me, he prayed silently. Then he took his time and gave the house a detailed inspection.

Finally, Eva returned, jubilant. Twisting her hands, she pronounced, "It's perfect for you!"

"Sold! I'll take them," Kidd said, referring to both the house and Eva. But she and the Realtor were too excited to hear.

—–⁂—–

"Come on, it'll be fun!" Eva said, finally convincing him to have a housewarming party. Personally, he couldn't care less. As far as Kidd was concerned, he could get by with a bed, a couch, and a flat-screen TV.

The first night he moved in, he sat on a box and stared at the moonlight through partially opened blinds. Kidd fell into a melancholy mood as he surveyed his surroundings. The living room was sparsely furnished, and pictures Eva had convinced him to purchase were waiting to be hung.

"Baby, I don't need pots, pans, and dishes," he had told her when she insisted on shopping for kitchenware. "That's why they have buffets."

Eva crossed her arms and arched a brow with a smirk. "You're not going to say it?" she teased.

"What?" Kidd was honestly clueless.

"You also have a woman who cooks."

He looked sheepish. "Well, ah, I didn't want to assume. But now that you mention it . . . thanks for the unlimited offer."

Wrapping her arms around his waist, Eva laughed. Kidd's piercing eyes searched her face. There was a brief period of silence as they both cherished the moment. *Ah, yeah. She is the one,* he mused. She was stunning, dressed in his favorite color—maroon. He counted the freckles—they were still there; her lips—still tempting; her eyes—still sparkling.

Reflecting on the day he might propose, Kidd thought of how he would address her father, *Mr. Savoy, may I have your lovely daughter's hand in marriage? I would say I'm doing something right.*

"Are you going to talk to me?" Kidd whispered, towering over her in the living room of his new home.

She frowned. "Weren't you listening?"

Was this a trick question, or something? "I didn't hear a word, but I read the expression on your face. You're happy."

"So you did listen to my heart?" She smiled.

"That's what I do." Once more, they embraced without saying another word.

For the rest of the day, Eva stayed on the subject. "Okay, the time for the housewarming will be . . ."

Kidd's emotions were fluctuating all over the place. With so many things for him to consider, some kind of change must be taking place in him. He recalled the time when he wouldn't have given a second thought to shutting out the whole world—if he felt so inclined.

Now he listened attentively as Eva rambled on. Was he supposed to invite his neighbors? Of course, there were his cousins. Parke and Malcolm had reached out with phone calls. Malcolm had even driven from his office downtown to North County just to take him to lunch. Thanks to Eva, Kidd accepted Malcolm's olive branch even though he wanted to decline. She convinced him that family would always have his back, a saying his mother had drilled into him as a boy.

Kidd surprised himself as he reflected on how much he cared about his present circumstances. He knew he couldn't shake Parke and Malcolm without breaking the children's hearts, so he decided to embrace the family wholeheartedly. Although he really did like them, he was too stubborn to admit it in a humble fashion. In their opinion, he had redeemed himself by capturing the bad guy.

Then there was another feather in his cap; he was still working at the nursing facility and keeping his commitment to watch over Grandma BB. If he were keeping track, that was a great accomplishment and should garner him a whole pan of brownie points.

Yes. Eva was the best thing that ever happened to him; she warmed his heart. But when she kissed him good-night and left that evening, his good mood suddenly turned sober again. He found himself comparing his old life in Boston to his new life in St. Louis. His fists were clinched together as if he was praying, but that was the furthest thing from his mind. Rather, he was doing some soul searching.

"What has been the purpose in my life—to have an invisible father, or a brother who is following in his pitiful father's misguided footsteps?" He truly wanted to know the answers.

As Kidd continued to contemplate his life, he knew Eva was the reason—the only reason—he didn't quit the nursing facility on day one. Looking back on his stint there, he actually had no complaints. No one demanded him to change diapers or do aisle cleanups. His main responsibility was to give elderly residents some attention—provide entertainment of sorts for them.

Two weeks later on a Saturday, Kidd was in the middle of moving the boxes of glassware and dishes Eva had made him purchase to the kitchen. As he prepared for his housewarming guests, the doorbell rang. *Now, who has the audacity to arrive early?* he thought.

A little irritated, he went to answer the door. On the way, Kidd smiled, wondering if it might be Eva. She had gone shopping for more party stuff, but she hadn't been gone long.

Swinging open the front door, he teased, "Back so soon—" Kidd was rendered speechless for a few seconds, then he stuttered, "Ma, Ace?" Engulfing them into a tight group hug, they remained united until Ace fought his way out of Kidd's stronghold.

"What are you two doing here?"

"We were invited, silly." His mother elbowed him out of the way as she and Ace entered. Glancing around, Sandra's eyes sparkled with approval. Kidd was glad he had hung the pictures.

"I can't wait to meet her," Sandra whispered. Immediately, she began her home inspection.

Kidd knew exactly who his mother was referring to. He was about to shut the door when Cameron swaggered up the walkway. *Now what was he doing here? Why did he come?*

This shindig was Eva's brainchild. He expected a few coworkers and neighbors who accepted the invitations she mailed. Her parents were out of town, but if they made it back in time, surely they would come. And of course, the St. Louis Jamiesons were on their way. Yeah. His woman was amazing. She really pulled one over on him; he wasn't expecting anyone from Boston.

"Whatz up, cuz?"

"What are you doing in town?" Kidd may have accepted Cameron's brothers, but he was another story. Cameron had become Ace's new crutch.

"You might as well let me in, because I think that pretty little lady needs help." Cameron smirked.

"And why didn't you help my woman?" Kidd shoved Cameron aside and hurried to rescue Eva from struggling with three assorted bags of party goods and food.

Gladly handing them over, she commented, "There are a couple of boxes in the trunk. Has your family arrived yet?"

"Yep, you little event planner. My mom and brother are here. My cousin Cameron's here too. How many people did you invite?"

"Oh, not many. Just the mayor, the entire police force . . ." She laughed. "Just kidding, pun intended. Did I do good?" She batted her eyes.

With a broad smile on his face that revealed his true feelings, Kidd steadied his breathing. "No, you didn't do good, woman. I don't even like those people," he teased.

"Behave. You know I can kick up some dust too, Kevin Jamieson."

As the late afternoon sun played hide-and-seek with her eyes and the wind tousled her hair, Kidd kissed her. After a lingering kiss, he took his time ushering Eva inside. Thoroughly enjoying their moment of solitude, he told her, "You know there's a small pond near here. Every time I jog past, it reminds me of you—peaceful, beautiful, and powerful."

After walking inside and taking the bags into the kitchen for Eva, Kidd returned to the living room. Ace and Cameron were sitting and talking over a beer. A few minutes later, he heard the sound of voices approaching the door. Kidd opened it in time to greet four Jamieson children bouncing up the walkway. The two oldest raced to the door as their makeshift finish line, while the toddlers took up the rear.

"Hi, Cousin Uncle!" Pace and Kami shouted in unison.

He was promptly hugged, squeezed, and then kissed by Kami. Whatever gifts they were bearing were definitely smashed in the process. Coming up behind them, Parke and Cheney were empty-handed, followed by Hallison and Malcolm, who was lugging an over-flowing basket.

Cheney stepped up first. "You are welcome to visit any time, but leave that gun at home," she whispered in Kidd's ear, as they embraced.

"Cheney, I'm really sorry about that. I did have the safety on it. I'm not used to being around children. But to my credit, I kept it in a safe place; it wasn't lying around."

"Doesn't matter. My children love to play hide-and-seek in their own house."

Kidd understood her point and nodded, then received Hallison's hug. Once the women entered, he was standing face-to-face with the brothers Jamieson.

"Forgiven?" Parke asked.

"Who? You or me?" Kidd questioned, narrowing his eyes.

"Let's call us even."

"Yeah. Sounds good." Kidd smirked and stepped back. Silently, it was the official signing of their peace treaty. When they walked in, his place suddenly came alive.

Angela and a reluctant Lance were the last of the guests to arrive. Throughout the evening, a few neighbors stopped by. Some coworkers came, enjoyed the food, and dropped off their gifts. Eva helped him open the abundance of presents. Watching her excitement over each gift, one might think it was her housewarming. Her constant expressions of *ooh* and *ahh* made him appreciate the offerings that much more.

Meanwhile, Cheney and Hallison's toddlers turned his two-bedroom home into a playground. Observing their innocence, he was reminded of Cheney's warning over the gun incident and truly understood what she was talking about. He would never want to see a child hurt because of his lack of thoughtfulness.

When their parents ordered them to be still, Kidd assumed his authority. "This is my house. Let them do what they want." He grinned.

"All right . . . spoken by a man who doesn't know how destructive little Jamiesons can be," Cheney said, while everyone laughed. Kami and Pace sat on the floor in the corner, content with playing handheld video games. Unrestrained, Paden and MJ continued having a field day, shredding gift wrap paper and littering it throughout the house.

When Kidd's mother spearheaded the cleanup, the women gathered in the kitchen and exchanged decorating tips for the house. It just so happened that he caught the moment when his mother slipped outside with Eva.

The Jamieson men were left alone in the living room to argue over sports—all in the name of good fun. Witnessing the scene, there was no doubt in his mind that, as Rodney King suggested long ago, the cousins could all get along.

Chapter Thirty-Seven

"You've done a good job." Tears filled Kidd's mother's soulful eyes, after Eva closed the sliding door. As the day was winding down, they were about to have a private talk on Kidd's small deck.

"Your son follows good decorating directions. Wait until Kidd sees the kitchen bar table set Cheney and I picked out as the Jamieson family gift. It should be delivered on Monday."

Sandra shook her head. "I'm not talking about this house," she spread her arms and turned from side to side, "or the decorating. I'm referring to Kidd. How on earth did you tame him?"

They walked down the stairs to put some distance between them and the house. "I didn't, Miss Nicholson."

"Please call me Sandra. When I spoke to you over the phone, I felt a kindred spirit as far as Kidd was concerned. Now that I have actually witnessed his happiness, it makes me want to have church in this yard."

Don't send out the invitations to the Holy Ghost party yet, Eva wanted to tell her. So far, Kidd hadn't scored a spiritual deliverance touchdown. He was still teetering on the sidelines.

"The Lord knows I've prayed for Kidd to be delivered from his angry spirit. Hatred is like a sponge. It picks up ugliness along the way until it's saturated with all kinds of filth," Sandra said with a faraway look. "I never thought when I fell in love with one man—who I didn't know was married—it would cause the son I brought into this world not to have room in his heart to love. I begged God not to make my sons pay for my mistakes. Then God spoke and corrected me. He said nobody can pay for my sins or the mistakes I've made—because He already did it."

Eva placed her hand on Sandra's arm.

"I'm so thankful," Sandra continued, "I now feel his spirit is finally settling. I haven't seen Kidd this content since he was a boy and knew his father was coming to visit. If you don't marry him, then . . ."

"Kevin has to ask, and I won't accept unless he surrenders to God. So it's three of us in the equation. At this point, I can't understand what's stopping him from repenting. It's frustrating."

"Welcome to my world. I'm surprised I don't have white hair by now, skipping the gray stage altogether." Her eyes sparkled.

Sandra Nicholson was a pretty lady with dark brown hair. Not a gray strand in sight. From what Kidd shared with her, Eva was surprised his mother had never married—ever. Well, who knows, maybe with her focus off her oldest son, she would concentrate more on her personal happiness.

"He's getting close."

"Sandra, I'm sorry to burst the bubble. But Kidd has come to church; he's walked down the aisle for prayer more than once. I've seen him reading his Bible . . . he respects me." Eva threw her hands up. "What is taking him so long?"

Sandra grabbed Eva's hands. "The race is not given to the swift, and we know Kidd's not running to the altar. So it looks like he's not in any hurry. Still, I believe once my son gets there, he will stay strong and endure until Jesus comes back."

"Only a mother's love would say that. I love Kevin, despite his stubborn ways . . . but a woman can only hold out for so long," Eva confided. She sniffed, determined not to cry. Then she welcomed Sandra's hug. "I'm sorry for venting. I know Kevin really is a good man, a wonderful boyfriend, and a very tenderhearted person."

"Hmmm, that's an interesting description for a man who left home as an angry Black man. But God can save anybody, even a moody man."

Laughing, they separated. Before rejoining the group, they exchanged a confident glance. A strong bond had just been formed.

Chapter Thirty-Eight

When the weekend was over, Kidd couldn't remember the last time he enjoyed himself so much with his family. His good mood lingered into Monday, until he walked into work and got the news. Miss Jessie passed away in her sleep hours earlier, making her the first resident to die in the facility in months.

Kidd kept an eye on Eva as she sat silently praying outside the elderly woman's room. The woman's only visiting relative sat inside mourning. It had been a display of uncanny timing. Miss Jessie's granddaughter was coming down the hall at the same time the head nurse was making the call to the next of kin for the death notification.

"Tissue and a glass of water never seem adequate when trying to console a family member," Eva told Kidd when she first learned about the death. "I'll pray with her granddaughter, if she wants me to." Eva had made it her standard offer. Kidd didn't comment when she added, "Only a few people have been so upset that they declined."

By the time he was making his third patrol through the hall to check on her, Eva hadn't moved.

Death. Kidd reflected on his own accomplishments and disappointments. Did Miss Jessie have any regrets in her life? What about his mother? His only regret in life would be if she didn't live long enough to witness his transformation. Movement broke his trance. Eva got up and disappeared inside the room.

Fifteen minutes later, she still hadn't emerged. As he rushed down the hall toward the room, Eva came out distraught. When she saw him, she practically fell into Kidd's arms. He nudged her into a corner for more privacy.

"Whoa. Are you all right?" He wrapped both arms securely around her. Eva shook her head and hiccupped, as she collapsed in his embrace.

For the next couple of days, Kidd ignored any whispers of death talk. Shaking his head, he dismissed the superstitious, inane sayings people have a habit of conjuring up by calling such things *stupid-stition.*

Eva slowly regained her cheerfulness. He had never seen someone grieve so hard over a person who wasn't a relative.

Back to business as usual, he performed his rounds of resident visits, ignoring the annoying ones like Mr. Johnston. Leaving his office, Kidd turned down the corridor to Mrs. Valentine and Mrs. Beacon's suite. *Let's find out what bizarre story Mrs. Valentine will be sharing today,* he joked to himself.

When he knocked on their door frame, Mrs. Valentine glanced up with merriment dancing in her bright eyes. The opposite was true for Mrs. Beacon who looked totally indifferent.

"Good morning, ladies."

"Hi, Adam, have you seen your Eve today?"

"Umm-hmm, and she's lookin' real cute too." Kidd winked and the old woman beamed, as if he was flirting with her.

"How ya been?" he asked her and then Mrs. Beacon.

"I've been better. I'm ready to go home," Mrs. Beacon said with weariness in her voice.

Kidd tried to engage Mrs. Beacon in a spirited discussion, but she pretty much ignored him. Standing to leave, he was surprised Mrs. Valentine didn't have any tales to pass on. He had just walked out when Mrs. Valentine called after him.

"You know what's wrong with your generation today?"

Kidd snickered. He knew it. Mrs. Valentine couldn't let him escape without some Black history lesson.

"I've been thinking about Jesus lately and all His promises. I also thought about the promised land and how the Lord was so mad at the children of Israel. He allowed them to get lost in the wilderness for forty years, until all the generations that had done evil in God's sight were consumed."

"So what are you saying, Mrs. Valentine?" Kidd folded his arms and waited patiently.

"Racism is an insidious form of sin. And when all the generations that are infected die out, folks will finally see the promises of God that have been waiting for them for many generations."

"That's a lot of generations," he responded, not wanting the conversation to go any further. Kidd felt he had enough of her lectures to last a lifetime. Changing the subject, he focused again on the stubborn and bullheaded Mrs. Beacon. "Soooo . . . what are the therapists saying about you going home?"

"They ain't. They say my attitude and determination are key to my comeback. And I've got plenty of both, but not lately. I'm tired. I think my old age of fifty-nine is catching up with me."

Mrs. Beacon didn't crack a smile, having just lied about her age. So Kidd kept his poker face, even though his belly was ready to explode in laughter.

"Yeah, but this isn't the *Biggest Loser* TV show. The therapists aren't about breaking you down. So you can refrain from cursing them out." Kidd grunted. "I heard your mouth is as bad as mine—or at least as bad as mine used to be," he corrected. "I don't need any competition up in here." He spoke with great authority and then left their room.

Kidd was determined to stay away from those two ladies—especially Mrs. Valentine—for a while. Although her stories were most times depressing, he mulled over what she had said about God's promises throughout many generations. Her words began to haunt his thoughts. "Did it skip me?" he mumbled under his breath.

A week after Miss Jessie's death, he and Eva had just returned from lunch when they got the news that another resident had passed away. This time, it was Mrs. Valentine. Kidd's heart dropped. He didn't realize how much of an impact she had on his life—until it was too late.

Suddenly it was his turn to be emotionally affected by a resident's death. He tried to recall all the stories she had told him when he was barely listening. At the moment, only the last conversation about generations dying out stuck with him. Maybe that was her way of saying good-bye—and a final warning to him.

"That's the second one," he heard Eva whisper. It was yet another death to deal with and another round of tears. She succumbed to a silent sob. "They go in threes."

Kidd wondered if Eva had picked the wrong profession. Death was inevitable, usually occurring at an accelerated rate within a nursing facility environment. Again he would have to keep an eye on her as best as he could.

"I've got to go into a meeting, text me if you need me. Okay?"

She nodded, sniffed, and walked back to the nurses' station.

Even though he loved his woman, he still didn't believe in "stupidstition." Nevertheless, Kidd knew he had to get his act together before it was too late.

Why haven't you repented? God spoke.

A chill went down his spine. He was momentarily in a state of shock. It wasn't a question, but a statement.

Come unto Me. You who are heavy burdened. My yoke is easy and burden is light, God softly beckoned.

"I'm coming, Lord. I'm coming," Kidd whispered in hope to appease God.

Hours later and he hadn't caught a glimpse of Eva, he went in search of her. Walking through the campus grounds, he ignored the whining and yakking coming from the petting zoo animals.

There he discovered Eva meandering aimlessly along a path. When she looked up and saw him, she waited as he took long strides to her. Her eyes were puffy. He crushed her to his chest and didn't let go until she began to struggle.

"I can't breathe."

"Sorry, baby." Letting her go, he remembered too that they were at work. However, his main concern was to console her. "Are you sure nursing is for you? I think you become too attached."

"I worked in the business sector for a few years and walked around numb because of office politics. Whether I was a nursing candidate or not, I'd still mourn for the lives of those who die. It doesn't matter if they were sick, killed in a car accident, murdered, drowned . . . it just makes me value life all the more. I'll miss her calling me Eve. And you know she was a great storyteller."

"Yeah, she seemed to know I was your Adam too." Kidd wasn't ready to admit it, but it seemed like her last tale was meant to put the fear of God in him.

"Come on, we'd better get back inside."

Kidd's iPhone buzzed seconds after he walked into his office, indicating he had received a text. Unclipping it from its holster, he read the message: *Dinner tonight for two. Bring Eva with you. Love, Cheney Jamieson. FYI, Eva has been texted too, in case you even think about declining.*

A bittersweet smile appeared on his face. Eva enjoyed spending time with Cheney as much as Cheney and Hallison raved about her. However, there was no way he thought she was going to be in a mood for socializing. He replied: *Let's reschedule. We had a resident pass away and Eva's taking it hard. I'll let her pick another time.*

Cheney texted back: *Oh, I'm sorry, Kidd. I'll be praying for my sister and the resident's family. Tell her to call me if she wants to talk.*

That Kidd wouldn't do. If Eva needed someone to talk to, she had two options—him or Jesus.

Mrs. Valentine's funeral was held a few days later at a little church called The Last Days. It was packed. More coworkers attended than either Kidd or Eva would have imagined, considering how much she irritated everyone with her continuous chatter.

The pastor, with a long biblical name, performed the eulogy in less than ten minutes. He closed with: "God gave her a gift of proclaiming His Word in parables, and she performed her task until her last breath. May her soul rest in peace until the great day when Jesus shall appear and rapture up those who are His. In Jesus' name. Amen."

Approximately two hundred–strong mourners released a resounding, "Amen." Afterward, Kidd and Eva waited in line to view the remains, then left. When they drove back to the facility's parking lot, two patrol cars were posted at the entrance.

Kidd exchanged glances with Eva. "Now what?" he asked, sighing.

He parked and they went inside. The place was buzzing with activity. The staff was in quite a frenzy. Eva stopped Dawn, who hadn't attended the funeral. "What's going on?"

"Haven't you heard?"

"No," Kidd and Eva said in unison.

"We were at Mrs. Valentine's funeral," Eva added.

"Yeah, right. It's Mrs. Beacon—" Dawn's voice lowered to above a whisper.

When Eva shook her head, Kidd placed his hand in the arch of her back for support. "Oh, no! God, please, not the third death in a row!" Her voice indicated a heightened level of anxiety that wasn't lost on Kidd.

God, I'm a strong man, but I can only take so much bad news. Kidd's body tensed for the rest of the news. "What about her?"

"She's missing."

Just then, two officers walked down the hall and headed to the administrative office. The director was frantic. "This has never happened here before. We take pride in the care of our residents. If the media gets wind of this, our reputation will be tarnished."

"Madam, we've checked her room for clues," said one of the police officers.

Kidd tugged Eva closer to him.

"The pond will be next," the same officer suggested.

Eva shuddered. "Death comes in threes," she whispered. "Please, Lord, let them find her alive," she pleaded, with her hands folded for prayer.

"Everything will be all right." Kidd hoped to reassure her, gently squeezing her shoulders.

"We have our divers on the way." The other officer reported to the director.

"Are you aware that all her belongings are gone?"

"What?" Eva gasped.

"Are you saying she escaped?" Kidd's frown was deep. Just then, his iPhone rang and he checked the ID. "Hey, Parke, ah, about Grandma BB—" Parke cut him off. Kidd's eyes bugged as he listened, then shook his head. Quickly, he disconnected and looked at Eva.

"Call off the search and rescue team," he told the officers.

Everyone turned to Kidd. "Why?"

"Grandma BB, Mrs. Beacon, isn't dead. She's at home."

Chapter Thirty-Nine

"*T*hat woman is pure drama," Kidd said to Eva, as they snuggled together on his sofa. Still trying to get over the shock of Grandma BB's escape, Eva managed a smile at his comment. At the moment, there wasn't much more to say about her. Mrs. Beacon had provided an unsettling end to an already mournful day.

Before they left work, Kidd had ordered carryout. Their plan was to spend the evening together. They'd been watching marathon game shows on cable to relax and recover from the events of the day. Eva seemed clingy, and Kidd didn't mind administering some tender loving care.

With the funeral still fresh in his memory, Kidd's mind jumped to Mrs. Valentine's death. Almost as if he felt a sense of guilt, he wanted to confide in Eva. Breaking their moment of silence, he began, "I didn't detect that Mrs. Valentine wasn't feeling well the last time I visited with—"

Then he paused, unwilling to complete his thought. He could still hear Mrs. Valentine's last words about sinful generations dying out. Was she talking about herself? Did she know she was dying? Perplexed by her veiled message, he cleared his throat.

To erase his troubling thoughts, he went back to their initial subject. "I can't believe Grandma BB was bold enough to post her escape plans on Facebook and Twitter all day yesterday. And after that, she had the nerve to follow through."

As it turned out, Grandma BB phoned one of her Red Hat Society girlfriends. She told her friend she had to get out fast before she was number three on the death hit list.

Eva expressed her concern. "What I can't understand is why she just didn't check herself out or tell you or your cousins to pick her up. I hope she has someone at home to help her, because she needs assistance."

"Parke's working on that now. I guess I would be spooked, too, if someone died in the same room where I was staying. That's kind of creepy to know that the death angel was waiting on Mrs. Valentine. She was that close."

Eva tapped "pause" on the remote and shifted around in his arms. "We're all *that close* to death. We just don't know how close. That's why we have to live right every day and constantly pray."

"Do you ever get tired of praying for me?" he whispered, lost in her beautiful eyes.

"I don't get tired of fasting and praying for you." She sighed and became contemplative. "I've just never met anyone who is so stubborn. Sometimes I feel like I took a chance on our relationship, but you won't take a chance on God. And as a God-fearing Christian, it's very frustrating—because I love you so much."

Kidd grunted. "I bet you never guessed your man would take you on an emotional roller coaster ride. That was not my intentions, but I did warn you about my demons."

"I knew you were trouble the moment I saw you." Eva smiled tenderly and leaned her head against his chest. "I love my man. There's a song I haven't heard in a long time." She began to sing the lyrics: "Somebody prayed for me, they had me on their mind. They took the time and prayed for me. I'm so glad they prayed . . ."

As she sang, Kidd was drawn into the melody. He closed his eyes and began to do exactly what the song suggested. Pray. He didn't realize his words were audible until Eva began praying along with him. When they finished with, "In the Name of Jesus," Eva whispered, "you are my heart."

"And you are mine." As Kidd stared in her eyes, a feeling suddenly came over him. However, as the emotion grew stronger, it became apparent that it was contrary to the intent of his prayer. A stirring ignited within his body.

"You've got to go," he said abruptly, startling Eva as he stood to his feet.

"What?" She blinked.

"Eva, your man is 100 plus percent male. I'm on fire for you, so get your purse and keys. I'm taking you home." He literally pulled her to her feet, then picked up the remote and aimed it at the TV.

"What is your problem? We've always controlled out hormones. We just prayed—"

"And we are going to be praying and repenting in a few minutes— if you keep looking at me like that."

Eva was taking too long to collect her things, so Kidd literally swept her up in his arms and carried her out the door, ignoring her protests. Unlocking the car doors with his remote, he stuffed her in the front seat as gently as he could. He was about to go around to the driver's side when she stopped him.

"Hey, caveman, do you mind getting my door keys? They must have fallen out of my purse while you were manhandling me." Eva asked, scowling.

He went back for her keys, relocked his door, and then dumped the keys in her lap when he got behind the wheel.

"What's the problem, Kevin? You've never treated me so disrespectfully."

Kidd's testosterone was raging, and she was accusing him of disrespecting her? If he stripped off her clothes and loved her the way he so desired, that would be disrespectful.

Setting the air to maximum cool, he rolled down his window and explained, "Baby, something came over me in there, and it would scare you for me to repeat it. I love you so much. But if I touch you one more time, I won't be able to control myself. Please understand."

Eva giggled, before she broke out into an uncontrollable laugh.

"I hope you have something funny to share with me—to take my mind off you." Irked by her carefree attitude, Kidd was trying not to dishonor her sexually, and here she was making fun of him for it.

"Baby, you are the sweetest man I know." She cleared her throat and relaxed in her seat. Then she adjusted the air to tone down the coolness. Folding her hands in her lap, she started, "Okay, here's something funny. I can't believe you survived your three-month probation at Garden Chateau. Although barely, considering you gambled with Theo—"

"Hey, the old man challenged me. How was I to know he had a stash of quarters? When I turned down that offer, he suggested his coveted desserts. I knew he was a diabetic, so I figured, why not?"

"Every nursing facility has some unforgettable characters. Miss Jessie Atkins' sweet spirit is one I'll always remember and try to emulate. And you—who would've thought you'd become so attached to a little old lady who amused herself with stories in her head—nothing more. She was ninety-seven. Slavery was long gone before she was born—legally, at least."

Kidd's temperature was beginning to come down. *Whew.* "The gambler in me says you're wrong." He blew another sigh of relief, glad he had gotten out of the house in time. Unable to fully explain the sudden lust that tried to overpower him, he drew a conclusion. Being at home alone with a beautiful woman was bad enough; being alone with a beautiful woman he was deeply in love with was unbearable.

"Really? Is there anything you won't place a bet on? We're going to have to do something about this gambling obsession you seem to have."

"You're my obsession now. Can't you tell? I say we go to the library and see if the history books back up all the stuff she said. Besides, we'll be in a public place." Then he added an incentive. "And how about this—if she was right, I'll treat you to a shopping spree in downtown Boston. What do you say?"

"Boston? That's going a long way to shop until you drop. Hmmm, tempting though . . . and what if I win . . . and we find out that Mrs. Valentine was simply a sweet lady who fantasized about slavery?"

"Then I'll treat you to a shopping spree and dinner in downtown Boston."

"Either way, it sure seems like you want me to go . . . to Boston."

"I want you to see where I came from, so you can see how I got here."

"I would love to visit Boston. Should I book my hotel room, or will you be doing that?" Eva lifted her brow.

"Woman, after what I just went through a few minutes ago?" Reaching for her hand, Kidd placed a kiss in her palm. "If I want to get you in my bed, then I'll marry you first."

"Only if I say yes."

"You think you've seen a storm raging . . . I can't take much more conversation with you and the word *bed* in the same sentence."

When they made it to Eva's condo, Kidd walked her to the door. "This can't go on for much longer, Eva," he warned. "We both know that." Backing away, he waited for her to go inside. He didn't ask for or offer a good-night kiss. "I'll pick you up tomorrow morning at ten, so we can head to the library." Kidd whirled around when he heard her lock click. Storming to his car, he got in and drove off.

"Lord, this is not even funny."

Chapter Forty

On Saturday morning, a receptionist at the St. Louis County Library ushered Kidd and Eva to the third floor where special collections of historical information were stored. Surrounded by bookshelves and cabinets, Kidd was clueless about where to begin to look for the information. Only one person seemed to be manning the desk, and she was White. *What does she know about African American history?* he wondered.

The curious couple approached the desk and read her name tag: Ruth. She listened intently, then stood and pointed out a wall of file cabinets. Housed within them were microfilms on anything from slave codes to property taxes paid.

As Eva listened to Ruth's information, a book on a nearby shelf caught her eye. Grabbing it, she sat down at a table to peruse it.

"My eyes are good and I want to keep them that way. I'll start with the books," Kidd responded to Ruth, referring to the microfilm.

"We do have records in books from every state, such as marriages, divorces, apprenticeships, morbidities . . ." Ruth rattled on.

Kidd snapped his fingers.

"That's it, the morbidity books. Do you have one for Mississippi?" Kidd's heart pounded. It could possibly validate Mrs. Valentine's intelligence or prove that she was senile and her ramblings were meaningless. Either way, Eva had already agreed to travel to Boston. He was a happy man.

Ruth fingered the spines of the books on the shelves. "It looks like we have the 1850 and 1860 volumes. The others must be on microfilm."

Which year did Mrs. Valentine supposedly quote? He thought a few minutes. Finally, he dismissed Ruth and slipped the 1860 book off the shelf. He then joined Eva at the table where she was scanning through another book.

The volume Kidd had chosen was well worn, but in good condition. He thoughtfully resisted manhandling it to preserve it for the next generation. Carefully, he opened the book and flipped through the pages until he finally reached the last names beginning with the letter N.

Kidd's heart slammed into his chest. "Eva, look at this!" He impatiently waited as she got up from the other side of the table and came around to peer over his shoulder. "Mrs. Valentine was right," he said in awe, fingering various first names. They all had Negro listed for the last name—from the top of the page to the bottom.

Eva took the seat next to him and became just as engrossed in the information. "It lists their ages, how they died, and the county where they lived. Everything is so detailed, so personalized—everything—except their identity." She shook her head sadly.

The two spent the remainder of the day in the special collections department. Numerous questions swirled in Kidd's head about his father, Samuel, and Samuel's father and Samuel's grandfather. Kidd approached Ruth countless times about how to research African American history in general. Eva seemed content reading one document from its beginning to the end.

"Do you know where Samuel was born, his parents' names, does he have any siblings, did he serve in the military?" Ruth fired off one query after another until Kidd had to confess he and his brother were not reared under the same roof with Samuel. It irked him that he didn't know the answers, and to make matters worse, it was a White person asking the questions.

He waited for the look of pity to flash in Ruth's eyes. Secretly, that was the main reason for Kidd's resentment toward Parke. It was because of his lack of knowledge about his own family. Parke made him feel— not intentionally he was now sure—incomplete when he talked about the Jamieson legacy.

"That won't stop us. That's what we're here for," Ruth said with determination, "to trace our roots."

Kidd had forgotten about Eva's presence until she came up behind him and slid her hand in his. Maybe she sensed his mood change. "Ruth, let me ask you a personal question. Considering my history, aren't you afraid of what I might uncover about your ancestors and what they might have done to mine?" he quizzed her.

"On the contrary, in the words of President Barak Obama, there is no blue America, white America, or red America. We're all Americans. I need to know the truth about our shared history. That way, I can help pass it down to the next generation. We need to warn future Americans not to repeat the past."

With a nod, Kidd smirked. The woman had passed his test. "I hadn't expected that answer." He exhaled. "By the way, you've been so helpful. I think it's about time I formally introduce myself. My name is Kevin Jamieson."

Ruth laughed. "Very nice to meet you. I detected a hint of surprise on your face. You look pretty intimidating, but I know who Jesus is."

Eva quickly came to Kidd's defense. "He's a teddy bear who roars like a jungle lion, but plays like a kitten."

"Sometimes," he added very simply. What his girlfriend didn't know about his past wouldn't hurt her. Eva already knew he carried a gun. Although Kidd had been reading his Bible and praying more, it didn't stop him from instilling fear into people by his demeanor.

"Not a problem, Mr. Jamieson. Let me know if I can be of any further assistance." She got up from behind the desk and walked over to another patron, who looked just as confused as Kidd was when he first arrived.

Deserted by Ruth and with Eva engrossed in some interesting factual data, he strolled to a shelf and randomly pulled out some books. Finally, he rejoined Eva at the table. Together they compared tidbits of enlightening information as they read.

Mentally, Kidd wondered what dirt besides Samuel's illegitimate children he could dig up. With the pride he held close to his heart, he refused to ask Parke. Whatever his mother knew, maybe this was a good time to find out.

"How fast can you pack for Boston?"

"Huh? What?" Eva blinked. "You're serious?" She closed the book she was reading.

"We can leave tonight." He didn't want to wait and a phone call wouldn't cut it.

"*You* can leave tonight. But if you're inviting me to come, then the earliest *I* can go anywhere is Saturday morning—next week."

"I'll take it."

Chapter Forty-One

Boston, Massachusetts

As Eva's plane touched down, she glanced out the window, wondering if this would be the first of many trips to Kidd's hometown—or her last. She loved him and he loved her. The question still remained, did he love Jesus enough to repent, be baptized, and accept all the gifts God had waiting for him?

Just like her mother's decision to take Eva's father back after their divorce, Eva had to make a decision whether to continue a relationship with Kidd or break it off. Their sexual frustration could only be held at bay for so long. After all, theirs was a relationship between an unsaved and a saved partner. How long would it be before the road could lead to sexual realization?

Eva took a deep breath and unbuckled her seat belt, as she prepared to depart the plane. Minutes later, she exited the concourse at Logan Airport. Her heart fluttered when she locked eyes with Kidd. In all of his "black-coffee-without-the-cream" handsomeness, she forgot her resolve. He was holding a large white sign as if he was a company chauffeur picking up a passenger.

What was the man up to now? She smiled. Did she not drop him off at Lambert Airport the previous morning before she went to work? They hadn't been away from each other for twenty-four hours.

The closer she came toward him, she could make out the words: *I'm looking for Eva Savoy, the woman I love.*

Eva prayed inwardly, *God, please save Kidd soon, for himself and then for me. I'm moments away from lusting, so I'm going to repent now and pray for strength. In Jesus' name. Amen.* In the back of her mind, she heard whispers of "don't settle, don't compromise, don't back down on your beliefs. Remember, his lack of salvation is a deal breaker."

Kidd didn't wait for her to reach him. His strides were long until he was inches before her. He plucked her carry-on bag off her shoulder and lifted her off the ground. "Mmmm. I've missed you." He snuggled her tightly to his chest.

She giggled while basking in his attention. "Since yesterday?"

"Every moment we're apart."

Releasing her, Kidd squeezed her hand. As he guided her to the baggage claim area, he said, "They say a day is like a thousand years to God—and me too."

Impressed, Eva lifted a brow and chuckled. "Is that Bible reference 2 Peter 3:8?"

"I don't know. It's in there somewhere."

Once at the carousel, they chatted and laughed while Eva watched her garment bag pass her by two times. Kidd had her so swallowed up in his "I miss you" hugs that she could barely get his attention.

Finally, with her single piece of luggage in tow, he guided her to his vehicle. Exiting the airport, Eva admired the passing structures, homes, and businesses in a city noted as one of the original thirteen American colonies. She wondered what it would be like to live in a place with such daunting historical landmarks.

She could feel Kidd's eyes on her despite him driving. "You're so beautiful. Thank you for coming."

She blushed. "Considering you paid too much for my airline ticket and the hotel that looks very nice online, you're more than welcome." Eva took a deep breath. "So what do we have planned?"

Kidd appeared relaxed and peaceful, wearing a smirk across his beardless face. Which look did she prefer? It was a toss-up—the beard or his smooth skin. "Well, I wanted to play tourist and take you to No Name for lunch, then to Faneuil Hall, the aquarium in the North End, and then on to shopping downtown on the cobblestones . . . and—"

She stopped him. "I don't want to eat at a place where you can't remember the name. Give me a tour of your life. Show me where you lived as a child, where you went to school, your hangouts. Show me how Kevin Jamieson went from a fifteen-pound bundle of joy to the handsome, full-of-attitude man you are today."

"Fifteen pounds?" His laugh was hearty. "I said I wanted to, but my mother can't wait to see you. She's first on the tourist attraction list. She likes you and hasn't stopped talking about you since that open house. It's never 'how are you doing, or how is the house shaping up?' Your name seems to dominate our conversations, and I ain't complaining one bit."

Eva smiled. Sandra was a sweetheart who loved her sons. How could Kidd remain spiritually defiant around such a praying woman like her? It made Eva wonder how instrumental she could be in leading him to Christ, short of cooking and serving the Bible on a plate for him to chew on it.

"Sandra's a jewel, Kidd."

"She is. That's why I became so angry growing up that my father could mess her over like that. Ma and I spent most of yesterday just talking about things. I asked her questions about Samuel that I didn't want to know before. Since you and I visited the library, I've had a hunger to know my roots. That was a startling revelation for my mother."

"Did you get answers?"

He shrugged. "Some. She didn't hold anything back and told me what she knew. All I know is that it's time for completion, if I can get it. I'm hoping you'll stick by me as I battle with my demons. Baby, just hang with me. Boston will be memorable, I promise you."

"Are you sure you want me to learn your deep, dark secrets right now? I mean, it's kind of personal. Don't you want to digest the news first?"

Reaching over, Kidd took her hand and squeezed it gently. "You're so interwoven in my heart, I can't untangle you. I want you to find out about Kidd Jamieson's past at the same time I do. That's just how important you are to me. Got it?"

"Got it." Eva mockingly shivered, as if she was afraid to disagree.

Kidd barked out a laugh. "Stop with the fearful expression. You know I would never hurt you, woman."

"Humph. What about when you pulled your caveman stunt on me a couple of weeks ago?"

"I was protecting you from me. I know my feelings toward you, and I know my body. I don't lose control unless it's in anger or passion. Trust me. I had to get you out of my house."

At least, he does have restraint. She thanked the Lord for that. They laughed together.

"I'll give you this minitour, starting from my childhood home in Mattapan. Unfortunately, now we call it 'Murderpan'. We've lost so many of our teenagers here." He pointed out some streets and bypassed others. "Here's Dudley, Washington, Forest Hill . . ."

Kidd continued driving until it appeared they were close to their destination. He turned on Northfolk Street, then Elizabeth, until finally, Kidd slowed on Astoria.

Eva swallowed hard. It wasn't a street where she would send her children out to play. So far, she had seen blocks and blocks of overbearing buildings. Two- and three-story residences—some brick, most with siding—all with small front yards, lined the streets.

302

A few questionable characters loitered out front, watching as Kidd's vehicle cruised by. Eva glanced to make sure her door was locked. Some seemed to recognize him and nodded; he waved. The mantra "only the strong survive" crossed her mind. Kidd was that—strong and tough—and, thankfully, he had survived.

"That's it there." Kidd pointed. "The white building. We lived on the second floor." He lingered in front of his childhood home and sighed. Then, nodding as if he was saying good-bye, he drove off.

"That's Almont Park where I played basketball and softball," he said, cruising by.

As his tour continued, their surroundings changed dramatically. They passed Roslindale and then on to Hyde Park.

"About three years ago, I moved my mother to where she lives today. Ace still lives there too—for now."

Eva listened hard, trying to hear what Kidd wasn't saying about his past.

He turned on Grantley Avenue. The block was lined with condominiums. Large bay windows highlighted the property; the sporadic landscaping gave the complex a touch of flair. Steep stairs led to the front door, evidence of energetic and able-bodied homeowners.

"Wow. These are nice. Talk about going from rags to riches."

"Not really." Kidd chuckled. "They're nice, but I can take you to some parts in Milton, which isn't far from here, or to Back Bay, and you'll see some properties that will triple your wow."

There was ample parking, so Kidd claimed a spot closest to his mom's place. When he came around to help Eva, he stole a kiss. Then grabbing her hand, he led her toward a corner unit.

His mother was standing in the doorway, waiting patiently. Sandra easily looked to be in her late thirties instead of flirting with her fifties. She was dressed in tan Capri pants, a white blouse, bare-footed with dark toenail polish, and curls that rested on her shoulders.

Sandra clapped with enthusiasm and smiled as though Eva was

headlining a show. Climbing the long flight of stairs, Kidd grinned proudly.

"I sure don't get smiles like that when I come home," he whispered, placing a kiss in his girlfriend's hair.

Eva bumped him as she held on to the railing. "Jealous?" She laughed.

Once they reached the landing, Sandra wrapped Eva in the same kind of soothing hug she had given her in Kidd's backyard a while ago. Her eyes danced with excitement. "Eva, you're more beautiful than before."

"Thank you," she responded gracefully.

Taking over, Sandra guided Eva into a spacious living room. Immaculate mahogany wood floors covered the first level, along with the stairs that led to the second level. A pencil-sketched portrait of two boys caught her eye. "A Mother's Love," was the caption beneath it. *Maybe one day, I'll understand,* Eva considered.

The living room's décor revealed that Kidd's mother had an eye for color combinations. Eva reclined in an overstuffed chair with Kidd, who seemed attached at her hip. Sandra left the room and returned a few minutes later carrying a tray filled with bottled waters, iced teas, and snacks. After she placed it on a glass-top coffee table, the charming woman sat on the sofa and beckoned them to come and join her.

Anticipating what she was up to, Kidd huffed and rolled his eyes as if he was annoyed. Eva grinned and pinched him. Then dutifully, she sat between the mother and son. The show began with a stack of photo albums that rested on a nearby table. Sandra took the album on top and, in reverence, opened it. Again, Kidd groaned as his mother recited the details of her two sons' antics as toddlers.

"Hey, Ma, do you remember how much I weighed as a baby?" Kidd asked, after the third album.

Eva lifted a brow in a teasing gesture, while he twisted one of her curls around his finger.

Sandra paused. "Hmmm. Yeah, you were a big one."

Eva snickered.

"I'd say you were a little more than eight pounds, which was hefty baby weight back then."

They were laughing when Ace opened the door; his muscular body filled the doorframe. A basketball was tucked under his arm. Eva watched him enter the room. Today he looked younger than his twenty-six years. When she met him in St. Louis, he reminded her of a teenager instead of a grown man.

"Hey, ya'll. Eva, it's good to see you again." With a lazy walk, Ace headed straight to the couch. Looking as though he was going to greet Eva with a hug or kiss, Kidd stood and intercepted.

"Ace, shower first. You know I don't play that on my furniture. Whew!" Sandra scrunched up her nose.

"And after you freshen up, don't even think about touching my woman," Kidd said, in a threatening voice. He towered over his brother and warned, "A simple hello will do from afar."

Ace grunted. "Chill, bro. She knows I'm the better-looking one."

Kidd threw a punch, but Ace ducked as if it was a ritual stunt between them. When their mother chuckled at their antics, it confirmed to Eva that the brothers were simply horsing around.

"Is he staying out of trouble, Ma, really?" Kidd asked, after Ace disappeared up the staircase.

Sandra folded her hands and sighed. "He has a probation officer who is on him about getting a job or enrolling in a training program. That could keep him out of jail. Cameron has stuck by him too."

Kidd didn't comment, so Sandra steered the conversation back to the snapshots. After an exhausting few hours of storytelling, he announced they were going sightseeing.

Their first stop was to fulfill his promise to take her downtown shopping, but there they purchased nothing. Not too far away, Kidd circled Boylston Street a few times to get a parking space near Filene's Basement.

There was no window-shopping this time. The result was three bags of bargains. Eva searched through racks of clothing to find styles she hadn't seen at home. Thrift store shopping with her mother had paid off. She could spot a bargain when she saw one. She even found some items for Kidd's house.

"Are you getting hungry, babe?"

Bargain hunting was hard work. Indicating that she was starving, they left. On their way to dinner, Kidd continued as a tour guide, advising Eva they were in South Boston. "We're heading to Fish Pier where No Name Restaurant has some of the best seafood in Boston."

Eva welcomed the fast-paced feel of the East Coast and the kiss of the Atlantic Ocean. It was such a contrast to the Midwest. Nevertheless, Missouri was her home and she loved the "Show Me State."

Immediately, she laughed when they arrived at the eating establishment. "It's really called No Name."

Finding a parking space wasn't a small task. When the mission was accomplished, Kidd helped her out of the car. Instead of holding her hand, he wrapped his arm around her waist and guided her inside. The worn wide-plank hardwood floors and wood tables gave the place a casual ambience. Eva didn't feel overdressed in her flirty, gypsy-styled, multicolored skirt and her minijacket over a plain white top.

After they were seated, she couldn't wait to scan the menu. Kidd made a few suggestions. None of them really seemed appealing at first, so their waiter offered the seafood platter. That way, she could sample a variety of selections.

"Hmmm. How about the salad with the lobster meat?"

Kidd arched his brow at Eva. "So you're trying one of my recommendations after all," he teased, then ordered glasses of water with lemon for them.

Eva shrugged and glanced around. Kidd watched her every moment, which made her feel so cherished. She loved him and wanted them to live happily ever after, but God . . . Eva blinked when Kidd reached across the table and gathered her hands.

"You know the saying, 'home is where the heart is'?"

She nodded.

He brought her hands to his lips and kissed them. "Although Bean-town is my home, until my 'heart' landed in Boston yesterday morn-ing, I wasn't home. You look pretty and smell good. You are my heart, and I love you." He rubbed her hands at the same time he trapped her sandal-covered feet between his loafers under the table. "Thanks for letting me kidnap you for the weekend."

"I love you so," she whispered, then looped her fingers through his. "You're my heart, Kevin, and St. Louis isn't the same without you." Eva had to look away because the stare he was giving her was smothering. As if somehow cued, the waiter returned with their glasses of water.

"So tell me why this No Name nonsense is so special?"

"It started as a simple diner for fishermen when they returned to shore. Soon the phrase caught on and the label 'No Name' stuck." His expression was unsure. "If I'm not mistaken, it's Boston's oldest restau-rant under the same ownership for almost one hundred years. Celebri-ties have been known to stop in . . ."

Kidd was still explaining the tale when their food arrived. He gave a sincere blessing over their meal and offered thanks for Eva's safe arrival. Her heart melted. Very few words were exchanged until almost every bit of seafood had been consumed.

"That was delicious. Seafood will never taste the same." Eva dabbed her mouth with a napkin. "I'm stuffed. I hope you don't mind if I go back to the hotel and rest up for tomorrow," she said, after he paid the bill and left a generous tip.

Standing, Kidd stretched and reached for her hand. "Of course not."

"I heard the East Coast church services are long."

"You have no idea."

Chapter Forty-Two

*T*he next morning, Kidd called Eva from the lobby of the Hilton Hotel. "Good morning, Miss Savoy. Your chauffeur is waiting." "I'll be right down, Mr. Jamieson."

Two minutes and counting, the elevator doors opened. The gold trim and lights reflecting off of a mirrored background gave Eva a celestial glow and rendered Kidd speechless. His eyes swept from her stilettos, to her shimmery stocking-covered legs, to an all-white, two-piece suit. Suddenly white was his favorite color.

Walking up to the elevator door, he stepped in and allowed the door to close.

"What are you doing?" Eva teased. She had to know exactly what he was about to do. Sweeping her in his arms, he brushed his lips across hers before taking her garment bag and small carry-on.

Eva let out a nervous giggle when the doors opened on the second floor. They both greeted a short woman with a wide church hat perched on her head as she entered the elevator. Kidd winked at Eva and then pushed the lobby button. When the doors opened again, he allowed the woman to exit first.

Standing in the middle of the lobby, he asked, "Can you get any more beautiful? You are stunning, baby." Kidd bent down and cupped her face until her lips touched his. He kissed her as if that moment was all he had to do for the day. Pulling back, she added a few more pecks on the lips and took a deep breath.

"Show off." Eva's smile was alluring. "You've never kissed me like that before."

Standing at the desk to check out, Kidd threw his head back and laughed. "Really? Maybe it's because you haven't worn my favorite color before."

"I thought maroon was your favorite color."

"It was."

Minutes later, he steered her toward the revolving doors. Continuing their conversation, Kidd made a declaration, "Let me be clear. As for the kiss, you are my woman and I love you, which means I can show off any time I want. You've got a problem with that?"

"I'll never complain again." She giggled.

"That's what I want to hear."

In the hotel parking lot, he placed Eva's luggage in the trunk. His mother opened the door to give the front seat to Eva. When she got out of the car, the two women exchanged a sincere hug.

"Sandra, you look so pretty in your classy hat and that elegant dress—so chic. I couldn't pull off that hat look." It was obvious to Eva that Sandra's style was simple, but sophisticated.

"You just haven't found the right one," she insisted and patted her lilac, wide-brimmed hat, trimmed in small beads.

"I didn't realize you were waiting. I hope I wasn't too long," Eva apologized.

"Not at all. Here, you take the front seat."

While Eva shook her head, Kidd took control and ushered his mother into the backseat. After nudging Eva to sit in the front, they were on their way. In less than ten minutes, Kidd turned from Blue Hill Avenue to Woodrow.

The pastor, Hershel Lane, stood at the top of the steps outside Faithful Church of Christ, speaking to everyone who entered. He was a large man with thick, gray sideburns that connected to his beard.

"Praise the Lord, Sister Nicholson." He nodded. "Kidd, welcome home! It's good to see you again . . . and with two lovely ladies on your arms."

His mother grinned proudly. Kidd exchanged greetings, introducing Eva before they proceeded inside. The worship service was already underway on the second level. They walked into a sanctuary that could easily accommodate hundreds. Glancing around, Kidd nodded at a few recognizable faces, whose names he had forgotten.

His memory was full of times when his mother dragged him and his brother to service. As he and Ace got older, however, Sandra's urgent pleas went mostly ignored. Today it was all about his free will and answering God's call to salvation.

All week long, God had been leading him to Mark 2:17. Once Kidd read it, the Scripture wouldn't leave his mind: *It is not the healthy who need a doctor, but the sick. I have not come to call the righteous, but sinners.*

The atmosphere seemed notably different to Kidd. The praise was in high gear as they followed Sandra to what was probably her favorite seat. This time when his mother and Eva knelt to give reverence, Kidd joined them. Neither seemed surprised by his actions.

Minutes later, Pastor Lane walked through a side door, dressed in a red and black robe. He took his seat in the pulpit. When invited to stand, Eva, along with other visitors, were acknowledged. Church announcements were next, followed by two selections from a small choir with powerful voices. Kidd was getting antsy. He was ready for the sermon and to get it over with.

Then Pastor Lane stood and requested another selection, almost as if to taunt Kidd. Eva squeezed his hand, which was linked to hers. She must have sensed his impatience. He loved her. Wasn't he about to make a commitment because of her?

Beside Me, there is no other, God spoke.

After the choir finished singing, Pastor Lane opened his Bible. He didn't give a Scripture, but immediately began his sermon.

"Life isn't fair. We've heard it, we've said it, or perhaps we've thought it," Pastor Lane stated. "Guess what? You're right, but that's in our natural mind. Cain killed Abel, and what did God do when Cain cried out because he feared for his life? God marked his head, so that no man would harm the murderous brother. Look at David, a big-time sinner. Yet he was an even bigger repenter, so much so that God called David a man after His own heart. How about God's chosen people, His elite generation—the Israelites—yet they served their enemies, the Egyptians, as slaves."

Kidd drowned out the congregation and was locked into the message. He didn't want to miss one word of the sermon.

"There were so many perceived injustices toward men in the Bible that I would be here all day running down the list. So what's your beef today? Nobody likes you on your job? Your father deserted you as a child? Your husband divorced you for another woman—or sometimes another man, these days . . ." Pastor Lane stirred up his members.

"That's right!" a few members shouted.

"Let's look at Jesus. He had it rough from the time He got here. The Son of God had to be born in a manger, in a barn filled with animals. Raise your hand if you were born outside in the cold. Hold them high." With his microphone in his hand, the pastor leaned on the podium, waiting to count hands.

"It wasn't fair that the Pharisees and Sadducees hated Him for doing good. . . . Have you ever heard of such nonsense? You bless someone with a thousand bucks and they turn around and get mad at you about it." He paused and lowered his voice, "This is your moment of self-examination. Be honest with yourself. You can't lie to God anyway. What's your injustice today that the Lord can't fix?"

As the pastor conjured up examples, Kidd's beef with his father seemed less significant. His mother and Eva never looked his way, but he wondered what they were thinking. Pastor Lane tossed out more common complaints. Kidd didn't realize that an hour had passed since he began his sermon.

He swallowed hard and his hands became sweaty. It had been more than a week since he'd thought about his bargain with God concerning his salvation. He had asked God to hold off a little bit longer. God had been calling him for weeks, maybe all his life, but Kidd had rejected the RSVP.

Will He call me again? Kidd wondered. *Or has my door of opportunity closed?*

His heart pounded, anticipating the moment was upon him. The pastor opened his arms wide and the congregation stood. As though it was a signal crafted specially for him, Kidd heard the pastor say, "It's time for you to allow Jesus to even the score in your life. The Bible says in Romans 8:18: *'I consider that our present sufferings are not worth comparing with the glory that will be revealed in us.'*"

He pounded the podium. "You need to stop listening to spiritually uneducated, silly-minded people! Stop carrying that burden that is weighing you down from sunup to sunset. Stop it! Come today. God is calling you. You've held off long enough with your stubborn, prideful, boastful self. Isaiah 64:6 says, *'All of us have become like one who is unclean, and all our righteous acts are like filthy rags.'*"

By now, Kidd was on the edge of his seat. Pastor Lane continued his invitation. "If you are willing to come, He's got something powerful to clean you up—it's called salvation. Jesus stands at the door. Obey the Scriptures: repent and be baptized for the remission of your sins. This is God's order, not mine. Don't say you'll come back another time, come today."

Okay, this is why you're here. It's your time. Go, his heart pressed him.

Don't be persuaded by this one sermon. Consider your options, a louder voice in his head mocked him.

Kidd looked to his left and right. Both his girl and his mother had their heads bowed and eyes closed.

Why haven't you come? God spoke.

Because . . . he struggled to finish the sentence.

I stand at your door and knock. I am Your Father. Why do you not let Me in? God asked. *The day you hear My voice, harden not your heart.*

"It's time to surrender," Kidd mumbled. He felt himself being propelled and stood up. As though a video was playing before his very eyes, Kidd saw a vision of Jesus' lifeless body lying on the ground. The gash in His side, with water and blood flowing to form a stream—it was a horrific image seared in Kidd's mind.

He stepped out of the pew and walked down the aisle on a mission. Coming face-to-face with one of the ministers, Kidd knew that simply receiving prayer this time wouldn't do. "Welcome, brother. What do you want from God today?" asked a man whose stature resembled a teenager, but whose voice was commanding.

"I want God to even the score. I've been carrying something for a long time."

"Then repent, brother. Be sorry for all your sins that you've committed in your heart, mind, and body. Confess them right now—not to me—but to Christ."

Come unto Me, those who are heavy burdened, I will give you rest. It sounded like a guarantee from God.

He nodded, although the young man hadn't said another word.

"Lord, I am sorry for my actions. I want to move on with my life. I want to be delivered. Please save me." Until he had finished, Kidd didn't realize he had spoken out loud.

"Brother, He's able. You've repented. Now let God do the rest. He wants you to be born of the water and the Spirit. If you're ready for a clean slate, we have ministers ready to baptize you. That's the next step. Then you'll have to continue in His Word."

Closing his eyes, Kidd nodded again. This was it. Either God was going to do what He said He was going to do, or He wasn't. Kidd was bouncing the ball back in God's court.

Prove Me, God challenged him. *I am not a man that I should lie.*

Opening his eyes again, Kidd followed several other candidates through a door behind the pulpit and proceeded down the stairs. The songs and praises seemed to follow him. Soon he was ushered into a small room to change into all-white garments: pants, socks, and a T-shirt. Within a few minutes, he and the others were led to a pool.

One by one, each candidate was baptized. Soon it was Kidd's turn to descend into the water. Taking the steps down into the pool, another minister who didn't look strong enough to support his weight, instructed Kidd to cross his arms over his chest.

Gripping the back of Kidd's T-shirt firmly, the man lifted one arm. "My dear brother, on the confession of your sins, your faith in God and the confidence we have in the Holy Scriptures, we indeed baptize you in the name of the Father, and of the Son, and of the Holy Spirit. God will give you His promises and will equip you with every spiritual gear to fight the devil and gifts you need to present you faultless in the day of judgment. Amen."

Swiftly, Kidd was dunked under the water and then yanked back to the surface.

He didn't even recognize his voice when he came up. "Praise God! I did it! I'm free!" Then Kidd shouted a series of times, "Thank You, Jesus!" while pumping his fist in the air. "Hallelujah!" Not an excitable person by nature, unless he felt threatened, Kidd couldn't believe his own theatrics. But he also couldn't stop himself from praising God. Nor could he control the tears streaming down his face.

Unable to remember how he got back to the changing room, the realization hit that he had made a commitment to God—and he was determined not to back out. He looked in the mirror as he dried off and donned his own clothes. Squinting, Kidd studied his face. There was no noticeable difference. But somehow, he didn't feel the burden of life overpowering him any longer, even with Samuel's absence. Taking a few more minutes to himself, he made sure that there were no lingering signs of his tears.

Kidd stepped out of the room and was guided down a corridor where he heard loud voices of praise, unrecognizable words, and jubilant singing. Although he wanted to join in their praise, he bypassed the room and kept walking down the foyer. He was anxious to rejoin his mother and Eva, who waited with open arms to receive him. Squeezing him in a group hug, their tears went unchecked. They patted his back and rejoiced with him. Kidd couldn't contain his joy and laughter.

Finally, stepping out of their embrace, they fixed their eyes on him.

"That was so simple," Kidd said with a sense of awe.

"Salvation is more than the water baptism. Now you've got to study the Bible and learn how to walk a different lifestyle," his mother said, sniffling, as Eva nodded in agreement.

"I don't know why I fought God so long." Kidd shook his head.

"Stubborn," Eva and Sandra said in unison. Neither woman cracked a smile.

Chapter Forty-Three

"We'd better hurry before we miss the boat," Kidd advised Eva an hour later. They were back at Sandra's condo, sitting and talking about Jesus. Kidd had questions about his experience, and his mother and Eva answered them as best they could.

When she heard him mention the boat, Sandra threw up her hands in disappointment. "I cooked Sunday dinner for you, and what do you do? Go and spend money on a boat."

Surely, today's baptism had changed Kidd's mind-set about gambling—surely. Didn't he know that a walk with Jesus involved letting go of old habits? Eva held her peace. He was now a babe in Christ and salvation meant crawling before walking. She was just ecstatic that Kidd took the initial steps toward a lifelong commitment to the Lord. The true test would be a different lifestyle, but God had the power to keep him from falling—if Kidd would accept it.

"Since we fly out late tonight, I wanted to take Eva on the Spirit of Boston for a dinner cruise."

Sandra would not be placated. "For almost a hundred dollars a plate?" She shook her head. "Why didn't you mention it when you saw me cooking all this food?"

"Leftovers taste great, Ma." Kidd wrapped his mother in a hug. "We'll be back." He kissed her squarely on the forehead and ushered a reluctant Eva out the door.

In the car, Eva stared out the window. She felt guilty leaving his mother, but giddy because what she wanted so much had actually happened.

"What's the matter, baby? I got baptized today. We should be celebrating my new birth. Right?"

"I am rejoicing. But I thought you'd want your mom to be part of it too. I'm hurt for her. She seemed so disappointed when we left." In the midst of her joy, Eva had to express her concerns. "Besides, I know that the boats at home are casinos, and they have restaurants to lure people in. Can't you cancel?"

"Have you ever heard the saying, 'You're not in Kansas anymore'? The Spirit of Boston is a cruise boat. We board at the Seaport World Trade Center. I thought you would enjoy the skyline. Besides, I wanted some time alone with my lady."

"Sorry," she mumbled, chastened.

Reaching over, he grabbed her hand and squeezed it. "Babe, you had so much faith in me before today. Don't lose it now. Okay?"

"I won't. I love you so much."

"And I'm even more in love with you. So relax, love. The decks are climate-controlled, and the buffet is scrumptious."

Eva did as he said and closed her eyes. Leaning her head against the headrest, she relaxed and linked her left hand with his right one.

"You want to do any more sightseeing?"

She shook her head. "Nope. The best Boston sight was watching you get your sins washed away. I'm good. Wait until I tell my parents and sister."

He chuckled. "Yeah, wait until I tell Parke and Malcolm."

Soon they had made it to the Seaport World Trade Center and parked in the Seaport Hotel garage. Eva couldn't hug Kidd enough, as they strolled to the majestic boat.

"Wow!" she exclaimed when they boarded.

Their host led them to a dining room that could rival any in a downtown St. Louis restaurant. With Kidd behind her, Eva followed the man up a spiral staircase to a top deck where many tables were set up for intimate dining.

When it came time to be seated, Kidd ushered the host out of his way. "I've got this, man," he said in a territorial tone. Pulling out Eva's chair for her to be seated, he then took his seat.

Blushing, Eva rested her elbows on the table to cradle her chin. "Show-off."

"Some things, Miss Savoy, will never change—even with salvation. You are still my lady, and I can take care of you. Do you think I'm going to let some other man admire your backside while he waits for you to sit down? Think again."

She scrunched her nose at him. Eva had no further comment concerning his covetousness. The closeness she felt with him was stronger than she had ever experienced in the past. She sighed in contentment as she glanced out the window. "What a beautiful sight. It's such a different world here. Are we going out to the Atlantic Ocean?"

"No. The Spirit of Boston travels within the inner harbor and the outer islands. Come on, let's eat."

Standing, Kidd reached for her hand. The buffet table was long and the seafood selection was endless. They stacked their plates with a sampling of everything and returned to their seats. Once Eva was settled, Kidd took her hands. Before bowing his head to pray, he stared into her eyes. "You are mesmerizing." He leaned forward and brushed a soft kiss on her lips.

"Lord, in the name of Jesus, thank You for keeping Your end of the bargain and giving me grace in my moments of stupidity. I didn't deserve Your forgiveness, but You gave it to me. I didn't deserve this beautiful woman I have, but You gave her to me anyway. And I plan on keeping both—You and her. Thank You, Jesus."

Warmth stirred in Eva's soul at the sound of Kidd's heartfelt prayer. It was music to her ears and a feeling of euphoria surrounded her like a dream. No, she did not want to share this moment with his mother. Before she opened her eyes, she added, "And by the way, Lord, please bless and sanctify our food. In Jesus' name. Amen."

Slowly, she met Kidd's eyes.

"Amen. Thanks for coming up the rear with that one." Kidd smirked then frowned. "I'm still trying to get over the fact that Jesus really is a sin-buster. I can't explain the feeling, except to say I feel care-free, with no burdens riding my back."

Eva smiled and nodded that she understood. "It's just the beginning. God will show you things that will make the Bible come alive in your life. Now you mentioned a bargain? What were you talking about?"

Kidd shrugged and reached for the butter. "The last time I was at your church and got prayer, I made up my mind that I would take the plunge—no pun intended—but I wanted my mother to witness my new birth. I guess it was my tribute to her, since she birthed me into the world. So the deal I made with God was, if He would let me hold off the whole commitment thing until I came back home, I wanted my mother to be present when I received Christ." He smeared butter on his bread and took a bite.

Eva frowned. "Kevin Jamieson, you played a dangerous game with God. Not only did God give you grace, you had a whole lot of mercy going for you since your so-called bargain with God. Do you realize you could have died in your sins before receiving the Lord's salvation? We're not promised tomorrow. God didn't have to allow you to live to see this day. That's why salvation is so urgent. When you hear His voice, you must not harden your heart. It's the most important step you can take in your life. You truly have a lot to be thankful for," she fussed. Then she praised God for His grace.

"He did say it, and here I am."

"Thank You, Jesus." Eva wasn't aware the boat had set sail until the music started to serenade them. A DJ was onboard, along with live singers. Their repertoire was impressive—from line dancing to country music to Motown.

Eva had never seen Kidd smile so much. He seemed so relaxed. They talked about silly stuff, laughed at nothing, and flirted with each other. Although they were stuffed, they nibbled on an array of desserts that were served at each table.

"Let's take a walk on the deck."

Lulled by the music, Eva followed him outside and admired the beauty of Boston's skyline. What seemed like a million lights twinkled from inside the tall buildings. Snuggling in Kidd's arms, Eva leaned back and closed her eyes. She was content with their moment of quietness.

Too soon, Kidd was steering her back inside. "Come on. It's getting chilly."

The entertainment was jumping when they returned to their seats. Minutes later, the DJ played an R&B tune, "Let's Get Married" by Jagged Edge. Kidd stared at her like he never had before. Eva's heart pounded, not sure of what was happening.

"I asked you once if you were getting married, and your exact words were, 'It's none of your business.' I didn't like that answer, but I respected your privacy. What was that all about?"

She shrugged. "I enjoy anything with a happily-ever-after ending—romance novels, romantic comedies, the weekly Bridal Bliss showcases from Essence.com, bridal magazines, and movies with a tender love story. If I mentioned my fascination to my mother, she would have ideas in her head that I'm either desperate or keeping a secret. I'm neither. I believe every woman wants to get married, but when a man hears the 'm' word, he assumes he's the prey and takes off running. That's a good way to lose the best thing in the world."

"Baby, you have never chased me away. I may have physically walked away when we argued, but you had already taken control of my heart. And there's no way a man can live without a strong, beating heart."

Eva's eyes misted. "I love you when you speak from that strong, beating heart of yours."

Kidd leaned forward and planted a soft kiss on her lips. "Let's Get Married" was still playing in the background. "Recently, when I was over at your place, I saw a stack of bridal magazines stuffed into a bag. And I started wondering . . . hmmm, is she feeling what I'm feeling? If so, then it's time for me to get down on my knee. I think we should give both of our mothers something to talk about."

Kidd stood, reached into his pocket, and took out something small that he concealed in his hand. Then he bent on one knee. Tears instantly streamed down Eva's cheeks, and he brushed them away with his free hand. With one flick of his thumb, he opened a velvet box.

"I saw this brand in one of your magazines I shoplifted from your place. Don't get angry—that was before Jesus cleaned me up! I am no longer a thief. Since I bought this at Jared's, I'm assuming I did good." He grinned sheepishly.

Eva was almost breathless as she managed to utter, "It's beautiful."

"Eva Savoy, you took a chance on this bad boy from Boston. I'm asking you to search my heart and know that deep down inside, I'm a good man who will love and protect you like no other man can or will. I've fulfilled all my requirements, including surrendering to the Lord and getting permission from your father. So now I ask you, will you marry me?"

Kidd talked to her dad? Was the song still playing and were the voices getting louder? Tears blinded her vision. She couldn't look around. Through tiny bits of clarity, Kidd came into focus. She nodded in the affirmative.

"Umm-umm. Not good enough." He smirked, still on bended knee.

The live singers, a two-man and one-woman trio, made their way to the table. They began singing the lyrics to "Let's Get Married." It had to be a setup. One guy handed Kidd his microphone.

Eva held her breath. Was Kidd about to serenade her?

"I'm waiting," Kidd whispered, inching the microphone to her lips.

"Yes, I will marry you," she said softly.

The place erupted in claps, whistles, and cheers. The DJ struck up the 1980s hit by Kool and the Gang, "Celebration." The singers bounced to the rhythm and danced away.

When Kidd got to his feet, he pulled Eva into his embrace where she cried uncontrollable tears of joy. She was still sniffling when the two-hour excursion came to a close and the ship returned to the harbor. A line of well-wishers congratulated them until they walked off the ship.

By the time they made it back to their vehicle, Eva startled Kidd and initiated a tender kiss that left him moaning.

"Wow!" Leaning against the car, he took a few minutes to catch his breath. "Woman, your subscription to those bridal magazines is about to pay off. You have forty-eight hours to plan our wedding."

Chapter Forty-Four

Kidd's mother cried and screamed her happiness at the news that her son was an engaged man. Sandra put the food fiasco on the back burner, as she and Eva hugged each other.

"Sorry to break up this tender moment, Ma, Eva, but we have a plane to catch. We'd better grab our bags."

Half an hour later, they were out the door and heading to Logan Airport. Today had been an extraordinary day. Kidd had gotten engaged to Jesus and his woman. Could it get any better? He was definitely a happy man.

On their return flight back to St. Louis, Eva snuggled up next to him. In the sexiest tone he had ever heard her utter, she sweetly gave him a piece of her mind. "Kevin?"

"Yeah, baby?"

"Although I agreed to be your wife," Eva sassed him, "you will not bully me into marrying you, as if I was nine months pregnant. It's mid-August now. I need at least until October, and that's a rush. After all the magazines I've studied, I really do want a fairy-tale wedding."

"Our first disagreement as an engaged couple." Kidd was amused, but succumbed to her terms. "Babe, I want you to have the wedding of your dreams. Whatever your parents can't foot, I will. That's just how much I want you."

Eva's eyes misted.

Uh-huh. Kidd couldn't take any more tears. He just knew how much he loved her, so he kissed her.

It wasn't even five minutes later when Eva voiced another concern. "I've been thinking."

"That's scary."

She slapped him on the knee. "Seriously, the fall semester starts in a few weeks. I can't do both—study for a degree and plan a wedding." She gritted her teeth. "Is there any way possible we can hold off until next fall? I can get through the semester, then—"

Kidd's mouth dropped open. "How much willpower do you think I have? No, that's not possible for a saved man, barely a worldly man. Absolutely not. I'm in love with you. I'm attracted to you physically, which increases my libido. Now, taking those things into consideration, how fast can you speed up the process?"

Her look of realization was priceless. His woman actually hadn't considered that men didn't hold out for sex unless they had power from God. Kidd had that now, but how long would it last?

"I told you a while back that I graduated from junior college. After that, I just wasn't motivated to go further. At least, until I saw your passion. I've decided to go back to school. It may surprise you that I like being in control—"

"Not you," Eva teased and wrinkled her nose.

"I know. Who would have guessed?" They laughed. "I'm going to get a business degree with an emphasis in management. Let's sit out a semester, or a year. Let's invest in our marriage first; then we'll enroll together next year."

"Now I've got a wedding to plan in six weeks . . . thanks to a fiancé who seems to have control problems," she mumbled.

Kidd groaned. "Okay, princess, but if I won't kiss you until then, don't blame me. I can only take so much stimuli for so long. Let's see how much self-control I'll have on our honeymoon."

Eva swallowed hard. She looked out the window, but Kidd could tell by her expression that her mind was still ticking.

"Well, one thing off our checklist is house hunting," Kidd said with a sigh.

Eva whipped her neck around. "What do you mean? That's *your* house."

"Huh? You said you liked my house."

"I do, for you. The kitchen is too small and so are the rooms."

Women. Kidd would never understand them, especially the one he was about to marry. However, he had a whole lifetime to try. "Okay, we'll move as soon as you have our firstborn," Kidd countered. When she didn't respond, he teased, "What's the matter? Cat got your tongue?"

Eva shook her head. "Nope. I guess I'd better start picking out names."

He was speechless.

On the way to work Monday morning, Kidd stopped by Walgreens to browse through the bridal magazines. Considering his selection, one cover in particular caught his attention. He plucked it out of the rack and, with a smirk, walked to the counter to pay for it.

The clerk lifted a brow. "Never seen a man buy one of these," she said, ringing up his purchase.

Kidd shrugged and slipped his wallet out of his back pocket to pay her. "Hey, there are some romantic guys around. I just happen to be one of them." Eva wasn't going to get the upper hand on him when it came to a fairy-tale wedding—he hoped.

At work, the news of a third death of a resident floated throughout the facility—Mr. Johnston. Kidd reflected on his former nemesis who had suffered a massive heart attack at the dinner table on Sunday evening. The attending nurse said he died before the paramedics arrived.

Kidd wished he had one more chance to try and be pleasant to Mr. Johnston, whether they respected their differences or not. It could have been his first act of kindness. He didn't know the whereabouts of Mr. Johnston's soul. But regardless of the man's belligerent attitude, he didn't want to see anybody end up in hell. It was a place Eva's pastor had described as "a never-ending remix of horror and suffering."

The second breaking-news item at Garden Chateau was his engagement to Eva. The report about Kidd's salvation seemed to take a backseat to most, except his break buddies. They had question after question on why Kidd lost his mind for Jesus. He answered as best he could.

Once when he passed Eva in a corridor, Kidd pulled her aside and looked in both directions before taking the liberty to deliver a quick peck on her lips. He was proud to have put a rock on her ring finger.

Every now and then, Kidd got a chance to stay out of sight. He would hide out in his office, pull his Bible out of the drawer, and continue reading in Luke where he had left off the night before. He couldn't quite put it in words, but he felt good about himself. Then when he decided to call Parke to share his news, he was denied the chance.

"Praise God, Kidd, on your salvation! It's a lifestyle change, but you'll never regret it. Knowing Jesus is your backup will surely make life easier when the trials come," Parke rambled on without saying hello.

"Cameron," Kidd stated in a matter-of-fact tone.

Parke laughed. "That's Cam. Whenever there's news to get out, you would think he was a CNN correspondent instead of an electrical engineer. Also, congratulations on your engagement to Eva. She's pretty and smart and knows how to tame the big bad boy."

Kidd smiled to himself and nodded. "She does. Let me clear the air."

Parke tried to interrupt him, but Kidd barged ahead. "I'm sorry I was a thorn in your side, foot, and anyplace else. I was consumed by anger. I felt that I'd been left out of the benefits of life because of what I didn't have—a father named Samuel. Once the rage took hold of me, I nourished it. But now things have changed. I've changed. I might as well get it over with. I need to confront my father. I want to have closure on my old life, so I can live this new life in Christ to the fullest."

"You got it. One important thing to remember, you're an eleventh generation of a royal African tribe—"

"Parke, just show me on paper. Okay? The other thing I want to say is thank you; or rather, I should thank Grandma BB in a twisted sort of way. If she hadn't had the stroke, and you hadn't admitted her to Garden Chateau, and you hadn't suckered me into working there, I never would have met Eva."

"Your journey started long before you came to St. Louis. Although Samuel Jamieson wasn't the example you needed, God used him to set in motion your steps in life. Your destiny is unfolding."

"Speaking of Grandma BB, how is she coming along at home?" Kidd glanced up when there was a light knock and someone opened his door. When Eva appeared, he smiled at his fiancée and waved her in, tuning out his cousin.

"Parke, I've got to run. Eva and I will probably see you this weekend. We might stop by and check on Grandma BB too." He disconnected, then realized he hadn't said good-bye.

"Are you busy?" Eva asked.

"Doesn't matter. You'll always have priority in my life."

"I can't believe you're getting married," Dawn said, ecstatically to Eva as she and Angela combed through Eva's arsenal of bridal magazines. "Hey," she said, lifting up a page with cake designs. "I vote for cupcakes by Helfer's Pastries!"

Eva was on a ripping frenzy as she tore out pages of hairpieces, dresses, jewelry, and other accessories that had caught her eye over the years. "Definitely, Dianna Castner for headpieces," she determined.

"This is so exciting!" Dawn gushed. "Finally, after all the weddings I've attended, I'll be center stage and—"

"The bride is the main attraction," Angela corrected. It was her turn to hold up a page. "Whoa, whoa . . . Eva, check out this feather and lace gown by David Tutera. It is absolutely gorgeous!"

"Yeah, I know that, Angela," Dawn interrupted. "What I meant is that it'll be more exposure for me . . . besides the bride, of course. My doomed marriage at the courthouse should have been my omen to run out the back door. Do you know what the odds are for meeting your soul mate at a friend's wedding?" Dawn rattled on.

"No, what is it?" Angela and Eva said almost in unison.

Dawn shrugged. "I don't know, but it has to be near one hundred." The three women shared a hearty laugh.

Lord, please help Dawn find a good man—soon. Eva prayed for her friend and turned to the next page of her magazine.

Chapter Forty-Five

*T*he following Saturday, Kidd sauntered up the winding pathway to Mrs. Beacon's front door with Eva by his side.

He recalled his last visit to her home being under semidangerous circumstances. And that didn't even describe the bust. Kidd could still see the expressions on the faces of the true-to-life thugs when he snapped their pictures. Every time he thought about it, he would have to hold back an explosion of laughter.

Adjusting the basket he was carrying filled with various toiletries, they walked hand in hand. It was Eva's idea to bring a gift. *Women,* he thought as he struggled with the heavy load. They climbed the steps to the porch, and Eva pushed the doorbell. Minutes later, a bigger, blacker, and taller man than Kidd opened the door.

Automatically, Kidd became suspicious. Parke said Grandma BB was on her second nurse's aide. He hoped this bear of a man surely wasn't the replacement.

"Good afternoon. May I help you?" The man greeted, as if he was the homeowner.

"We're here to see Mrs. Beacon," Eva said, as Kidd and the man were in a stare-down duel.

"Sure." He turned, and Kidd opened the screen door for them to follow, leaving Eva to trail behind them.

"And you are?" Kidd asked.

"I'm Dino. Grandma BB's live-in nurse."

"Live-in nurse or live-in lover?" Kidd glanced back at Eva and whispered.

With her mouth swinging on its hinge, she swatted him. "That's just plain gross. Maybe she got him off the runway after a Chippendale performance." Eva whispered back.

"Don't drool, sweetheart. You'll have your very own Chippendale on our honeymoon night."

The front door slammed behind them. Eva jumped. Grandma BB's boisterous and high-strung neighbor, Imani, glided in wearing stilettos, tight jeans, and a suggestive halter top.

Eva pinched his arm.

"Ouch. What did you do that for?" He frowned in shock.

"Oh, just to keep you focused until our wedding night." Her smile was sweet and mischievous. Kidd didn't trust her for a moment.

Imani mumbled a greeting and turned her attention toward Grandma BB's nurse. "Hey, Dino. I brought homemade soup. I hope you're hungry."

Kidd whirled around and asked her, "So he really is a nurse?"

"Oh, yeah, and I'm keeping an eye on D. His bedside manners are impressive." Imani grinned wickedly. "Especially after I twisted my ankle." Suddenly, she had a slight limp.

Wearing a grin that stretched across his entire face, the man reached for the bowl. "Thanks. I'll just take this to the kitchen." When he stepped away, Kidd couldn't help but wonder if Grandma BB would even get a taste. The huge man looked like he could murder some food.

They walked into a large room where Grandma BB sat in a highback chair with her bare feet stretched out on a thick cushioned ottoman. Silent Killer was posted at her side, his ears perked.

"Well, if it isn't my bodyguard from Garden Chateau and his new fiancée."

"The grapevine around here is like a high-speed light rail," Kidd complained, while Eva beamed. At least his fiancée was happy. "Uh, we brought you a basket."

"Grandma BB, we're praying for your recovery," Eva added.

"You do that." The woman nodded. "So, who was the third sucker who got knocked off at the place? You know what they say, death comes in threes."

"What? You didn't get the memo on that one?" Kidd said sarcastically. Just then he thought about his new walk with Christ. He shouldn't have provoked her. Kidd apologized, but she ignored him.

Instead, Grandma BB beckoned to Dino. "I'm ready for my foot therapy now." Then she sneered at Kidd. "Watch it. I may not be able to outrun you for getting smart with me, but Silent Killer is as fast as a bullet." She winked.

Even a stroke can't keep a good woman down. "Well, Eva and I just wanted to check on you before we head to Parke's house." Kidd reached for Eva's hand and squeezed his affection. They turned to leave.

"When is the wedding?" Grandma BB called after them before they made it to the front door. "And I expect an invitation. You know I'm family, and I always get a front-row seat."

Kidd eyed Eva, daring her to change her mind again.

"October," Eva replied, with a charming smile.

"I'll be there in a wheelchair or on a walker. But make no mistake about it; me and my Stacy Adams will be there. So put aside a bouquet just for me."

Chapter Forty-Six

K idd's thoughts were elsewhere on the drive to Parke's house just a few blocks away. His prayers and the Bible studies couldn't subdue his pounding heart. He was about to know the whereabouts of his father, so he could have a man-to-man talk with him.

In his heart, Kidd recited John 8:32 more than once: *"Then you will know the truth, and the truth will set you free."*

"God, help me not to be afraid of the truth—whatever it is," he prayed.

"Kevin, I'm going to be honest. I don't know what you're feeling, and I don't even know if you can or want to tell me. But . . . what purpose will this possibly serve?" Eva asked softly before adding, "You barely tolerated Juneteenth."

He didn't believe in backing down. To confront his father in a civil manner, after all these years, was a test that Kidd had to pass. He had to believe that when he got saved, Christ nailed his feelings of envy, jealousy, and rage to the cross. However, he wasn't sure about his feelings toward his half brothers and half sisters. That was up in the air.

I will keep you in perfect peace, when you keep your mind on Me.

Trust in Me, God spoke Isaiah 26:3.

"Samuel wronged me, and the Bible says I have to forgive him and anyone who trespasses against me. That's a lot to ask of a man who believed in taking matters into my own hands all my life. If I'm going to be a Christian, I have to right Samuel's wrong. With that said, I'm not seeking to foster a relationship with him. I'm not even trying to like the man."

He swallowed. "I will admit I'm struggling with a bit of revenge. I want to see pride in his eyes for the man I've become. Of course, he'll have no choice but to admit he can't take any credit. I'm fighting against some conflicting emotions. On one hand, I want to hurt him for hurting me, my mother, and my brother. On the other hand, God wants me to forgive Samuel and give God control of my life. So, for Samuel *and* me, God saved me right on time."

"Would you really hurt your own father? Really?"

"You're asking me that question on the right day of the week, because now I'm determined to live for Christ. Before Christ came into my heart, I seriously would've left my mark on Samuel—because I hated him."

"Strong word."

"Strong emotions, babe, but God is handling those now. I just have to keep remembering that."

Kidd parked and turned off the ignition. Eva reached over and rubbed his hand. "Let's pray, sweetie."

He nodded.

"God, in the name of Jesus, we come before You for comfort. We ask that You calm the storm of rage trying to overtake Kevin. Please stop it. God, You saved him for a purpose. Now let him pass his first test. Thank You in advance. In Jesus' name. Amen."

"Amen." Kidd sighed. "Thank you, baby. Okay, let's get this over with," he said with conviction and got out of the car. He came around and helped Eva. This time, instead of walking hand in hand, Eva wrapped her arm around him. He leaned on her small strength to steady his feet as they climbed the stairs to the porch. Eva rang the bell. It was Kidd's first visit back to the place where he called home until the day he was put out, or he left, depending on whose version a person would believe.

Parke opened the door. "Hey, man." He engulfed Kidd into a hug and then kissed Eva's cheek.

"Don't get too comfortable doing that," Kidd threatened, nudging Parke aside and allowing Eva to enter first. "Humph, Jesus or no Jesus, nobody messes with my stuff or my woman."

"I've got a wife," Parke taunted him.

Eva rolled her eyes. "Testosterone."

Cheney strolled out of the kitchen, laughing. "Pay them no mind." She exchanged hugs with Eva. "Yep. Congratulations to the future Mrs. Jamieson. I'm so excited for you to join the elite club of Jamieson wives!"

"Thank you." Eva chuckled, as her eyes sparkled.

"On the downside, it gets worse after marriage."

Cheney's toddler came out of nowhere and raced across the room to Kidd. He swooped down and lifted the boy above his head. Paden giggled.

The bell rang, not once, but in a familiar sounding off-beat pattern. When Cheney opened the door, Malcolm and his family entered.

"What are you doing here? Did I intrude on a family game day? I thought this would be something personal between Parke and me." It was humiliating enough for Kidd that he knew so little about his father.

"Think again." Malcolm clasped Parke's hand in a shake and then did the same with Kidd's. Turning, he planted a kiss on Cheney's cheek, then Eva's.

"Would you all keep your lips off my woman? And that is not a request," Kidd advised, his nostrils flaring.

"So, Cheney, it doesn't get better with the ring on my finger. Huh?" Eva groaned.

"Nope," Hallison answered for Cheney. "Congratulations and welcome to a family of strong Black men." She hugged Eva.

"There's nothing personal between the Jamiesons. If it concerns you, it concerns me." Malcolm folded his arms and leaned against the wall, as if he dared Kidd to differ with him.

"That's right," the elder Parke agreed, as Papa P. and Grandma Charlotte strolled through the door. The grandchildren went wild, vying for their grandparents' attention.

"We're here because you're here to uncover information about one of the Jamieson descendants. Samuel belongs to all of us—just like you—whether he's a good guy or not," the elder Parke explained.

Kidd disagreed, but he wasn't going to dishonor Parke's father. He held his tongue.

"Okay, let's get started." Parke walked into the dining room where newspaper clippings, folders, printouts, and other documents were spread across one side of the table. Covering the other half was an array of healthy fruit and veggie snacks, ready to be devoured.

The visit had begun as a typical Jamieson family gathering. But now the moment became sobering, as the adults claimed seats around the dining room table. Kami and Pace followed and stood on either side of their father; the younger children were interested in the snacks alone. Parke powered up his laptop. Malcolm picked up a red folder and began reviewing its contents.

Eva stroked his arm to remind Kidd of her presence.

"Can you hear my heart pounding?" He reached over and whispered to her.

She laid her hand over her heart and then placed it on his. "Our hearts are beating as one." With that gesture, there wasn't a hint of doubt that Eva loved him with all of her being.

"Ready?" she asked.

Kidd nodded.

"Okay, cuz, I can recap everything that I'm sure Cameron already told you," Parke advised, while he waited for his computer to load.

"Start from the beginning. I barely paid any attention to Cameron. I still don't."

"Okay," Parke said. "First up, you do know that researching our ancestry will also bring to light some things people thought they buried six feet under."

Our? What a joke. "Parke, I expect nothing glowing about Samuel Jamieson—nothing at all." *Lord, You took the bitterness away. Why is it resurfacing?*

Fight the good fight of faith, God answered.

"Paki Kokumuo Jaja was born in December 1770 in Cote d'Ivoire, Africa," Parke began, rolling his tongue to authenticate an African dialect. "Landing in Maryland, Paki was indoctrinated into servitude. He was automatically separated from his bodyguards and sold for a couple hundred dollars in front of Sinner's Hotel, of all places. Ironically, the woman who would later become his wife was the slave master's daughter, Elaine.

"They had five sons: Parker was the eldest. They adopted the name Jamieson because a Robert Jamieson helped them escape along the Underground Railroad. First settling in Alton, Illinois, it didn't become a free state until 1818, so they had to keep moving. Your eleventh great-grandfather Orma was born in 1807. He was the youngest son after Parker, Aasim, Fabunni, and Abelo. This is where your history becomes interesting. Orma means 'born free,' yet he sold himself back into slavery for Sashe, a Kentucky runaway. When she was recaptured, Orma went with her, basically exchanging his freedom for bondage to be with her."

"Commercial break," Malcolm interrupted. "From a Christian standpoint, it's just God setting people free from their sins. But some freely return to their vomit—God's words not mine—their sins."

"Thanks for the Christian commercial, honey." Hallison kissed her husband.

"Yeah, thanks." Parke continued, "Orma's brothers attempted

several times to rescue him, but he refused to go without his pregnant wife."

"Hold up, Parke. How did you find out this stuff?" Kidd asked, as he leaned his elbows on the table.

"By piecing together old documents from county court records, census records, slave code books, draft registration cards, tax records, slave schedules . . ."

"Okay. I get it."

"Through bill of sale records, I found Orma's name, Sashe, and one son, Kingdom. In a bittersweet way, thank God Sashe's owner believed in selling runaway slaves instead of almost beating them to death."

"What a choice," Kidd said, dryly. "You're right. So far, I'm not liking any of this."

"They actually named their son Kingdom?" Eva asked.

"Yep. It makes you wonder what they were thinking," Malcolm replied.

"Their other children who lived were Candy, Paradise, and Harrison. Five others died."

"Five," Cheney whispered.

"It wasn't uncommon. Diseases like consumption, irritable bowel, pneumonia were common. Anyway, Kingdom named his firstborn, King. For the next sixty years, or over four generations, the firstborn sons were named King II, III, and IV. I found King II on the Freedom Bureau marriage registry online."

Parke pulled it up and turned the laptop around for Kidd and Eva. Pace perked up. He rubbed the boy's hair, as they began to read:

"*Date: September 11, 1865: Man's Age: 35 years old; color: dark; father: dark; mother: mulatto; lived with another woman 1 year, separated from her by sale. Woman's Age: 33 years old; color: copper; father: white; mother: brown. They unitedly had 2 children; the man by previous connection had 0; the woman by previous connection had 3.*"

"Hmm," was Kidd's only response.

"Amazingly, his son King III also registered his marriage, but his story wasn't so pretty."

Squirming in his seat, Kidd waved him off. "I don't want to see that one, just tell me."

"The Freedom Bureau reported that King III was removed three times from prior connections, which meant relationships, but to us—marriage. In plain English, he was probably sold. Forty years later in 1887, King IV survived a vigilante attack, but the good news is he was able to amass large plots of land to become a wealthy Jamieson. In 1890, he tweaked his firstborn son's name to Kingston. The census records are sketchy in 1890 because a fire destroyed most of them. Kingston was a complex dude. He served time in jail for a murder that was described as self-defense."

Parke frowned. "For some reason, Kingston had an alias and went under the name of George Palmer Jamieson. It's a mystery that will take me some time to uncover, but my family can do it. Slavery was over, but he was married three times. On to Kingston II; he served in WWII with an honorable discharge."

"Stop right there. I'm on overload. Sorry I asked." Kidd was about tired of this classroom session.

"But his son, Kingston III, was your grandfather." Parke eyed him.

Kidd regained sudden interest. "Okay, I can relate to a grandfather, but the others are too far back to have an impact on my life today."

"I could argue with your assumption, but I won't," Parke said.

"Good. I've never lost an argument, and I don't plan to today. So skip your commentaries."

Eva elbowed him, so Kidd plastered on a smile. "Please."

Cheney must have kicked Parke because he yelped and frowned at her. "What did I do?"

"Play nice." This time Cheney smiled and batted her eyes.

After rubbing his leg, Parke went back to tapping on the keyboard. "Kingston III was born in 1935. It looks like he didn't care about lineage because he abandoned the name and your father, Samuel. Your dad appeared to be the only child born to Kingston III and Hulda Robertson. Evidently, he was light enough to pass as a White man and he did. He changed his name to Sam E. Walker. He, along with some other entrepreneurs started a hotel chain in Cincinnati, Ohio."

Abandon? That's all Kidd heard. His father was dumped. Then he turned around and deserted Kidd. "A trail of emotional destruction," he spoke out loud. Kidd couldn't and wouldn't do that to his child. *God, help me.*

Call on My name and I will do it, God offered comfort.

"Unfortunately, yes," Parke said softly. "It started with Samuel's father's marriage to Hulda."

"Okay, enough. Where is my loser of a father now? And how many other lives has he destroyed?" Kidd spat out the venom that was trying to poison his spirit.

"Kevin," Eva whispered.

Kidd glanced at her angelic expression and immediately his anger was deflated. "I'm sorry. I'm working on this forgiveness angle, but God help me when I see him."

Parke cleared his throat. "You won't, cuz."

"What do you mean?"

"Samuel Jamieson is dead."

Eva gasped and covered her mouth with her hands. Kidd held his breath, shocked.

"I'm sorry," Parke said.

Kidd stared. The strike to his heart was heavy. In shock, he remembered to swallow. Then all he could do was blink. Every bit of boasting about hating him throughout the years quickly dissipated to yearning.

"When?"

"About seven years ago," Parke answered.

"Where?"

Parke tapped on his computer. "I found this online obituary. Why don't you read it for yourself?" He angled the laptop toward Kidd again.

"*Samuel Jamieson was the son of Kingston III and Hulda Robertson. He was united in holy matrimony to Eillian Ivy and to this union seven children were born: Saul, Jayson, Mayson, Zaki, Benjamin, Giselle Rayford (Jacob); and Lacey Jamieson of Hartford, CT; years later, he was united in holy matrimony to Zenita Pope and to this union two daughters were born: Suzette and Queen of Tulsa, OK; and he also was the father of Kevin and Aaron Jamieson of Boston, MA,*" Kidd read aloud.

The room was silent as he digested the information. "Well, he ran up some frequent-flyer miles," he concluded in disgust.

In death, he and Ace were included, but in life, Samuel excluded them. Kidd needed a moment to process the information. Who wrote the obituary? "Someone knew about us? Why hadn't they reached out?" he asked rhetorically.

Shrugging, Parke took back his laptop. "Maybe they were as resentful as you because of their father's choices."

"Yet someone listed all our names. My brother and I were acknowledged—in death only, not in life." Kidd's nostrils flared. He needed space. He had to get out of there for some serious damage control. Kidd got up hastily. As he was storming out of the house, he heard Parke say, "Let him go," in the distance. Parke was a smart man when it counted. At that moment, he knew his cousin couldn't be responsible for his actions.

God, I wasn't prepared for this. I got cheated. I got robbed.

He walked—no, marched—aimlessly down Darst Street. The massive historical homes surrounding Kidd seemed to taunt him. The windows adorning the three-story houses became eyes that reflected the pity he felt.

"God, why? You know I hated him. You know . . . why didn't You let me have the satisfaction of seeing him face-to-face? I wanted to prove to You and myself that I could forgive him and move on. Why, God?" Kidd swung at the wind. He approached a growling dog on the lawn of a large house. Balling his fists, Kidd roared back.

I give you power over beasts on earth and in the air, God spoke from Genesis.

"But I had no power over my life. With one good punch, I can knock the wind out of that mutt," he said in anger.

Yes, but you have no authority to take the animal's life. I grant permission over life and death, God spoke.

What does that dog have to do with anything? Kidd asked himself. Reeling from the shock of the news, it was difficult for him to remain focused. His mind was scattered, yet the Lord broke through with a message Kidd would not forget.

He was your natural father, but I am your heavenly, permanent, and forgiving Father. I have already set a work in you, and I will finish it. When you close your eyes, I am there.

"Yeah, but he wasn't there for me and how many others? Lord, I can't comprehend this." Kidd sniffed, but dared a tear to cloud his vision. He kept walking and crossed Hereford Street, continuing until he reached January Wabash Park. Flopping down on a bench, he said aloud, "Thanks, Dad, for being a loser and planting that seed in me and my brother."

I purchased you with a price. The old is dead, God spoke to him. *I washed your sins as white as snow.*

With his head down and eyes closed, Kidd began praying. He couldn't remember what words he uttered, but he knew he was pouring out his heart. Suddenly, the sound of a horn penetrated his consciousness. He ignored it until the driver became persistent.

Opening his eyes, he watched as Eva parked Cheney's car. He didn't have the strength to stand and meet her halfway, so he just stared as she approached him. Immediately, her presence gave him renewed courage. As soon as she was within arm's length, he reached out and wrapped his arms around her waist. Kidd had no words; resting his head on her stomach spoke volumes to her.

Eva rubbed his back and kissed the top of his head. "I love you, Kevin. Please tell me that means something to you right now."

He didn't want to share this mental breakdown of devastation, disappointment, and sorrow. But his Eva was there, and he thanked God for her. He glanced up into her eyes and saw love, not pity. "Right now, and until I take my last breath, your love means everything to me."

Kidd didn't track the time they remained glued to each other. The couple looked like an exquisite ebony figurine suspended in a moment of eternal embrace. Finally, he pulled back and was about to kiss her. At that moment, he was mesmerized by the hint of a smile on her lips. Eva's lids fluttered, but her eyes didn't open.

She looked so peaceful in the face of the emotional storm that was raging within him. Although Kidd was typically portrayed as being fearless, fear was beginning to grip him on the inside. Darkness tried to overpower him, taunting him with the charge that he and his brother were cheated.

"Eva," he whispered, as he tried to regulate his breathing.

"Hmmm." Sitting quietly by his side, she answered.

"Will you pray for me?"

"Say no more. I'm already talking to God. Why do you think my eyes are still closed?"

Chapter Forty-Seven

The last weekend in September

*T*he organist played the prelude to the bridal procession.

"Show time," Eva whispered, then inhaled deeply and exhaled. She waited for her cue to make her entrance. Her father lovingly patted her hand that was looped through his arm.

Her wedding dress was exquisite, crafted with yards and yards of white taffeta and satin. Tiny pearls were sprinkled throughout the bodice and dotted her long sleeves in a pattern of miniature roses. For a personal touch, her bridesmaids—Angela, Dawn, Cheney, and Hallison—placed fresh pink and white rose petals on her long train. When she walked, some would fall and create a trail of flowers.

Eva was sure Mrs. Beacon stole the show. Since neither she nor Kidd had grandparents, and they had become fond of Grandma BB, they included her in the ceremony. Their request seemed to encourage her to work harder at her therapy. Her only demand—as if she had a right to have one—was for Dino, her boy toy and nurse, to usher her down the aisle.

Looking lovely and graceful, the bride and groom's mothers were escorted to their seats. Following them, Eva was sure her flower girls, Kami and Shayla—Eva's cousin's daughter—were crowd pleasers. Earlier, the two girls primped in front of the mirror in the makeshift dressing room, chatting, and shaking their long curls. As they walked to the altar in their pale pink tea-length dresses and satin slippers, the girls released butterflies from rose-decorated birdcages. The seventy-plus degree temperature was perfect for the butterflies to take flight.

"Eva, you are so beautiful. You know your future husband is counting the minutes. If we don't start down that aisle soon, he'll come looking for you," Kenneth told his daughter.

Eva gave a nervous chuckle. "You were right, Daddy. Kevin was the one."

Kenneth winked. "I know. I'm convinced he'll be faithful to you and God. We had a very long talk—twice. You can't get better husband material than that." He kissed her on her cheek.

Eva smiled; she knew that basically her father threatened Kidd. Now the time had finally come. She took the first step, then two, and before long, Kidd's image came into view. The angry Black man she had first met, God had delivered. In his place, God gave her a good Black man to love. *Thank You, Jesus, for that.*

Never taking his eyes off her, Kidd didn't wait for Eva to make it to the altar. Instead, he made an unrehearsed move and marched up to her father. Kenneth wasn't prepared for the unexpected change in plan, but he gave his daughter another kiss and allowed the anxious groom to take her the rest of the way.

Once at the altar, their eyes locked until her pastor, Elder Taylor, cleared his throat. He was ready to begin.

"Dearly beloved, we are gathered here today in the sight of God and before these witnesses to join together this man and woman in holy matrimony. Kevin, do you take Eva to be your wedded wife, to live together in marriage? Do you promise to love, comfort, honor, and

344

keep her—for better or worse, for richer or poorer, in sickness and in health, and forsaking all others, be faithful only to her—so long as you both shall live?"

When Kidd answered, Elder Taylor asked Eva the same questions. Then he addressed Kidd again. "Kevin, I understand you have something to add to your vows."

What was he doing? This wasn't part of the script. Eva knew whatever he was about to say, it would make her cry and ruin her beautiful smoky eye makeup Dawn so artistically applied. Taking a deep breath, she braced herself.

"Eva, you are really my Eve. I believe God reached into my stony heart and placed you there. I was a lonely man until God brought us together. Part of me was missing—and that part was you. I will be forever grateful to Him for giving you to me."

A tear dropped from Eva's eye. She sniffed and wished that she had a tissue. But she couldn't look away; she didn't want to break the trance.

"Thank you for becoming one with me, for forsaking all the doubts and misgivings you had about me and loving me anyway." Kidd kissed her hand. Then he allowed Elder to finish reciting the vows until the conclusion.

Elder Taylor bowed his head and Kidd and Eva followed. "Lord, in the name of Jesus, we thank You for the union of this godly couple. Strengthen them when they are weak, rebuke the spirit of division, and bind the forces of any man or woman who would try to tear them apart. Lord, may You get the glory out of their lives, so that others may be encouraged to know that marriages do work and last. In Jesus' name. Amen. Before these witnesses, I now pronounce you husband and wife—Mr. and Mrs. Kevin Jamieson."

Guests cheered. The Jamieson groomsmen: Ace, Parke, Malcolm, and Cameron, whistled and hooted with pride. Grandma BB stood, aided by Dino, and whirled her cane in the air. Flashes of light exploded around them when the photographer and guests snapped photos of

345

their first kiss as a married couple and their jumping over the broom.

At the reception less than an hour later, Kidd swept Eva off her feet when guests circled them for their first dance as husband and wife. Ace scooted a chair into the center that was decorated with satin ribbons and a pick satin cushion. Once Kidd placed her on it, the string quartet serenaded them.

"What are you doing?" Eva whispered through clenched teeth. She wanted to be all smiles for the cameras. This was also not part of the program. She and Kidd had agreed to skip removing her garter in front of their guests. Eva wanted that to be a private moment shared between the two of them.

"Trust me. Close your eyes."

When she did, Kidd began to pluck the pearl-covered hairpins that Dawn had strategically placed to keep Eva's hair swept up. Guests cheered him on, as flowing curls cascaded to her shoulders.

"Do you have any idea how much time it took to do that?" she asked, opening one eye.

Then she felt the weight of something on her head. Opening her eyes, she reached up and fingered . . . a crown? Kidd came around and knelt before her.

"What is this?"

"I figured since I'm royalty and all, I deserve a queen. And baby, you are my crowning glory. Plus, I got the idea from one of your bridal magazines. Great tips."

Kidd winked and kissed her passionately.

BOOK CLUB QUESTIONS

1. Compare Kidd's attitude with that of someone in your life.

2. Why didn't Kidd's mother, Sandra, feel her sons were paying for the sins of their mother?

3. Discuss Kidd's bargain with God. Have you ever bargained with God and what was the outcome?

4. What is the message you are left with at the end of the story?

5. How did Parke and Cheney's children affect Kidd?

6. Was Eva's father right to give Kidd a heads-up?

7. Eva used her mother forgiving her father as an example of being patient with Kidd and his commitment to God. Agree or disagree?

8. When did Kidd's relationship change with Parke?

9. Eva's friend Dawn was determined to meet men. Discuss her tactics. Were they appropriate?

10. How often would you visit your friend or relative in a nursing facility?

*W*e shouldn't always believe everything we hear.

God can block the sins of the father with blessings to his children.

Aaron "Ace" Jamieson is living a carefree life. He's good-looking, respectable, can hold down a job, but his weakness is women. If a woman tries to trap him with a pregnancy, he takes off in the other direction. It's a lesson learned from his absentee father that responsibility is optional.

Taleigh Reed has a bright future ahead of her. She's pretty and has no problem catching a man's eye, which is exactly what she does with Ace. Their chemistry is undeniable and their passion explosive, but there's one catch. Trapping Ace Jamieson is the furthest thing from Taleigh's mind as she is determined to be a good parent, whether she remains single or blessed to find a good man who loves her and is willing to accept her child and possibly adopt him.

But Ace's big brother and cousins don't plan to let the child who represents the twelfth generation descendant of a royal African tribe leave the fold. Whether Ace decides to accept his responsibility or not, his family embraces Taleigh to Ace's shame.

The family has decided to turn Ace over to the Lord instead of laying a guilt trip on him to accept the responsibility of his child and choose the blessings from his heavenly Father to overpower the sins of his earthly dad.

I hope you have enjoyed Kidd and Eva's story. If this is your first introduction to the Jamieson family, welcome.

I first started the *Guilty* series while I was researching my family tree. I decided to incorporate some of my genealogy findings into *Guilty of Love*, thus creating my Jamieson characters as tenth generation descendants of a royal African tribe. As a unique tool to track down relatives from my family tree, I decided to give a few characters the names of my ancestors with tidbits about their lives. My hope is that some of the readers would connect the dots and locate me.

I started with Charlotte—my maternal grandmother—and gave that name to Parke's mother. I had no specific reason why I chose the last name Jamieson, except that it had a distinguished ring to it, or so I thought.

While writing, I continued searching for my maternal grandmother's grandmother, whose name was also Charlotte, with a last name of Wilkerson. But I ran into some problems when I got to the 1870 census. Charlotte Wilkerson, along with her two sons, William (my great-grandfather) and his brother Samuel, were nowhere to be found. So I asked some fellow genealogy enthusiasts for their help based on the information I had.

What they were able to uncover blew me away. It appears that Charlotte was actually a Jamieson all along. I felt it was confirmation from God that I was on the right track.

On the 1860 census, Robert Jamieson was the slaveholder over Charlotte, giving her the name Jamieson. In his household, lived John Wilkerson (my great-great grandfather) who was listed as a teacher in the academy. Needless to say, my heart still beats wildly when I think about how God manifested His will in my writing career.

In this story, Miss Jessie Atkins was my grandmother who passed away in a nice nursing facility. And yes, my hand was on the door handle when the staff was calling me for death notification. I got to her bed-side and was able to rejoice that I had a grandmother in my life for more than forty years. The year she lived with me, Grandma often thanked me for taking care of her. I will always remember her saying, "I thank you. You never know whose hand is going to give you that last piece of bread."

HERE IS MY PATERNAL GRANDMOTHER
JESSIE BROWN WADE COLE ATKINS'S FAMILY TREE:

Jessie was a twin to Louis Wade. They were the third generation of twins.

Jessie's mother was Minerva Brown (my great-grandmother). She was born in Arkansas in 1891 and died in 1988 in St. Louis.

Jessie's father was Odell Wade (my great-grandfather). He was born in Arkansas in 1888 and died in 1972 in St. Louis.

Minerva had twin brothers: Ellis (who lived to be 100 years old) and Louis. Minerva's mother was Nellie Palmer (my great-great grand-mother was a twin to Solomon). Both were born in Arkansas in 1874. Nellie's mother was Minerva Palmer born 1848 in Arkansas. Yes, I also have three generations of Minervas in my family.

Minerva's father was Joseph Brown. I am still researching his side. With a last name of Brown, it's not easy.

Odell's mother was Callie Young Lowe (my great-great grand-mother and of the Choctaw tribe). She was born in Arkansas.

Odell's father was Winston Wade (my great-great grandfather) was born in Tennessee in 1856. His date of death is unknown.

Winston's mother was Manurva (my great-great-great grand-father). She was born in North Carolina in 1822 or 1828.

Winston's father is unknown, but his father was born in Virginia.

Manurva's father was possibly Jacob Jordan (if so, my fourth great grandfather). He was born in 1801.

Whew! That's all, folks.

ACKNOWLEDGMENTS

I'm proud to be an alumna of Emerson College in Boston. It was fun to revisit and give my tribute to "Beantown" for the memories.

Shout out to my play bro, Mik Johnson, who welcomed me into the family as his eleventh sister—no kidding. Ma Johnson had ten daughters and five sons, so while I attended Emerson, I was a card-carrying member of the Johnson family. Mik answered his phone ready to take my calls.

I praise God for Faithful Church of Christ on Woodrow Avenue in Boston, Massachusetts, where Suffragan Bishop Hershel Langham, placed me—this baby saint of a few weeks old—under the watchful care of the Johnsons to nourish me and help me grow into the saint that I am today. Praise the Lord!

To the First Lady of Bethesda Temple in St. Louis, Missouri, Sister Juana Johnson, who has been a fan since book one. Thanks for setting aside time to take my calls and share your stories on your journey to become a director of nursing.

To Guilty Series Fan Club captain, Mia Danielle, for letting me pick her brain as a nursing student and all the captains of the Guilty Series Fan Clubs across the country who are supporting me by getting the word out about the Jamieson Legacy. I am so blessed to be loved, encouraged, and supported.

Thanks to author, Tim Pinnik, for sending me copies of old newspaper articles.

I could handpick my brothers and sisters at Bethesda Temple who have blessed me, but I'm afraid I would leave someone out. So thank you all for the thumbs up when I walk into the sanctuary.

To my wonderful agent, Amanda Luedeke, with the MacGregor Literary Agency. If it wasn't for the ACFW conference, I never would have found a jewel. Go, Amanda, it's your birthday!

To the readers, friends, book clubs, and churches who have lifted me up in prayer every time I begin a new chapter, thank you.

To my former editor, Joylynn Jossel, may God bless you for embracing my vision. To freelance editor, Chandra Sparks Taylor, you have been holding my hand from the beginning. May God bless you for blessing me. The staff at Lift Every Voice Books—thank you for letting me take you on the Jamieson Legacy ride.

Now on to the really important folks:

Jesus—my Savior, Wonderful Counselor, King of kings, Lord of lords, Redeemer, Deliverer . . . thank You for using me as Your vessel to inspire, entertain, and show readers the richness of Your promises.

To my husband, Kerry, after 28 years of marriage, his support is unwavering, especially since he wants to retire and have me take care of him for a change—that's a lot of pages to write.

LOL to my recent graduate, Simi—congrats and to my firstborn, Jared—oh, the testimony is coming!

To my sweet, supportive, and wonderful cousins who are descendants of Coles, Browns, Carters, Wilkerson/Wilkinsons, Jamiesons, Brownlees, Wades, Jordans, Palmers, Lamberts, Thomases . . . and in-laws Simmons, Sinkfields, Crofts, Sturdivants, Stricklands, Downers.

ABOUT THE AUTHOR

*P*at Simmons considers herself a self-proclaimed genealogy sleuth. She is passionate about researching her ancestors, then casting them in starring roles in her novels. She has been a genealogy enthusiast since her great-grandmother died at the young age of ninety-seven years old. She enjoys weaving African American history into local history.

She describes her Christian walk as an amazing, unforgettable, life-alternating experience. She is a baptized believer, who is always willing to share her testimonies about God's goodness. She believes God is the true Author who advances her stories.

Pat has a B.S. in mass communications from Emerson College in Boston, MA. She has worked in various media positions in radio, television, and print for more than twenty years. Currently, she oversees the media publicity for the annual RT Booklovers Conventions. She has been a guest on several media outlets, including radio, television, newspapers, and blog radio.

She is the award-winning author of *Talk to Me,* ranked #14 of Top Books in 2008 That Changed Lives by *Black Pearls Magazine*; she also received the Katherine D. Jones Award for Grace and Humility from the Romance Slam Jam committee in 2008. Pat is best known for her Guilty series: *Guilty of Love, Not Guilty of Love*, and *Still Guilty,* which was voted the Best Inspirational Romance for 2010 by the RSJ committee. Her newest release, *Crowning Glory,* is receiving rave reviews. Her fans are eagerly awaiting the next books in the Guilty series: *Guilty by Association* and *The Guilt Trip* in 2012.

Pat Simmons has converted her sofa-strapped, sports-fanatical husband into an amateur travel agent, untrained bodyguard, and GPS-guided chauffeur. They have a son and daughter.

THANK YOU FOR READING GUILTY BY ASSOCIATION

www.thejamiesonlegacy.com

- *Post a review on Goodreads.com, Amazon.com, bn.com, cbd.com*
- *Write a review on your blog*
- *Like the Guilty Series Fan Club Facebook page*
- *Watch for the other books in the series:*
  The Guilt Trip (June 2012)
  Free of Guilt (January 2013)

LEVB
LIFT EVERY VOICE BOOKS

STANDARD DATA
RATES MAY APPLY

Against the Gates of Hell

ISBN-13: 978-0-8024-0169-4

Twins. Kerby and Herby (Junior) Wilson. One, a police officer. The other, a functional addict. Kerby Wilson finds himself duped by his own pride and going down a desperate path. As the bottom falls out of his life and darkness consumes his soul, he trades all he holds dear for an elusive state of peace. Junior, Kerby's twin, is caught up in his own battle of resentment and bitterness. He denies having a hard heart while trying to shut his wayward brother out. This debut novel reveals an inside look at the internal and external struggles of two men who find themselves in need of God's grace, love, and forgiveness as they fight for their lives against the very gates of hell.

LIFT EVERY VOICE BOOKS

lifteveryvoicebooks.com

Fifteen Years

ISBN-13: 978-0-8024-6885-7

Josiah (JT) Tucker, the son of a substance dependent and neglectful mother, spent most of his childhood years in the custody of the state, living in foster homes throughout Atlanta, Georgia. At the age of fourteen, he was taken from the foster family that he had grown to love, the Smiths, and returned to his negligent birth mother. Enduring the hardships faced while living with his birth mother JT manages to make something of his life. However, fifteen years after being taken from the Smiths and at the peak of success, he finds himself feeling empty and at his lowest. When he decides to reconnect with the Smiths, JT hopes to find his faith in God renewed as well.

LIFT EVERY VOICE BOOKS

lifteveryvoicebooks.com

LIFT EVERY VOICE BOOKS

Lift every voice and sing
Till earth and heaven ring,
Ring with the harmonies of Liberty;
Let our rejoicing rise
High as the listening skies,
Let it resound loud as the rolling sea.
Sing a song full of the faith that the dark past has taught us,
Sing a song full of the hope that the present has brought us,
Facing the rising sun of our new day begun
Let us march on till victory is won.

The "Black National Anthem," written by James Weldon Johnson in 1900, captures the essence of Lift Every Voice Books. Lift Every Voice Books is an imprint of Moody Publishers that celebrates a rich culture and great heritage of faith, based on the foundation of eternal truth—God's Word. We endeavor to restore the fabric of the African-American soul and reclaim the indomitable spirit that kept our forefathers true to God in spite of insurmountable odds.

We are Lift Every Voice Books—Christ-centered books and resources for restoring the African-American soul.

For more information on other books and products written and produced from a biblical perspective, go to www.lifteveryvoicebooks.com or write to:

Lift Every Voice Books
820 N. LaSalle Boulevard
Chicago, IL 60610
www.lifteveryvoicebooks.com